SF Books by Vaughn Heppner

DOOM STAR SERIES:
Star Soldier
Bio Weapon
Battle Pod
Cyborg Assault
Planet Wrecker
Star Fortress
Task Force 7 (Novella)

EXTINCTION WARS SERIES:
Assault Troopers
Planet Strike
Star Viking
Fortress Earth

LOST STARSHIP SERIES:
The Lost Starship
The Lost Command
The Lost Destroyer
The Lost Colony
The Lost Patrol

Visit VaughnHeppner.com for more information

Invaders

By Vaughn Heppner

ISBN-13: 978-1539316657
ISBN-10: 1539316653
BISAC: Fiction / Science Fiction / Adventure

-1-

I was driving fast when it happened.

It was a moonless night as my Chief Cherokee Jeep topped a hill on a single-lane road in the middle of Nevada. My high beams showed endless desert. I was almost to Station 5 of Western Sunlight Inc., a vast solar-collecting plant in the middle of nowhere. The vehicle's air-conditioner was humming, and the radio was barely playing tunes from a station in Las Vegas.

We had two new security hires. I was thinking about cutting the headlights and rolling in to see if they were asleep at their posts.

I bent forward as I saw something in the starry sky. The best way to describe it was like a ripple in the higher altitudes. It was faint, but it definitely rippled. Maybe it was a heat wave of some kind.

I gripped the steering wheel tighter with my head shoved too far forward. I tracked the ripple. It seemed to speed up—

It reached the area high over the Chief Cherokee. At that moment, the engine cut out. The dash lights died and so did my headlights. The air-conditioner quit spilling its delightfully cool air.

My fists clutched the steering wheel with manic intensity. A bump and a lurch smashed the top of my head against the windshield.

I thumped back against the seat and fought the steering wheel as I raced over desert sand and rocks. I couldn't remember having left the road, but clearly, I had. I slammed upward against my seat belt as the jeep caromed off a boulder. The steering wheel tried to jerk free of my grip. By main strength, I regained control of the vehicle, straightened out and finally turned back toward the road.

I listened to the wheels crunching across sand as I lost momentum, finally coming to a stop on the shoulder of the blacktop highway.

I panted, blinking stupidly and kept thinking, "What in the hell just happened? What was that ripple?"

I pried my fingers off the steering wheel, frowning. Could I have seen an electromagnetic pulse, an EMP? Real people didn't see things like that. Yeah, maybe in the movies you would, but not in real life.

I tried the ignition, but there was nothing. My jeep was dead.

I took out my cell phone. It was dead, too.

Whatever that rippling event had been, it had messed with all electronics.

Could something bad have happened at Station 5? Could the newbies have caused…I don't know, something that made a ripple in the night sky?

Why would the ripple have started in the high altitudes then? It would have been a low-level thing like a Warthog attack.

The Warthog was the Air Force's A-10 ground attack plane. The flyboys hated them, but in my humble opinion, they were the best thing in the air-jockey outfit.

I used to be in the Marines myself. That had been ten years ago, or as I liked to count it, five jobs and one marriage ago.

I got out of the jeep and looked up at the stars. They blazed overhead like gems. A cool night breeze blew.

I muttered a few choice words, collected my .44 and shoved it into the holster of my shoulder rig.

I was wearing a cheap suit and cheaper dress shoes, but I decided to hoof it to the station. It was approximately six miles away from here. If they'd lost power, too—

A chill fear worked down my spine.

"Get a grip," I told myself. "There's an easy explanation for all this. You've just got to find it."

I felt a little better after the pep talk. So I locked the jeep, and started walking down the blacktop toward the station.

The first few miles were easy. Then, the shoes began to pinch my feet. Despite the breeze and the time of night—a little past midnight—I was sweating too much. I thought about tossing the jacket, but slung it over my back instead, switching hands from time to time.

I used to be a Marine, but I hadn't exercised as much as I should have these past few years. My legs started getting tired, and the cheap dress shoes meant I'd have a blister soon. During the next mile, I berated myself for not grabbing the .38 this morning instead of the massive Smith & Wesson. The weight of the .44 meant the rig dug into my flesh more than I liked.

Finally, I heard gravel crunch underfoot. I stopped, using my jacket to wipe sweat from my forehead. I knelt, feeling the gravel with a hand. The rocks were uniformly round and small. That meant I'd reached the outer limits of Station 5, the gravel apron.

I should have seen lights from here. There were several large block buildings in the center of hundreds of acres of solar collectors. There were massive underground batteries to store the solar energy before operators sent it away along the power lines.

The eerie feeling I'd had at the beginning returned with renewed strength. I had seen something rippling, all right. If the station was dark—

My head jerked upward.

I heard a weird, loud whine coming from the sky.

My mouth was dry, and—

I froze as a column of dull red light stabbed down from the stars. It was a big pillar of illumination, like something from a science fiction movie. The event lasted two, maybe three seconds. The giant beam illuminated the block buildings as it put a huge round circle on the parking area before the main building.

One second, the parking area was empty. The next, three tank-like vehicles appeared within the diameter of the beam. It seemed like a stage-magician's trick, the kind where he shows the crowd his hands and then—presto—he's holding roses for his assistant.

The tanks were...different. They had treads, but had a boxlike main body and a bubble turret on top. Even weirder, each tank had a narrow cannon. It was more like a .50 caliber barrel but much longer than it should have been.

Pain spread outward from my chest, growing into a throb until I sucked down a gasping breath.

As suddenly as it had appeared, the beam vanished. Thankfully, the awful whine quit a second later.

It took several heartbeats before my mind started up again. It felt sluggish, though, as if from a hangover. Was I in shock?

I squeezed the bridge of my nose, forcing myself to breath regularly.

Once I had reestablished my breathing pattern, I craned my neck, searching the night sky for a sign of a blimp or a heavy transport plane. Either of those would be a reasonable explanation for the origin point of the beam. Obviously, the beam had not originated in space.

Yeah, I'd seen the sky ripple earlier. But that didn't mean a beam could teleport three tanks onto the Western Sunlight grounds of Station 5.

I wiped beads of perspiration from my upper lip. I had to get a handle on myself. Teleportation beams... No, no, the tanks must have already been there. The beam had simply highlighted them.

I laughed with relief, finally realizing what must be going on.

I must have stumbled onto a war game, maybe one that had gone awry. Sure. There was an Army proving ground west of here. Even farther beyond that was the old Nevada Proving Ground where the government used to explode their aboveground nuclear weapons. The last of those had gone off in 1962—a lifetime ago. A platoon of Army tanks must have gotten lost here.

"Searchlight," I said, snapping my fingers. The dull red beam had been a searchlight for the war-game officials. They'd used it to pinpoint the lost vehicles.

I smiled, feeling better and far superior to the former me from six miles ago at my jeep. The tanks had gotten lost because the Army had been testing new equipment. I'd seen the effects of that equipment as a ripple in the night sky. Maybe I'd never seen tanks like those before, but that didn't mean anything.

What would be the best way to play this?

The smartest thing was to go over there and explain why I was out here. Maybe I could help the tankers, give them directions back to the Army proving ground.

With that decided, I started down the gravel apron and then stopped abruptly.

One of the tanks started up with a soft purr.

I frowned at that. I'd been in a single war game while in the Marines. I'd heard a tank then, and it hadn't sounded anything like that. The tank back then had roared like a prehistoric monster.

The tank down there sounded like a regular car. What did that—?

"Come on, Logan," I told myself. "Quit freaking out over little things. Go see what's happening."

I blew out my breath and started down the slight depression again. It was time to find out what had happened and check in with the two newbies.

-2-

I descended along the gravel apron, soon reaching pavement, a flatter area with the first of the solar collectors. It was like a giant black tabletop tilted at an angle so it could catch the first rays at dawn.

There were thousands of similar collectors, and they presently hid the tanks from view. If I arched up onto my toes, I could see the tops of the dark block buildings. I only did that once, as that caused the shoes to pinch my feet harder than ever.

I debated pulling off my shoes, but that seemed wrong. Besides, I'd get sand in my socks. Then I'd have to toss the socks. They were the most expensive items of my wardrobe other than the Smith & Wesson.

It was a decent gun despite its age, a revolver. I'd practiced with it more times than I'd hit the gym. I was okay with the gun but no pistol marksman.

I snorted softly.

The .44 wouldn't do a thing against a tank, so I don't know what I was thinking. Just a case of nerves, I guess.

I was bigger than average. I'd played football in high school as a tight end. I'd had good hands and had been hard to tackle, as I'd been bigger than most of the linemen. Those had been the days.

My imagination must have gotten the better of me as I continued to pass collectors. I suddenly found myself holding my S&W. I couldn't even remember drawing it.

I almost shoved the gun back into its holster.

Then, I wondered why the tanks had maneuvered near the buildings in the first place. If they were Army vehicles, wouldn't their commander have had the sense to stay away from the fragile collectors?

I couldn't knock a collector over, but a tank could crush one. It could leave a swath of destruction. I doubted the Army wanted a costly bill from Western Sunlight.

I realized I'd already been hearing their treads smashing collectors.

That seemed so dead wrong that I halted my progress. I crouched, with my butt resting on the top of my heels. Slowly, I put the .44 back into its rig so I could clutch an upright collector-strut with both hands.

I listened to the ongoing destruction. The tanks weren't coming toward me, but leaving, heading east. The Army proving grounds were due west. I'd come up from the south, from the direction of Vegas.

The sky-whine started up again. A second later, the dull red beam reappeared.

I shot to my feet and shaded my eyes out of habit. I squinted as I peered up into the sky, searching for a blimp or transport plane. Failing to spot any, I followed the column of light as far as I could with my eyes.

The hairs rose on the back of my neck. The red light seemed to reach into space. It made me dizzy, with vomit burning the back of my throat. I was starting to believe I'd stumbled onto something truly weird and definitely dangerous.

Abruptly, the dull red ray died away. I noticed the silence and realized the whine had been louder than last time.

The silence did not last. I heard faint voices that made my gut clench. The voices were creepy, buzzing noises like enormous insects might make.

I broke out in a cold sweat. I'd seen far too many science fiction and horror films, and I'd read too much for my imagination. The implications of all this—

Wait. The buzzing sounds were easy to explain. There must be soldiers down there wearing combat suits. I'd read about futuristic fighting gear before. The chief obstacle was a lack of small but powerful batteries. As batteries improved, the military would be able to make some truly impressive individual fighting gear. Maybe the military had chosen this location so they could easily recharge their suit batteries.

My shoulders slumped with relief as I realized the buzz must be coming from experimental equipment.

Yeah, okay, Logan, old pal, my suspicious half said. *Now explain to me what the giant red beam just did.*

I frowned, having a hard time coming up with an explanation that made sense. Maybe the light had been some kind of targeting thing. The soldiers had…made a night drop. They must be airborne soldiers practicing a night insertion. I simply hadn't seen them drifting down in the darkness.

I nodded, breathing easier.

As I crouched there, the sounds from the tanks dwindled, allowing me to hear wood beginning to splinter. I had no doubt what that signified. The soldiers were breaking into the block buildings. That seemed to confirm my idea of their need for the stored energy.

It would seem they were stealing the energy, and I was in charge of security…

What had happened to the two newbies? I'd forgotten all about them in the excitement.

I had to investigate, and I had to make sure my men were okay. If nothing else, I had my cell phone. I could take pictures of the Army experimenters destroying Western Sunlight equipment. That would save my employers a lot of money later.

I climbed to my feet as my determination grew. Then I remembered that my cell phone was dead. I brushed that aside. My eyes and memory would have to do when I gave my testimony in a court of law.

Taking a deep breath, I increased my pace. Had the Army paid off the two newbies with bribes? But if the Army had done that, why wouldn't they have just asked Western Sunlight for permission to use the facilities? The Army always had money to spare, and Western Sunlight would have grabbed at the money-trough opportunity.

Events weren't adding up, and that made me apprehensive. With great care, I headed toward the sounds of men kicking in doors.

-3-

I eased around the corner of a block building. As swiftly as I could in my foot-pinching shoes, I hurried along the side of the building. Finally, I peered around the next corner.

Flashlight beams played on the ground farther away. Three tall men were walking toward an unsullied entranceway to an untouched building. The men wore dress suits, although theirs looked more expensive than mine. Each of them wore a fancy hat like a Hollywood gangster.

The sight shocked me, and I froze, but not before the toe of my left shoe struck the wall, making a scuffing noise.

The three men stopped. The buzzing commenced between them, although I couldn't see their mouths. A second later, the flashlight beams swept toward my building.

I jerked back so the back of my head rested against the cool concrete of the building. The buzzing sounds grew more insistent. A second later, I heard the sound of their shoes quickly striking the pavement as they ran toward me.

I exploded off the wall, rushing toward the nearest solar collector. It seemed terribly important that I stay hidden.

I reached the collector, grabbed the nearest strut and swung myself around. At the same time, I threw myself onto the pavement. I hit with an "oof," knocking the air out of my lungs. I dug out the Smith & Wesson a second time, clutching it with both hands as I rested my arms on my elbows.

The three men came around the corner at a run. They played their flashlight beams on the ground. Maybe there wasn't enough sand on the pavement for me to have left tracks.

One light went along the base of the building. At a buzzing order from one of them, another sprinted along the side in that direction. The man had something in his other hand. It was hard to get a good look at it, but it was definitely a weapon of some kind.

The three no longer seemed like Army personnel to me, which shattered my previous guesses. I reanalyzed the situation. Something bothered me about these three, something I couldn't quite pinpoint.

The suited runner reached the other corner. He jumped around it, holding the weapon in one hand and the flashlight in the other.

The other two waited at the first corner.

I squinted, trying to see their faces better. Illumination from a flashlight helped, and it finally struck me what seemed wrong about them. Their faces were more like wooden masks than living flesh and blood. It made me think of zombies or beings who wore human disguises.

The one who had been sprinting opened his mouth. The buzzing seemed to come from somewhere deeper inside him. It was a fast noise, like a machine or a giant insect might make.

The sight and sound made my flesh clammy. I had to concentrate to keep myself from groaning in dread. What were those things? I didn't believe they were human.

The waiting duo played their beams on the ground and the nearest collectors. I remained in my prone position, trembling, but ready to fire if any of their lights washed over me.

Somehow, none of them did.

Unfortunately, my elbows were getting sore, and the .44 had begun to shake in my grip.

Finally, the three retreated around the two corners, one in one direction and the other two in the other. None of them buzzed the others before going. They just did so in unison.

I lowered the S&W and felt myself collapse against the pavement. I lay gasping for air. The situation had become surreal.

I swallowed in a dry throat. It was one thing watching little green men from Mars on the big screen while trying to make out with your date. It was another thing to find yourself all alone in the Nevada desert after witnessing red beams, boxlike tanks and buzz-talking freaks.

What would have happened to me if their flashlight beams had caught me?

I thought about priorities. I'd heard stupid stories about abducted people. In those, the extraterrestrials liked to practice experiments on their victims. If they caught me, would the tall men jab an insect growth into my gut? Would it grow while I ate ice cream at a prodigious rate? Would I have to watch my belly swell and see an alien burst out of me?

Western Sunlight wasn't paying me enough for that.

I squeezed my eyes shut as hard as I could. Was this the right interpretation of what I'd just seen? The buzzing had been too wrong. I hadn't imagined it, either.

Back in the Marines during embassy duty, I'd faced screaming protesters waving knives at us. I had held my post and attacked on command with my buddies. I would never have let my squad down.

No one would know if I slipped away now, though. Did I have an obligation to face these horrors? The two newbies were likely dead or long gone from the premises. How did my getting killed help them in any way?

I drew up to my knees, climbed to my shaky feet and began to stagger away from the block buildings. I wasn't sure of directions just then. But I knew I wanted separation from the freaks.

I found breathing difficult and my eyesight kept blurring. I was dead tired and now I was frightened and confused.

I—

"What are you doing here?"

I yelped as a tall man shined a flashlight beam in my eyes. I hadn't heard him approach, had no idea how he'd gotten ahead of me.

I raised an arm, shielding myself from his beam. He lowered it so the light shined on my chest. Then, he repeated the question. I squinted at him. He had the dead-eyed stare of a fish, but he hadn't buzzed the words with an open mouth. He'd spoken English...even if he had the slightest of accents.

"Who..." I took a draught of air and tried again. "Who are you?"

He looked to be anywhere from forty to fifty. He had a round face, and he was taller than me, although not by much. He was skinny, though. His somber face told me he was a no-nonsense man—if he was a man.

"This is private property," he said. "You are trespassing."

I just stared at him.

"Why are you here?" he asked for the third time.

"Jeep," I said, waving a listless arm.

"You have a vehicle?" he said in his unemotional manner.

I nodded.

"It runs?" he asked.

Did I detect a note of surprise? That helped me collect myself. Finally, my mind started whirling again.

"My, ah, jeep broke down," I said. "I've been looking for a gas station."

He studied me with his fish-eyes.

"You are lying," he announced. Without further ado, he reached under his jacket. I had no doubt he was reaching for a shoulder-harnessed weapon.

With an oath, I lunged at him. I didn't hit him, but I grabbed the arm going for the weapon. My hands latched onto a thin arm—thinner than it had a right to be. But that wasn't the terrible thing. He radiated a dreadful heat.

"Do not touch me," he said in the same emotionless manner that he'd spoken everything else.

He took his hand out from under his jacket as he flung his arm. I gripped the arm as hard as I could. That caused me to lift off the ground and launch away from him. I'd never heard of anyone with that kind of one-armed, standing strength. It was inhuman.

I flew away, but I didn't let go. My weight jerked him off his feet. I fell onto my back, pulling him over me as if I were some kind of kung-fu champion. I'd like to say I planned all that, but it was stupid luck. I let go then, and he sailed away from me.

Adrenaline kicked in. Like a coiled spring, I bounded onto my feet, swiveling toward him.

He hit the ground, and his flashlight flew from his hand. It landed and skidded, but managed to focus its beam on him.

His face never changed expression. I saw the arm dart under his jacket again.

My .44 was already in my hands.

BOOM!

The slug plowed the pavement beside him, blasting cement chips everywhere. That hadn't been the plan. I concentrated, aimed the hand cannon on his necktie and squeezed the trigger two times.

BOOM! BOOM!

I blew chunks out of him as black gunk jetted upward. It was too gooey to be human blood. He didn't have bones. At least, I didn't see any. Instead, he seemed to be made entirely out of some kind of dense meaty substance.

I'd taken out a good portion of his upper chest. Even so, the bastard sat up. A part of my mind screamed at me to run as far and as fast as I could away from this zombie. Another part of me told me I'd better keep my act together or I was a dead man.

Deliberately, I retargeted.

BOOM! BOOM!

I blasted his head, spraying gunk and bone in two shattering globs, and sending the hat spinning from the wreckage of his skull.

He fell back with a thud.

The shakes hit and I dropped my Smith & Wesson so it clattered onto the pavement. Weird alien noises—buzzing—came from several different directions.

"Logan," I hissed to myself in warning.

Despite the hammering in my chest and my shaking hands, I picked up the revolver. I had one bullet left. I shoved the big gun into its holster and clicked the strap into place.

Three steps brought me to the dead thing. I picked up his flashlight and shined it on him.

He was one ugly corpse with the black gunk bubbling out of his chest and shattered head.

I had one thing going for me, a curse, you could say. I screwed up easy jobs and pleasant relationships, finding it hard to do what everyone else found easy. Maybe as compensation, I found it easier to do the things that froze others. I could think and act normally in crazy situations.

With a grunt, I reached into his sticky suit and yanked out the weapon. It was pistol-shaped but wrong. There was no orifice for a slug to eject from—the end was solid. It reminded me of my raygun toys as a child.

I clicked off the flashlight, gripped the raygun harder than ever and listened. Approaching feet struck pavement and crunched on the gravel nearby.

The others were closing in on me. They were aliens. I might be the only human who knew about their existence, and I was alone out here at Station 5. The two newbies I'd come to see were either dead or long gone.

I knew one other thing. For the good of the human race—for my own well-being, too—I couldn't let the aliens find me.

-4-

I backed away from the corpse. Then, I turned and ran. As I did, I realized that might cause me to panic.

The funny thing about the human psyche is that it often follows what your body is doing. I'd learned that during my year in college. I'd been a waiter in a fancy restaurant. I'd often come to work angry, but I'd never left like that. The reason was simple. I'd forced myself to smile at the customers in order to get good tips.

"Hi, I'm your waiter, Logan," I would say, grinning or smiling if the woman at the table was particularly cute.

That smiling put me in a good mood. I know. That sounds shallow, like, what kind of goof was I? But try it sometime. When you're bummed or depressed, force yourself to smile and mean it. Sooner than you realize, you'll be feeling better.

This principle could also work negatively, as it was doing to me at Station 5.

Panic welled up in me as I sprinted from the extraterrestrial's corpse. I found myself breathing hard, with an itch crawling along my spine. I could imagine a red ray beaming me in the back, burning me down. That made me sprint faster as the gibbering monkey-brain in me tried to take over.

I swore softly at myself. With a stronger effort of will than it should have taken, I made myself stop.

Even then, I found myself trembling.

I swore to myself again, clenching my teeth together so they wouldn't chatter.

I wouldn't survive the night if I couldn't start thinking. Panic could kill a man faster than just about anything else. I might accidently dash myself against a collector strut if I wasn't careful.

"You gotta think this through, Logan," I whispered.

I wiped sweat out of my eyes, which caused me to gouge my forehead with the solid tip of the raygun clenched in my right hand. The pain made me flinch, and that made me mad.

Deliberately, I set the raygun and flashlight on the pavement.

My forehead throbbed. I touched it, feeling wetness there. I couldn't believe it. I'd cut myself with the end of the raygun.

Head wounds bled the worst. If I wasn't careful, I'd leave a trail of blood for the freaks to see.

I blotted my forehead with my jacket sleeve. In the old days, a man had a handkerchief in his front suit pocket. I could have used one about now.

How had the alien popped in front of me before? The original three hadn't spotted me. They'd played their flashlight beams everywhere but where I was hiding—

I hissed at my stupidity. That was it. That had been the giveaway—if I'd been awake to what had been going on. They'd spotted me and had made a show of looking everywhere but where I'd hid. They had played me.

Did that mean the extraterrestrials had better night-vision than humans did?

I listened intently, but couldn't hear them anymore. I imagined the tall, skinny, human-looking aliens moving silently in the dark. How hard would they look for me? Had they found the dead alien—

I spotted a glowing red light and whipped my head around so I could see more clearly.

The image of what I saw stamped itself into my memories. One of the expensively suited men—an alien, I told myself—held a similar raygun to the one I'd taken. And it was a raygun, all right. I saw a red beam stab from the solid orifice and strike the corpse. The corpse glowed, reminding me of a bad 1960s

TV special effect. Then the body began to slowly disintegrate. A dark oily smoke drifted from the glow, and an oily residue stained the pavement where the corpse had been.

After the entire corpse had vaporized, the raygun beam disappeared. It left afterimages on my eyeballs.

I looked away, closing my eyes, desperately wanting my night-vision back.

That clinched it for me. No way did the U.S. have hand weapons that could vaporize a body with a beam. We had red laser lights that kids used to drive cats crazy and flash on movie screens, but nothing lethal like I'd just witnessed.

I wasn't a math whiz, but I could do simple arithmetic. A red teleporting beam from space, boxlike tanks, buzzing instead of speech, fantastic strength from a rail-thin arm, radiating heat and lastly, a real raygun: that all added up to extraterrestrials on old Planet Earth. Worse, for me, they were in Nevada at Station 5.

Once more, I blotted my bleeding forehead with a sleeve.

The aliens had teleported down three tanks and a squad of goons from space to a remote desert location. My jeep and cell phone had died. The aliens must have blanketed the area with a—

I don't know what they'd used to do that. But as I said, I'd watched a ton of science fiction TV shows and movies. I'd read my share of SF novels, too. The aliens had arrived on Earth in spaceships no doubt presently orbiting the planet. That implied a Faster-Than-Light Drive, an FTL starship.

I looked up at the stars. Humanity wasn't alone. Right now, I wished we were.

If these bastards had a starship, was it scanning Station 5 for me? Would it work like that? Maybe the collectors made a scan difficult. Maybe if I ran out into the desert, I'd show up like a neon light on their scanners.

I listened more intently, straining to hear any telltale sounds.

What did it mean that the aliens looked and dressed like humans? That seemed to imply that they were trying to blend in among us. One of them had even spoken to me in English. These aliens had clearly studied mankind.

I began to feel lightheaded.

In the starlight, I examined my purloined raygun. The aliens appeared to have hands and fingers just like us. Were those their real bodies, or were the bodies…a disguise?

I noticed a stub where the trigger should be. With the lightest of touches, I depressed it a tiny bit.

I heard the faintest of whines inside the weapon as it started to vibrate just a bit in my hand. The tip glowed with an almost invisible red color.

I jerked my finger off the stub. Clearly, that's how I could fire it.

The faint whine cycled down. The vibration stopped.

I blotted my forehead again, mopping away blood and sweat.

I had a weapon to use. But what good would my one raygun do against their many?

I grimaced, determined to make a fight of it. I'd already killed one of the bastards. I could kill more if I had to. What right did they have to come down onto our planet and start destroying property? Maybe they had killed my two men, as well.

I had another thought. If their scanners were so good, why had they teleported down while I was here to see them? Did that mean they were arrogant, sloppy or less capable than I thought?

A noise to my left caught my attention. With deliberate slowness, I turned my head, staring, trying to see something other than indistinct black shapes.

I thought I could see something moving over there.

My heart began hammering and I started trembling. What should I do? Had an alien seen me? If he had, why hadn't he fired at me?

I heard a scraping noise from that direction. I estimated the black blot to be about sixty feet away. A low-sounding beep and a faint green glow were coming from it.

The primitive monkey-brain part of me screamed with certainty. The alien had a detector. The creature from another planet had spotted me with it.

Before I was quite aware of making any plans, I aimed the raygun at the greater darkness and firmly pressed the trigger stub.

The alien gun whined just like before, but louder and brighter this time, then vibrated and shot a pencil-thin beam. The light illuminated a tall alien in a human suit. It held a device that could have been a detector. I saw all that as the beam flashed past him, hitting a collector farther behind him to the left.

I adjusted, bringing the red ray onto him. The alien had lousy reflexes. The beam struck him square in the chest area just as he began to lower the device. He hadn't ducked, sidestepped or done anything more than move his arms a bit.

He glowed immediately, finally made a convulsive effort to escape and collapsed onto the pavement. That caused my red ray to overshoot him.

I lifted my trigger finger. I could hear something new in the distance. I didn't need to disintegrate him all the way—I just needed to take him out of play, which I'd done.

My heart raced. My gut boiled. I wanted to sprint like a mad fool for the desert and get the Hell home. Instead, I began walking to the right.

I was certain I would be an easy target in the desert. And I wanted to live. Despite the fuzziness of my thoughts, I actually had a plan. Now, it was time to see if I could pull it off.

-5-

As far as I could see, the trick was surviving the night. Later, I would have to tell someone what had happened.

Clearly, people would think I was nuts…unless I had incontrovertible evidence. The evidence would be my raygun. I didn't plan to use it again tonight, as I didn't want to drain whatever juiced the disintegrating beam.

The plan was simple and elegant. I'd learned in the Marines that complicated plans usually went awry because of friction.

In military terms, friction was all the little things that went wrong, often at precisely the worst time. A man named Mr. Murphy had a law about that, the kind of law few people could ignore and get away with it.

Because of friction, easy plans were usually the best ones. The more people one involved in a plan, the more friction it caused.

I was going to hide in a basement—in a battery storage area. I would go to one of the places that they'd already raided. In hide-and-seek, one of the best spots to hide was in a place a seeker had already searched. In hide-and-seek, doing the opposite of what the seeker expected was also a good bet.

The aliens would surely expect me to run away.

I heard one of them to the right. Slowly, I lowered myself until I was crawling across the pavement on my belly. In the interest of survival, I'd taken off my shoes. I held one in each hand along with a rolled-up sock stuck inside each. That made holding the flashlight and raygun harder, but I could manage for a while.

I was going to have to walk out of here later, tomorrow, most likely. I didn't want to do that in my bare feet or without socks.

I stopped, badly out of breath under a collector. Belly crawling was hard, sweaty work. It had also been too long since I'd had a drink of water. I was beginning to feel dehydrated, and I was definitely hungry.

It took me several tries to swallow and a few more seconds to focus again. I could see the block buildings from here. Three of the dress-suited aliens were carrying huge boxes through one of the smashed-apart doors.

I would skip that building.

After a minute of observation, I began to crawl again. Thirty seconds of it left me panting too hard. I was never going to get where I wanted at this rate.

It bothered me that I couldn't force myself to stand right away. Fear had a lot to do with that. Maybe it would be better to head into the desert after all.

"No," I whispered. "Stick to the plan. Don't chicken out."

Trembling, I climbed to my feet. Crouched over as if that would help keep me hidden, I crept from one solar collector to another. Finally, I neared the building opposite the one the three beings had entered.

I would first have to cross an open area to reach my building. I looked around and didn't see or hear any aliens.

I grimaced to myself, but I knew that the sooner I started, the sooner I'd be safe. I tottered into the open. My stomach clenched and my spine tingled. I felt as if an alien sniper had a bead on me. The bastard was playing me, knowing my fear was eating up my nerves.

I was shaking badly by the time I threw myself against a wall. I looked up, gulping air. This had been a terrible idea—

I cursed under my breath and started moving again. I had the raygun in my hand, the trigger finger hovering over the stub.

I stopped at the corner, peered around it and saw a tall alien exit a building. He held something up against his left ear. It must have been a communicator. He stopped, looked around, held the thing before his mouth and made soft noises I could not hear. Finally, he resumed walking, disappearing around another building.

I darted out, rushed to a smashed door and zipped inside the building. I promptly crashed against a low box, sprawling over it. I lost the flashlight and raygun. They both clattered over the floor. I barely caught myself in time. If I hadn't, I would have used my nose to do the landing.

I panted in terror, certain I was about to hear aliens come running to inspect the noise.

None of them did, though.

I climbed to my feet and winced as I tried to move my left wrist. I must have sprained it. I crawled on my knees, using my good hand to search the floor. Finally, I found the flashlight. I kept looking for the raygun and had no luck, although I did find my shoes. I took thirty seconds to put them on.

Afterward, I asked myself what was the best option.

I clicked on the flashlight, playing the light across the floor. Ah. There it was. I clicked off the light, collected the alien weapon and headed for the stairs.

Soon, I eased down the metal steps. I feared using the flashlight again, so I went slowly. I reached the bottom and fumbled around, finally bumping against a giant storage unit.

This was no good. I didn't even have starlight anymore. It was pitch-dark, the kind that made a hand in front of your face invisible.

I clicked on the flashlight, and my hopes sank. I'd guessed wrong. Friction had reared its ugly head.

As I moved past the first storage unit, I saw an alien contraption. It was square-shaped, about the size of a large dinner table and it was pulsating rhythmically as if it were a giant heart.

I took several steps closer. The thing radiated heat. I noticed cables plugged into it. Those were energy cables from the batteries, but I didn't see the ends plugged into the pulsating gray…thing. The flesh—if that was flesh—engulfed the plugs.

I circled the gray, square-shaped, pulsating creature. I looked for eyes or a mouth, but found nothing like that. It seemed to be all one pulsating piece.

What was the thing supposed to do? What was its function?

I knew I had to get out of here. If the aliens had plugged this monstrosity into the storage batteries, they were going to come back eventually.

I spun around and took a step toward the stairs.

I heard buzzing. It seemed to come from inside the building on the main floor. Another alien seemed to reply to the first.

Were they headed toward my basement?

I flicked off the flashlight and peered from around a storage unit. I saw light up there. They seemed to be heading this way, all right. The footsteps drew closer—

I held my breath.

The door opened all the way, and a light shined down the steps. An alien put a foot down the first staircase.

I had to make a decision. A second alien followed the first. They both had flashlights.

I aimed the raygun and depressed the stub. The weapon whined, vibrated and shot a thin red beam. It struck the first alien in the chest. I held the beam on him as he began to smoke.

The second alien dropped his flashlight. Faster than I had seen any of them move, the second alien pivoted on the stairs. This one moved like a lizard, leaping upward.

I moved the raygun, sending the beam at him. The red beam struck the doorframe as the second alien darted out of sight.

Now what was I going to do?

-6-

I think I realized it was over for me then. Depression welled up. I'd hoped to take them both out and get out of here.

Likely, it was too late for that now.

I snarled a curse, tightening my grip on the raygun. I wasn't beaten yet, damn it. I had to think this through. I needed to act before it was too late.

I clicked on the flashlight. The first alien had one hand on his chest, trying to stanch the flood of black gunk from the hole there. His other hand wiped at his belt, trying to drag out his raygun. His skin had turned a nasty shade of green. Did that mean he was dying?

I raced for the stairs, trying to beat him to the punch. His other hand finally latched onto the raygun, and he began to draw it out of its holder.

I pressed the stub, drilling him a second time with my beam. He smoked, and part of his upper body disintegrated. I quit firing, bounding up the stairs. Unfortunately, I slipped on black gunk that had dripped down several steps.

I released both the flashlight and the raygun in order to catch myself, but it was too late. I slipped on the alien blood and went down hard, striking my chin on a metal step.

I must have knocked myself out.

The next thing I knew, my head and jaw were aching. A few of my teeth felt loose. I lay at the bottom of the stairs. When I tried to get up, I groaned in agony. I thought I might have broken one of my ankles.

I didn't hear anything from the top of the stairs. Was the first alien dead? I had no way of knowing. I tried to think, but that was getting harder by the second.

If I'd broken an ankle, it was all over.

I dragged myself along the floor, searching in the darkness around the stairs. After a time, I found the flashlight and clicked it on. Soon thereafter, I had the raygun again.

I checked my left ankle. I couldn't tell if it was broken, but it had swollen to the size of a grapefruit and the skin was discolored.

I glared at the dead alien on the stairs.

Friction had nailed me in the end. Those stupid little things one didn't consider had ended my chances. Instead of feeling sorrow or pity for myself, I realized I still had to do my part for the human race.

There was another factor to my next action. The aliens were going to kill me. Of that, I had no doubt. That made me angry. I wanted to hurt the bastards who were going to steal my life from me. I could lay an ambush for the next ones to show up, but maybe they had battle tech to take care of the situation. There was only one way I could see to hurt them now.

On my belly, I crawled for the storage units. The light jiggled as I crawled. Finally, from on the floor, I stared at the pulsating gray matter. I'd like to know what the thing did. Why had they hooked it up to our power?

I set the flashlight on the floor so the light was aimed at it. Afterward, I took the raygun in both hands. My hands no longer shook. They were rock-steady as I depressed the stub. The thin beam struck the pulsating gray thing that drank our collected solar energy.

I expected it to glow, but that didn't happen. The pulsating gray matter seemed to resist the beam. The flesh darkened around the spot of the beam, but that was it.

I kept beaming the thing, hoping to wear it down. My raygun vibrated and whined louder than ever. I noticed that the gray flesh-cube pulsated less than before. That was something, at least.

Finally, I quit beaming and dragged out my revolver. With a loud boom, I sent my last bullet into the quivering alien flesh. Then, I resumed beaming it.

Everything was different after that. The thing quivered like mad. It began to glow this time, and awful smelling smoke billowed from it.

"Die!" I shouted.

The first piece of flesh disappeared soon thereafter. Black gunk spilled out of the area and gave off terrible fumes. For an instant, I saw lights inside the quivering square of table-sized flesh. Was this a weird, alien cyborg unit?

I beamed until my raygun cycled off. Just before that happened, more of the gray-flesh square disintegrated. Gallons of black gunk jetted out of the rest, and the huge square began to deflate like a slowly leaking balloon.

At that point, my raygun gave up the ghost. I heard it click several times, and then it stopped altogether. I'd used up its power pack.

The alien gray square dying like that did something bad to the batteries, which should have been impossible. The huge batteries began to hiss and shake, and suddenly they discharged electrical bolts. A smell of ozone mixed with the foul alien odors.

I climbed up and hopped away on my good foot.

Something I couldn't see began to crackle with fire. Electrical smoke added its stench. I had to get out of here before I burned to death or was electrocuted.

I hopped several more times and crashed against the bottom of the stairs. I didn't let that stop me, not now. I began crawling up on my hands and knees.

Maybe the half-disintegrated alien still had his raygun. If so, I could use that. The slippery black gunk had already started to harden, but not enough for my tastes. It soaked through to my knees and got on my pants.

The dead alien was still holding a raygun, but the weapon was melted in places and therefore useless.

Carefully, I negotiated around him, continuing up the stairs until I reached the door. I heard aliens out there. They were coming.

I hopped again, and took out my Smith & Wesson. I was out of bullets. I should have had extra rounds with me, but wishing wasn't going to help me now.

My bad ankle throbbed. Alien blood clung to my clothes. My time on Earth was rushing to a close. It left me bitter, I admit it.

I reversed my hold of the .44, gripping it by the barrel. I would use it like a club. It was the best I had. If only I'd taken a flip-knife with me.

The first alien hurried through the main smashed door. I clubbed him as hard as I could on the back of the head. It was a terrific hit. If he'd been human, I'd have dashed him to the floor. That had been my hope, as I'd planned to relieve him of his raygun.

Instead, the alien stumbled forward without going down. He buzzed as if cursing with pain. I hopped at the bastard, but that only made me an easier target for the next thing through the door.

"Stop," an alien behind me said in English.

I didn't stop because I knew there were no percentages in it. This was it. I wasn't going to go out trussed up or given a lecture before one of them shot me. I was going to go out fighting—if I could get close enough to the first alien who had ruined my chances for escape.

I hopped on one leg as hard as I could. It would have made my old high school track coach proud. I had done the hop, step and jump in track, and had done well enough to go to the meets.

The hops jarred me enough to click my teeth together. That might have alerted the first alien.

He took his hands from the back of his head and turned around to face me. The second alien—the bossy one—buzzed a warning, I suppose.

I snarled, raised my gun-club and found an alien fist smashing me square against the nose. Everything went blank after that.

-7-

I grew aware again as a constant vibration played along the length of my prone body. I felt it mostly in my hands, which were pressed down before my aching face.

A hump of sorts on the floor caused my butt to stick up. A grinding noise up ahead made me frown, and my body lurched as gravel crunched somewhere nearby.

What was going—?

Oh. I was in a car. They'd put me on the floorboard in the back seat. I felt something in my good hand. I played with it in my fingers, crinkling…a hard candy wrapper.

Slowly, I unraveled the wrapper and slipped the hard candy into my mouth. I wanted to crunch it. I was ravenous, but I sucked it instead. It was cinnamon flavored—

Wait a minute. This was from Strings. I always grabbed a fistful of these as I left the restaurant. I felt the carpet, felt the way the vehicle moved—

The bastards were carting me out in my own jeep.

My anger brought a touch of greater awareness to my foggy brain. I felt something on my back. I lay there, trying to decipher the feeling. Finally, the thing on my back shifted.

An alien was using me as a footrest. I must have twitched then. I couldn't help it.

The alien using me as a footrest spoke. "The creature is awake."

"Has the creature spoken to you?" the driver asked.

"No. He is silent. I believe he is trying to understand the situation."

The alien was right about that. I desperately wanted to understand. My mind was sluggish, though. One thing made me curious. They didn't buzz to each other. They spoke in slightly accented and stilted English. There was a reason for that, and I would have liked to know what it was.

"Ask the creature its name," the driver said.

The alien with his feet on my back did just that.

"Logan," I answered.

"Does the creature possess the customary two names or merely the one?" the driver asked.

"Why not check my driver's license?" I said.

Neither of them spoke. Finally, Mr. Nasty Feet-on-my-Back dug out my wallet. He soon told the driver my last name.

"How about letting me sit up," I said.

"The creature feels humiliated," the one said.

"That is interesting," the driver said. "It makes my hypotheses even more likely. I submit it is the only answer to what we witnessed."

"Why would it wield such primitive weapons then?"

"It used our weapons against us, which was an ingenious move. It also maneuvered skillfully to the most delicate point of our process. It rendered the achiever into a null state. That should make the reason for its apparent primitiveness self-evident."

"I do not understand," the backseat alien said.

"The primitive weapon aided its disguise," the driver said. "The aboriginal-style assault almost deflected us from the true nature of its being. Luckily, I have a Class 5 understanding of the Galactic Guard's deception techniques."

"The Organizer will surely add several percentage points to your haulage fee because of your greater education."

"That is my estimation as well," the driver admitted.

I frowned with my forehead pressed against the carpet. These two did not sound like deadly space invaders. It almost seemed as if the driver was bragging about himself. And what was this about a haulage fee? Were these two contractors for someone calling himself the Organizer?

"Who are you?" I asked.

"The deceptive Earth-disguised creature is becoming demanding," the backseat alien told the driver.

"Cause him pain."

The alien dug one of his heels against my back, making me squirm.

The squirming caused me to use my left foot and I yelled. That sent pain shooting through my bad ankle, which made me lurch upward.

"He is attempting an escape."

"Shock him into submission," the driver said in the same emotionless voice they'd both been using the entire time.

"Wait a minute," I said.

It was too late. A prod sizzled against me that sent electrical currents coursing through my body. I went rigid at the pain and collapsed in a heap once the alien removed the shocker.

"You will not make demands of us," the rear-seat alien told me. "You will await the next phase in docile contentment."

"Sure," I gasped, "whatever you say. Just don't shock me anymore."

"He is attempting to negotiate a better deal," the backseat alien said.

"Shock him again," the driver said.

"No! Wait!" I said.

"He demands you desist giving me orders," Mr. Backseat said.

The driver slammed on the brakes. That threw me against the back of the front seats. The jeep skidded across the road until we came to a stop.

I heard the front door open, and then a back door opened. With iron-like fingers, the driver grabbed my broken ankle. He dug those fingers into the tender flesh.

I yelled loud and long, trying to kick my foot free of him. He dug harder, finally letting go.

I wanted to whimper at the pain, but refused to give him the pleasure. My foot throbbed horribly and a cold sweat had broken out along my body.

"You will not make demands of us," the driver said. "We know about your deception. I realize you want to goad us into killing you. This will not happen. You will now serve us, or I will cause you endless torment."

I panted, remaining silent.

"He is stubborn," the backseat alien said. "He refuses to acknowledge your order."

"What do you want me to say?" I shouted.

"Is that another demand?" the driver asked the other.

"No," I said. "Look. I'm different from you. I'm not trying to order you around or to disagree. I'm confused, and you're hurting me."

"Is this more deception?" the backseat alien asked.

"Yes," the driver said. "The Galactic agent is exceptionally skillful. He seems very convincing. Listen to me, Guard-man. Will you do as I demand?"

"Yes," I said.

"This is your given bond?" the driver asked.

"Yes," I said.

"How can a guard-man have become so weak?" the backseat alien asked.

"Perhaps they stationed him on this dirt ball for many cycles," the driver said. "He has become lax like the aboriginals."

"How the mighty have fallen."

"Do not show so much awe toward the Galactic Guard," the driver said. "If the Organizer ever heard you speak like that…"

"I am ashamed of my words," Mr. Backseat said.

"It is forgotten," the driver said. "Logan-creature, are you awaiting my speech?"

"Yes," I said.

"You will remain stationary for the remainder of the journey. If you attempt any subterfuge, Z17 will administer pain. Do you acknowledge my command?"

"Yes," I said.

"He has a great fear of the pain," Z17 observed. "I would not have believed it before this example."

“We will use this fear to keep him docile until we reach the destination,” the driver said. “Then, he will deliver the ship into our hands.”

“He would do this for us?” the backseat alien asked.

“You heard him. He will do anything to escape the pain. Now, watch him closely. He may attempt a trick.”

“I am ready for any deviousness,” Z17 said. “I will pain him greatly if he so much as twitches the wrong way.”

Without another word, the driver returned to the front, slammed his door shut and revved the engine. With a lurch, we started moving again.

I had no plans of trying to escape for now. But what did the driver mean I was going to deliver a ship into his hands? What kind of disguise did he think I maintained? Had he called me a Galactic agent?

Clearly, he’d taken me for someone else. Probably, this was the only reason I was still alive. I had to use that against him. I believed I could. Because from what I’d heard so far, the aliens had stopped impressing me. That gave me hope—and I needed something to give me an edge. Otherwise, I was never going to survive the next few hours.

-8-

The rest of the car ride proved uneventful. None of us spoke further. I slept in a half-dazed state, hungry, exhausted and shivering at times.

I wondered what would happen to me once I failed to deliver this ship to them. What were the other aliens doing in Nevada? Why had they appeared at Western Sunlight, Station 5? These two hadn't sounded as if they belonged to an alien invasion force making a beachhead on our planet. What did that make them then?

I noticed that bright lights shone through the windows. I tried to roll over to see where we'd arrived.

"Remain still," Z17 told me.

"How about telling me where we are then," I said.

"Do not interrogate me or I will prod your flesh."

I hated being a prisoner, but it was better than being dead. How had the Good Book put it? *Even a live dog is better off than a dead lion!*

I felt like a dog, all right. Back at Station 5, I had been a lion. Maybe if I lived long enough, I could reverse the situation again and roar once more.

Even as I told myself that, I began shivering uncontrollably. I imagine it was due to shock from the broken ankle, maybe shock at my predicament as well.

The jeep stopped. The engine quit. The driver's side door opened. He must have opened a back door, too, because I still felt Z17's feet on my back.

“We will move him to the plane,” the driver said.

Z17’s feet stepped across my back, over my butt and across the back of my legs.

“Sit up,” he said from outside.

I rolled over and worked up to sitting position. We were at a well-lit field, with massively bright lights shining down on us.

Z17 grabbed an arm, hauling me out. His grip was hot and he was inhumanly strong.

I groaned as I bumped my bad ankle on the jeep, but I managed to balance on my good leg outside the vehicle.

“He is weak,” Z17 said.

“Bring him,” the driver said.

“I dislike touching his cold flesh,” Z17 complained. “It reminds me of the Doppler fish on Quintus Five.”

“Prod him then,” the driver said. “Just make sure he is in the plane by the time we leave.”

With that, the driver walked away toward what looked like a large warehouse.

I had a second to scan my surroundings. For a wild moment, hope flared anew, as I thought we were at a local airport. That was wrong. Past eleven bright lamp-poles that circled a large warehouse, there was nothing but more Nevada desert. I saw several Learjets and an old WWII Mustang parked nearby.

“Go,” Z17 told me, pushing against my left shoulder.

I hopped, crashing down onto my good foot, barely managing to stay upright. He shoved again, and I hopped again, barely staying up a second time.

“Hey,” I said, turning toward him. “Why not point to where you want me to go. I’ll hop there as fast as I can. If you keep shoving me, I’m going to fall down.”

Z17 looked at me deadpan.

As he did, I studied him. He was taller than me by a few inches. He was rail thin and wore a dark silk suit and the fancy hat. The face was too round and the eyes too dead-seeming for him to pass as human. I was betting the hat hid something monstrous. His facial color was passable as a too-white

Russian or Canadian. His hands were gray, though. He should have worn gloves if he wanted to pass as human.

"You are inquisitive," Z17 said. "I find it distressing. Therefore, you will not look at me."

I averted my gaze from his face.

"You are properly docile," Z17 said, "and you are quick to heel to my commands. That is prudent. I wonder, though. Why do you continue with your Earther disguise?"

I shrugged.

"Go that way," Z17 said, pointing.

I hopped toward a Learjet. As I lurched one hop at a time, I realized that an eerie whine was emanating from the warehouse. It set my teeth on edge and made the hairs on the back of my head stir. I tried to ignore the sound, but it drained much of my remaining strength.

Halfway to the jet, I sagged to my knees, panting from the strain.

"This is not the destination," Z17 said behind me.

I peered back at him. Had I clubbed him earlier with the .44? Had I—

He drew the prod from under his suit, clicking it on so a spark of discharge played on the end.

I groaned as I straightened, hopping again. My good leg had become shaky, the knee sore. Sweat drenched my clothes. My vision began to narrow, never a good sign. I wondered if I was close to passing out.

That seemed likely. As much as Z17 didn't want to feel my cold skin, I didn't want to feel his hot hands. It wasn't a pleasant heat, but like a creature let out of Hell for a season. The alien didn't belong on our world.

As my vision swam, and my hops grew shorter each time, I became convinced the aliens were here to steal some precious resource from the planet. They were thieves, plundering our world of items we would need in the future. They did this in a greedy manner, the way strip-miners tore apart a beautiful mountain for several pounds of gold, leaving nothing but ugly rubble.

At last, my hands crashed against the side of the jet. That made me twist away because of my sprained wrist. I'd forgotten about it. The pain caused me to fall onto my back.

"Get up," Z17 said.

I stared at him from the ground.

He pulled out the prod.

I closed my eyes, exhausted, having given my all. A second later, I bolted upright as a jolt of electricity coursed through me. I crashed against the jet, managing to hold the position, resting the side of my face there.

"You are a remarkably lazy creature," Z17 said.

I had no comebacks. I simply breathed, sweated and trembled.

I heard something *click* and looked up to see that he had unfolded a staircase from the plane.

"Go inside," he said.

I worked around on my good leg, hopping up a step at a time, finally sliding onto the carpeted floor. I dragged myself to a cushioned seat, standing and plopping into it, exhausted.

The interior was plush, with expensive-looking equipment, but nothing out of this world.

Z17 climbed in, pressing a switch to bring up the stairs and closing the entrance. He regarded me, waving a hand before his face.

"Offensive odors radiate from your being."

"You overworked me," I said. "That makes me sweat, which releases an odor from my sweat glands."

"Earth creatures are biologically suited to this low gravity world," he said. "Therefore, your statement is illogical."

"You can move around as easily on a broken leg as on two good ones?"

He pulled out the prod.

"That wasn't an interrogation," I said. "That was a statement answering your question."

Z17 stared at me with his fish-eyes. "Explain your remark more fully."

"My ankle is likely broken. That means I can't use it. If your ankle was broken, you would be limited in mobility as well."

"That is illogical. My ankle would never break."

I blinked at him stupidly. "Maybe you don't have bones like we do."

"You liken me to an Earth creature?"

"Not if you take that as an insult," I said.

"They are vertebrates," he said. "They lack healing speed and are easily immobilized. How could likening me to an Earth creature be anything other than an insult?"

"How about we change the subject," I said. "I'm famished and thirsty. I'm not going to be able to deliver any ship to you unless I…replenish my strength."

That seemed to freeze him as he considered my words. Finally, "You claim to be an Earth creature indeed?"

I could see where I might have made a mistake. If they thought I was a Galactic agent *pretending* to be human…

Z17 shoved the prod into a holder under his suit and took out a communicator. He watched me as he pressed a tab on the communicator. Then, he opened his mouth and buzzed words.

Seeing and hearing it up close made my flesh crawl and my vision narrow again. I opened my mouth and tried to hyperventilate so I wouldn't pass out. It worked just enough.

As my vision expanded to something normal again, Z17 put away his communicator. "You have attempted a sly play, Earth creature. We will have to rig you for the next phase. Put your arms on the two rests."

I blinked at him, debating my chances for a last attack. I realized they were less than slim. So, I put my arms on the rests.

He pressed something in his pocket. Tentacle-like bands flew around my forearms, securing them in place.

Z17 promptly went forward, passing a curtain. A few moments later, he returned with something that looked like bolt cutters.

"This will hurt," he said.

"What are you doing?" I asked, alarmed.

Without further ado, Z17 knelt on one knee, opening the pseudo bolt cutters and reaching for my bad ankle.

"Hey!" I shouted, kicking my leg.

That didn't help. He neatly caught my ankle with the sheers. The cutting parts weren't metal, but two crackling lines of power. He snapped the handles inward. The crackling, buzzing power-lines sliced through my flesh and bone, and my foot and part of my ankle dropped to the floor, separated from the rest of me.

My eyes bulged in shock and dismay. A terrible groan slid past my lips. Blood poured from the ankle, and I began to buck in my seat, trying to tear my arms loose from the metal tentacles.

"Desist in that," Z17 said.

More blood leaked out of my half-cauterized ankle.

Z17 drew his raygun, grabbed my maimed leg and beamed spots around the ankle. Pain exploded, causing me to black out.

I jerked upright what must have been seconds later. This time, I howled in agony, continuing to thrash in the seat.

Z17 was on his feet, staring down at me as he held my bloody foot in his hot hands. He reopened the Learjet entrance and jumped outside, heading for the big warehouse that made the strange whines.

Where was he taking my foot, and why? I frowned as I realized something else. My right triceps throbbed. I stared at my triceps and saw a growing spot there. Spurts of blood leaked. If I were to guess, I'd say Z17 had shoved a needle into my arm the few seconds I'd passed out. What had he injected into me?

Before I could derive a conclusion, existence faded from my consciousness as I blacked out a second time.

-9-

I came to by slow degrees. I was aware of vibration and a loud noise. My position lurched then, seeming to go up and down.

My vision was foggy and it felt as if someone had stuffed cotton balls in my mind. I'd been in trouble. I'd...gone somewhere in the dark, with bright stars overhead—

Nevada. I had gone to Station 5 to check up on the two latest hires. Yeah, my jeep had stalled, and—

Aliens!

The last few hours came flooding back. I lurched upward and stared down at my foot.

It was there!

I checked the other foot. It was there, too. I had both feet.

I couldn't help it. I laughed, grinning like a maniac. I checked my hands then, rotating both wrists. They were good. They were strong. Neither was sprained.

In fact, I felt invigorated. As my mind began to chug into a higher gear, I realized I had never felt better in my entire life. As the fogginess departed, a new feeling of strength and well-being filled me.

That made no sense at all.

I closed my eyes and opened them, repeating the procedure several times. Finally, I gathered my bearings.

I was inside the Learjet. It droned loudly as midsized airplanes do while in flight. It was dark outside so I could clearly see the stars. There was also a bottom glow along the darkness.

I looked across the aisle. Z17 or his twin sat in a seat. He wore darkly tinted goggles with buds in his ears. Was he watching an inflight movie?

The alien turned toward me, making a clicking sound with his mouth. Maybe that was his way of acknowledging that I was looking at him.

I turned away, moved my arms—the metallic tentacles no longer secured them. I slid over a seat and stared out the window.

I wished I hadn't.

I stared down at the Earth. We were high up here, what NASA might call low Earth orbit. I knew Learjets did not fly this high. Big jumbo jets did not fly this high. Nothing other than the Space Shuttle and satellites had reached this height.

How could the Learjet be up this high?

The answer was obvious. The aliens had modified the plane. Maybe they had gravity control, or something.

I turned from the window and grabbed my foot. Z17 had used power-line cutters to snip it off and a raygun to cauterize the wound. I examined the foot. There was a hairline scar all the way around my ankle.

I rotated my ankle. It felt fine. I put my foot down and put weight on it. There was no pain.

"Can I speak to you," I shouted over the engine noise.

Z17 turned toward me. He removed the earbuds and took off the goggles. For just a moment, his eyes were a glowing red color.

Just like a demon, I thought. Had the aliens been on Planet Earth before? Were the people who believed in UFOs correct? Had aliens visited Earth in the distant past and managed to get into our myths?

Z17's eyes turned from red to dark black. It was as if he made the change through an act of will.

I shoved my unease aside and pointed at my foot.

"You will soon need your full strength, Earthling," he said loudly.

"You just cut if off. Now, it's there."

"I am not a veterinarian or a xeno-surgeon," he said.

"I don't understand what you mean."

"You Earthlings possess crude mechanical bio-machines for bodies. You claimed a part of your body was broken. I took it to the fabricator. He repaired it for me. I simply reattached it afterward."

I blinked several times, taking in his implications. "You might have given me painkillers before you did that."

He made a gesture that seemed to indicate my words were meaningless.

"You are disposable," he said. "We use pain to prod you to correct action. Why would I bother giving you pain-inhibitors? I would rather give you pain-heighteners so you would leap to obey me the first time."

His frankness surprised me. I filed away the "You are disposable," and decided to ask him more while he was in a talkative mood.

"Why do I feel so much better?" I asked.

"Interrogations will—"

"I know, I know," I said. "Do not interrogate you. I'm not."

"You dare to correct me?"

I grinned.

"Now you bare your incisors at me in a hostile gesture."

"Z17," I said.

His face rippled as if worms moved under his skin. It was ghastly, and it made me gag in revulsion.

"Do not pronounce my designation," he said. "I find it…distasteful in the extreme. You will obey promptly in this."

I figured he meant I wasn't supposed to call him "Z17," again.

"Yes," I said.

That seemed to settle him, as his skin stopped rippling. After sitting still for a few seconds longer, he asked, "Do you mean to suggest that you feel intensely healthy?"

"Yes," I said, realizing that's exactly how I felt.

"When I reattached your ankle, I found your body infested with a vast array of diseases and malfunctions. That would hinder the reattachment, which would degrade your usefulness to us. Thus, I gave you a booster shot. It has given…" He seemed to consider what it had given me. "You now have perfect human health. You may be the only creature on this dirt ball to possess that. It has aided the healing, and it will aid in the ship-recovery."

"Okay—"

"You will now remain still and silent for the remainder of the journey. Otherwise, I will prod you for a prolonged time and lock you into your position."

"Yes," I said. "I understand."

He looked at me with his dead eyes.

I faced forward to show him I would do exactly as he said.

Finally, out of the corner of my eye, I saw him pull the goggles over his eyes again. He put the earbuds in place and settled back in his cushioned seat.

I looked out the window.

The modified Learjet continued to drone through space. I wondered if the aliens had done something to the outer skin, giving the jet stealth ability. If not, what did the various tracking stations on Earth make of us?

I leaned against the interior skin, peering out the window. I shuddered to see the northeastern edge of the North American continent. I could make out the upper edge of the U.S Eastern seaboard, New Brunswick and Newfoundland of Canada and then the vast wilderness of Quebec. We left the landmass and headed out over the Atlantic Ocean.

A lurch caused the Learjet to shift. The engines droned louder, and it seemed as if we increased speed. The jet began to shudder, and I pressed my nose against the glass, leaning as far back as I could to try to see the front of the jet.

The darkness around us rapidly dwindled as we began to reenter the blue of Earth's atmosphere. Before we did that, though, I spotted a new landmass. Most of it was ice-white. That made sense. It looked to me as if we were headed for Greenland.

Why would we go to that ice-locked island?

Long ago, during a planetary warm period, Viking explorers, led by a man called Eric the Red, had settled on the southernmost tip of Greenland. Eventually, the Greenland

Vikings had died out. Historically speaking, nothing else of importance had ever happened on Greenland.

So why would we be headed down to the ice island? How could I help them recover a ship on a piece of land almost continuously sheathed in arctic ice?

None of this made sense to me. If this ship was in Greenland, why had Z17 joined a bunch of aliens appearing in Nevada?

I flexed my left hand and rotated my formerly broken ankle. The aliens had fixed me like a broken toy. Now they expected me to help them. They figured I would do so in order to escape more pain. At first, they had thought I could help because I was a Galactic agent in disguise. They no longer seemed to believe that. So how could I help them as a mere Earth creature?

It seemed that I would find out when we landed. I needed a plan, but I had nothing. That meant I would have to wait for an opportunity. It didn't have to be a good opportunity. Otherwise, I might wait too long to do something. It just had to be a chance to hurt these intruders.

I vowed to myself that I would do exactly that when the moment came.

-10-

If the aliens had gravity control, it didn't show itself on the long glide down to Greenland. The modified Learjet shook, and the roar became like a cyclone. I had to clamp my hands over my ears and clench my teeth together. By the time the shaking lessened into something bearable, my jaw muscles ached as if I'd chewed ancient bubblegum for a week.

Z17 had never changed expression as he'd watched whatever he did on the darkened interior of the goggles. The noise hadn't bothered him in the slightest, and he'd ridden out the shaking with what seemed to me as contemptuous ease.

The Learjet skimmed across a vast field of ice and snow. We moved at nearly supersonic speed, rising a few times as we whipped past icy mountains.

Finally, the jet began to slow. The landscape outside was as bleak and desolate as ever. I couldn't see any sign of the sea, the ocean. I imagined we were in the middle of the monstrous island. I'd exchanged a desert of sand for a hellishly icy one.

The landing gear must have finally deployed. The Learjet lowered, and the noise became slightly less invasive as we touched down.

It was a hard landing as we bumped, rose, descended roughly again and skidded and slid for miles. Finally, we moved slowly enough for me to unhook myself and stare out my window.

There were snow-cats in the distance, another midsized jet and a large white warehouse building. It looked exactly like the one in Nevada except for the color.

Our pilot taxied us near the other Learjet. Finally, he shut down the engines. That allowed me to hear and feel the wind buffeting the plane.

"Stand," Z17 said.

I glanced at him. He'd put away the goggles and earbuds. He seemed ready to go.

"Can I ask you a question?" I said.

He stared at me. I had no idea what he was thinking. "Speak," he said.

"Do you have parkas for us?"

"Explain your meaning."

"Do you have heavy clothing?" I asked. "It must be cold outside."

"You desire space gear?"

"No," I said. "I need heavy clothing to protect me from the cold."

"That is illogical, as it is unlikely you will live long enough to experience any debilitation from weather extremes."

I let that settle in before I asked, "Don't you need thicker clothing for outside?"

I hardly saw his hand move as he pulled out the prod, lunged with a fencer's speed and jabbed me in the stomach.

A terrific jolt slammed me backward against the window. He held the prod against me longer than before—letting it zap repeatedly—and he seemed reluctant to remove it.

I lay on the floor gasping.

"Do not speak obscenely again," he said.

"Yes," I whispered.

"Come," he said, as he put away the prod. "Hurry to your feet."

I climbed slowly back to my feet.

The former driver swept past the curtain. He barely gave me a glance as he opened the entrance. Bitter cold howled into the compartment. Without a qualm, the driver walked down the steps into the icy wind. He began crunching through the snow toward the warehouse.

Z17 shoved me from behind so I stumbled to the entrance. I climbed down the steps and immediately began shivering from the cold. Icy particles struck my face and began numbing my skin. I turned up to Z17 in the Learjet's doorway.

"I'm going to freeze to death before I can deliver the ship to you," I said.

"Hurry to the snow-cat," he said. "You can wait in there."

I picked the closest one, staggering through the snow and bitter cold. I'd started last evening in the Nevada desert. Now, it was morning, and I was in the middle of Greenland. My body was acclimatized to hot weather, not to this mind-numbing cold.

My teeth began to chatter and my shivering inhibited my progress. I soon stumbled and hugged my arms against my body, rubbing myself to generate a modicum of warmth.

I hardly remember reaching the cat. Z17 opened the passenger-side door. Hot hands grabbed me, throwing me inside. He slammed the door shut, remaining outside.

While my teeth chattered, I looked around. Unbelievably, there was a parka in here. I put it on, even though the sleeves were too short and it bound tightly against my chest. With the hood over my head and my freezing hands in front of my mouth, I tried to warm myself the best I could.

It finally occurred to me that Z17 wasn't watching me as closely as before. He kept his gaze on the warehouse. He had to look over the cat's hood to do that. He only occasionally glanced to the side at me.

When he looked over the hood again, I quickly searched the forward compartment. This seemed like an ordinary Earth-made snow-cat. Slowly, I opened the glove compartment. A mid-sized screwdriver lay there among folded papers and an unopened package of Certs.

I stuffed the mint-flavored Certs and the screwdriver into a parka pocket. The screwdriver wasn't much, but maybe at the right moment I could jab it into one of the aliens.

I recalled how densely meaty the aliens had been. Z17 had seemed to imply earlier that he did not possess a spine or bones of any kind other than the skull that I'd blown away in one of them last night. That likely meant it would be hard to drive my screwdriver into one of them. If an opportunity presented itself, I'd have to plunge the screwdriver in as if I were trying to shove it through a concrete wall.

I kept searching the compartment, finally spotting a flare gun. It seemed too big to hide on my person. I picked it up and checked the load. There was a capsule in the tube. Maybe if I could get Z17 or the driver to bite down on the end of the tube, I could launch the flare into his gullet. Otherwise, would the flare incapacitate either one enough to do me good?

Maybe it could disable them long enough for me to grab one of their rayguns.

Z17 had made it plain. I was disposable, unlikely to last the morning. That meant I had to make my move soon.

Before I could formulate a plan, Z17 opened the passenger-side door. Fortunately, I'd already set the flare gun aside.

"Climb into the back," he said.

Without going out into the icy wind, I climbed over a seat, sliding in back.

Z17 climbed in, shutting the door. A few seconds later, the driver opened the other door, hoisting himself inside.

The driver looked at me before looking at Z17.

"The creature is weaker than we suspected," Z17 said. "It cannot tolerate the slight chill."

"Then it is indeed an Earth creature," the driver said.

"That is my conclusion as well."

"Kill it," the driver said, as he reached for the door handle.

"Is that prudent?" Z17 asked.

The driver froze, slowly turning to face Z17.

"We have used a transport vehicle to move to Location One," Z17 said. "The Organizer might note this if he demands an audit after the mission."

"The Earth creature is of no value to us if he lacks Galactic agent codes," the driver said.

"Is that precisely the case?" Z17 asked.

"A non-Galactic guard logically does not possess Galactic Guard codes," the driver said. "We need the codes to bypass the auto-defenses."

"That is true," Z17 said. "But we have noted the Earth creature's cleverness in Location Seven-A. That exhibition of cleverness was not natural to the species."

"This is interesting," the driver said. "Continue with your analysis."

"You noted this incongruence in the creature. To your astute mind, it suggested a Galactic agent in disguise."

"You agreed with my assessment," the driver said.

"I did indeed," Z17 said. "I am not attempting a blame-shift."

"It appears to me that you are."

"Bear with me, Q11."

"Continue," Q11said.

"You rightfully connected the link between the Earth creature and the Guard. In some manner we have not yet discovered, the Galactic Guard used the Earth creature toward its hindering ends."

"That is an interesting speculation," Q11 said. "You have a subtle mind, Z17."

"At first, I wished to have an explanation in mind in case of an audit. Now, I have begun to wonder whether my subconscious mind has not stumbled onto the truth."

"This is not stumbling," Q11 said. "This is a stroke of genius. With it, you have divined the Galactic agent's technique. We will continue with our original plan, using a slight modification with the aboriginal."

"We will insert a Bemis Six tracker into it?" Z17 asked.

I held my breath as I slowly moved my right hand into my parka pocket. The fingers curled around the screwdriver handle.

"Yes," Q11 said. "I will insert a deep tracker in the Earth-creature's intestinal track."

"Deep trackers are exceptionally painful to the host," Z17 said.

"That does not matter to us."

"It could," Z17 said. "The Earth creature might not survive such a placement long enough to perform its task."

"If it might not survive, that logically means that the Earth creature might survive the placement. You will inject the Earther with—"

"Excuse me," I said, interrupting.

Q11 shifted in his seat, looking back at me. I lunged at him with everything I had. I struck his head with my body, using my left hand to clutch the back of his head. Then I shoved the screwdriver as hard as I could at an eyeball. For once, I had perfect targeting. The tip of the screwdriver smashed into the eye. It was softer than the rest of his body. With my weight, I shoved the screwdriver blade deep into his brain.

Q11 violently jerked away from me. Because of my left hand on the back of his head and my fierce grip on the screwdriver handle, he dragged me over the front seats.

Z17 reached up, grabbing my legs.

I shoved my feet against his torso. Given my position, that propelled him hard against the passenger-side door. Maybe it hadn't latched properly before. The door swung open and the alien tumbled out of the snow-cat into the snow.

Q11 was twitching violently in his seat. I released him and felt an elbow smash against me, driving out my breath, but I still managed to draw his raygun from its holster. I beamed Q11 at pointblank range. He twitched even more violently and then sagged as if deflating.

I twisted around as Z17 climbed to his feet. For a second, our eyes met.

"See you later, dude," I said, beaming him in the chest.

He disintegrated in seconds, his fumy ashes sprinkling onto the snow outside.

By that time, black gunk from Q11 had soaked my parka.

My chest heaved as I sucked down air. This was an insane situation. These two freaks had been about to put a tracker in my gut—

I shook my head. I didn't have time to worry about that. I had to act while I could. With an effort, I pulled my thoughts together, formulating a rough plan. It didn't matter if it was freaky, practically impossible. I was in this mess, and unless I kept everything together, I would die, possibly in a hideous manner.

Aliens were real. Rayguns were real. I actually was in the middle of Greenland. If I played everything straight, I just might get out of here alive.

That helped me control my breathing and put the situation into perspective so my mind could continue to function. I had taken my opportunity, and it had worked twenty times better than I'd expected. Now, I had to keep doing that. I had to keep taking whatever these space bastards gave me.

I checked the warehouse. No one came running out of it. Luckily for me, the snow-cat's passenger side was on the opposite side as the building. Thus, the cat had blocked some of what I'd done.

I dragged Q11 from the snow-cat, dumping him onto the snow. One thing I learned then, these aliens were heavier than they looked.

I left the screwdriver in his brain, but I kept his raygun. Then, I checked his pockets, coming away with a communicator and a small device with several buttons on it.

I stared at him, looked over the hood at the warehouse and decided I couldn't stay here. If I could have, I would have liked to head back to Nevada in the Learjet. But I had no idea if I knew how to fly it. I was fairly certain I could drive the snow-cat, though.

Shivering, I climbed back in and slammed the passenger-side door shut. I slid to the driver's side while putting the raygun on the passenger-side seat.

The key was in the ignition. I turned it. The engine roared. I immediately turned on the heater to full blast. Precious and most welcome warmth blew out of it.

I glanced at the warehouse again. No one had come out of it since the last time I looked. Was anyone even in there?

I lacked the balls to go check. Instead, I put the snow-cat into gear and hit the gas. The treads began to churn, which made the main vehicle lurch. It was easy to decide where to go. I would follow the tracks in the snow heading out.

As the heater began to fill the cab with warmth, I wondered what I was going to do next. I was no longer a prisoner, and I'd killed two more aliens, but I was stuck out here in the middle of Greenland with no way home. I had an ill-fitting, bloody parka, a snow-cat and a raygun. How could that help me survive the next few hours? It was time to do some serious thinking.

-11-

I almost stopped the snow-cat and ran back to Q11. I might need his hat. The aliens wore them to look more like us—it seemed like a reasonable conclusion anyway. Maybe I could wear one to look more like them.

I peered back at the dwindling warehouse. Despite the wish to have an alien, Earth-looking hat, I couldn't force myself to turn around and go back.

The way I saw it, I had three options. I could follow the tracks and try to find this Galactic Guard-ship. Maybe I could worm my way onto it and contact Galactic Guard Headquarters. That seemed very chancy at best. The bad aliens had hinted that weapons or traps of some sort protected the ship. Why would I have any more luck getting past those weapons than the creepy aliens?

For the sake of argument, I would ditch option one. That left the last two. I could take the cat and head for the coast. I would have to hope the coast was near enough, that I had gas enough, and that I could find a human-owned ship or settlement to take me in.

That option seemed almost as risky as the first one.

Option three was heading back to the warehouse. That option had two variants. I could try to kill everyone in the warehouse, or I could try to slip onto a modified Learjet and fly out of here.

That option had far too many iffy variables to seem worth the effort.

So where did that leave me?

It would appear that I had selected option four: freeze to death in the middle of Greenland.

I shook my head, disliking option four the most.

Before I could reassess the options, the flat-shaped communicator buzzed. It lay beside the raygun on the passenger-side seat. I picked it up and realized my mistake right away.

The entire flat area showed me another alien, a spitting image of Z17. The aliens all looked alike to me. Maybe they thought the same thing about humans.

The alien on the screen opened his mouth and made the obscene buzzing sounds at me.

I stared dumbly at him, revolted almost as much as the first time I'd witnessed this.

"Who are you?" he asked, switching to slightly accented English.

"Ah…this is Z17," I said.

"Answer me correctly," the alien said. "Who are you?"

I depressed a button to no effect as I repeated my answer.

"Z17?" the alien said. "Why have you transformed into that hideous Earther shape?"

"I, ah, have devised an option to our original plan," I said.

"Speak further of this," the alien said.

I nodded, deciding to run with it. "In case the Galactic agent's protective devices kill the Earth creature, I will make a second attempt as an Earther."

The alien stared out of the screen at me. "That is illogical. My analyzer has also detected your falsehood. You are indeed an Earth creature as I first suspected. Give your device at once to Z17."

"Yes, at once," I said.

I opened my door and pitched the communicator outside. Quickly, I slammed the door shut. Then, I put my foot on the accelerator, increasing speed. I figured the aliens could track me through the communicator.

Twisting back in the seat, I could barely make out the warehouse. It seemed as if dots ran out of the building, but it was difficult to be sure. Soon, I saw puffs of smoke chugging from two snow-cats. That was certain. Clearly, the aliens had decided to give chase.

That would severely limit my options.

I shrugged fatalistically.

Maybe that was just as well. This way, at least, I knew what I had to do. It was option one now all the way.

I twisted back again. I'm not sure what I expected to see. Maybe I figured disc-shaped UFOs would appear, skimming the ice after me. Instead, I could make out two snow-cats giving chase. The warehouse had already dropped out of sight.

I laughed because that was better than howling in despair.

They had found me. But I was a free agent again. I'd slain them, paid them back in full for what they had done to me. There were worse ways to go in life than battling for your planet.

The way I saw it, I was winning against the aliens. I had become a huge pain in the ass for the rest of them. Maybe dumb luck had played a part. So had my willingness to go onto the offensive the first chance I'd had.

I twisted back once more. It looked as if the two snow-cats had gained on me just a little.

I debated plans and rejected them almost as fast. It seemed to me that keeping my morale high was half the battle. If I let myself get depressed, I would lose fast. If I kept believing I could do something against them, I'd at least try. I had won several encounters by trying.

I gripped the steering wheel, bouncing up and down in my seat as the cat crawled over a rocky patch. The clattering treads moved me toward a large canyon in the distance.

I wondered if the Guard-ship was out there. Who was this Galactic Guard anyway? Did that make these space invaders criminals? That would give the whole thing an entirely different spin.

My stomach rumbled. I was hungry. I searched as I drove, but there was nothing to eat in here. Finally, I remembered the Certs.

I tore open the package, eating them slowly one by one. It did little to assuage my hunger, but I'm pretty sure I had the mintiest breath in Greenland.

I thought about what the last alien had asked me, "Why have you transformed into that hideous Earther shape?"

Did that suggest the aliens were shape-changers? They lacked a spine and bones. They had dense meaty bodies, and they had humanoid appearances. Maybe the Organizer used these particular aliens because of their one amazing talent, the ability to shape-shift into the aboriginal form—us.

I thought about that and old Earth myths. Werewolves were supposed to be able to shape-shift after a fashion. Vampires turned into bats according to some of the legends. Demons took on the shapes of people or animals. Maybe those ancient legends held a tidbit of truth. That would imply the invaders had been here before. Vampires were supposed to be stronger than humans were. The same held true for demons.

I snorted. It was a fanciful thought that didn't make a bit of difference to my situation. Aliens were on my tail. Did anything else matter?

I studied the snow-cats behind me. Since I'd been holding the pedal to the metal, our distance had remained the same. I might even have pulled away a little.

It was a good thing they didn't have any guided missiles. I thought more deeply about weaponry. Just how far did these rayguns fire? Maybe the disintegrating beam dissipated over distance. Maybe they were only good at short range.

What did Nevada and Greenland have in common? What did the aliens do in those warehouses? They had said Nevada was Location Seven-A. That implied at least seven landing points. Here in Greenland was Location One.

The canyon had grown as I traveled. Worse, I saw two snow-cats heading toward me from there. I squinted into the distance. I thought I could make out another warehouse at the edge of the canyon, but I wasn't sure.

I thought up a wild plan. I would leap out of the snow-cat, first making sure it headed straight for the others. I would then wait in the snow for the two cats following me. Like an Indian (feather not dot), I would rise out of the snow to wreak havoc on these shape-changing invaders.

The problem with the plan was waiting in the icy cold. I'd finally started to get comfortable. On no account did I want to open any of the doors and brave the arctic chill.

That meant playing a game of chicken with the aliens heading toward me.

I debated how that would work. Two snow-cats against one would be poor odds. Yet, I'd beaten Z17 and Q11 at much worse odds. True, I'd had surprise on my side…

I remembered some of my Marine training. Surprise was a force multiplier. I also remembered grade-school multiplication. One times anything was still that number. But a force multiplier would be one times three perhaps. That would give me a force of three instead of just one.

I nodded as the distance between us closed.

The two vehicles headed straight at me. If each snow-cat contained two aliens, they had a force of four. Did they have better weaponry than me? That was questionable. Clearly, if each alien had a raygun, together they had four times my firepower. I noticed something else. The approaching snow-cats did not fan out, but came at me one on one like braves on the warpath. Was there a reason for that?

I twisted back in my seat.

I couldn't make out the vehicles well enough to see if they had done the same thing.

Why did the approaching cats come at me one on one? Could the area around the snow trail be full of landmines?

I grimaced. I knew too little. Maybe that was just as well. If I knew the real odds against me, I might never have gotten the balls to try anything.

I had to use surprise against them if I hoped to survive.

I turned the steering wheel, veering sharply off the trail. The treads churned snow. I was still headed for the long ravine coming up, but I no longer headed toward the approaching cats.

I kept my eye on those two.

The seconds ticked away into a minute. Neither of the approaching snow-vehicles followed me off the trail into the snow, although they still closed the distance between us. Now, however, they did so at an angle to me.

My heart began to beat faster and my breaths were shorter. I squeezed the steering wheel.

"Let's think this through," I said. Hearing my voice helped my battered morale a little. "It's possible you're going to reach the ravine before any of them do. What do you do once you're there?"

I tried to analyze that, but kept staring at the two approaching vehicles instead. I did not like it that neither of them had left the safety of the trail.

"This is what you have to do to win," I told myself. "This is just like pocketing the screwdriver."

My snow-cat lurched suddenly. I looked around as I heard a great splintering sound.

Sweat beaded my forehead. Should I put the cat into reverse? I clicked on my seat belt, noticed a shoulder strap as well, and clicked that into place, too.

I kept moving the machine forward. The noises had stopped, and the cat did not lurch like that again.

I wiped my forehead, glanced at the nearing enemy machines—

An explosively splintering sound and a sickening lurch downward told me I'd been right in one fashion. This wasn't a minefield but it was dangerous leaving the trail. My vehicle plunged down. I had time to see whiteness flash past me. Maybe I had been driving across a glacier and this was a giant crevice.

Sickening squealing noises and terrific buffeting told me the worst. I was indeed in some kind of crevice, sliding against the walls. With a slam and a jolt, the ride ended as suddenly as it had begun.

I sat there dazed, my mind wanting to shut down, my body too tired to keep doing this. I tried to reason this out. Instead, I sat there with my mouth open, remaining in a semiconscious state. Maybe it was time to let go of my consciousness and take a break from reality…

-12-

My shivering brought me back to reality.

I realized the cat must have shifted while I'd sat here in a daze. I stared into an icy depth. It seemed to go down forever, an opening into Hell perhaps.

The straps holding me constricted my breathing. I glanced to either side of me. Icy walls had pinned the snow-cat. The light came from above, likely through the hole I'd created by falling through.

I'd lost the game of chicken with the aliens. I had flinched.

A tapping noise confounded me. It came again, from behind. I twisted around and saw one of the aliens at the back window, the highest point of the snow-cat at present. The bottom of his dress shoes gently landed there.

I realized in a sick instant that I had to act now before it was too late. I searched the passenger-side seat, but failed to see the raygun. Then I saw the alien weapon on the windshield where it had landed after the fall.

Using my legs, I braced myself against the windshield, pushing upward enough to release the tension from my seatbelts. I clicked myself free of each of them.

I heard a heavy thump from the back window, another, and then glass shattered. A shower of glass pieces struck my seat back. A few hit my head. They all rattled against the windshield like hail.

Twisting upward, I saw the alien floating feet-first into the snow-cat. I imagined he had a harness around him.

"Do not move," the alien said. He aimed a raygun at me from between his fancy dress shoes.

"Please, save me," I wailed. "I'm hurt. I can't move even if I wanted to."

His raygun made a soft whine that I recognized. The tip glowed red. I tightened my muscles. So this was it. He was just going to murder me. Why had he come down to do that? He could have—

A beam flashed past my face. It struck the raygun on the windshield, melting it into uselessness and fusing it into the windshield glass.

An animal instinctiveness motivated me. I knew capture meant my death in the short term. Z17 and Q11 had proven that beyond doubt. My only opportunity for further life was to strike now.

I gathered myself and leaped upward, clawing at the front seat in the process. The fingers of my right hand reached upward just as he lowered another fraction. I grabbed a foot, pulled myself higher, and latched my other hand onto the same foot.

He must have fired the raygun again. I heard it whine. At the same time, I yanked him to the side and got lucky. The beam grazed his leg. That must have caused him to release the trigger stub.

The whine quit. His leg smoked, squirted black gunk and he jerked convulsively.

That dislodged my grip.

I slammed down against the glass-littered windshield. That caused the snow-cat to creak with metallic complaint as it shifted the tiniest and most ominous bit.

"Cease this resistance," the alien said.

I jumped up again, clawed at the driver's seat again and grabbed the silky fabric of his pant leg. Like a monkey, I hoisted myself higher.

He moved the raygun downward so the solid tip struck my head.

Bellowing like a madman, I latched onto his wrist and twisted savagely. I yanked down, pulling him a little. My feet touched the windshield. I snarled as if I'd gone berserk, and I bit his wrist as hard as I could. It was like chomping onto hot tree-bark.

His fingers convulsed just the same, releasing the raygun.

I snatched it, let myself collapse out of range of his hands and aimed the weapon up at him.

We looked at each other. I realized he wore a silvery belt with a great glowing gem in the front center. Wait. There were glowing gems on each of the four points of the compass on his belt. The fingers of his left hand moved toward a disc that appeared to be affixed to his left palm.

I fired. The beam drilled him between the eyes a second before his fingers could connect with the disc.

I stopped firing.

His head slumped forward as black gunk jetted from the hole in his forehead.

I scuttled out of the way along the windshield, avoiding the dripping gunk.

Once more, the snow-cat screeched metallically against the sides of the icy crevice. I peered down, still not seeing a bottom. That made my stomach lurch as I shivered with dread.

I had to get out of here.

Looking up at the alien, I noticed his body slumped around the silvery belt. I did not see a rope trailing up from his body. Was the belt some sort of gravity flying device?

That seemed likely.

While pocketing the raygun, I stood up on the windshield. I tried my best to ignore the metallic and icy creaks and groans around me. The snow-cat was going to plunge farther soon. This part of the crevice was narrower than the area beneath us.

I climbed the front seat to reach the dead alien. He had to be dead, right? He certainly hovered in position.

I fanned through options, knowing I had to act in seconds. I didn't have time to strip the gravity belt off him. Besides, how would I control it? Maybe if I took the belt off him, it would float up, relieved of his dead weight.

That gave me an idea.

I climbed upward, finally reaching the shattered back window. I reached behind me and grabbed the alien's hat. I pulled him upward. The hat seemed fixed to his head. He also seemed to have what I would call neutral gravity. He neither floated up nor sank down on his own.

The opening in the ice up there was a long way from me. I thought to see two more aliens drifting down the crevice toward me.

I had to get out of here.

Wrestling the dead alien out of the snow-cat, I maneuvered him to the side of the vehicle.

I was sick with fright, did not want to do this, but I didn't see any other way. This was another opportunity, and I was going to take it while I could.

I wrapped my arms around the alien. Then, I shoved off with my legs and quickly wrapped them around him—or it—as fast as I could.

I held my breath. Would we plunge down as I half expected? No, we began to sink, but it was at a steady and not particularly fast rate.

I grinned wildly. I was doing it.

We sank past the snow-cat and headed down toward the unseen bottom. As I silently congratulated myself on my ingenuity and daring, I heard more metallic screeching.

Craning upward, I saw two disintegrator beams strike both sides of the snow-cat. The rays devoured metal and ice. That allowed the trapped vehicle to slide along the walls. The vehicle gained speed—and suddenly, the snow-cat was plummeting after me, zeroing in on me like a guided missile.

-13-

Death plummeted toward me. I had seconds to act, no more. I used the Third Law of Motion—for every action, there is an opposite reaction.

I hurled myself from the slowly sinking alien corpse. That sent the corpse in one direction and me in another. I twisted in the air clumsily due to the parka and my oversized frame. I scrambled for an icy hold for the second before I gained too much velocity.

I dropped nevertheless, scratching at the raspy ice. Then I slammed against a ledge.

The snow-cat hissed past, missing me by a whisker. I felt the air displacement of its passage. Instead of looking down and watching, I closed my eyes and fought to keep from groaning. I struggled to keep myself still even though I wanted to twist in agony at my impact against the ledge.

I hardly breathed as I lay there.

Soon, I heard the snow-cat hit the bottom. A moment later, I felt my icy ledge quiver at the shock.

Now, I opened my eyes. I lay on more than a mere protrusion of ice. This was a slick rocky ledge, and there was an indentation against the wall as well. I would have liked to have a cave, but an indentation in the ice-wall might serve me, too.

I rolled until I couldn't move any farther. The aches and pains had receded enough that I could begin to think again. I had the floor space of a tiny tool shed. The outer lip was maybe half that size.

I kept myself still, waiting for it, waiting for it—

I inhaled sharply but silently as an alien in a silk business suit floated past my hiding spot. He wore the same glowing belt as the first alien had done. A moment later, another alien floated past me on his way down to the bottom.

I waited several heartbeats. Then, I forced myself to move. I began trembling violently before peering over the ledge. I hated heights.

The two aliens flicked on some kind of light, beams. They played them down into the darkness.

I rolled back into my depression. My shivering changed soon enough from fear to cold as the iciness began to seep into my bones.

If I hadn't started with perfect health, I doubt I would be awake now. I felt utterly exhausted. My morale sank to its worst so far.

Yeah, I'd escaped death and capture, but I was just about as lost as a man could be. This seemed like the end of the line for me.

An indeterminable amount of time later, the two aliens floated upward. One of them carried the third gravity belt. Maybe they had gone to retrieve it instead of seeing if I was dead or not. Neither of them had a detector out. It led me to believe they figured I was history. I was just an Earthman, anyway. I knew the invaders had a low opinion of humanity. At the moment, that was fine with me.

I waited, shivering harder as time passed. Finally, I leaned out of the opening, peering upward. I saw clear sky up there, nothing else.

I didn't want to look down. Instead, I rolled back into the depression.

The aliens possessed gravity belts. In another time and place, I might have thought that fantastic. Now…

I was becoming sleepy. I shook my head, squeezed my eyelids together and opened them wide.

I'd just won a fantastic hand-to-hand battle against an alien. I'd fought my way out of a precarious snow-cat to land here.

The aliens had stopped chasing me. If I did nothing, I would soon freeze to death. So, unless I bestirred myself right now, the game was over for me and the aliens would win.

I had two choices if I wanted to live. I could climb up or I could climb down. If I wanted a quick suicide, I could jump off the ledge.

My only tool was the raygun. It might be enough. Up or down, that was the only decision I had to make. Creating tiny handholds with the raygun would be easier if I climbed up. That would mean hoisting myself each time. That would quickly tax my remaining strength. Making footholds downward would be harder, but climbing down would be easier than going up.

"Uh..." I said. "What do you do once you reach the bottom?"

I peered up at the distant opening. I didn't believe I had the strength to reach there. Besides, what would I do once I got outside?

It was time for another roll of the dice.

The only way I could win would be to reach the Galactic Guard-ship. The implication seemed to be that the ship was in the ice. Why else would the aliens have a base camp beside a gigantic ice canyon in Greenland?

Before I could overanalyze this, I slid my feet toward the edge. Immediately, my trembling worsened.

I knew I didn't have a choice, though. I forced my feet over the edge and slid my legs downward. I gripped the edge with my left hand, tilted out just a little, concentrating on my feet the whole time. I pressed the trigger stub, beaming the ice in two locations. I waited a few seconds before sliding down a little farther. The toe of each shoe slid into a melted step.

My descent was incredibly tedious, and gut-wrenching, too. It did not get easier the longer I did it. I did get better, however, at making the footholds. I tapped the trigger-stub now.

If I'd climbed up, I might have used the heated tip of the raygun to make the holds. I couldn't do that going down because I didn't dare reach down that far.

By the time the raygun ran out of juice, my arms were trembling from exhaustion and the cold had sapped my strength. I pocketed the useless gun, rested one side of my face against the ice and then resumed the descent.

I managed another few feet before I slipped. A ragged shout tore out of my throat. I fell, plummeting like a rock and struck another outcropping, driving the air from my lungs. I struck a second outcropping, a third, which flipped me, and slammed against the bottom.

I groaned painfully. That unlocked my lungs so I gasped for air.

I lay there, just breathing, afraid to move and find the extent of my injuries. I imagined I'd fallen another one hundred feet or more to the bottom. It's possible the outcroppings had saved my life by slowing me down, provided I hadn't broken any bones.

Just how far could a body fall and survive?

I discovered several pieces of luck. One, I'd fallen onto a heavy patch of snow. It might have cushioned my fall just a little.

The snow must have reached here from my initial breakthrough.

The second piece of luck was the last flip. It had moved me just enough so I'd missed the crumbled snow-cat to my left.

I tried sitting up. Several muscles immediately cramped, and a few spasmed. I let out another groan of pain before rolling over, clamping my hands over my mouth.

I didn't know how much noise it would take for the aliens to detect something.

My back muscles were the worst, twitching with cramps as I lay there. I contorted several times, breathing raggedly.

I flexed my back muscles briefly, but stopped that as agony lanced through me. Finally, the process stopped.

Gingerly and painfully, I climbed to my feet. I didn't straighten, but stood there like a bent old geezer with arthritis in every joint. I shuffled around the smashed snow-cat not sure what I was looking for.

I finally realized I couldn't do this normally, so I eased down onto my hands and knees. I crawled over the smashed metal, being extremely careful around jagged and sharp metal edges.

After an eternity of searching, I found a flashlight, the flare gun and the half-melted raygun. I found pliers and a bottle of aspirin. It must have come from the same toolkit as the flashlight.

I took my treasure, sitting away from the wreck in the little spot of sunlight that reached down from the opening. I took six aspirin, force swallowing them one at a time. I used some of the fallen snow, putting it in my mouth and melting it before sipping. The drinking took time, but that was fine. I wanted some time for the aspirin to give my body a hand.

Finally, I used the pliers, working over the half-melted raygun. After considerable effort, I found what I took to be the power pack. It appeared to have survived the beaming. I pried it out, soon shoving it into my powerless raygun.

I decided to test the weapon later when I needed it. At this point, I didn't want to waste any energy.

The process must have taken me longer than I realized. I could stand and straighten almost all the way. The aspirin had worked like magic.

First pocketing the flare gun and some extra flares, I clicked on the flashlight, looking in the darkened areas. The bottom was larger than I'd realized. Some of the walls were composed of rock. Other parts were blue—ice. There were no tunnels, no caves, no way out of the crevice bottom except up.

I might have sat down and quit except for one thing. I still had the raygun, a possibly charged raygun.

Once more, I returned to the wreckage. After a while, I found the various chunks of the dead alien. One of the chunks had a communicator. On a third chunk was another device.

I left the communicator and took the other device. Might this be a detector?

I held it in my cold fingers, realizing this was my only hope for survival. After a desperate search, I found the controls. After a little experimentation, I turned it on.

I aimed the device one way and another. I did that a second time, pressing more controls this time. After ten minutes of rational, systematic experimentation, I got the screen to glow green if I aimed it a certain way.

With a fatalistic shrug, I decided that would be my route, as it pointed at an icy wall, not rock. Now it was time to use the raygun.

With the flashlight in one hand and the raygun in the other, I pressed the trigger stub. To my great delight, the disintegrator ray struck ice. I began to burrow my way into the ice, planning to continue for as long as this sucker worked.

I dearly hoped I'd put a fully charged power pack into the raygun and not one nearly empty.

-14-

The biggest problem proved to be melted water. The second was steam.

Water kept trickling out of the tunnel, at times pooling in and under the slush. That soon soaked my pants and chilled my legs to the marrow. The steam made me cough and caused moisture to cling to my face. The fur that lined my hood was soon as soaked as my pants.

There was nothing else to do but to keep tunneling. I paused from time to time to check the detector—if it was a detector. It showed the same green glow that had caused me to start in this direction.

Shivering, with my teeth chattering, I held the beam on the ice before me, as I'd been doing for a while now. This time, the ice disintegrated and melted, and the beam poked through into something behind the ice.

I quit beaming and slid up to the hole, for once unmindful of the slush. With the flashlight beam poking through, I peered into what seemed to be a natural cave.

I drew back and rammed my shoulder against the ice. With the sound of crackling and splintering, I broke through to the other side.

A few seconds later, I climbed out of my slushy tunnel into a cavern. I played the flashlight beam everywhere. The cavern grew larger the farther the beam traveled.

Setting the flashlight on the ground, I pulled off my hood and debated ideas. Finally, I took off my shoes, my wet socks and pants. I rolled them and twisted, wringing out as much water as I could. Soon, I put my pants back on and did the same with my damp socks.

I was seriously freezing. I probably already had hyperthermia.

Despite my dire predicament, I was finding it difficult to keep my eyes open. An oppressive drowsiness had settled over me. I knew one thing. If I took a nap, I doubted I'd wake up on this side of life.

Once more, I was thankful that Z17 had given me perfect human health. I would never have lasted this long otherwise.

I was sleepy and ravenous, but I still had reserves of fat in my body. This was a matter of will power. I could keep going if I could stay awake.

The aspirin had done wonders for my aches and pains. Necessity had also kept me going. If I'd guessed correctly, I must be nearing the last lap of the quest.

I checked the detector. It gave me the same information as before.

Picking up the flashlight, I forced myself to jog. It turned into a shuffling gait soon enough, but that was fine. I was moving. That would help keep me warm after a fashion.

As I traveled along the cavern, I used the flashlight to scour ahead. Then I heard a noise.

I clicked off the flashlight and dug the raygun out of my parka pocket. I realized what it was—alien buzz talking.

That must mean I'd made it into their excavation site. I nodded but couldn't think much more. My primary need was to get warm—fast.

Groping in the dark, I continued toward the buzzing. Soon, I saw light in the distance. I noticed something else, too. I was no longer traveling through a rocky tunnel, but a corridor with metal walls.

Increasing my gait, knowing I wouldn't last more than another ten minutes, I readied myself for a final fight.

The light ahead intensified. I stopped, crouched and let my head droop. The next thing I remembered was snapping my head up. I'd fallen asleep. I rubbed my aching eyes and stared.

An alien hover-pad neared. I couldn't have been asleep more than a minute or two. Two aliens stood on the pad shining beams on the walls. I glanced at the walls—

Shock made me shiver harder. Egyptian-style hieroglyphics adorned the metal walls. What did that signify?

I snorted softly to myself. What did it matter?

The hover-pad slipped out of sight then.

I blinked stupidly, wondering if they had teleported away. My sluggish mind understood a second later. The hover-pad had turned into a different corridor.

I knew I had to act while I still could, so I clicked on the flashlight, shouted feebly and shuffled after them. Maybe I wasn't thinking clearly anymore. The hover-pad seemed like an angel of mercy just then. If I let it get away, I was going to go to sleep forever down here at the bottom of the world.

I took the turn into the new corridor and almost bumped into the slowly moving hover-pad. One of the aliens turned around.

I beamed him in the stomach. I did the same thing to the other one. They both half disintegrated and flopped onto the pad. The hover stopped moving after they both collapsed onto it.

Groaning like a lunatic, I rushed the floating pad. It was several feet off the floor. I put the raygun away, jumped and levered myself onto the pad with them.

One at a time, as I luxuriated in the hot gunk that must have been alien blood, I dumped each of them overboard.

I was closer to collapsing than I had realized. "You have to keep moving," I told myself.

Food, I thought. I need food and I have to get warm.

Finding it too tiring to argue with myself, I cleaned my hands, stood and began figuring out the hover's controls. It proved pathetically easy to drive. In moments, I was heading back for the turn.

With my flashlight beam leading the way, I traveled down long metal corridors away from my entrance point. Occasionally, I shined the beam on a wall, seeing more hieroglyphics.

I didn't worry about the hieroglyphics anymore. I didn't think about how they'd gotten here or who had put them on the walls. I didn't worry about how old they might be. I was drugged with fatigue and hyperthermia.

The passage of moving air helped to dry my clothes. Heat from the pad did even more for me. In near apathy, as I struggled to keep my eyes open, I traveled under the Earth.

I heard a noise later, heard it again and finally realized there were lights headed toward me. I craned my neck forward. With a shock, I saw more hover-pads approaching me.

I turned my pad, racing away, taking different corridors. Soon, other hover-pads blocked my passage. I turned around again and tried yet another passageway. I zipped into the largest corridor of all. Behind me, the aliens followed. I wasn't sure, but it seemed as if they had dropped farther behind.

At the last moment, I saw a wall loom before me. Fumbling at the controls, I brought the pad to a halt. A few taps more made the hover-pad sink to the floor. I had reached a dead-end. Behind me, the aliens approached at what seemed like a crawl.

I jumped off the pad and approached the wall. Playing the flashlight beam on it, I saw a line in the middle that reached from the floor to the ceiling.

What did that mean?

"Idiot," I slurred. This was two big doors pushed together. I'd reached a portal.

I played the light behind me. That way represented death. I played the light on the doors. I pounded on them, shouting for an automated entryway to let me in. I kicked the doors. I—

Finally, I stopped shouting, stopped pleading and approached what seemed like a keypad along the side. Each button had a hieroglyphic on it. I pressed one. It sank in and stayed there. I pressed another one.

A nozzle protruded from a hidden slot. I heard clicking, rasping and a vile substance dripped out of the nozzle.

Was it supposed to have sprayed me, gassed me?

I kept pressing more buttons.

Another thing popped out of a wall. It glowed. I felt heat, but then something clattered and the glow and heat stopped.

I looked back at the approaching aliens but forced myself to turn back to the keypad.

I pressed another—

A great sound like giant millstones grinding caused the two doors to open a smidgen. A loud squeal and another grinding noise foretold the doors' abrupt halt.

A terrible dry and ancient odor billowed out from the narrow opening. It caused me to sneeze several times and then begin hacking.

I didn't care.

Covering my mouth with the sleeve of my parka, I staggered from the keypad. I forced myself through the narrow opening into the ancient room, cavern, whatever I'd found.

The aliens were coming and I had to keep going. If I was right about this, I'd found a way to the Galactic Guard-ship.

-15-

I finally stopped coughing but still found it hard to breathe in here. The air was stale and evil seeming. It made me dizzy. The longer I staggered, the more unfocused my eyesight became.

Through dogged determination, knowing that to stop was to die, I kept moving one foot ahead of the other. I'm not sure what I saw, as strange images swam before my vision.

At one point, I thought I saw men and women in individual glass cylinders. They wore odd, metallic seeming clothing. Some had star symbols. Others—

I can't remember.

I staggered, wheezing, feeling a pounding in my brain. I fumbled open the aspirin bottle. They all poured onto the floor, but I had no time to pick them up. I could feel something closing in, aliens presumably.

I began to laugh, feeling unhinged.

Tears slid down my cheeks, and I wiped them away. That was the first time I noticed my skin wasn't freezing anymore. Instead, my cheeks felt hot.

Was I delirious?

I stumbled past banks of controls. They seemed complex…and maybe even a little sinister. I did not like this place. It had a bad aura. Yes! I could almost hear screaming souls begging for mercy in here. But this place did not know the meaning of mercy. It was cold, clinical and exacting. A powerful intelligence, a brooding malignancy seemed to throb inside this chamber as if it were watching me.

I kept glancing over my shoulder, balled my fingers into fists—

I halted in shock. I saw more of the glass cylinders. There were rows of them this time. In them were frozen men and women in all manner of positions. Some had their palms pressed against the glass. They were big, squat and hairy with low foreheads. I'd seen people like this before. Neanderthals!

My heart thudded. My breathing quickened. I took a step toward the nearest cylinder. What was this place? How had Neanderthals found their way into these cylinders? It seemed as if someone had experimented on them.

I halted once more as my shoulders hunched. The sense of coldness, exactness, experimentation—the powerful intellect behind this—

I broke into a staggering run, desperate to get out of here. The underground complex had the feeling of great age. How long had this place existed in Greenland? Who had built it? Why did the aliens seek it?

My breathing became ragged as I staggered past other chambers. My eyes narrowed in one as I spied smaller, prehistoric hominids. Just like the Neanderthals, they were frozen in various poses in yet more glass cylinders. They did not seem fully human with their furry bodies but like something from my high school biology textbooks, those that claimed they were apemen or apes evolving into men or proto-humans or whatever.

From a far distance came a loud squealing.

I shouted hoarsely, startled by the noise.

The noises were loud and metallic, as if giant metal teeth slowly and painfully clacked against each other. My breath whooshed from my lungs as I realized the aliens were coming. They must be forcing the giant doors. That caused my knees to give out.

I stumbled, crashed against a solid object with my head, bounced off it and slammed against the floor. I twisted in pain, wanting to curl up and forget the whole thing. My body throbbed. My head hurt, and I heard strange words coming from nearby.

I began to shake. With a last shred of self-control, I raised my head off the floor, opening my eyes. Something was wrong. I dragged a shaking hand across my face. I felt sticky…blood. There was blood on my face.

I heard more metallic screeching in the distance. The terror of this place propelled me. I crawled blindly, bumping against more objects before finding my way around them.

I heard strange words again coming from nearby. I forced myself to consider that.

"Is someone there?" I asked, hating the tentativeness of my voice.

"Indeed someone is," the voice said in English. "Are you human?"

The voice didn't strike me as evil, or even cold and clinical. Still, the thrust of the question troubled me. It took several tries. Finally, I forced myself to say:

"Yes, I'm human, a Homo sapien."

"You are an aboriginal of the planet then?"

I hated my helplessness. I hated these bizarre questions. "I just said I am. Who are you?"

"This is distressing. I can't seem to visualize you. Can you…see me perhaps?"

"I can't see anything. Either my eyes are damaged or I can't wipe away the blood pouring over them fast enough."

"Oh, this is even more distressing. I detect pursuit of you by…others not native to the planet."

"That's right," I said. "Aliens are coming. I think they're shape-changing aliens."

"A moment, please. There seems to be a discrepancy in my receptors. How long have I…" He stopped talking as if something bothered him. Several seconds passed before he said, "It appears you are correct. Unguls are in pursuit of you. But that can only mean…"

Once more, he stopped talking. I waited, listening to the Unguls, I presume, forcing the giant doors. If this person knew the name of the shape-changing aliens, did that make him an alien, too? It seemed likely, especially as he'd asked if I was human, an aboriginal of the planet.

"This is becoming more perplexing by the moment," he said. "I am unable to contact the fathership or raise my agent. How did you pass the auto-defenses?"

"Dumb luck," I said.

"The odds of that are infinitesimal. I must have been right when I detected a residual malevolence at work here. The discrepancies in the situation are pressing me to the obvious choice. It appears I must break protocol and initiate a first level contamination. Quick, human, you must follow my voice."

"Who are you?" I asked.

"That is unimportant at the moment. We must act together for our collective benefit. I take it you wish to continue your existence."

"Yes," I said.

"Then follow my voice. You will reach me soon. I have a means of escape—I cannot understand why my agent hasn't returned yet."

"What agent?" I asked.

"Pay no attention to my ramblings. But you must hurry if you hope to survive the Unguls. What is your name?"

"Logan."

"Follow the sound of my voice, Logan. I will aid you if you agree to aid me."

"I already said I would."

He paused again before saying, "Excellent. I detect honesty in you, which would make you a man of honor."

"That's me."

"Know that I also have honor. You can trust me. Now move, human. We have little time left."

He guided me with his voice, warning me when I was about to bump into an object. That finally bothered me, as he'd said earlier that he couldn't see me.

"If you can't see me," I said, "how are you able to warn me if I'll ram against these various objects."

"I cannot presently see you in the visible spectrum. I do have a heat sensor, though, and a schematic of the portal area."

"Are you in any way connected with the Galactic Guardship?"

"How do you know about that?" he asked sharply.

"Unguls caught me before and spoke of it."

"I find this distressing indeed. I may have made an error. Are you one of their aboriginal tools perhaps?"

"No way," I said. "I killed Unguls to make my escape. They invaded my workplace. I've been trying to stop them ever since."

"What is your regular capacity?"

"Uh…I'm a security guard, if that's what you mean."

"Earth security?" he asked.

"No. I work for a company on Earth, though."

"Then we have similar occupations, although of vastly different scales. I am here to thwart those like the Unguls and their superiors."

"You're part of the Galactic Guard then?"

He didn't respond.

"We're helping each other, remember?" I said. "If you're not part of the Guard, though…"

"I understand your distress. Know that I am an advisor to a Galactic Guard agent. Trust me that it is not in your future self-interest to know more."

That made sense, I suppose. If the Galactic Guard had kept itself hidden from us so far, what would they have to do to me later to make sure I wouldn't talk about them?

"What is this place?" I asked.

"It is part of a serious crime against Earth," he said.

"So you're investigating it?"

"You have almost made it. Now climb up quickly. An Ungul combat party has almost reached this area."

I climbed onto what felt like a large steel pad, crawling to a disc-shaped object there.

"You must pick me up and hold me," he said.

I rotated from on my knees, feeling the floor for him.

"One, two, three," he said. "One, two, three—"

"Got you," I said. My hands latched onto what seemed like a flat cell phone.

“Stop,” an Ungul shouted from farther away. I could tell it was an alien because of the odd accent. “You must stop your evasion tactics at once.”

I heard a strange humming and felt an even stranger sensation. Then, disorientation struck. I heard a garbled command. Heard what sounded like a disintegrator beam—

Then, all sounds vanished. I felt nothing. It’s possible I floated in limbo. I don’t know how else to describe it. I felt as if I tumbled end-over-end but there was no more matter, nothing but—

I slammed against a floor. I heard splintering and crackling, and I felt something break apart under me.

“What’s going on?” I shouted.

“It appears there has been a serious malfunction,” the flat device said. Was it a comm unit?

“What does that mean?” I asked.

“I must reconfigure my matrix. Please do not move from this location. There is a paradox at work, some malignant force threatening our continued existence. Unless we act with extreme circumvention, we might succumb to it, as well.”

Afterward, he fell silent.

-16-

A nearly total weariness threatened to send me into oblivion. But I had to know what this “serious malfunction” meant. I rolled over crackling objects. Something about them freaked me out. I rolled faster and fell over an edge to land several inches down.

I lay there for several seconds. Nothing dire happened, and I noticed it was warm in here. With painful slowness, I twisted out of the parka. Once I was free of its binding confines, I used the inner jacket and pressed it against my forehead to soak up the blood, then pulled a sleeve inside out and wiped my eyes. That made no difference to the situation. I still couldn’t see a thing.

Was I blind or could there be another explanation?

I fumbled in the parka pockets until I found the flashlight. I clicked it on while holding my breath. The light shone brightly. I exhaled with relief. It had just been dark in here.

I shined the light around…

It looked like I was in some kind of compartment. There was a small dais with strange discs on the ceiling directly over discs on the bottom. I pushed up to my knees, still holding the parka against my bleeding forehead, and froze in disbelief.

I saw what had crackled earlier. It was a man-sized skeleton. There were bits of material around it, a strap holding an ancient pouch and several rusted devices. What freaked me out the most about the skeleton was that it had a tail, well, a skeleton of a tail, anyway. I don't mean it had a prehensile tail. That was a tail. The dead creature on the teleport dais—

I thought I must have teleported from the excavation site in Greenland to wherever this place was. If I were going to bet, I would say I'd made it onto the Guard-ship. The reason the Guard-ship had never left Earth was that the Galactic Guard agent had died the last time he or she had teleported. Given the brittleness of the bones and the almost nonsexist clothing, the dying had been countless millennia ago.

It was warm enough that I stripped off the rest of my clothes. I was a mass of black and blue bruises.

I could no longer fight my exhaustion, so I rolled up the parka, lay my head on it and promptly fell asleep.

***

I had no idea how long I slept. I woke up by slow degrees, aware I'd had nightmares. Upon fully waking, I remembered everything that had happened to me so far.

It had become pitch-black in the chamber. I fumbled in the dark for my flashlight, found it and clicked it—off. I'd forgotten to turn it off before I'd fallen asleep. I'd slept long enough to drain the batteries.

That was just great.

"Hello?" I said, in the darkness.

I felt the stillness of a tomb around me. For a wild instant, I wondered if the Guard-ship was buried deep underground. Just how long ago had the Guard-ship landed on Earth?

I recalled the Egyptian-style hieroglyphics I'd seen on the walls. I remembered the Neanderthal men and women and the smaller hominids in the glass cylinders. That had all been in a giant underground complex in Greenland. Who could have built that? During historical periods, Greenland had been ice-filled. Was I supposed to believe people would have first dug into the ice and then drilled underground? Either our scientists didn't really understand the past or the Guard-ship had landed on Earth a very long time ago.

So far, everything I'd seen in Greenland under the ice and seen on the Guard-ship pointed to extreme age. What had caused me to sense a powerful intellect while I'd viewed the glass cylinders? I still didn't like thinking about it or them.

"Hey," I said, hating the darkness and my continued helplessness. "How long does it take to reconfigure your matrix, anyway? Do you hear me?"

Apparently, he didn't hear me. Maybe it was time to force him to listen. I gathered my resolve, crawled onto the dais and soon felt the brittle bones.

I tried to leave them as I found them. Soon, I picked up the flat cell phone-like object. I let my fingers rove over it as I searched for controls. It was smooth, all of one piece.

I used my fingernails, trying to find anything I could tear apart. I—

Something slid to my left. I heard the noise as a distinct sound. Blinding lights snapped on all around me.

I cried out, throwing my hands in front of my eyes.

"Do not fear," the device said. "I am dimming the lights to their lowest setting. I take it you can see now?"

"Yes," I said, peeking from between my fingers.

I took my hands from my eyes, able to open them all the way now that he'd dimmed the lights.

I'd heard a hatch slide open. A round object the size of a vacuum cleaner floated into the room. It was silvery, with antennas sprouting from the top along with a short and ugly tube that was pointed right at me.

"What is that?" I asked, indicating the round thing.

"That is a Mark III Mobile Ship Defense Unit," the device said. "It is aiming a flamer at you."

"You don't trust me now that I've helped you?"

"I have taken a precautionary measure, nothing more."

I studied the device in my hand. "You're a computer, aren't you?"

"That is a primitive-level assessment. But it shows you have a rational side. I am grateful for that. I am a sentient crystal entity from Rax Prime, trained as a Galactic Guard Advisor Unit."

"You're saying that under this sheathing of metal you're a piece of crystal?"

"Sentient crystal," he said.

"You're alive?"

"That is what it means to be an entity."

"How can a piece of crystal be alive?" I asked.

"You have a biological bias, a primitive failing, I'm afraid."

"I'm not trying to insult you. I'm…trying to understand all this." My gaze slid to the bones with the skeleton tail, the bits of fabric around it and rusted tools. "Was that your agent?"

"That is my present speculation, as well. There are serious incongruities, however, for that to be true. The first is the seeming age of the bones, which would indicate a long passage of time."

"When did you come to Earth?" I asked.

"I do not believe Galactic time measurements would have any meaning for you."

"I suppose they wouldn't," I said. "What was happening on Earth when you landed?"

"We are temporary allies, human. Thus, the less you know, the less the Guard will have to scrub from your memories later."

"Look," I said. "I'm not dumb. That complex in Greenland must be ancient. Those bones are ancient. That means you must be ancient, too."

"Did you not hear me when I spoke of incongruities? The most pressing is the apparent passage of time regarding my agent's remains. Whatever else you believe, we did not land on Earth in your dim past. We came…"

"Yes, you came," I said, trying to pry it out of him.

"Do you recall that I spoke of a malignant will earlier?"

"I sure do. I think I felt it before, too."

"While that is interesting—your sensing of it—that is not germane to our present dilemma. I suspect this evil agency caused the odd situation regarding my agent."

"What's that supposed to mean?"

"There is a mystery regarding your planet, one the Guard intends to solve. Unfortunately, the Unguls have complicated the situation by breaking Galactic Law, entering a prohibited zone and landing on a banned planet. I suspect their superior—"

"It's someone called the Organizer," I said.

"That is an alias, I assure you. But it speaks well of your intentions that you relay the information to me. I appreciate this."

"So why is Earth a banned planet?" I asked.

"I am proving garrulous, a fault of sentient crystals, I'm told. If I had motive power like one of you biological units... Enough," he said, as if to himself.

"So what are we going to do?" I asked.

He didn't respond.

"We can't just let the Unguls roam around the underground Greenland complex."

"Before I do anything," the unit said, "I need to understand what happened to the Guard-ship and to my agent."

A red light flashed on a panel. Several lights in a pattern played along the unit in my hand.

"What are you doing?" I asked.

"I have come to a conclusion," the unit said. "We are in danger in this place. I must move the ship as soon as possible. But... Human, will you continue to assist me?"

I stared at the unit, the metal sheath that supposedly held a "living" crystal inside. I'd definitely seen humans, Neanderthals and smaller, apish hominids in glass cylinders in the Greenland complex. I'd learned Earth was a banned planet in a forbidden zone. The Galactic Guard was real and these shape-changers, the Unguls, sounded like some kind of criminal organization, maybe like a Galactic mafia.

"I'll help you," I said. "But I want to know more. For instance, what was that place? What was with all the glass cylinders under the Greenland ice? Why did they hold hominids, and why did I sense a malignant intellect?"

"You have great curiosity, I see. That speaks of high intelligence on your part. Know then that my agent and I learned this landmass was once called Thule."

"Thule is a name from ancient Greek legend," I said.

"It is from an even older civilization than the ancient Greeks, I assure you."

"Are you talking about the Antediluvians?" I asked.

“Logan,” he said. “Instead of exchanging data, we should be acting. A suspicious power-drain is taking place in this location. We must move the ship as quickly as possible.”

“Sure,” I said. “How are we going to do that?”

The ugly nozzle on the defensive robot retreated into the smooth metal. A cover *snicked* into place over it.

“First, we must go on a reconnaissance mission,” he said. “It will entail risk and involve physical adjustment on your part. Otherwise, I cannot see you surviving the various encounters. Since I may need your help for a prolonged period, I desire that you remain intact for as long as possible.”

“What kind of adjustments are you talking about?” I asked, not liking the sound of it.

Instead of answering, the living crystal must have caused the discs above and below me to glow with power. I felt the same disorientation as before, and everything disappeared from sight.

I was teleporting somewhere—right back to the excavation site under the ice in Greenland I suspected.

-17-

"I urge you to remain silent," the unit whispered.

I found myself in total darkness again, unable to see anything. Cold hit me immediately, and I realized I was naked. I'd forgotten to put my clothes back on before teleporting. I lacked the flashlight, the raygun—everything except for the sentient crystal in my hand.

Normally, I would have berated myself for something so stupid. Instead, I realized the extent of my exhaustion.

A clang sounded in the distance, startling me.

"What was that?" I whispered.

"I suspect it is more Ungul interference," he said softly. "We will have to move quickly."

"Unguls," I said. "So we're back in the underground Greenland complex?"

"We are indeed."

"Why is it dark this time?"

"Yes. That is interesting. Perhaps the Unguls have caused a blackout."

"Look," I said. "We have to teleport back to the ship."

"There is no longer enough power for that. We must find energy cells and another way to the ship in order to bring the cells to the engine room."

"But I don't have any clothes, any shoes or socks. I'm going to freeze to death before we get very far."

"Oh my," the unit said. "You are right. That is my error, I'm afraid. Let me think…think… Yes. I will have to accelerate the timetable. Are you familiar with right-left, forward-back directions?"

"Sure. I was in the Marines once."

"I do not understand your answer."

"The Marines are like the Galactic Guard, only tougher."

"That is impossible, as Earth creatures are frail by nature."

"I got this far, didn't I?"

"I concede the point in your favor. Let us begin."

"Wait," I said. "If you're going to guide me in the dark, I'd like to know how you can see all of a sudden—unless you were lying to me earlier about not being able to see."

"Active deception in the line of duty is no crime," he said.

"So you did lie to me."

"I practiced caution. If it puts you at ease, know that I have a limited ability to scan my surroundings. That is how I see."

"Okay," I said. "By the way, do you have a name?"

"I do. It is YTR-129987-Q233-78B."

"Uh...that's too long for me to say every time. Is it okay if I call you Rax?"

"Because I am from Rax Prime?" he asked.

"It's like calling a guy from Texas Tex."

"I am familiar with the concept."

"I'm glad to hear it," I said. "I'm ready to get started any time you are, Rax."

"Then you may proceed by taking five steps to your left."

I followed Rax's instructions as the Unguls continued to make clangs and clanks in the distance. Then, I heard a muffled explosion. The floor shook for several seconds, followed by rumbling.

"What are they doing?" I whispered.

"In my estimation they are blasting and drilling for the master chamber."

"Do you know what's in the master chamber?"

"I do not," Rax said. "Go left three steps..."

Soon, I felt a draft, and I began shivering. Five minutes later, my teeth began chattering.

"Stop," Rax said later. "Rotate your body fifty degrees to your right. Now, take seven steps forward. Halt. I am about to give you precise instructions. It is important you follow them exactly. First, you must set me down."

"Why?"

"We do not have time for extended explanations. If you wish to be warm, follow my parameters—"

"Sure," I said. "Keep talking. I'm sick of being cold."

The unit made a clicking noise as I set him on something metallic. From there, Rax instructed me. I moved backward, lay down—

Something soft but unyielding clamped onto my arms, legs and torso.

"Rax," I said. "What's happening? I'm confined to a table."

"Do you remember that I spoke of physical adjustments earlier? Some of the procedures could be painful. You must endure in silence. Otherwise—"

I didn't hear the rest, as a needle stabbed me. It sank much too deeply. I squirmed, wanting to howl, but managed to bite down on my lips before I did.

The table rose as the needle pulled out. Something smothered my face. I panicked, tried to jerk free and inhaled something sweet smelling. I realized there was a mask covering my mouth and nose. It seemed to be a breathing mask.

As I assessed that, the table turned upside down and went down. I splashed into a sludgy substance. I shivered at the cold. I think electricity might have surged through the solution, and I felt as if I were bathed in fire.

What had the little crystal done to me?

My recollections became fuzzy after the electrical discharges. I must have dreamed the rest. I could see my reflection in glass as a soft glow bathed a Frankenstein chamber of horrors. I wore a mask in the dream while I floated in a green solution. Needles with tubes behind them zeroed in on me, driving into my flesh like mini-torpedoes. More electricity struck me. I lost sight of the reflection. In the dream, my body became rigid in agony. Fire roamed throughout my body. It burned away dross and did something to my cells. Cold, heat, stretching and compaction seemed to be remolding my flesh like clay. I wasn't in the hands of God, but some demonic monster trying to replicate the creation of Eden.

Instead of receiving the breath of life, a gust of searing agony made my fingers tingle and my toes pulsate with the change.

What was the change?

I had no idea, but I in my nightmare I seemed to recollect the little bastard's words.

I hated the Galactic Guard. I hated the crystals from Rax Prime. I hated the Unguls who had intruded upon my life in Nevada. I wanted to hunt them all, drive them all from my planet. By what right had they come down onto our dirt ball, as the Unguls had called it?

Finally, the nightmare ended and I slept the sleep of pure exhaustion.

Too soon, I stirred, my eyelids twitching. I heard the former clangs and clacks. I felt the rumble and heard what sounded like gigantic drills, no doubt burrowing into the earth.

I realized I was awake somewhere in the dark in this labyrinth-like underground madhouse.

"Logan?" Rax said.

"What?"

"You survived the treatment. I suspect you will be glad to know that that considerably heightens our odds of success."

I sat up in the dark, ready to destroy the living crystal. The only thing that gave me pause was that I was far hungrier than when I'd fallen for Rax's trap.

Trap! I felt around and picked him up.

"Give me a reason why I shouldn't smash you into pieces," I said.

"I admit I practiced a deceptive tactic," Rax said. "Before my agent's demise, we believed we had stumbled upon the machine's purpose. It was and is quite ingenious. If he was correct, you are considerably tougher than before."

"*If*?" I asked. "You mean you don't know exactly what the machine did to me?"

"I am still in the middle of an investigation," Rax said. "I took a risk for the good of the team."

"I took the risk, you little bastard."

"We both took risks in different degrees. Without you, it is possible the Guard investigation will fail. That is a first order magnitude disaster. You merely risked your own life."

"Yeah, but it's my life!"

"I do not understand the thrust of your philosophical assertion."

"We don't have time for this," I snarled. "I'm still naked, weaponless and hungry. And I feel as if I'm going to faint from fatigue."

"Then we must clothe you and reach a food source," Rax said. "If you would turn left forty degrees and sprint seventy-nine steps as rapidly as you can…"

I followed the crystal's instructions, fully expecting to bang my shins against something at any moment.

"Be ready to halt in seven steps," he said.

I slid to a stop.

"Take two steps forward. Stop. Rotate to your left ninety degrees…"

Rax spoke and I followed the byzantine instructions. Finally, without warning, an electrical discharge sparked from Rax to a receiver on a wall. That caused a locker-sized section of the wall to slide up. Several uniforms hung in there.

I couldn't see anything after the spark died away. Fumbling in the darkness, I felt one-piece uniforms. Picking the one that seemed the largest, I shoved my feet into it. The fabric stretched but didn't feel binding. I sealed it by pressing the halves against each other. It seemed as if the fabric bonded together and to my skin, covering me from my neck to my toes. It was thin, but I no longer felt the bite of cold.

"There is footwear in the bottom," Rax said.

Sure enough, there was. I doubted the shoes would fit, but what the heck, I tried them on. The substance was tougher than the fabric, but it also stretched, fitting to each foot.

"How does that feel?"

"Surprisingly good," I told him. "Now, what about the food you've been promising?"

"You will begin by rotating to your right and walking…"

-18-

The food was in a bin. I'd torn off the lid and begun eating. It was stale, dry and crunchy, but I ate it ravenously, one handful after another. I had no idea what it was. Frankly, it reminded me of dry dog food but went down like kettle corn-flavored popcorn.

My stomach bulged and still I devoured the stuff. I felt as if I could eat until the last trumpet sounded.

"Water," I said, with a mouthful of the crunchy food and with crumbs spilling from my lips.

"There is some two feet to your right."

I reached over in the dark, picking up a sloshing container. The water was metallic-tasting, but I guzzled it as if I'd just finished a marathon.

I don't recall ever having eaten like this before. With each handful, some of my weariness departed. It felt as if my body had already taken the sustenance I shoveled down and begun using it like building-block material.

I continued crunching one handful after another, interspacing them with more guzzling. I realized I'd been working in a mental fog for some time. My mental acuity now sharpened with startling speed.

I lowered a palm of crunchy bits, facing the direction I'd last heard the crystal speak.

"What did the electrical bath do to me?"

"It strengthened you," Rax said, "and made you more resistant to sickness."

"Will I heal faster?"

"I believe so."

"How?"

"It induced cellular changes within you. To be precise, you have leaped several millennia ahead of your fellow primitives in evolutionary development."

"And that makes me hungrier than ever?"

"You are now burning up your bodily resources quicker than before as your internal systems effect repairs."

"That doesn't make me more evolved. I used to be a general pattern human, able to survive in a host of environments. Now—"

"You are more specialized," Rax said. "But the specialization will improve your chances of surviving the Unguls."

I thought about that as I continued eating and drinking. Abruptly, I became full. I should have been drowsy after eating like that. Instead, I felt invigorated, positively hopping with energy.

"Something has been bothering me," I said. "This place is ancient. Your agent's bones were ancient. Yet, you claim your Guard-ship landed recently."

"I spoke about incongruities," Rax said.

"So…what are you suggesting? This evil intellect caused your agent to age several millennia in a manner of moments?"

"I wonder if the intellect did so while my agent used the transporter. Our scientists have not yet discovered all the ramifications to teleportation."

"Wait. Are you suggesting this intelligence has been around since the time of the hominids?"

"I am unfamiliar with your time scales or hominid theories, but you seem to be implying a great stretch of time regarding the intelligence."

"That's right."

"If you had listened more closely, you would realize that I have suggested nothing of the kind. Perhaps the malignant intelligence can hold itself in suspended animation for long time periods, only resurfacing at pre-selected intervals."

"Why would this mysterious being do this?"

"That is an excellent question, Logan. Discovering motivation is halfway to solving a mystery. However, we should discuss this later, as our present position is too exposed. The longer we are in this upper area, the more likely it is that the Unguls will discover our presence. We must use surprise against them, as surprise is a force multiplier. We will need serious advantages if we are going to reenergize the ship."

"Marines know all about force multipliers," I said.

"That is thoroughly reasonable," Rax said. "As that is one of the first sciences primitive peoples uncover."

"What's the plan?"

"A surprise assault on their main drilling operation," Rax said.

"That seems too risky," I said.

"The drillers contain power cells convertible to the Guard-ship's energy requirements. We will also need the drillers to reach the ship. Without the ship, we will remain helpless against the Unguls and the Organizer. With the ship, I can contact the Guard vessel in Jupiter orbit. That should end the crisis for Earth's aboriginals."

"All right," I said. "But I'll need weapons if we're going to attack the Unguls."

"I agree," Rax said. "Unfortunately, here is where the process becomes tricky…"

***

I crawled through what must have been an access tube, a very tight-fitting one. If I inhaled too deeply, that expanded my chest too far and halted all progress.

I kept Rax in a front pocket, navigating the maze at his directions while taking shallow breaths.

Finally, I reached a grate blocking my way. I tried to push it off, but something held the grate in place.

"Can you reverse your position so you can use your feet to kick it off?" Rax asked.

"Not bloody likely," I said.

"Then I suggest you bash the grate off with your fists."

"I'll break my fingers and maybe my knuckles if I do that."

"Once, that might have been true. That is no longer the case."

"You're saying my bones have hardened?" I asked.

"That is correct."

I thought about that and the amount of dry food I'd eaten. Had I needed sustenance to complete…whatever the bath had started with me?

"Bashing my fists against the grate will shred my flesh."

"Your flesh will heal."

"You're crazy if you think I'm going pulverize my hands for you."

"Unless you have another method," Rax said, "you must follow my suggestion to break through into the needed chamber."

I crawled up a bit more, braced my body, put my palms on the grate and pushed as hard as I could. My body slipped backward. I re-braced myself and tried it again.

The screws, bolts, whatever, began to creak and groan. Then, the grate shifted under the pressure. But in the end, I lacked the strength to shove the screws out of the metal wall.

"Sudden force applied in judicious locations should force the grate off the wall," Rax said.

I closed my eyes, breathing deeply as I thought about that. Could Rax be right about my bones? How could a short electrical bath have changed me so fundamentally?

"Is my flesh denser than before?" I asked.

"Not categorically so," the crystal answered.

I repositioned myself. It was hard in the narrow confines of the tube. Finally, I managed to draw my arm back. I punched ahead of me. It was awkward, much less forceful than I would have liked and exceedingly painful.

"This isn't going to work," I said between clenched teeth.

"You are holding back. You must attack the grate by hammering it off. Do not worry about your hands."

"You're not the one feeling the pain."

"You are the active unit, I am the control unit. You must excel in this physical endeavor or you will fail to break into the chamber. Your planet could face dire consequences if the

Organizer is allowed to continue his depredations unchallenged."

I decided Rax was right. So, I kept hammering at the grate. Each blow hurt as much as you'd imagine striking solid metal would be. I cut my flesh, bled and moaned after repeated blows. I became claustrophobic and, barely controlling the panic, used it to hit the grate harder and harder.

Suddenly, the metal flew off the wall. It fell and clanged against the floor.

I collapsed, keeping my aching, bleeding hands in front of me.

"There is no time to rest," Rax said. "We must collect weapons and return through the tube."

My hands throbbed and tingled. I'd felt a similar sensation as a kid when I'd almost frozen my hands by digging tunnels in the snow, really deep tunnels. Finally, the tunnels had collapsed on me. I'd dug my way out, but my mittens had thoroughly soaked through. My fingers had been icy cold. As they had thawed out in the house, they had tingled as they did now deep in the Greenland complex.

I huddled in a corner, keeping my hands in front of my body. The pain subsided shortly. I wondered what the flesh of my knuckles looked like. I wouldn't have been surprised if I had indentations on my bones.

"Your breathing has become even," Rax said. "That should mean you are ready for the next phase of the operation."

"Can you scan my hands?"

"Yes," he said, sounding reluctant to answer.

"Are they going to be okay?"

"It is not a matter of a future event. Your hands are sound right now."

"Everything is healed?" I asked.

"No. But your hands are functional. You need to begin collecting weapons and power cells."

I stood, gingerly moving my fingers. I wasn't ready to feel the torn flesh yet. If I had to do it over, I don't think I could have started bashing the grille again.

"What am I looking for?" I asked.

"I have already found the weapons. You must merely collect them, transport the lot through the access tube and we can move into our assault position."

"Fine," I said. "Are we gathering rayguns?"

"I am unfamiliar with your terminology. You will take a Class III Pulse Rifle, a satchel of energy cells, another of shock sticks, a force knife and a resonator."

"What in the heck is a resonator?"

"I will need it later to recalibrate the alien energy cells for the ship."

"The Ungul rayguns are better than any pulse rifle," I said.

"Do you mean the Class IV Disintegrator Ejector?"

"I guess so."

"The ejector is a viable close-quarters weapon. For our requirements, it is too short-ranged."

"Where do I find this arsenal anyway?" I asked.

I followed the crystal's instructions, and soon found myself loaded down with his laundry list of war-fighting equipment. I shoved it all into the access tube, suppressed my shivering and climbed back in.

For the next ten minutes, I slid the rifle and pouches ahead of me.

"Wait," I said, pausing at an access junction. "You're giving me different directions. We didn't come in this way."

"That is an amazingly astute observation. You have a keen sense of direction. Do you feel this is due to your conversion, or did you possess this directional sense in your former state?"

"Why are you changing our route?" I asked.

"There is nothing nefarious about it, if that is your concern. We are moving toward our assault position. If sensations of fear are dampening your resolve—"

"I'm in," I said. "Don't worry about me. I've been waiting for a chance to hit back at the Unguls. I feel like I'm in a horror movie, and one key thing in those is to hit back as hard as you can instead of running away in terror."

"I applaud your warrior spirit. It is the correct emotional response for our present situation."

"Yeah," I said. "So how about we keep moving."

-19-

After much crawling and later walking through dark corridors, we finally reached a lit area. I hunkered down and examined my hands, expecting to find shredded, blood-dripping flesh. There were scabs and some of the flesh looked pulped. Yet, the damage was less than I'd expected.

"Are you satisfied?" Rax asked.

I touched the battered flesh. It was normal after a fashion. I couldn't understand the less-than-spectacular damage.

"I couldn't have healed that much in so short a time," I said.

"If you are referring to your hands, you are correct."

"I don't get it."

"We discussed this earlier," Rax said. "It is time to concentrate on the mission."

"I have to understand what the machine did to me. Am I still human?"

"That is a metaphysical question, one that I am ill-equipped to answer. If it is any consolation, I suspect you are now like some of the ancient Earth heroes."

"What heroes?"

"This is mere speculation," Rax said, "but after having read the briefing papers on the subject, I suspect you are like the mythical champions Hercules, Achilles and Gilgamesh."

"Say again," I said.

"Could the mysterious being have given similar treatments to such early heroes?" Rax asked. "Remember, they went on to achieve fame on your barbaric planet. Perhaps Hercules and others simply had accelerated strength, an ability to absorb greater damage and an ability to heal faster and more thoroughly than the base population."

"Why would the mystery aliens do that to them?" I asked.

"That is a primary question the Guard has yet to solve. Before I leave your planet, I hope to have an answer."

"You're kidding me?"

"While your education could use substantial broadening," Rax said, "this is neither the time nor the place for it. Are you ready to begin the assault?"

I peered down a long corridor. We'd reached hieroglyphically adorned walls again, this corridor dimly lit with overhead lamps embedded in the ceiling. In the distance, I could hear churning drills and occasional explosions.

"Do you detect any Unguls keeping watch?" I asked.

"None," Rax said. "I doubt they expect trouble at this junction. That should prove beneficial to our assault."

I nodded slowly.

"Time is critical," Rax said. "We must move into position."

I picked up the pulse rifle. It was longer than I would have liked and much heavier, although it wasn't as heavy as a .50 caliber machine gun. I slipped both pouch carrying-straps over my shoulders and started down the corridor.

I could finally see my one-piece. The uniform was metallic-looking but as soft as silk. It kept out the cold, and was adorned with several stars. I'd seen similar garb among the first set of humans in the glass cylinders.

Despite everything I'd been through, I felt unnaturally spry. If I was like Hercules, did that make me a superhero?

I shook my head.

I'd never seen any movie superheroes shred their hands as I'd done. They would have smashed off the grate without a problem. Therefore, I wasn't in their league, although I was no longer in the bush league, either.

"Is there another access tube nearby?" I asked.

"No. You will walk ahead one thousand, four hundred and thirty-seven steps—"

"You mean waltz right up to them?"

"Essentially, that is correct."

"We need surprise, remember?"

"This is how we will achieve our surprise. Logan, I detect a rapid heart rate, which undoubtedly indicates nervousness. I suggest you trust my strategic and tactical judgment."

"The last time I charged ahead—I'm talking about Station 5—I ended up getting captured. I doubt I'll survive a second capture."

"In that, I agree. My plan does not entail your capture, but enemy elimination in the local area."

"Have you broken into their communications or something?" I asked.

"I have," Rax admitted. "They have a tight net and use a code I am still trying to break. My analysis of the comm chatter leads me to believe they do not expect any enemy interference. However, I do believe they are expecting a possible situation once they break into the place they are drilling. That, no doubt, is why each of their personnel is armed."

"How many are in the local area?"

"Nineteen effectives," Rax said.

"That includes the drill operators?"

"Everyone," Rax said.

I thought about Station 5 and the Unguls I'd faced there. I thought about Z17 and Q11. I remembered how Z17 had lopped off my foot. They'd likely killed the two new hires in Nevada. The Unguls had cut me, chased me, driven me from my latest employment and destroyed my former work world. Who knew what they planned to do to the planet as a whole.

"Do you have a sniper location in mind?" I asked.

"This is an excellent suggestion," Rax said. "Yes, firing from concealment. I approve of that, and will add it to my tactical configuration."

The crystal's latest comment changed the dynamics between us. Until that moment, I'd believed in his Galactic superiority. Rax belonged to a society and civilization that built and flew starships. They were light-years ahead of anything we could do. But did that mean Rax had plain old-fashioned common sense?

If he hadn't known enough to already figure I would try to kill the Unguls as a hidden sniper, then the crystal lacked the most basic common sense of all—how to survive a firefight.

I would do this exactly how I believed was the best way to do it. I would no longer let his Galactic Guard qualifications awe me. He might be sliced bread in the spaceship department, but I was the former Marine. I was the security expert, and I was the flesh and blood action unit between the two of us.

"Explain the shock sticks to me," I said, as I hoofed it down the corridor.

"The procedure is simple," he said. "Twist the top arming mechanism…" He went on to tell me how to set it as a time bomb, and how to ensure maximum blast.

I got the jitters as I broke into a jog. It had been one thing in Nevada crawling in the dark on my home turf. It was another charging down an underground corridor toward an alien drilling site. The whining grew louder. The occasional explosion shook the corridor, causing me to slow down and once to stop because I staggered too much.

"What kind of chamber are they trying to break into?" I asked.

"That is not germane to our present mission," Rax said.

Did the crystal know, or did he not want to admit that he didn't? None of it would matter if I couldn't kill the aliens.

From here, I could see that the Unguls had set up in a vast chamber. It was more like a giant cavern. To my shock, I realized it was a cave, as the walls here were rock instead of metal. Huge lights hung from the ceiling with thick cords trailing down from them.

The Unguls must have put those in. The original invader had a tidier style.

The corridor shook again and rock-dust drifted into view as I staggered closer. Soon, I saw a glimmer of natural light coming from the opposite point of the cavern.

Carefully, I slid along a corridor wall, my palms sweaty and my breathing rapid.

"Are you scanning?" I whispered.

"Affirmative," Rax said. "Several Unguls are aimed in our direction, although I doubt they can see you in here."

I halted, and I reminded myself I had to do the combat thinking for the both of us. I slid onto my belly and began to crawl.

"This manner of locomotion substantially lowers our assault speed," Rax said.

"Getting hit by enemy fire will lower it even more."

"Perhaps you do not yet comprehend," Rax said. "I have already factored that into my calculations. You can absorb more damage than you would expect. Even better, you will heal from secondary strikes—"

"You're not the one absorbing damage," I said stiffly. "So, I'll rely on my own judgment in this."

"I hesitate to state the obvious, but it is in your own best interest to take advantage of my superior strategic and tactical skills."

I continued crawling, too intent on watching for Unguls to argue with the crystal.

As I approached the main cavern, I got a better idea of the situation. The cavern was circular and huge like the Oakland Raiders Coliseum. Just like the coliseum, it had levels. Parked hover-pads were on the main level. Three tiers down were three floating drillers. They were oval-shaped with a big drill in the center. Large scoops pushed the rubble to the sides.

I exited the corridor on my stomach and felt the cooler air on my cheeks. A stack of boxes stood nearby. I crawled toward them.

"We have a problem," Rax whispered. "I have detected more Unguls headed down. They are in the main thoroughfare, using tracked vehicles."

I reached the boxes and climbed to my feet. I checked the pulse rifle. Everything seemed ready. Before I engaged the power cell, I leaned out. The rifle had a fancy scope. I experimented and soon got the hang of it. One by one, I began to locate and count the enemy.

"Why do you not open fire while you have the opportunity?" Rax asked. "This excessive caution is unwarranted. The Unguls will present themselves once you begin firing. Why are you practicing this pre-combat location?"

"It's a Marine tradition," I muttered, my mouth too dry to say more.

"I suggest—"

"Shut up, Rax. Let me concentrate."

The crystal fell silent.

I counted twelve Unguls. Rax had told me there were nineteen in the drilling area. That left seven I hadn't found. That was too many, especially with the snow-cats coming with reinforcements.

I eased back behind the boxes, put the rifle on the ground and began placing shock sticks beside it.

"I realize you desire quiet," Rax said, "but this delay strikes too close to home as cowardice. If you cannot—"

"Rax, we're going to enter a new phase in our working relationship. I hereby demote you from your leadership role. You're unsuited to tactical management, anyway. Instead, I am reinstating you in your traditional role as an advisory unit."

"I feel I must inform you that you lack Guard rank status to—"

"I'm doing this on my authority as a United States Marine sergeant," I said, interrupting him.

"That lacks all credibility in the Galactic Guard."

"You're wrong," I said. "Now, shut up like I told you. My stomach is in knots, and I have to be steady."

"Are you about to attack?" he asked.

"Yeah," I said, my mouth now totally dry.

I picked up the rifle, flipping several switches as Rax had instructed me earlier in the gun-locker chamber. The pulse rifle purred as it began to vibrate.

I leaned out, laid the end of the barrel on a box and sighted the first Ungul. My palms were slick with sweat. My breathing had increased and I had the shakes.

I began to hum. It helped a little. Ever so gently, I squeezed the trigger—

The weapon vibrated more as its whine increased, and with a *spat*, an orange pulse-bolt ejected. When I say orange, I mean as bright as a Christmas light. I don't know how Rax figured I could snipe the Unguls with this thing. The pulse-bolt glowed so brightly that everyone in the cavern had to see it.

The pulse struck the targeted Ungul. He glowed brighter than if I'd hit him with a raygun. He tumbled to the floor as a charred piece of alien meat. If the pulse-bolt didn't disintegrate him, it definitely killed him, which is all that counted now.

I gritted my teeth, targeted a new Ungul and fired another pulse. One after another, I targeted and fired. This was a speed contest, and I had range on them.

The drilling stopped. The explosions ceased. Some of the Unguls sprinted for cover. They ran faster than a human could. I killed two of the runners. Other Unguls took out their rayguns, firing back at me.

The boxes took hits. Smoke roiled from them. Some of the boxes lost sides, spilling small glittering contents.

I shot eleven times before pulling back behind what remained of the boxes. I had hit and killed six Unguls for sure, maybe cut down another two. That was eight out of nineteen.

With a trembling hand, I picked up the first shock stick, twisted the top cap and stepped out from behind the boxes. I reached back as if trying to throw a long bomb across the length of a football field. I heaved the stick, watching it twirl. Then, I dove behind the boxes as two rays slashed past me.

I heard a loud *crump*. The shock stick worked, at least. Had it taken out Unguls?

I picked up another stick, twisted the cap and hurled it over the top of the boxes.

"Unguls are flying here commando-style," Rax said.

I gave a maniacal laugh. I'd been expecting that.

Now, jetpack infantry sounds cool. Flying into battle must have a high all its own. But there was one thing I knew from the Marines. Cover in combat counted for a lot. Flying at a man didn't give one any cover, but completely exposed the individual.

I leaned against the boxes, took a deep breath and poked around with the pulse rifle. The Unguls flew up from the pit, three of them like bats out of Hell.

I sighted and fired. A pulse-bolt hit one. The alien tumbled backward. The others fired at me. One lost control of his belt and shot up at incredible speed, striking the ceiling. I imagined that Ungul was either dead or incapacitated.

The last one zoomed closer, had almost reached me in fact. I hurled a stick in his direction and ducked.

The stick made the crumping sound. I looked up in time to see the Ungul smash against the wall to my left. He bounced off and flew toward me again.

I shot him at nearly pointblank range, melting enough of the belt to deactivate it. He struck the floor with a thump.

Now, though, three snow-cats roared into the cavern. Each stopped, and out jumped more Unguls. These wore combat gear and carried rifles.

"You must retreat," Rax said.

"What about the energy cells down there?"

"They are meaningless, as you cannot acquire them and live. I need you alive, Logan. I have to admit, though, that was a stirring exhibition of combat prowess. You are an uncommonly good soldier for a human. I would not have believed it unless I had actually seen it."

"They're going to chase us."

"They were about to chase us in any regard."

"What do you mean?" I shouted.

"First, we must escape the battlefield. I will tell you then."

"You mean you lied to me about the reason for our assault?"

"That is one interpretation. Please, Logan, retreat. You have done much better than I expected. The Unguls are about to use heavy weaponry against us."

With the pulse rifle in one hand and the rest of the shock sticks in the other in a pouch, I pivoted for the corridor and sprinted like mad.

-20-

"What's happening back there?" I wheezed from inside the corridor.

"The Unguls have acquired a fix on you," Rax said. "I believe they will initiate a full-scale search until they have you in captivity."

I raced down the corridor as air burned down my throat. Behind us in the cavern, I heard snow-cats rev.

"Why did we make the assault if it couldn't succeed?" I panted.

"The attack was dangerous but necessary," Rax said. "Remember, I am a top-rated strategist and have plans within plans. I have also been analyzing you since the beginning. The percentages were high that you would balk if you knew the truth."

"What truth?" I shouted.

"You only had a thirty-seven percent chance of survival. I did not anticipate such a bloodthirsty manner of assault on your part. Clearly, these Marines are a formidable combat organization."

"You're just buttering me up," I said. "You don't really believe what you said."

"Turn left," Rax said.

"Balls!"

I slid to a stop, turned around, got on one knee and aimed the rifle down the corridor.

"That is unnecessary," Rax said. "And it lowers our odds of survival. We have engaged them as needed. Now we must—"

The rifle whined as I fired, sending an orange pulse down the corridor. I watched through the scope. Two Unguls who had raced into the corridor ducked back out of sight.

I sprang to my feet and went left, as Rax had suggested. A hover-pad waited there in the shadows. Instead of berating the crystal about not telling me about it sooner, I pitched the rifle onto the pad, jumped up and pressed controls.

"We will travel into the darkness as I navigate," Rax said.

I panted as I followed his instructions. We zipped into darkness except for the control lights on the steering panel. Riding instead of running was a vast improvement. Sweat slicked my forehead, but it was less than I'd expected.

"What else have you kept from me?" I said.

"We activated equipment—the machine in particular. It appears the Unguls have been monitoring the interior complex. I detected an increase in comm chatter. The probability was high that they were about to hunt for us. A first strike on our part seemed judicious."

"That doesn't make sense," I said. "If they were going to hunt us, we should have ambushed them in the corridors instead of attacking head-on in an area where they could deploy their superior numbers."

"The reason why we attacked should be obvious to you."

"Well, it's not," I snapped.

"I am disappointed in you, Logan. We did not attack to gain the energy cells or even to retard their search for us. We attacked in order to throw them off the real trail. The ship is recharging even as we speak."

"How can it do that?"

"Through an osmosis subterfuge method," Rax said.

"That's not what I meant. You said the ship was in a location with a power drain."

"It was. Something has interrupted the power drain. That allowed me to use regular Guard techniques to recharge the ship's power cells."

"That doesn't make any sense."

"It is another incongruity, I agree," Rax said. "There are factors here I cannot directly sense, although I fathom their presence. Yet, that is beside the point. The critical factor is that the osmosis subterfuge method is not completely secretive. If the Unguls make a careful study of their readings, it is possible they can counteract the process before we can escape."

"I think I'm tracking your meaning. Instead of looking into a power drain somewhere, you want the Unguls chasing me?"

"Chasing *us*," Rax said. "I have put myself in jeopardy as well. That should show you how critically I view the need for our deception tactic."

"When are you going to start trusting me and telling me these things up front?"

"I trust you now," Rax said. "You have shown yourself to be both brave and resourceful. Yes, you are Galactic Guard material, Logan. There is no doubt about it."

I didn't let his praise go to my head, because I didn't know if he really meant it.

"How long are we going to let them chase us?" I asked.

"An hour should—oh no."

"What now?" I asked.

"The Unguls are deploying hover-pads. We must accelerate and attempt several high-speed maneuvers. Are you able to concentrate?"

I rolled my shoulders to loosen them. "I'm ready," I said.

For the next fifteen minutes, we flew faster, turned sharper and worked deeper into the complex. I hunched over the controls, tapping the panel the instant Rax gave a new instruction.

"Stop as quickly as possible," he said later.

I did.

"It is time to begin leaving shock sticks," he said. "You will set them as proximity mines."

"How do I do that?"

He told me. I told him I needed light to do that. He instructed me to pull him out of my pocket. Like a regular cell phone, he shined a light on the sticks. I adjusted several, turning them into proximity mines. Afterward, I readied to drop the first one onto the floor.

“What are you doing?” he asked.

“Deploying the first proximity mine,” I said.

“If you set them in place, our proximity will activate the mine. You must throw them into position, making sure we are far enough away so the mine does not immediately detonate.”

I did as he instructed. Soon, we sped into the darkness again. After three minutes, maybe four, I heard explosions.

“Excellent,” Rax said. “We damaged a hover-pad. That should spur on the rest to chase us vengefully.”

I frowned to myself. Was that the goal—to anger them? Why would that be the goal?

“I think I get it,” I whispered. “You want them chasing us instead of drilling because they’re not trying to break into some key place in the complex, but about to reach the Guard-ship.”

“Please, Logan—”

I laughed. “It’s a basic strategy. I’ve seen a crow do something similar, cawing and diving at me as I went to inspect its fallen chick. The mother wanted me to follow her instead of her defenseless chick.”

“You must internalize such comments,” Rax said. “It is possible the Unguls are monitoring us closely enough to pick up our speech.”

“Fine,” I said. “But I—”

“I detect—error, there is an error. A Min Ve has descended to the drilling pit. This is a catastrophe. The probability of a breakthrough has increased one hundred fold. I must advance to a Phase 4 Initiative. Are you ready, Logan?”

“For what?” I shouted.

“It may already be too late, but we must transport this instant.”

-21-

I materialized inside the Guard-ship. I found it blinding, as lights blazed inside the chamber. I staggered, covered my eyes and strained to adjust to the greater illumination.

"We must hurry to the piloting chamber," Rax said.

"You have to give me a minute. It's too bright in here."

I heard a click.

"Is that better?" Rax asked.

I peered from between my fingers. It was far better, dimmer. I watched my step—

"Hey," I said. "What happened to the skeleton? It's gone."

"The robot has been tidying up," Rax said. "Please, Logan. You must hurry."

Jumping down from the transporter dais, I hurried though a sliding hatch and raced along a short corridor with a solid deck. There were five other hatches to the sides and a lone forward hatch. It slid up as I neared it.

I rushed into a forward sloping chamber with controls along the sides and two large cockpit-type windows, with two seats in the front area.

Lights snapped on outside the windows. It showed rock. The Guard-ship was in a solid rock cavern. Even as I studied the rock, stone chips fell from the ceiling and sprinkled onto the windows. That made me start. Then the tip of a drill burst through the ceiling, sending more rocks and gravel against the ship's upper glass.

"Hurry, Logan," Rax said. "You must sit in the pilot seat and turn on the controls at my orders."

"Can't I shove you into a slot so you can drive the ship?"

"I have always thought that would be an excellent idea," Rax said. "A quorum of Rax Prime crystals once threatened to leave Guard service unless they gained such a privilege. The High Council vetoed the idea, and the crystal quorum backed down at the last minute. Their Galactic patriotism outshone their need for equal rights."

I plopped onto the pilot seat, setting Rax into an obvious slot on the controls. At his instructions, I tapped the controls, lighting up panels. A hum began somewhere inside the ship, and my seat vibrated the slightest bit.

As this happened, the drill widened its breach as more metal whirled into view. I looked up, watching the drill disappear up its hole.

"They could drop explosives on us at any moment," Rax said. "You must activate the shield."

"How do I do that?" I shouted.

At the crystal's instructions, I tapped more controls. A green nimbus suddenly glowed around the Guard-ship. Seconds later, two black objects tumbled out of the ceiling-hole. Instead of striking the windows above me, the objects halted on the glowing nimbus.

"Prepare for impact," Rax said.

The two objects exploded. I stared upward in sick fascination. In slow motion, the shock blew the shield downward until it struck the hull. Metal groaned as the ship shook. That threw me out of the seat, causing me to crash against the controls.

A klaxon wailed. The ship shuddered worse than before, and the shield darkened.

"Get back into your seat," Rax said. "If they drop more explosives, the Unguls might make a breach into the ship."

I slumped groggily onto the seat, and in a daze, I buckled on seatbelts. Afterward, I continued to follow the crystal's instructions.

"They are readying a beam, Logan. You must engage the thrusters."

"Are you sure? You said earlier—"

"Engage, engage," Rax said. "Be ready for the shockwave, but engage this instant."

I tapped the needed control, and all Hell broke loose around us. Rocks flew everywhere, as hot exhaust must have smashed against the chamber walls. Flames licked around the ship. We shook. My teeth rattled and my body strained against the straps looped around me.

The roar increased, making it almost impossible to hear Rax's instructions. Then, the ship lurched as we shook harder. Rocks began raining down on us. Some broke through the weakened shield, striking the outer hull with ear-shattering clangs.

All at once, like a fishing bobber on a geyser, we shot upward. The ship smashed against the weakened ceiling rock—I'd seen hairline fissures everywhere. We bounced left, thrust right. My head seemed to snap back and forth. I dreaded ricocheting metal shredding the interior compartment and obliterating my skull.

Then, we were through!

"Rotate the ship, Logan. Engage the laser cannon. Shoot them this instant."

"What do you mean shoot them? How do I shoot them?"

The ship had broken out of its resting place and into the main cavern. I wondered how it had gotten there in the first place. I recognized the drilling ovals. I saw a snow-cat near an entrance with outer illumination. I also saw Unguls wrestling with what looked like an artillery piece. This piece lacked a muzzle opening, but had the solid tip a raygun would have.

With dread, I realized it was a ship-killing disintegrator ejector. The Unguls were trying to line it up with the Guard-ship.

"How do I fire the ship's cannons?" I shouted.

Rax explained as the Unguls lined up the artillery-sized disintegrator. The tip glowed with a hellish color.

I slapped a control. The Guard-ship shot forward, heading for a wall.

"Turn, turn," Rax shouted.

For the next few seconds the ship lurched in one direction and side-swiveled in another. A thick beam flashed past, barely missing us. The beam quit, and the Unguls readjusted for a better shot.

"You must calm down," Rax told me.

"You calm down and start telling me how to fly this thing."

The crystal spoke deliberately. That helped steady my racing nerves. The Unguls lined up the cannon. At the same time, I brought the ship around. The disintegrator's tip glowed with terrible promise. I stabbed the repeater switch. Laser bolts struck the ground in front of the disintegrator. The enemy piece began to beam. At that moment, the shelf in front of the enemy weapon fell apart. The piece tilted toward the pit. The Ungul crew waved their arms in desperation as they slid down with their gun. Then, both the gun-crew and the weapon plummeted for the bottom of the drilling pit.

"While I applaud your cunning," Rax said, "it is far from the optimum gunnery pattern you should employ in the future."

"You're welcome!" I shouted.

After I calmed down, I maneuvered the Guard-ship, using the cannon to obliterate the drills, the scoops and the snow-cats. Afterward, I targeted hiding and then sprinting Unguls. They proved to be excellent gunnery practice. By the time I killed the last alien, I felt as if I had the hang of flying and firing this thing. It was actually quite responsive. To tell you the truth, all my hours of videogame playing came in handy. I was used to maneuvering combat ships like this at my computer console.

"Have you gained sufficient confidence to fly us through the tunnel?" Rax asked.

"It will be a piece of cake," I said.

Soon, the Guard-ship roared through a rocky tunnel. One area seemed like it would be too narrow. I used the laser cannon, widening the way just enough.

Seconds later, the Guard-ship burst into the open with a blue sky and shining sun. We'd reached the Greenland surface, although I flew in the bottom of an icy canyon. I took us up, brought the ship around and hammered the alien warehouse with laser bolts.

I shouted gleefully. The Unguls had terrorized me. They'd likely killed my Nevada guards and thought to have their way on Earth to do as they pleased.

"Let's shred the other camp," I said.

Rax didn't respond. I had no idea why, but I wasn't going to let it spoil my fun. Using the tracks in the snow, I followed the route to the base camp with the modified Learjets.

After three passes, the warehouse, Learjets, cats and personnel were either burning or dead in the snow.

"Where do we go next?" I shouted. "Personally, I suggest we strike them in Nevada before they know what's going on."

Rax still did not speak.

"Is something bothering you?" I asked.

"Indeed," Rax said. "According to my scanner and calculations, the chief alien orbital vessel has located us."

"That doesn't sound good."

"We are about to find out," Rax said. "The Organizer's communications officer is making her final request to speak with you."

"Why does she want to speak with me? Why doesn't she want to speak with you?"

"There is an unfortunate bias in Galactic Society against beings such as me."

"What do aliens have against intelligent crystals?" I asked.

"Are you willing to speak with the communications officer?" Rax asked.

"Sure, why not?"

"Your manner is far too glib, considering the situation. Yet, you have agreed to the conversation. That meets standard operating protocols."

"You're making it sound as if it's a bad idea to talk."

"I have one suggestion you would do well to heed," Rax said. "If she insists on using Galactic Standard Speech, tell her as an Earth-assigned agent you will only communicate in the aboriginal tongue."

"I'm thinking my talking to her might not be such a good idea after all."

"I have already accepted the call on your behalf," Rax said. "Refusing now would be tactically unsound."

A screen rose from a panel. The screen was fuzzy for just a moment. Then, it cleared, and I found myself staring at another alien.

She was blue-skinned, with pouty lips and seductively green eyes, and she had the longest, thickest hair I'd ever seen. She didn't strike me as an Ungul, and her face was too angular to be human. But she had an exotic sexy way about her that I found appealing.

She spoke gibberish but did so in a sexy purr.

I recalled Rax's warning, and decided the Organizer's people would expect arrogance from a Galactic agent. Thus, I sneered at her without saying a word.

She cocked her head, spoke again and waited.

"I am on Earth," I said.

She asked another gibberish-sounding question.

"Because I am on Earth," I said, "I will only communicate in the aboriginal tongue."

She cast a glance to someone off screen. I heard off-screen gibberish this time. It had a rough, male quality. She frowned, nodded and faced me once again. She reached out, tapping unseen controls. Only then did she stare into my eyes.

There was a shock at the base of my skull, and my groin, and I felt even more attracted to her than before.

Her lips moved. A second later, I heard, "This is a crude and time-wasting protocol. The planetary species has a limited vocabulary."

"You should have gone elsewhere then," I said.

Her eyes radiated intensity, and despite my best effort, I found myself grinning at her. Maybe we could talk over a drink.

"The situation does not concern you, Galactic," she said. "We have letters of marque from the High Min Ve Council. Thus, we are engaged in a legally correct action. Your interference threatens an open rupture and possibly war. Are you prepared to accept the responsibility of such dire consequences?"

War sounded bad, and serious, but I wasn't sure how to respond. Thus, I kept studying her compelling features, wanting to see more of her.

"You are zealous," she said, "and perhaps you were unaware of the legality of our action, as our presence here is unusual. Fortunately, in his grace, the Organizer will allow you to depart the planet and the star system in peace. He will also forgo seeking punitive damages in the Galactic Council. But if you attempt to destroy more of the expedition's property and personnel, I am instructed to tell you that we shall employ maximum force defending ourselves."

"Threats don't scare me," I said.

"You are outgunned, outmanned and outdated," she said. "There are no Galactic starships in the vicinity. This is a derelict planet and an abandoned region of no concern to the Guard."

"That's not how I see it," I said.

She leaned closer to the screen, and a frown curved her lips.

"There is something amiss here," she said. "Your speech patterns, your leering insolence—you are out of sync."

I shrugged as if indifferent, uncertain what she meant.

"Are you aware that no one knows of your existence here?" she asked. "Thus, no one will care if you die. Consider my question carefully, Galactic. Will you cease your resistance against the Organizer?"

"We should consider her offer," Rax said softly.

"No!" I said, startled the crystal could say that.

The blue-skinned beauty stiffened. She must have taken that as my answer to her.

"You're a stubborn fool," she said. "You have just sealed your death."

"Listen—" I said.

Abruptly, the screen went blank. That seemed terribly ominous. Had I screwed up?

"Why should I have accepted her offer?" I asked Rax. "She's bluffing, right? You said there's backup near Jupiter."

"A lie at the right moment often buys one extra time," Rax said. "Ours is a frail position. A little verbal maneuvering would have—

"Warning," he said. "The orbital vessel has locked onto us with its targeting computers."

“What should I do?” I asked.

“Listen to me precisely, Logan. You must do this correctly the first time, or you and I shall both cease to exist.”

-22-

I flew the Galactic Guard-ship faster across the snow and ice. It reminded me of coming to Greenland. It was hard to believe I'd only arrived this morning. My time in the tunnels and complex seemed like a lifetime now.

"So what's the plan?" I asked.

"Please hold your questions," Rax said. "I must give my full attention to my calculations." Several seconds later, he said, "I have it. We have less than three minutes before they launch."

"That seems like an awfully long time for them to warm up their disintegrator cannons."

"You are working under a false assumption," Rax said. "The orbital vessel is not a warship."

"Then why are we running away? Let's go upstairs and blast them to smithereens."

"For all your sophistication, you are a barbarian, Logan, with simple solutions."

"Yeah," I said. "Well, sue me."

"That does not make sense."

"Neither does your chicken-liver attitude," I said.

"Theirs is a pirate vessel."

"What's that even supposed to mean?"

"From their pirate vessel," Rax said, "the aliens engage in piratical activities. You heard the Jarnevon. She sought to color their activities with a legal fiction—I am referring to the letters of marque from the Min Ve Council. Earth is a banned planet in a forbidden zone. Not even the Min Ve can wriggle out of that in a Galactic court of law."

"I'm not worried about that," I said. "I want to know why their vessel should worry us if it's not a warship."

"While the orbital vessel is technically not a warship, it possesses weapons pods. The pods and the pirate ship's shields are several orders of magnitude more powerful than my Guard-ship's shields and weapons arsenal."

"That still doesn't explain why they haven't fired their beams yet."

"They are not going to use beams."

"What are they going to use?"

"A missile," Rax said.

"Let's knock it down before it strikes us."

"It is a ZeLoran Hell-Burner," Rax said. "It is heavily armored with a nuclear warhead."

I stared at the crystal. "You're kidding me? The aliens are firing nukes at Earth?"

"The reason is legality," Rax said. "A nuclear attack is a Class IV violation, making it a minor offense. Using spaceship-class disintegrator beams from an orbital location is a Class II violation—a felony."

"Using nukes is just a slap on the wrist?" I asked.

"The hell-burner will wreak greater devastation on the planet," Rax said. "But it is less likely to notify the aboriginals of Galactic origin technology."

"That's a big whoop-de-do," I said. "I take it the hell-burner can vaporize the Guard-ship."

"With ease," Rax said.

"So what is it again that we're trying to do?"

"Look to your right, Logan. Do you see the ocean?"

I peered out the window. The Guard-ship zoomed from the airspace over Greenland, flashing over the choppy waters of the Arctic Ocean.

"Take us down into the water," Rax said.

I zoomed down.

"Error," Rax said. "Desist from your watery insertion at once."

I took us up.

"You must slow down before you enter the water," Rax explained. "Otherwise, we will either skip off the surface or crumple bulkheads."

"Roger that," I said.

Within thirty seconds and too many Gs from hard braking, I maneuvered the Guard-ship into the sea. It was an eerie sensation to watch the green water slosh over us. At a steep incline, I headed down.

"You do know water pressure increases the deeper we go, right?" I asked.

"I have already increased the pressure inside the ship."

Around us, the bulkheads began to groan in complaint.

"Turn to your right," Rax said, "and activate the outer screen."

I did.

"Tap the red control," Rax said.

We headed down, but at a slower rate. We also launched a buoy, attached by a thin line to our ship.

It bobbed on the surface.

"Scanning…" Rax said.

I studied the screen. By whatever tech the ship possessed, I watched higher Earth orbit. At first, there was nothing. Then, I noticed a shimmering but otherwise invisible ship. It was huge, bigger than the biggest aircraft carrier. The shimmering dulled until I could barely make out the alien vessel.

It wasn't round, oval, or even octagonal shaped. Instead, it looked like an erector set that had visited a planetary junkyard, welding masses of scraps onto the girders. Some of the rearward pieces glowed.

I took that to be propulsion.

A forward pod slid open. Bright light shone out of it. Then, a sleek-looking missile popped out. It drifted toward the atmosphere. After ten seconds, a rocket engine ignited. The missile leapt, speeding for lower Earth orbit.

"I have calculated the warhead's size," Rax said. "It is several magnitudes larger than I expected. We are unlikely to survive a watery detonation."

I wiped my lips with the back of my wrist. Aliens had just targeted us with a hell-burner, a thermonuclear-tipped space missile. This had to be a first for the Earth.

"How many megatons is the warhead?" I asked.

"It is many times more powerful than Earth's biggest nuclear weapon."

"Can't the ship's shield protect us from the blast?"

"In no way," Rax said.

"So that's it? We're toast?"

"I did not say that. Unfortunately, the only successful maneuver will devour most of the ship's pirated energy. It is possible the enemy will also detect our deception, which will render it useless."

"A nuke like that will also destroy a lot of Arctic life," I said. "We have to destroy the missile before it detonates."

"This is not a dream, Logan. This is reality. Wishing does not make—"

"Yeah, I got it," I snapped. "So what do we do?"

On the screen, I saw the missile's heat shield glowing as it burned through Earth's upper atmosphere.

Rax began spitting out instructions. I had to unbuckle, race to various parts of the piloting chamber and tap in precise codes.

I glanced over my shoulder at the missile on the screen. It was streaking straight for us, presently passing through to the lower part of the atmosphere. A running number indicated how many kilometers from impact. It was less than three.

"Rax," I said.

"Get back in the pilot's chair. Hurry, Logan. We have less than twenty seconds to achieve transfer."

"What are you talking about?" I shouted.

"Press the blue tab."

I did.

The ship's engine whined at its highest setting so far. But absolutely nothing happened. I glanced at the screen. The missile streaked under the kilometer range. It headed at an angle for the water.

"Are we dead?" I shouted.

"Tap in this sequence," Rax said.

On the screen, the missile struck the water, coming for us like a torpedo.

I looked out the window. The water seemed to fade from view, growing lighter and lighter colored. A feeling of disorientation struck me. The water vanished. We seemed to tumble. Suddenly, I heard what sounded like a sonic boom. The ship shuddered, tossed to-and-fro as rushing water swirled around us. I expected it to get worse before the end, before oblivion, but by some miracle, the water and the ship's shaking began settling down.

"What's going on?" I shouted. "Did we survive the detonation after all?"

The screen activated. I watched, glued to the set. A great hump appeared on the surface. I had no idea of its size. Then a great column of water shot toward the sky.

"What's happening?" I shouted.

"The hell-burner has detonated," Rax said. "I am recording the aftereffects."

"That wasn't the blast hitting us?" I asked.

"By no means," Rax said.

"How long until the blast reaches us then?"

"It won't."

"That doesn't make sense."

"We teleported, Logan," Rax explained. "We moved the ship halfway across the planet into the Pacific Ocean near Hawaii. I had you create a displacement bubble ahead of us. The water rushing in was the boom you heard."

I stared at the screen, at the column of dirty water thrown up by the alien hell-burner. What was that going to do to the Arctic environment? Likely, millions of fish and other organisms would die. Nations would notice the nuclear warhead having gone off. It might cause accusations to fly between nations. It might even ignite a war between the nuclear-armed countries.

"This is awful," I said.

"The Organizer is brazen," Rax said. "He has to find and kill us now. Otherwise, the Galactic Guard will hunt him to his death for what he just did. He will know this, of course. I am afraid I have miscalculated the size and intensity of his greed. He must know—"

Rax stopped talking.

"You were going to say," I prodded.

"By launching the hell-burner, the Organizer has given us license to eliminate his operatives and destroy his vessel without warning or quarter."

I digested that. "Will he move openly on Earth now?"

"There is no telling."

"So, what do we do next?" I asked.

"Yes," Rax said. "That is an excellent question. It is time for me to make deep calculations."

-23-

I sat in the pilot's chair inside a Galactic Guard-ship. For the first time in countless hours, immediate death wasn't staring me in the face. I peered out a window, wondering how far we were underwater. I saw a curious shark in the distance circling our craft.

I'd gone to work last night in my jeep. Now, I sat in a freaking spaceship, having dealt with at least four different kinds of aliens. There were the shape-changing Unguls, Rax the crystal, the Min Ve, which I hadn't yet seen, and the sexy Jarnevon. The Organizer had launched the big daddy of all nukes just off the coast of Greenland. For the moment, at least, the bastard must believe we were dead.

"Okay," I said. "I think I know what to do."

"I doubt your idea will be Guard approved," Rax said, "but what is your suggestion?"

"We have to lay the evidence before the President of the United States. Once he knows the score, he'll order a counterattack against the alien vessel."

"There is a problem with that," Rax said. "Your species does not possess a space fleet."

"I know," I said. "But we have plenty of ICBMs. If we launch enough of them, I'm sure we could knock down the Organizer's pirate ship."

"What are ICBMs?"

"Intercontinental ballistic missiles," I said. "They can reach orbital space and have a nuclear payload."

"I see," Rax said. "Yes, in theory your suggestion has merit. The flaws in actuality are many. Once the Organizer sees the massed missile launch, he will immediately counter-launch, raining nuclear death on your country. I suspect his vessel also has enough countermeasures to destroy whatever missiles make it into orbital space."

"You suspect, but you don't know."

"Did you not hear me regarding the nuclear devastation you would unleash on your country?" Rax asked.

"We would have to launch a surprise attack," I said. "Maybe we could hammer him first with the Guard-ship. You know, keep him occupied while the U.S. launches its missiles."

"Logan, you fail to grasp the reality of the situation."

I'd figured all along that my idea had holes, but I'd decided this might be the best way to get Rax to talk. I was sick to death of his secretiveness.

"What reality?" I asked in my most sneering tone.

"Firstly, Guard policy mandates a stealth approach on primitive planets and doubly so on a banned one."

"The Organizer's hell-burner just wrecked your cover," I said.

"That is in no way true," Rax said. "My cover is intact. I doubt the aboriginals are aware of the Organizer's vessel, either. It has remained cloaked the entire time."

"Yeah," I said. "Well, what about all the Unguls roaming around Nevada in tanks? Someone is going to report them. I bet someone must have seen the Learjets flittering about in low Earth orbit."

"Could you explain that in further detail?" Rax asked.

I filled Rax in on my adventure in Nevada and the trip to Greenland. I finished it with, "So, according to Z17, there are at least seven active sites on Earth."

"That is not necessarily the case," Rax said. "In fact, I highly doubt it. I do not believe the Organizer would squander his resources in seven different locations at once. At most, there are three sites but more probably two: the one in Greenland and the other in Nevada."

"I don't know, Rax. The way Z17 talked, it sure seemed as if there are more than just the two or three places. By the way, what's the Organizer after, anyway?"

"I am afraid I cannot say."

"That's a bunch of crap," I said heatedly. "I've risked my life helping you, helping the Galactic Guard. The least you could do is let me know what it's all about."

"Logan, I am under strict orders never to divulge such highly sensitive information. I have already told you that Earth is a banned planet. That means only specially authorized personnel can land on its surface."

"Why is Earth banned?"

"Because it is a danger to the rest of the galaxy," he said.

"Come on, Earth? Oh. I get it. Are we humans the greatest soldiers in the universe?"

"I do not follow your logic," Rax said.

"It's easy. You Galactics have banned anyone from coming here because you fear what would happen if the human race broke out into the stars. Likely, we can kick everyone's ass, and then some."

"That is a preposterous notion. While I admit you are a warlike species, you are far from the most savage or the most notorious."

"So, we're not banned because of humanity's dangerousness to everyone else?"

"I have already said too much," Rax told me. "I am on your planet by special authority of the Galactic Guard, which gained the privilege through the highest channels. I have a suspicion as to the true nature of why my agent and I came, but I am not at liberty to explain that to you."

"I'm beginning to get the picture," I said. "This malignant intelligence you've spoken about has your Galactic panties in a bunch. That's what you're investigating."

"Let us change the subject," Rax suggested.

I stared at the crystal, looked up at the ocean waters and unbuckled the straps around me. I stood, beginning to pace. I thought back to what I'd learned in the last few hours. Suddenly, I snapped my fingers.

"How come you haven't contacted your fathership yet?" I asked.

"Logan—"

"You told me before it was in Jupiter orbit."

"That is true. I did. It was an error on my part to speak about it."

"Forget about that," I said, becoming excited. "Have you secretly contacted them?"

"No."

"Why not?"

"Because I cannot detect them," Rax said.

"Have they gone into stealth mode?"

"By all indications, the starship has left the solar system."

"Without first trying to get in touch with you?" I asked.

"It is yet another incongruity in the case, I admit."

"You've said that before, about these incongruities. What do you mean by it?"

"Very simply that the facts do not logically fit together."

"Can you give me a for instance?" I said.

"I could but will not."

"Well, maybe we should sneak off-planet then and go after the fathership, flagging it down. We need some serious backup."

"How do you propose we go after them?" Rax asked.

"I don't know. First, we have to get enough power, I guess."

"It is not a matter of power," Rax said. "I believe you are working under a false assumption. This is an infiltration Guard-ship. It was built for localized missions."

"What are you saying?" I asked. "You can't hop between star systems in this thing?"

"That is correct. The ship has a limited capacity for operating in a vacuum environment."

"Okay, okay, are you saying it's a shuttle?"

"I do not understand your reference point," he said.

"This thing is for getting down from an orbital starship to a planetary surface. But it's not for journeys to Neptune or even Mars."

"We could reach either planet," Rax said, "although I am not sure we could return to Earth from Neptune."

I nodded, pinching my lower lips as I thought about that. "So you're saying your fathership just up and left you and your agent high and dry. Is that normal Guard procedure to cut and run like that?"

"It goes against all protocols," Rax said.

"That's just like the Marines—don't leave your buddy lying on the battlefield."

"A quaint saying," Rax said, "but accurate regarding Guard procedure."

"Here's the number one question then," I said. "Why did your parent ship hightail it from the solar system without first rescuing you?"

"It is a mystery indeed, one among many."

"Unless…they thought you were dead," I said. "Maybe they waited around and finally gave up because it was taking you or your agent too long to call in."

The crystal did not respond.

"Maybe this has everything to do with the reason for your agent's bones turning brittle."

"You are a curious being, Logan, and your logic centers are highly developed but prone to running wild with speculation. I suggest we ponder more immediate problems."

I returned to the piloting chair, sitting down.

"Let's see if I understand your plight," I said. "You're stuck on a banned planet, one with a dangerous mystery. This Min Ve Council has gotten bold or greedy. It's finally gotten the balls to send a privateer to Earth, to try to gain control of whatever power scares the hell out of you Galactics. The Organizer has the upper hand here, as you lack all means of contacting your Guard friends. Your only partner is me, a barbarian aboriginal, one you are not supposed to divulge any Guard secrets to."

"I congratulate you," Rax said. "You have stated my dilemma succinctly."

"Should we go back to the Greenland complex and poke around?" I asked.

"The radioactive fallout from the hell-burner is too great for that."

I wondered how many people had died in the nuclear holocaust. The more I thought about it, the angrier I felt.

"Do we have enough ship power to do anything?" I asked.

"We are low on power, but that will prove to be the least of our problems."

"Look, Rax, I can't do all the thinking here. Either you talk to me or you can drop me off, and I'll try to put my life back together the best I can."

"Such an action would be irresponsible of me," Rax said, "as I cannot risk you contaminating the other aboriginals."

I eyed him. "You're saying I already know too much."

"Yes," Rax said.

"So we're at a serious impasse. If you were telling me the truth before, you need me to fly the Guard-ship. So, you can't just up and kill me without stranding yourself. But there's no way I'm going to work for you, if you're going to keep me a prisoner for the rest of my life."

"I have a sworn duty to the Guard," Rax said.

I snapped my fingers. "There's the answer, Rax. I'll give you my word to keep silent about you and the Guard. I won't tell a soul."

"While I suspect you are giving me a genuine offer, I cannot trust your capricious human nature."

I shook my head.

"You're in a pinch, Rax. You can't keep your prissy rules and hope to win. Either you learn to bend a little and realize we can scratch each other's backs, or you might as well commit suicide. Because I don't see you solving anything without my help—and I'm not going to help you if I don't know what's going on."

"How can I scratch your back?" Rax asked.

"You don't like the Organizer breaking Galactic Law by coming to a banned planet. I don't care about Galactic Law, but I care about my planet. I don't want the Organizer dropping more nukes or killing more humans. I have a feeling he'll do more of both before this is over. That means I want to stop him. While I don't imagine myself as a world-saver, I realize

I'm in the hot seat. I didn't ask for this, but I'm here. I have a duty to the rest of the human race to fight for our united survival. Maybe that's not the issue, but maybe it is. Maybe the Organizer will destroy humanity in order to cover his tracks. I can't take that chance. Thus, I'm willing to do what I have to in order to stop him."

"You never did stop being a Marine, did you, Logan?"

"I don't know. Maybe not."

"You make a logical case," Rax said. "I am impressed, and I need your full cooperation. I suppose I could invoke the Antares Clause. I will have to support my decision before a full board later. That could cost me my provisional citizenship, but the situation is dire and I have few options. I believe the Galactic Guard Commandant will support me, but Heaven help us if we fail.

"Logan," he said. "In a nutshell, this is the extent of what the Guard knows concerning the present case. Hmm, I suppose I will have to give you a brief history so it makes sense. Know, then, that starting a long time ago, few ships ever returned from this region of space. In time, the Guard narrowed the focus. The Old Guard learned that Earth was the focal point of the danger. The Guard of those times sent several expeditions to the planet. Only one returned, but with their personnel scrubbed of memories. After that, the Galactic Council declared Earth a banned planet and the local region a forbidden zone."

"What do you think happened to all those ships?"

"There are competing theories, each equally ridiculous. We can go into the theories later—"

"Why did you and your agent come if it's so dangerous?" I asked, interrupting him. "Why did the Galactic Council change its mind about Earth?"

"That is the pertinent question," Rax said. "The present situation started several years ago when treasure hunters found ancient script buried deep on the fourth planet in the Canopus Star System."

"Where?" I asked.

"The Canopus System is roughly three hundred and thirteen light-years from Earth. It is the brightest star in the constellation of Carina."

"Oh," I said.

"According to the barely legible text—written in Linear D, mind you—the scroll claimed to belong to the mythical Polarions. Have you ever heard of them?"

"Polarions?" I asked. "No. Should I have?"

"I had hoped—never mind. It does not matter. 'Polarions' in Galactic terms is like saying 'the gods' in human terms."

"You mean like the Bible was God-inspired?"

"The gods denotes many powerful entities of divine nature, which is different from the singular claim of one divine Creator. It is more like claiming that Zeus, Apollo and Athena are real, or were real, and that humans could find Zeus's thunderbolts or Thor's mythical hammer if they looked hard enough."

"The Polarions were gods?" I asked.

"Not exactly," Rax said. "But they hold a mythical fascination for certain Galactic races. They supposedly fashioned incredible technological marvels at the dawn of Time. Later, they disappeared. There are a thousand hypotheses as to why they departed. None of those matter to our mission.

"In any case," Rax said, "most rational beings would have brushed aside the scroll's claims. There are countless forgers in the galaxy, preying on people's gullibility in order to gain profits. This seemed like an obvious prank despite the alleged proof of the scroll's antiquity. However, the treasure hunters had also found a weapon. The weapon was smaller than my ship. That is all the Guard knows concerning it except that it also obliterated a Rigellian battle fleet. One moment, the Rigellians maneuvered toward an enemy planet. The next, the weapon vaporized everyone, including the treasure hunters who had wielded it."

"How big was the battle fleet?"

"Twenty-eight maulers and their accompanying support vessels ceased to exist in one moment of time," Rax said. "It was a dreadful example of the power of the Polarions. It showed to perfection the foolishness of dabbling with energies better left untouched."

"What does any of that have to do with Earth?" I asked. "The treasure hunters died with their fantastic weapon, and they found it on a planet in the Canopus System, three hundred and thirteen light-years from Earth."

"Firstly," Rax said, "not all the treasure hunters died. A Min Ve survived. The Guard learned that he claimed the scroll spoke about another cache of marvels. The scroll also spoke of dire curses and warned in no uncertain terms the risk anyone took in trying to uncover the cache."

"I take it the scroll spoke about Earth."

"It did indeed," Rax said.

"Then why hasn't the universe coming running to knock down our doors to find these super-weapons?"

"It hasn't because the entire universe doesn't know about the claim," Rax said. "Only a handful of beings are privy to the information you have just heard. There is another reason, which I have already stated. Earth has a terrible reputation. Few spacefarers have ever returned from this cursed planet, my agent now included in that list."

"That doesn't make sense," I said. "We humans have done just fine here for thousands of years."

"It is a great mystery, I agree."

"So you're saying that somewhere on the planet are Polarion super-weapons?"

"I have come to believe so," Rax said. "I also wonder if these weapons are too powerful for anyone to wield successfully."

"Meaning what?" I asked.

"Meaning that tampering with them could bring about terrible devastation to the galaxy. I am afraid the ancients wisely banned anyone from coming to your planet. I have heard a saying while here. 'Let sleeping dogs lie.' We should let the Polarion technology molder for another millennia, lest we bring about a stellar Armageddon."

"Clearly the Min Ves don't agree with you," I said.

"Most Min Ves do, but there is a criminal cabal in their midst. The criminals must have strong-armed enough council members to sanction their foolish expedition."

"Why do you think the Polarions chose Earth to stash some of their super-weapons?"

"I have no idea," Rax said.

"Why have we been immune to these terrible weapons all this time?"

"It is a mystery, as I have repeatedly said."

I scratched my head, my curiosity burning brighter by the minute. "That's a good story, Rax. Now, what are you and I going to do about it?"

"Perhaps we should do nothing and let the ancient devices devour the pirates."

"Did you even listen to your own story?" I asked. "The treasure hunters used the weapon against a battlefleet, wiping it out. We have a duty to try to stop the pirates from finding these ancient weapons. While I might not have believed your story two days ago, after what I've seen in Greenland, I'm a believer in the possibility of Polarions."

"You have a point."

"Damn straight, I do," I said.

"Yes," Rax said. "Let me calculate our various options."

The crystal fell silent, and I waited. It proved a long wait, more than twenty minutes. That was long enough for me to get up, search for the head, use it and sit back down in the pilot chair.

"We are already on Earth," Rax said. "As long as I live, I have a responsibility to follow my oath of service. You stated your duty to your race, and you have a good heart. We should continue to work together to stop the Organizer from unleashing a possible reign of terror on the universe. That means we must stop him from finding or taking weapons too powerful for any mortal to wield."

"Sounds like you have plan," I said.

"Yes," Rax said. "First, we must siphon power through the osmosis method. Then, you and I will scout out the Nevada excavation site, given there is one. We will go armed and alert, and learn more about the Organizer's progress. Afterward, we can decide on the next move. Perhaps by then, another Guard starship will have arrived in the solar system."

"Let's hope you're right," I said. "How are we going to do this scouting?"

Rax began to explain.

-24-

Siphoning the power proved easy, as Rax had said. We parked underwater a mile offshore from Oahu, Hawaii, and for the next several hours, we sucked energy from the power grid.

Rax explained a little more about operating the ship. I watched the energy levels rise until we finally had full banks.

"I've been wondering about something," I said.

I was piloting us through the deep like a submarine. We were using an advanced scanning system to stay clear of underwater sensing gear and prowling submersibles. It was weird to realize that I could see the expensive national military toys, but they had no idea I was cruising circles around them.

"How are we going to slip unnoticed onto the Nevada excavation site?" I asked. "While the Organizer must believe he destroyed us, I'm sure he has someone watching his scanners."

"The Guard-ship will remain underwater for the duration of our scouting mission," Rax said.

"You're suggesting that we teleport to the site?"

"We cannot directly teleport there for several reasons," Rax said. "The chief one being that I have yet to fix the location."

"Do you have a cloaking device or something?"

"Not like the Organizer has on his orbital vessel," Rax said.

"When we teleport, do we make a big red beam like I saw in Nevada?"

“The Guard possesses advanced teleporting systems superior to what the Min Ve Council has given the Organizer. But to answer your original question, you and I will leave the ship, appearing near your Western Sunlight’s Station 5. We will have to track the tanks from there. You have a decided advantage as a pseudo-agent. You are an aboriginal. Thus, the Organizer’s people cannot easily detect you as Guard affiliated.”

“They must scan from space, right?” I asked.

“That is correct.”

“And they won’t be able to spot our teleportation?”

“There is a small possibility of that, which is why we will teleport only when their vessel is on the other side of the planet.”

“Can’t they detect you?”

“These things are matters of probability, not yea or nay. My metal sheathing helps to screen my true nature. If I take the proper precautions, it is highly unlikely anyone on the enemy ship will detect my presence while I am on the planetary surface.”

“But if you—”

“Logan,” he said, cutting me off. “Let us prepare. We have this one chance to do this correctly. We must strive for a perfect insertion and be ready to accelerate our timetable at any moment.”

“Sure,” I said. “Let’s prep. What do you have in mind?”

***

I managed to modify the little crystal’s plan. The hardest part was convincing him it would be okay to let me mingle with other humans. The key leveraging point proved to be supplies. While he could teleport me just about anywhere in Nevada, plopping us into the middle of a desert would be a good way to leave us stranded in the middle of nowhere.

In the end, Rax decided to trust me because I convinced him that stopping the Organizer was in my own best interest.

He transferred us into my apartment in Las Vegas. I didn’t have any keys on me and the building had good security. If I’d had to break in—instead of just teleporting inside as we did—

that would have likely proved troublesome. This way, I grabbed my emergency credit card, changed into regular clothes and put on an extra shoulder rig. Instead of the cannon-like .44, I wore a smaller .38.

Rax hadn't loaned me any of his advanced Guard weaponry or allowed me to take the Greenland force-blade. Instead, I had my backup revolver with plenty of ammo, a spring-assisted flick-knife, a compass, a small spyglass, a canteen and a satellite phone. I wore desert hunting gear with a good pair of boots.

I raided my refrigerator, polishing off just about everything in there, including an old jar of dill pickles and a questionable carton of milk.

"I'm definitely eating more," I said.

Rax remained silent.

I carried him in an inside jacket pocket. I had a tiny earbud in place, so he wouldn't have to speak through the fabric.

I had a little over four hundred dollars in the apartment, and put it all in an old wallet I found in the top drawer of my desk. I'd lost my regular wallet, which held the rest of my credit cards and my driver's license. I took an old license, figuring that was better than having nothing.

I went to the bank first, taking out one thousand, two hundred and fifty dollars, leaving two hundred in the account. Afterward, I went to a rental agency, getting myself a powerful Chief Cherokee Jeep.

I figured what the heck and bought an AR-15 on credit, loading up on ammo.

I loved Nevada, especially as compared to the Socialist State of California. I used to live in California. It had great people and an amazing climate, but a crappy state government that taxed people as if the state thought *they* were the Feds. The state government also had oppressive laws against just about everything. I'd grown up in California, but I had always felt myself breathe easier in the state next door.

I headed north from Vegas with the air-conditioner roaring full blast. I had a full tank of gas, new tires, a new rifle and a new purpose.

"I've been wondering," I said. "If you're right about the two sites, the starship is going to be scanning the local Nevada area twenty-four/seven, as Greenland is history."

"Despite all that," Rax said, with his tinny voice in my left ear, "I suggest we head for Station 5."

"In order to pick up the tank tracks?" I asked.

"That is one reason. The other is to study the station. That will tell us much concerning the Organizer's mindset."

"What do you mean?" I asked.

"Did his people repair the damage to the station? Did they set up a camouflage screen around it or did they leave it smashed?"

"Oh, I see. How hard is he trying to conceal his actions or not conceal them? If he's trying to conceal them that means he's still operating secretively on Earth."

"Precisely," Rax said.

I settled back for a long drive and turned on the radio. I was glad I'd bought a new pair of sunglasses. It was bright out here.

The songs lulled me, which I appreciated now. Every time they stopped playing songs for an advertisement or some news, I switched stations. I didn't want to hear about a strange occurrence in Greenland. I realized after an hour that I wanted to absorb the regular life I might never have again. By a freak happenstance, I'd been thrown into a new world that included talking crystals, shape-changing aliens, spaceships and ancient space gods.

I shook my head. Why me? Why did I have to be the guy thrown into an alien freak show? Sure, I had perfect health now, was stronger than the toughest NFL lineman, and I could heal like a lizard re-growing its tail. I also had to face this alone, without anyone knowing what I was doing.

"It's just you and me, kid," I said.

Rax didn't answer. What did he think about all this? What did a non-moving crystal think about life, about honor, patriotism or even sex?

I sat up while listening to a crooning love song.

"Tell me about the Jarnevon," I said. When the crystal didn't answer, I said, "Rax."

"What is the problem?"

"Are you asleep?"

"I was in meditation mode," Rax said. "It is akin to human sleep. Its primary function is data storage rearrangement. I can only hold so much short-term data. Then, I must process it into long-term crystal storage regions so I can empty the short-term capacitors."

"That makes sense," I said. "I'm sorry about that. Go back to sleep."

"I cannot do that now," Rax said. "Entering meditation mode is a complex process. I am no longer in the correct mood to attempt it."

"Oh," I said.

"What is that wailing I hear?"

"It's the radio. Do you like it?"

"It is awful and mind-numbing. Why do you torture yourself with it?"

"We call it entertainment," I said.

"I am not amused."

"I'd turn it off," I said, with a grin, "but I might fall asleep if I did."

"Then I will endure."

I lowered the volume some anyway.

"That is more agreeable," he said. "Perhaps if you gave it another few taps…"

I did as he requested.

"I can begin to self-rationalize now," he said.

I laughed. "Are you telling me you can't think if I have the music on too loud?"

"Ah. I believe I have finally inferred your reasonableness concerning the radio. You wish to interrogate me and are attempting to lighten my mood."

"You and the Unguls," I said. "Questions aren't necessarily interrogations."

"What is your question, Logan?"

I nodded. "What do you know about Jarnevons?"

"Are you referring to the Organizer's comm officer?"

"I guess so," I said.

"Did you find her attractive?"

I raised an eyebrow. "Do you know about that?"

"If you are referring to sexual liaisons, yes, I am aware of the mammalian male attraction to a comely female. However, a Jarnevon is not human, although there are many similarities. If you are asking about their sexual nature, I believe it is quite similar to yours. Some have theorized that Jarnevons and humans are descended from a prototype humanoid. I suppose that is possible, but it would negate the evolutionary theory presently maintained by your world's educational personnel."

"I didn't realize until this moment what an egghead you are, Rax. But I guess that makes sense. What else does a sentient crystal do but think all the time?"

"Is that an insult?"

"No," I said. "It's an observation. But you were telling me about Jarnevons."

"First, let me collect some data," Rax said. "Did you enjoying staring at the comm officer?"

"I did."

"Would you like to mate with her?"

I laughed. "Are you a prude, Rax? Would that bother you if I wanted to?"

"According to my briefing, humans form attachments to those that they sexually engage with. This special bonding lessens if the lover engages with multiple partners in a short time period. Are you a sexually aggressive male perhaps?"

"I like the ladies, if that's what you're saying."

"No. Do you engage in repeated liaisons with multiple partners in short time spans?"

I shifted a bit on the seat as I said, "I'm not a player."

"Then I suggest you forgo any thoughts concerning the Jarnevon. As a comm officer, she is highly ranked aboard the privateer. That means she is a thorough opportunist. According to my data, the correct saying is, 'She would eat you alive.'"

"I don't know about that," I said. "Are Jarnevons sexually active with other species?"

"Jarnevons are highly aggressive and often engage in mercenary actions. She is likely combat trained, psych-ops certified and predatory to an unusual degree. If she used her sexual charms to arrest your attention, it would be solely for reasons of gaining an advantage over you."

"Sounds like a challenge," I said.

"I am sorry. Have I offended your vanity?" Rax asked. "It is simply a correlation of species parameters. Jarnevons use whatever they can to advance their social rank. Humans appear capable of love and forming lasting commitments. The Jarnevon would only let you fondle her if she thought it would gain her an advantage."

"Okay, forget about it. She was easy on the eyes. Let's leave it at that."

I readjusted the seat, switched stations to old hard rock music and watched the monotonous desert terrain. As I did, I kept thinking about the Jarnevon and her intense green eyes.

How alien where Jarnevons? It sounded like they had more in common with humans than with Unguls. What was the real scoop on human origins? Maybe our old ideas needed some readjustments.

"Quick," Rax said. "Stop the jeep."

I slammed on the brakes so the vehicle swerved. "What's going on?" I shouted.

"Get out of the vehicle and run. Do it now, Logan."

We were still moving, but I didn't hesitate. I opened the door, barely remembered to unbuckle and heaved myself out. I hit the ground rolling around twenty miles an hour, spinning over gravel.

The jeep kept going. I looked up from on my back, and barely saw what looked like a dark streak come from the sky and slam against the jeep with a crunching roar.

The Chief Cherokee exploded, with metal flying everywhere, some of the pieces slamming against the ground around me.

"Rax!" I shouted.

"I am aware of the danger," he said.

Another dark streak flew down leaving a luminous trail in the sky, this one heading straight for us. The sky lost color as I watched. That wasn't the worst. I saw the thing in an instant of time. It looked like an iron rod half the size of a tetherball pole. It had a needlepoint, maybe to slice through the atmosphere the way it did. The thing slammed into my chest at supersonic speed and exploded with unleashed kinetic force against the ground.

I'm dead, I thought. Then I wondered how a dead man had the ability to realize he was deceased. What was going on here?

-25-

The answer should have been obvious to me. Rax had used the teleportation machine, bringing us back to the Guard-ship.

"Why didn't you teleport us out of there in the first place?" I asked. "Why did you have me leaping out of a moving vehicle?"

I'd torn my clothes, gained several bruises and my left elbow had become stiff. I'd dusted myself off for several seconds after stepping off the transporter dais.

"I did not have enough time for an immediate transfer," Rax said. "I detected the guided rod too late in its descent. In other words, the attack surprised me. In retrospect, I should have been more alert. If they had attacked us while I was in meditation mode, we would both be dead."

"Thank God for the radio," I said. "By the way, what in the world is a guided rod?"

"I am surprised by the question. Your own country has devised similar technology, although they have failed to deploy them yet."

"What are you talking about?"

"In your country it is called a THOR missile," Rax said. "In essence, it would be a space pole waiting in orbit, initially guided onto target by small maneuver rockets. Seconds before impact, a terminal guidance sensor searches for the targeting parameters, steering the rod onto the objective. The Organizer used a more advanced version of that to demolish the jeep. One pound of metal moving at orbital velocity unleashes a twenty-pound equivalent of TNT. The rod aimed at us was at least twenty pounds."

"That's crazy. The rods were launched from the alien orbital vessel?"

"That would be my guess," Rax said. "The second rod was there to kill any survivors. It was insurance. That shows the Organizer is taking us seriously. That is bad for us, but shows wisdom on his part."

"You said it's a rod. It came down from orbit like a meteor?"

"Precisely," Rax said. "It is another Class IV violation. This is my error. I thought he would believe us dead and thus forgo such extended precautionary measures."

"Why didn't he use the rod on us in Vegas? Why did he wait until we were so close to Station 5?"

"You have answered the question by asking it. Like anyone, the Organizer has a limited amount of time, equipment and personnel. He must have decided on a particular area around the station. Anything entering that zone would have to endure a scan. He must have detected me, as I doubt his scanner could be so refined as to pick out a particular human."

"If you're right about that," I said, "it proves Station 5 is still important to him."

"That is a logical assumption. Yes. Logan, we must go to the science chamber. Once you exit the transfer chamber, it is the second hatch to your left."

I exited the chamber and entered a larger room. It had several seats and screens with various consoles against the bulkheads.

"Please sit down on the first chair," Rax said.

I did.

"We will use a tiny spy drone," Rax explained. He teleported the drone into position and turned on its directional sweep.

"You're allowed to use the drone and scanner?" I asked.

"That is self-evident," Rax said. "While I am not allowed to pilot the ship, under the Antares Clause I can use the transporter and other devices."

I nodded.

"We shall attempt a passive scan first," Rax said.

I watched the screen, soon seeing the drone's view of the blacktop road leading to Station 5. About a mile from the site, everything went fuzzy.

"Is that due to enemy interference?" I asked.

"That is correct," Rax said. "The extent of the anti-scan leads me to believe they have set up a force screen at the station. That makes sense given the convertor you destroyed in a basement."

I recalled the pulsating gray cube I'd shot. "What did the thing convert?"

"The stored solar energy, of course," Rax said.

"Was the convertor alive?"

"Not in the sense of you and me. It was more akin to a mechanical plant."

"Like a cyborg plant?"

"That is an apt term. But back to the force screen. I could attempt an aggressive scan and possibly break through. Such a scan would alert the Organizer to the spy drone. He might be able to track the drone's signal back to our hidden location."

"Maybe he's already spotted the drone and is actively doing as you suggest," I said.

"The drone is difficult to spot, as it is minuscule and sheathed in radar-resistant material. Once the Organizer spotted the drone for what it is, the backtracking of the signal would be easier. Thus, if he had spotted the drone, we would be facing another hell-burner or possibly a massed rod bombardment. Since neither has occurred, I believe the drone is still hidden from him."

"Unless that's what he wants us to believe."

"That is over-subtle," Rax said. "If the Organizer could, he would kill us."

I nodded.

"How badly do we need to see what's behind the force screen?" I asked.

"It would give us greater illumination concerning the Organizer's thoughts, but the fact of the force screen shows us that he is still using the station. That is interesting. It must be a staging area, which implies that the excavation zone is nearby. Let us see if we can find tank tracks."

I watched the desert terrain on the screen. Rax went back and forth in a broad sweep for about ten minutes.

"I am ready to concede defeat regarding the tank tracks," Rax said. "I believe someone has swept the tracks from view."

"That means we have no idea about the location of the excavation site."

"Untrue," Rax said. "It must be near the base camp—Station 5. Besides, I am not thwarted from an object so easily. Let us consider various possibilities. What direction did the tanks go last night?"

"East," I said.

"We will begin with an eastward sweep."

Time ticked away as the screen showed the Nevada terrain. Slowly, it changed, climbing a mountain range, entering valleys, up, down, up, down…

I grew drowsy as my eyelids became heavy. My chin soon rested on my chest. I might have snored. I definitely snorted, blinking sleepily.

I raised my head. "Did you say something?" I asked.

"I beg your pardon," Rax said.

"I dosed off," I said. "I thought I heard you say something."

"Oh. I did. I said, 'This is odd.'"

"What?" I asked.

"Excuse me?"

"What's odd?"

"Oh, yes," Rax said. "It is a little thing, but it is interesting nonetheless. Observe, please."

I studied the screen. It showed a low mountain range with brownish grass and some clumps of flowers sprinkled about. Clouds drifted in the sky. I saw a road, more of a dirt track, really, with grass growing between the wheel tracks.

"Did you notice the oddity?" Rax asked.

I closed my eyes tightly, opened them wider than before, and searched the screen. "What am I supposed to notice?"

"I will replay it," Rax said. "Watch closely."

I did, not seeing anything different. I saw a dirt road, grass, flowers and jackrabbit moving around. There was nothing here to get excited about, unless you were a crystal, I suppose.

"Do you not find it odd?"

"Rax, I'm not tracking you. It looks like Some-place, Nevada. So what?"

"Did you not notice the sparrows? I will replay the scene again."

"Sparrows?" I asked. "What do they have to do with anything?"

"Just watch," Rax said.

I saw a small flock of sparrows. They flew up from a clump of grass, winging it for some sage bushes.

"Hey," I said. "Where did the sparrows go?"

"Precisely," Rax said. "That is my question, as well."

"Replay it again," I said.

The scene shifted once more. I watched the sparrows fly up, maybe twelve of them. They flew fast and abruptly disappeared from sight. It was as if they simply flew off the edge of reality to somewhere else.

"Rescan the area," I suggested. "See if you can find the sparrows."

"I suggest a different approach," Rax said. "This is the first anomaly I have found. It is the first clue that something is amiss. It was a slight thing that possibly only a Rax Prime crystal would have noticed."

"You did well, if that's what you want to hear. What do you think is causing that? A Min Ve force screen?"

"No, I would have sensed such a screen. This is something completely different, something…beyond Min Ve science."

"Are you suggesting this has something to do with Polarions?"

"Notice what happens," Rax said. "The sparrows fly, moving to a place where they simply cease to exist. They are not flying under a force screen or a camouflage screen."

"How do you know that?"

"Because I would detect a slight distortion as the sparrows slipped under such a field. What we are seeing is something of a different magnitude."

“Do you have any idea what could do that?” I asked.

“I am uneasy seeing this. It strikes me as magical, and we Rax Prime crystals do not believe in magic.”

“So this is another of your incongruities?” I asked.

“That is so.”

“What do you suggest we do about it?”

“We must explore the area in person,” Rax said.

I raised my eyebrows.

“That doesn’t seem smart,” I said. “The Organizer will probably detect you like before and rain more rods down on us.”

“That is a possibility, but I doubt it. There is no sign of tank tracks, no sign of any activity, space pirate or human. This seems like a desolate region of desert. There is certainly no sign of an excavation site. Yet, the place has this strange occurrence. We should explore it in person for a short time, teleporting back with our conclusions.”

I nodded slowly. “I’m game if you are. What do you think we’re going to find?”

“I hope for a clue. Otherwise, we will have to resort to riskier endeavors.”

“A clue it is,” I said.

Rax brought the drone back onto the Guard-ship. I shut down the science station and headed to the transfer chamber.

-26-

We materialized beside the dirt road with grass growing down what should have been the centerline.

I looked up, shading my eyes from the sun. The ball of light was almost directly overhead, meaning it was nearly noon. I did not spy any rods, but that didn't mean much. The Organizer hadn't had time yet to spot us and launch an orbital assault.

I looked around. We were in a valley with low mountains on either side. The northern mountains were bone dry, with plenty of naked boulders and shale. The southern mountains had yellow grass blowing in the breeze. I did not see any telephone poles, buildings or other signs of civilization. The road was the only marker that humans had ever been here.

I saw a jackrabbit eying me. There were more sparrows, while high in the sky drifted a vulture or hawk.

"Which way do we go?" I asked.

"Cross to the other side of the road," Rax said.

"Are you sensing any anomalies?"

"None," he said. "And that frightens me because it lends credence to the idea of the Polarions. The sparrows disappeared earlier, but nothing I know or can detect explains what I saw."

I drew my .38 and started across the road. I stopped midway, crouching to inspect the dirt.

"What do you see?" Rax asked.

"Tire tracks."

"Is that unusual?"

"It's comforting," I said, "because it means someone has used the road since the last time the wind blew strongly or it rained."

"Logical," Rax said. "Let us continue."

I stood, looking up at the sky again. It held the lone vulture or hawk and a vast blue expanse. With a shrug, I moved across the road and headed north.

I increased my pace, listening to the crunch of my boots on the ground. Nothing extraordinary happened. Dust rose in some places. In others, I stepped on dry grass. I walked steadily, waiting for Rax to say something. The crystal kept his own counsel. After a quarter of a mile, I figured he should have said a few words by now.

"Well?" I asked.

Rax did not respond.

"Hey," I said. "What's the prognosis? Is this a rabbit trail, or have you figured something out yet?"

If he had, Rax did not want to say.

I scowled, deciding it was foolish holding my revolver for no reason, and shoved it back into its shoulder holster.

After clicking the strap into place, I looked up again. The sky was empty.

"The vulture or hawk is gone," I said.

Rax remained silent.

"Okay, I've had enough of this. What are you thinking?"

Rax refused to speak.

I finally dug him out of the inside jacket pocket and shook him.

"Are you listening to me, Rax?"

He still did not respond.

For the first time, a stab of panic touched my chest. Something was off. I looked up into the sky again. The vulture or hawk couldn't have dived out of sight. What had happened to the soaring creature?

I shaded my eyes and scanned the sky from one end of the horizon to the other. There was nothing. I did it a second time. My head swayed back as I noticed a swath of green grass on the northern slopes.

Those mountains had been bare before. I stood on the valley floor, staring at the green area. That had definitely not been there earlier when we'd stood beside the dirt road.

I looked up at the sky and then at the grassy area.

"You're somewhere else," I said aloud. "You crossed a barrier. This place doesn't have a vulture or a hawk, and here, one area of the mountains has water."

I looked at the metal-encased crystal in my hand. Was it possible that Rax did not work in the place that was almost like Nevada?

I tried to think this through. We hadn't crossed under a camouflage screen. What sort of barrier had we crossed?

I looked around, made a thirty degree turn and trudged toward the dirt road in the distance. This one didn't have any grass in the centerline.

A chill blossomed in my chest. The cold tightened, and I found that I had to force myself to breath.

"Okay, Dorothy," I said. "You're not in Kanas anymore."

The attempt at levity did not lighten my mood. I took a deeper breath and began walking along the road. Sure, I could turn around and go back to the place where Rax had functioned. How would that help me, though? If this had something to do with Polarions, I wanted to find out what.

I trudged approximately two miles. At that point, the dirt road changed into a concrete one. I kept walking beside it, and I spied a house in the distance. It had a fence—

I stopped.

The house had a telephone pole. Wires on the pole led to another telephone pole. That led to another and so on. The poles soon followed the road, which dipped about a mile away. There were no poles behind me, just ahead. That house over there was one of the ends of the lines for this place's telephone service.

My mouth was dry as my sense of unreality increased. It was too bad I'd lost my canteen in the destroyed Chief Cherokee. I'd lost the AR-15 as well.

After another half mile, I trudged upward on the road. I spied something flickering to my left and frowned. The flickering worsened, and it seemed as if I could see something behind a shimmering ghostliness.

I detoured off the road, took out the .38 and neared the shimmering area.

I shouted hoarsely and dropped onto my stomach. Then, I began to slither over dirt and through grass, closing in on what appeared to be three alien tanks hidden behind a camouflage field.

I stopped about forty feet from the flickering field. It was like something from a science fiction movie. I lay there, scanning for signs of Unguls.

No one moved inside the field. Nor did I see any tank tracks leading to the half-hidden vehicles. That seemed weird.

Did Unguls wait inside the tanks, ready to blow me away? I began to doubt that. Surely, they would have noticed me walking down the road. The tanks must have heavier disintegrator beams than the rayguns the Unguls carried.

I stood, dusted myself off and put away my .38. Then, I strode for the flickering field, slowing as I neared it. I took a breath and plunged through the distortion.

The three tanks had parked one behind the other. I couldn't see any open hatches. Each was the size of a U.S. Abrams M1, although a little taller. Nothing moved on the tanks. Each had antennas and what I now realized were disintegrator cannons. It would seem each tank could also cast a camouflage field to hide itself.

"Okay," I whispered, beginning to move. I approached the rearmost tank and noticed dirt clods in the tracks and a clump of grass. I touched the tread. It was real. I climbed the bulldozer-like tread and used the flat of my hand to bang on a side of the tank.

Nothing happened. By this time, I hadn't expected anything to occur. I finally noticed a hatch and tried to force it open.

After five minutes of futile effort, I jumped down and approached the second Ungul tank. It, too, resisted my efforts to enter.

I backed away, observing them. I noticed footprints in the dirt. The Ungul had worn shoes, and it looked as if they had headed for the road.

I rubbed my chin. The Unguls had set up a camouflage field around their parked tanks. That would seem to indicate they had voluntarily left their vehicles.

I looked up at the sky. Had the Unguls contacted the orbital vessel? If they had, why hadn't the Organizer sent reinforcements. If the Unguls hadn't contacted the orbital vessel, why wouldn't they have retreated from this odd place and told the Organizer about it?

I kept remembering the disappearing sparrows and that Rax hadn't detected anything to account for that. The little crystal had suggested a magical possibility.

I'd read enough science fiction to be familiar with the Arthur C. Clark saying, "Any sufficiently advanced technology is indistinguishable from magic."

If the Polarions existed, wouldn't their tech seem like magic to the rest of us? But if Polarions existed, why had they left their Greenland laboratory intact with frozen specimens from bygone eras? What did it mean that Greenland had once been known as Thule to a civilization that greatly predated the ancient Greeks?

Should I follow the road to see where it led or should I retreat and get back to the Guard-ship? We'd already picked up more data. Maybe Rax had held back certain info from me. The more I thought about that, the more likely it seemed.

I would keep going. If the Unguls wanted to investigate this place on foot, then so did I. I'd just have to make sure the Unguls didn't capture me.

-27-

Several miles later, I lay on dry grass in the shade of a boulder, looking down a hill on a small Nevada town. The municipality had a main street with a general store, a bank, a post office, a hotel, a diner and a church. There were big shade trees throughout the town that couldn't have a population of more than eight hundred to a thousand people.

The one unusual aspect of the place was a tall white tower on the other end of town. The tower loomed over the buildings and was maybe three times the height of an old Saturn V rocket, the kind that had shot Apollo spaceships to the moon.

The tower had a futuristic feel to it. It gleamed in the sunlight like polished metal. There was a large plaza around it at ground level. The plaza—a circular area—looked like it had a plastic coating, spreading out the length of a football field all around.

People congregated on the plaza until a siren blared that I could hear from here. Half of the people headed for the tower. The other half headed for their homes, it would appear.

I watched those heading for the tower. A door opened at the base of the tower. The people lined up, slowly filing inside. When the last person disappeared into the tower, the doorway vanished.

From where I lay on the hill, the door didn't seem to close or slide shut, the opening just disappeared. Was that more Polarion magic?

If I were to bet, that's what I'd lay my money on.

I went back to studying the town. Yep, the majority of those who had left the plaza went to the various homes. A few people headed for Main Street.

I counted twenty-three cars, nine trucks and estimated around one hundred bicycles. Three of the trucks—older model pickups in mint condition—headed up the road. It would seem they headed for the country houses.

I kept watching for another twenty minutes or so. I saw a sheriff's patrol car move along the streets. Soon, it drove to the hotel, parking there. A sheriff wearing a cowboy hat got out, looked around and then headed for the hotel.

What should I do?

In the end, I slid out of sight, climbed to my feet and headed down toward the road. Before I reached the road, two Unguls in natty business suits and old gangland-style hats rose from behind a large boulder. One of them aimed a raygun at me. The other spoke into his cuff.

I kept my hands away from my body.

"Do you boys have a problem with me?" I asked.

The Unguls glanced at each other. The cuff-talker opened his mouth.

"Why did you climb the hill?" he asked.

"I'm giving my friend a surprise party," I said. "I wanted to make sure he hadn't made it into town yet."

"That is a lie," the Ungul said. "You have followed us. We have watched you for some time."

I shrugged. "You're new here," I said. "I'm curious about you. We don't get many visitors way out here."

"You are curious about us?" he asked.

"That's what I said."

The two exchanged glances before the talker regarded me again.

"Do you live in the town?" he asked.

"No. I live in the country."

"What transpires in the tower?" the Ungul asked.

"You mind putting away your gun?" I asked. "I don't like having people aim those at me."

"Approach us," the talker said.

I came closer.

The talker's eyes narrowed. "Your clothes are a different style from those the town folk wear. You do not belong in this place."

"So what?" I said. "Neither do you."

"You will tell us why you followed us."

The gunman slid his weapon into a rig under his suit jacket. As he did, he stepped near, reaching for me with one hand and pulling out a small flat device with the other.

"Z5 will use an agonizer on you," the talker informed me. "He will inflict pain until I am convinced you speak the truth."

Z5 grabbed one of my wrists with a hot hand. I suppose he was relying on what he believed to be his greater than human strength. He moved fast, pressing the agonizer against my neck. It felt like being branded with a white-hot iron.

I yelled and twisted my captured wrist with violent force, wrenching it out of Z5's grasp. I think that surprised him. While he was stronger than a human, now I was, too. I swung at him as hard as I could, hitting him in the face. He catapulted off his feet, and his head snapped back against the ground as he crumpled.

The agonizer fell from my neck. Z5 stirred on the ground, but he didn't get up. The talker peered at me with dislike.

I stepped toward him, slugging him the gut. He folded around my fist and went back several feet, staggering, but remained upright. He shoved his hand under his jacket, likely to grab his raygun.

I followed him, grabbing the spring-assisted flick-knife in my pocket. My thumb pushed the tiny protrusion and the blade flicked into position. He drew his raygun. I stabbed him in the brain, the blade smashing into his cranium. He jackknifed backward, yanking the knife out of my grasp.

The talker landed on his back and began twitching violently like a death-shot cat. He humped and twisted faster than the eye could follow, the raygun lying uselessly on the ground where he'd dropped it. A few moments later, the jerking movements subsided and he lay perfectly still.

That's when his flesh began to melt, tearing away at the business suit. The process happened fast until he was gray-colored, hairless and possessing large alien eyes. In its true form, the Ungul proved shorter than a human with bulges in odd places.

"That just leaves you and me," I said. I scooped up the agonizer, approaching Z5.

The dazed Ungul made a buzzing noise and reached under his suit. Before I could reach him, I heard an audible click. He began to glow a second later. Three seconds after that, he disintegrated in a red glow, leaving fumy ashes on the ground where he'd been.

Z5 seemed to have used a disintegrator bomb, apparently preferring death to interrogation. Unfortunately, that had also destroyed the raygun lying on the ground. I'd been planning to take it.

I felt nauseous at witnessing the suicide. Repulsed, I hurled the agonizer as far away as I could.

Who were these Unguls anyway? By the one's appearance—as many people imagined aliens to look from various UFO stories and shows—it seemed other humans had witnessed Unguls in the past. But if Earth was a banned planet, what had the Unguls been doing here over the decades?

Maybe this wasn't the first time that aliens had searched the Earth for Polarions.

I was tempted to turn around and hightail it out of here. I wanted to talk to Rax about what I'd seen. I would have also liked to get back aboard the Guard-ship.

I recalled the hell-burner. The Organizer would do whatever he had to in order to get his grubby Min Ve hands on the ancient treasure. I hated the idea of more alien nukes hitting Earth. That meant I had to keep going.

It was time to go to town and find out why this place had a gleaming white tower, and if that had anything to do with the mythical Polarions.

-28-

I walked past a regular-looking Nevada sign that said,

Far Butte
Population: 941   Elevation: 693

I'd never heard of Far Butte, Nevada. But I'd never heard of thousands of small towns, U.S.A.

It was clean. That was the first thing I noticed. The homes had pristine yards with perfect fences. I didn't see any dogs or cats, though. Nothing barked at me. I couldn't see any litter, any garbage, or peeling paint on the homes.

In some ways, it felt as if I'd walked into a TV version of the 50s. Despite the white tower and the weirdness of the situation, the town itself felt good. In some ways, it felt as if I was coming home.

I realized why a moment later. It reminded me of my childhood. I longed for the good old days. But maybe that's what most people wanted as they got older. My dad used to tell me stories of what he'd done as a young buck, making it sound like it had been the best time to be alive. Had his dad, my grandfather, told him similar tales of his youth?

Anyway, that was my first impression of Far Butte, a clean place with the old small town values, the America that had won WWII.

My stomach growled, as I smelled steak, French fries and coffee. I could use plenty of all three. So I headed for the diner that was beside the hotel.

I walked inside to the tinkling of an overhead bell. All the tables with red checkerboard tablecloths were taken. Most of the people looked up at me as the door closed, and the bell made its tinkling sound again. They stared as if I were a stray dog with two heads.

Some of that good feeling evaporated. In fact, I might have backed out, but I noticed three Unguls at a corner table. They sat stiffly, each sipping coffee and studiously avoiding looking at me.

Huh. If they served fancily dressed aliens pretending to be humans, they could serve me, too. I headed to the counter where there were two open spots.

I sat beside a big man with rolled up sleeves. He had a cigarette pack in his front shirt pocket and hairy forearms. He had a brush-cut, seemed to be in his thirties and looked strong. He struck me as a handyman. He was eating hash browns and eggs and drinking a Coke.

"How's it going?" I said.

He gave a nod and a side-glance before returning to his fare.

"You're in the sheriff's spot," the counter woman told me.

"I'm sure the sheriff won't mind," I said.

She stared at me. I figured she was in her upper thirties, early forties. She wore a dress, had brunette hair in a bun and a small restaurant hat, used too much makeup and had a nametag that said, DEBBY.

"Do you have a menu, Debby?" I asked.

"I'd slide over a seat if I were you," Debby told me. "The sheriff won't stand for you being in his spot. The deputy on the other hand…" she shrugged. "The sheriff will probably tell him to go check around while you eat."

"You got it," I said, sliding over, sitting beside a rangy old guy wearing a black leather jacket that said BAR HOPPERS on the back. He definitely needed a shave. Sprouting white whiskers covered most of his sun-leathered face.

"You chose a bad time to visit Far Butte," Debby said, sliding me a menu.

"Why's that?" I asked.

"Them," she said, indicating the Unguls in the back.

"What about them?" I asked.

Debby stared at me for several seconds, almost as if it was taking time for her to manufacture a reason.

"They're…" she said, looking puzzled. "Everybody will be on edge while they're here," she blurted, finally getting out the words. "People will wonder if you're an undercover agent working for them."

"Me? You're kidding, right? I don't like their looks any more than you do."

She gave me a funny stare before turning to go.

"I'm ready to order," I said. "I'll have two orders of steak and eggs and three orders of French fries."

"The sheriff doesn't eat steak," she said.

"Okay…" I said.

"Isn't that what you're doing? Buying him his meal?"

"No. I'm hungry."

Debby eyed me dubiously this time before finally smiling. It made her look years younger. "I'll say one thing. You're nothing like those three. They're only drinking coffee. I don't think they trust our cooking."

I nodded, and Debby seemed disappointed I didn't add to that. She went to the back counter and spoke to the cook on the other side. The heavy man eyed me before starting on his next order.

I propped my elbows on the counter and listened to what was going on around me. Debby talked a little to the various counter customers. There was another waitress for the tables. None of those sitting at the lunch counter said much to Debby. They ate, sipped their drinks and eventually pushed their empty plates away. Debby brought them their check. Most of them just signed it. She took that and pierced the check on a nail by the cash register. At that point, the customer left, soon replaced by another person coming in. It almost seemed as if people waited outside to come in to eat when it was their turn.

I glanced at the people at the tables. They seemed more animated than the lunch-counter crowd. The table people spoke quietly among themselves. A few hunched forward, maybe so they could whisper to one another. I would have liked to know what they were saying.

"Hey, Walt," someone said in a whiny voice behind me. "Someone took my spot."

I swiveled around. Walt was a big man with a cowboy hat, a tan sheriff's uniform and a badge pinned to it. He had a big gun in the holster with the usual police paraphernalia, handcuffs, spray, that sort of thing.

"You're new here, mister," Walt declared. He had a deep voice, sounding and looking like someone you didn't want to mess with.

The deputy was a lot older and thinner, wearing a regular police hat. His thin hands twitched as he looked at me. "You're in my spot," he said.

"I'll be out soon," I told him.

"Yeah, but I'm hungry. It's my turn to eat."

"Your turn?" I asked.

"George," the sheriff told the deputy. "He's new in town."

"I know," the deputy said, his hands twitching more than before. "But you know I've been out—"

"George," the sheriff said, making it sound like a warning.

The deputy got a hangdog look. "Don't think I won't forget this," he told me.

I nodded.

"When it's your turn to go to the—"

"George!" the sheriff said sharply.

The deputy's head snapped back as if the sheriff had struck him. A moment later, the deputy's shoulders deflated. He turned around and headed outside, ringing the bell as he left.

The sheriff climbed onto his stool, making his police belt creak. He picked up the cup of coffee Debby had thoughtfully poured for him. Good old Walt took a long sip, the cup clicking as he put it into its saucer. Then he half-swiveled to face me directly.

Debby had returned with my first plate of steak and eggs, putting an extra order of French fries beside it.

“When did you come into Far Butte?” the sheriff asked.

“Give me a minute, would you?” I was seriously famished, my stomach growling. Picking up a steak knife and fork, I sawed at the meat, popping a sizeable piece into my mouth.

I looked up and smiled at the sheriff as I chewed.

He didn’t like that. His face became noticeably stiffer, but he didn’t complain, either. He turned forward, taking another sip of coffee.

For the next few minutes, I worked over my first meal, polishing it off faster than seemed necessary. Soon, I used fries to soak up spilled egg-yolks, gobbling the fries in short order.

“Whew,” I said. “That’s better.”

Debby removed the plate and set the next one down.

The sheriff slapped the countertop with a meaty hand. It made my plate jump and a few of the others sitting at the counter.

“Do you mind, Walt?” the handyman beside him asked.

“I asked you a question, stranger,” the sheriff told me.

“Sure,” I said. “When did I get here? Well, let me see. I heard the shift-change siren and hoofed it here as fast as I could to the diner.”

I must have said the wrong thing. The sheriff’s face closed up even more than before, while the others at the counter became wary.

“Is the siren the town secret?” I asked.

“Shut your pie-hole,” the sheriff said.

“Done,” I said, turning to my second meal.

There was something more than a little weird going on. It was beginning to make me antsy, but I figured it would be smart to fuel up first. So, I cut the second steak and ate, slower this time. I pretended not to notice the sheriff casting dark glances my way. He ate a hamburger and coleslaw, foregoing any fries. That was his loss, as these fries were fantastic.

At last, Debby took my second plate away, putting down my third order of fries. She seemed nervous, giving the sheriff a worried look.

“I’ve never seen anyone eat like that,” the old man with the leather jacket said. He seemed amused, and he struck me as little less scared of the sheriff than everyone else was. "You been in the backcountry for a time?" he asked.

"I have that," I said.

"You tried to get out, huh?" the old-timer said.

For the second time, the sheriff slapped a meaty hand on the countertop. "That's enough, Parker."

"I'm done anyway," Parker said. The rangy old man slid off his stool, scribbled something illegible on his tag and left in a bow-legged stride.

A few seconds later, a Harley roared into life, and Parker left on a chopper with high handlebars.

I knew it now without a doubt. I'd stumbled into some kind of Twilight Zone. There was something very wrong here. I'm not sure why that should have surprised me. I'd already faced aliens. Why not a place that shouldn't exist?

I turned to the sheriff, wondering what line to take with him. Before I could decide, the three Unguls approached.

"Do you represent the law here?" the first Ungul asked the sheriff.

The sheriff looked over his shoulder, sat straighter when he saw who addressed him, and swiveled all the way around to regard the three in their expensive business suits.

"What was that, magistrate?" the sheriff asked.

"You wear a badge and carry an open weapon," the lead Ungul said. "I believe that means you represent the law."

"I'm a representative of the law," the sheriff said, as if that was a clarification. "Do you wish to report something?"

"We believe that man has committed a felony," the Ungul said, pointing at me.

I noticed the Ungul wore gloves. He must have known his gray hands would give him away to ordinary people.

The sheriff glanced at me differently this time. He was deadpan now, his eyes studying and gauging. I'm sure he noticed that I carried a gun under my coat. Finally, he regarded the three again.

"What kind of felony?" the sheriff asked.

"We believe he killed our…companions," the Ungul said.

"There are more of you?" the sheriff asked.

"Yes," the Ungul agreed, "there are more."

"May I ask on what grounds you are pressing charges, magistrate?"

The head Ungul blinked several times. "If he is carrying a small electric disc, that will prove he killed our two friends."

"I need probable cause to search him," the sheriff said.

"Can you not ask him to empty his pockets?" the Ungul said.

The sheriff turned to me. "I don't like strangers coming into my town, bringing their stink here."

"I don't have any problems with them," I said.

"Why don't you empty your pockets, stranger?" the sheriff said.

"Why don't they?"

Big Walt slid backward off his stool, his right hand dropping onto the butt of his holstered gun. "Empty your pockets," he ordered me.

Judging by his face and the stiffness of his stance, I knew he was going to force the issue. I wasn't sure about the Unguls. I couldn't figure out their game plan. Maybe they had tried to leave this place, as Parker had suggested, and found it impossible to leave. Now, I wish I had tried.

"Sure, Sheriff," I said. I emptied my pockets, putting the .38, Rax, my old wallet and a few old tangled pieces of dental floss on the counter.

"There is more," the chief Ungul told the sheriff.

"Sorry, nope," I said. "What you see is what I have."

"Turn around," the sheriff ordered me.

I obliged, putting my hands on the counter. The sheriff stepped behind me, patting me down, coming up with nothing extra because I'd already emptied my pockets.

"Don't touch anything on the counter," he told me. Walt then faced the Unguls. "He doesn't have this small electric device. What was it supposed to do?"

"It was a call unit," the Ungul said.

"Where are your dead companions?" the sheriff asked.

"Outside town by Observation Hill," the Ungul said.

"I do not wish to anger you, magistrate," the sheriff said, "but how do you know that's what we call the hill?"

“I am not angered,” the Ungul said. “We know because we have interrogated—interviewed several people.”

“Are you staying at the hotel?”

“Yes.”

“I hope you enjoy your stay, magistrate,” the sheriff said. “If you need anything, please don’t hesitate to contact me. I’m either in the prowl car or in the sheriff’s office.”

The chief Ungul pointed at me. “He is a dangerous ruffian. He is—”

“Magistrate,” the sheriff said, interrupting. “Are you making a second accusation?”

The Ungul regarded me. What did the alien think? Did the sheriff’s deference surprise him? Did the Ungul know what was going on, or was he improvising as I was doing? By some hidden signal, the three of them filed past us without another word, heading outside.

The sheriff watched them go, finally climbing onto his stool as the door swung shut and the bell rang. He put his left hand on my .38, sliding it to his coffee cup and saucer.

“I’m going to hold onto this for a while,” Walt told me.

“Any reason why?”

“I don’t trust you.”

“And you trust those three?”

“They are...*different*,” the sheriff said. “You, on the other hand, strike me as an obvious vagabond.”

“What’s with the tower?” I asked.

The sheriff blinked several times before he picked up his cup, sipping coffee.

“Did you know those three have rayguns?” I said.

“I don’t want any trouble,” the sheriff said mechanically.

“You’re kidding me, right?” I asked. “Those three just accused me of a felony. They told you *I’m* trouble. Then you disarmed me and didn’t even check to see if they have weapons. Why are you helping the aliens, Sheriff?”

His head jerked up. Across the counter, Debby gasped, shaking her head.

I glanced at her. She had become pale and had started to tremble.

"Yeah, I said aliens. That's what they are. They're not just different. How can you believe that when you're in some bizarre place cut off from—?"

I must have said too much. Hands reached out, grabbing me from behind. Men and women pinned my arms. At the same time, the sheriff rose, shouting like a madman. Spit foamed at the corners of his mouth.

He began to punch me in the gut harder than anyone had ever hit me. I tried to jerk my arms free to defend myself, but there were too many of them. The sheriff kept pummeling me. I coughed explosively; certain he was breaking bones and rupturing organs. Our eyes met. Despite his apparent rage, he seemed calm, deliberate in what he was doing.

A huge fist headed for my face. That was the last thing I remembered.

-29-

I woke up aching all over, with a puffy upper lip. It was dark outside. I could see stars through a high upper window. In the distance, a coyote howled a lonely cry.

With a groan, I sat up. I was on a cot behind bars. This must be the town jail. It was small, several cells clustered together with a wooden door leading somewhere. A small light shined above the door, the only illumination other than the stars.

My jacket was hanging on the back of a chair in the cell. I felt incredibly lousy, but given my beating, I suppose I should be grateful I could move at all.

If the sheriff had broken bones and ruptured organs, maybe they had already healed, or almost healed. I'd had a gutful of food in my belly, the necessary ingredients for my new and improved body to do its magic.

Then again, maybe I hadn't fully healed. My stomach hurt as I sat here. My arms felt like lead as I pulled the chair to me and checked the jacket pockets. A feeling of relief swept over me. Rax was still in the inner coat pocket. At least the sheriff hadn't stolen the crystal.

Why had the sheriff pretended to go crazy? Why had the people held my arms for him?

I fell back onto the cot, making the springs complain. My vision swam and my head was pounding. The sheriff had hit me hard. He was another person stronger than ordinary. Had he undergone the same kind of treatment I had? If I poked around long enough here, would I find men in star uniforms, Neanderthals and various apish hominids frozen in stasis tubes?

As Rax would say, there were definitely incongruities here. The old man in the black biker jacket—Parker—had asked if I'd been trying to get out. That was interesting on several levels. That—

The door hinges creaked. I glanced up and saw someone slowly opening the door.

I almost pretended to be asleep. I didn't want to face the sheriff right now. Instead, I just watched with my head on the pillow.

The door moved even more slowly as if the person behind it wanted to be as quiet as possible. A foot appeared wearing a white Keds sneaker. The door opened a little more, and a woman crept into the room.

I didn't recognize her. She was wearing jeans and a Levi's jacket and had long brunette hair that fell well past her shoulders. She had a Klieg flashlight in one hand, which was presently off, and a ring of keys in her other hand. She was pretty and seemed vaguely familiar, but I had no idea who she could be.

She aimed the flashlight at me and clicked it on, shining the beam on my face. I blinked and shielded my eyes.

"What's that for?" I asked gruffly.

"You're alive," she said, sounding genuinely surprised.

I recognized her voice. It sounded like the waitress, Debby.

I opened my eyes. She aimed the flashlight beam so that it no longer shined on my face, but illuminated my cell more.

"Who are you?" I asked.

"What do you mean?" she said. "It's me, Debby. Did the sheriff scramble your brains?"

"Debby is older," I said, as I studied the woman. This woman couldn't be older than twenty-five. Debby had been in her upper thirties on her best day.

"I wear a lot of makeup when I work," she said.

I blinked stupidly. "You wear makeup to make yourself look older?"

"I have to," she said. "Otherwise, some of the men bother me too much."

"What are you doing here in the jail?" I asked.

"Can you sit up?"

I pushed myself up, biting my lower lip so I wouldn't groan.

"What are you?" she said, as she moved closer to the bars.

"A stranger," I answered.

"That's not what I mean. I saw the sheriff beat you. I was sure you were dead, or the next thing to dead. But maybe you're not human and that's why you can move."

"I'm human, all right. You know I am."

She shook her head. "If you were human, you'd be torn up inside. I've seen the sheriff beat people to death. He didn't hold his punches with you. I watched. That's what he wanted, you know. He wanted me to see. He wanted me to know you couldn't do anything after this. But he was wrong, it seems. And that's weird. The sheriff is never wrong. He had to have believed he busted you up or he wouldn't have left you like this."

"I heal faster than normal," I said.

"Real people don't do things like that," Debby said.

"What is this place?" I asked, wanting to change the subject. "What is the white tower? What does it do? Why did old Parker ask me if I'd tried to get out?"

Debby grew pale as I asked my questions. She stared at me more intensely than before and bit her lower lip in apparent indecision.

"Why do you heal so fast?" she asked. "I have to know. I have a right to know."

"Sure," I said. "I was in a place in Greenland. I underwent an operation there. It changed me."

She digested that, finally saying, "You look and act human except for your crazy healing. I can see your confusion, too. You're like Jeff in that way. The sheriff killed Jeff and buried him out in the desert."

"What?"

"Listen to me," Debby said, coming close enough to press against the bars. It seemed as if she'd made a decision. "The sheriff is going to come back soon and take you out into the desert. He'll probably strangle you and have the deputy bury you."

"What are you talking about?"

"What's your name?" Debby asked.

"Logan."

"Logan, you're a stranger, the kind of stranger the sheriff doesn't like. He has a nose for those who can fit in and those who can't. I don't know why he didn't kill me when I came, but that doesn't matter now. He killed Jeff, and he killed Martin Cruz. I was going to run away with Martin. Sometimes, I think the sheriff is toying with me. He doesn't trust me, but I still work in the tower."

"What is this place?" I asked.

"If I help you," she said, "will you help me escape?"

Was she setting me up? "Why did you come to the jail if you thought I was too beat up to do anything?"

"Because I'm afflicted with endless hope," she said. "I also had to make my play. I'm going crazy here and I don't want to go back into the tower. I'm afraid I'm going to lose my mind soon. That's what happens to everyone else. They lose their spirit. They give up inside. Then they're just a drone until someone newer comes along and takes their place."

An outside light shined through the upper window. I heard wheels rolling over concrete.

Debby looked up at the window, moaning in dread. "He's back. I thought he'd be gone longer. He must have found—we have to get out of here, Logan. Do you think you can walk?"

I shoved up from the cot, grabbed my jacket and eased my arms into the sleeves as I tottered to the cell door.

Debby turned the key, swinging the door open. "I'm probably making another mistake. The sheriff might kill me this time. But there's something different about you. It seems as if you have a plan."

"That's me," I whispered. My gut hurt as I walked. I wasn't sure how far I could go.

"Come on," Debby said, grabbing my coat and tugging me toward her. "We have to slip out the back before the sheriff comes in."

She put an arm around my waist, helping me out of the cell and through the door. We entered the main office. It had two desks, a rifle rack, a coffee table—I heard car doors slam outside.

"What are we going to do with the body?" I heard the whiny deputy ask.

"Leave it for now," the sheriff said. "I want to talk to the stranger first."

"Quick," Debby whispered, urging me toward the back.

I knew we'd never make it. So I lifted my arm from her shoulders and headed for the rifles, for the five of them in the gun rack.

"What are you doing?" Debby whispered, following me. "We have to get out of here."

I saw my mistake. The rifles were locked in place by a bar.

"Logan," Debby whispered with urgency and despair.

That's when I got angry. I was angry at my weakness, angry that the sheriff had gotten the drop on me and almost beaten me to death, angry that I'd screwed things up for Debby. The woman was trying to help me.

I gripped the lock in my hands and twisted suddenly and savagely. It wasn't a big lock, but it was big enough. The lock resisted my newfound strength. I snarled, grabbed a rifle barrel and wrenched it as hard as I could. Wood splintered as I tore the rifle from the rack.

"Did you hear that?" the deputy whined. "What's going on in there?"

The sheriff didn't respond verbally. He broke into a run. I could tell by his heavy, rushing footfalls.

Debby moaned, with her hands in front of her mouth.

I ripped open a drawer, tore bullets from a box and shoved them into the rifle. It was an old-style, lever-action Winchester, just like the ones in old movie Westerns.

The front door banged open as the sheriff entered with a big revolver in his hand.

I levered a bullet into the chamber and fired from the hip. The sound was deafening inside the office. One after another, I levered more bullets into the chamber, firing each one at the sheriff.

The bullets sent him staggering backward. Then, he went down hard, the gun flying from his hand.

The deputy ran up with his own gun in hand. I'd hoped the man would run away. Flames burst from his barrel as he shot at me. The splintering sound told me he'd hit wood to my left.

I shot the deputy three times until he sprawled outside on his back.

Behind me, Debby moaned more piteously than ever. "Now you've done it," she said. "Now you've done it."

I approached the sheriff.

"No, Logan," she said. "Watch out."

I glanced back at her. She screamed, seeing something in front of me.

I whipped around in time to watch the sheriff sit up. The front of his shirt was torn, and there were marks on his flesh—pseudo-flesh, I guess you'd call it. Underneath the marks gleamed bright metal.

"He's a robot," Debby said. "Don't you understand? You can't kill him. Now he's going to kill us."

-30-

A cold, terrible feeling struck me as I watched the sheriff climb to his feet. He actually was a robot. Were they all robots in Far Butte? I didn't believe that. What about old Parker with his chopper?

I had another question. How many of the Far Butte people had guns? I was betting not too many of them did.

"You are under arrest," the sheriff said. The head moved minutely as he took in Debby. "You have aided and abetted a criminal escaping from justice. Your time has come, Debby."

I shot him in the head. He staggered. I ran at him as I levered another bullet into the chamber. I fired, pumping bullets at him. He staggered out the door and tripped as his heels struck the dead deputy.

"Come on, Debby!" I shouted. "Follow me."

I vaulted over the fallen robot, landing on the street. Swiveling around, cocking the lever-action Winchester, I aimed at Walt as the robot sat up again.

Debby screamed, sliding to a stop. She was in the doorway with the robot blocking her way.

I pulled the trigger, hearing the rifle click. I was out of bullets.

If you can imagine this, the robot smiled. What kind of robot would smile knowing someone had run out of bullets? I'm guessing it had to be an advanced model with sadistic programming.

I swung the rifle by the barrel, smashing the butt against his head as if it were a baseball. I knocked him down again, this time onto his side.

"Debby," I shouted.

She ran and jumped, landing beside me as she grabbed my jacket for balance.

"Get in the car," I told her.

"What car?" she shrieked.

"The police car," I said. "See if the keys are still in the ignition."

The sheriff began sitting up for the third time. I batted him down before he could get his balance.

Debby ran to the police car, opening a door and jumping in. She fiddled for a second before the engine came to life with a roar.

The robot sat up faster this time, and he—it—dodged my swing. I clubbed it on the return swing, causing the rifle butt to blow apart. The robot absorbed the blow and shot to its feet.

Bellowing, I charged, jabbing what remained of the rifle against its torso. I shoved and it tripped over the doorjamb. I figured I'd used up all my remaining luck for the next ten years. I pitched the bent rifle at the robot and sprinted for the police cruiser.

The tires spun, squealing on the pavement as smoke billowed. The car whipped out of its parking location. Debby jammed on the brakes, stopping the car amidst a smoky haze.

I opened the passenger-side door and leaped in. She punched the gas pedal, making the tires spin and squeal again. Then she screamed.

I twisted around. The robot was coming. Just before it could grab me, the car shot forward, the passenger-side door striking the humanoid machine just enough to throw it off balance.

We sped away from it down Main Street.

I opened my partly shut door and slammed it closed. I looked back, fully expecting to see the robot sprinting after us and gaining. Instead, the sheriff just watched. The machine kept watching until Debby took a corner fast, making the tires squeal once more.

"Now what do we do?" she shouted.

That was a damn good question.

Debby kept accelerating as we roared out of Far Butte.

***

"Why don't you pull over there?" I said several miles later. Far Butte was behind us. We were out in the desert.

Debby glanced at me before doing as I suggested. She brought the car to a stop under some trees, turning off the ignition and killing the headlights. Her shoulders slumped in the darkness.

I opened the passenger-side door. A cool breeze blew in, and I heard a windmill thump as its vanes spun overhead. Tree leaves rustled, adding their sounds. Stars twinkled brightly, but there was no moon tonight.

"Thanks for coming to get me," I said.

Debby did not respond.

I turned toward her. She'd bowed her head with her face in her hands. I think she might have been crying, but it was so soft that I couldn't hear.

"Hey," I said, as I patted her shoulder.

She looked up and tried to smile. "I'm scared," she said in a small voice. "I think…I think I did it this time. The sheriff will kill both of us. I went too far."

"Did you grow up here?" I asked.

"No! None of us did. Mr. Gaines says—"

"Who is Mr. Gaines?" I asked.

"That's the old-timer in the leather jacket, Parker Gaines. He used to be a biker in the Bar Hoppers. He told me once that he took a turnoff while traveling Route 50. He said it was the worst mistake of his life. That's how he got stuck in Far Butte."

"What is Far Butte?"

"I'm not sure," she said.

"How long have you been here?"

"Eight years."

"How old are you?"

"Twenty-three."

"You were fifteen when you came to Far Butte?" I asked.

Debby stared at me in the darkness. "I ran away from home. I was stupid back then. I thought I had a rough life. My dad, my real dad, died in Operation Ripper in South Korea."

"What?" I asked.

"My dad was drafted into the military," she said.

No one had been drafted into the U.S. military since the Vietnam War. Was she saying she wasn't an American?

"Uh…"I said. "Your dad fought and died during Operation Ripper?"

She nodded.

"I never heard of it," I said.

"It was in the news. General Ridgeway—"

"Ridgeway?" I asked. "You can't mean General Ridgway who led the 82nd Airborne during World War II."

"That sounds about right," she said. "He also took over from MacArthur in South Korea during the Korean War."

Her words weren't stacking up.

"Uh…" I said for a second time. "This might sound like a stupid question. But what year did Operation Ripper take place?"

"1951," Debby said.

I stared more intently as the weirdness intensified.

"What's wrong?" she asked. "Why are you staring at me like that?"

"Ah…how old are you again?"

"I already told you. Twenty-three."

Debby looked and sounded twenty-three, but if her dad had died in Operation Ripper in 1951, did that mean she'd been born around 1950? If so, she had to be approaching seventy.

Debby turned away. "You don't realize yet, do you?"

I guess I didn't. "Are we in some kind of alternate reality?" I asked.

"No, nothing like that," she said. "I could only wish it were that. It's worse."

"How could it be worse?"

"This place—Far Butte, the surrounding desert—is out of phase with the rest of the planet. Sometimes though, ever since 1951, it opens a little and a few luckless souls wander in. Most of the time, the sheriff interviews them. If they pass, the latest inductees get to work in the tower."

"What happens in the tower?"

Debby pushed her lips out. "It's hard to remember. Most people can't. Not too many of them worry about that, though. You get used to it. With a few, though, remembering becomes an obsession. Eventually, Walt takes those few out into the desert and no one sees them again."

"You remember, though, don't you?" I asked.

She looked down. "A little," she admitted.

"What do you do in the tower?"

In a soft voice, she said, "I polish a strange, giant ornament until the pieces gleam. Some of the pieces have cracks in them. I remove those from time to time and insert special crystals into the vacant areas. It's very complicated and only a few people get to go where I do."

She seemed to become uncomfortable. "I hear voices sometimes as I work in there. Horrible voices telling me awful things."

She began to weep softly.

I hesitated. Her story was starting to freak me out. Was she saying we were in some kind of 1950's time warp? That didn't seem quite right. It seemed as if she meant *out of phase* as if this was a pocket separate from the regular world.

Finally, the weeping got to me. I slid farther into the car and held her. She put her face on my shoulder and cried a little harder. Soon, I found myself stroking her hair.

"I don't go into the tower all the time like the others," Debby said quietly. "Mostly, I work in the diner, helping to feed everyone. But every once in a while someone finds the right kind of crystal and I have to see if it will fit in the matrix."

I thought about my crystal from Rax Prime. It seemed odd the sheriff hadn't taken Rax when he—when *it*—had had the chance. Maybe the sheriff hadn't realized Rax was a sentient crystal inside the metal sheath. That might have saved Rax from going into the special room inside the tower.

"You said we're out of phase. What does that mean exactly?"

"Just what it sounds like," she whispered. "We're hidden from everyone else on Earth. We're out of phase from normal time or maybe from normal space. I can never remember which."

"What changed in 1951?" I asked. "You said ever since 1951 a few luckless souls have wandered into this out-of-phase place. Operation Ripper couldn't have caused that."

"No, of course not," she said. "Parker has a theory about why things started happening in 1951, but I don't know if he's right. Back then, America began testing nuclear weapons in Nevada. Parker thinks the explosions woke something up here, something in the tower that's been hiding for a long, long time. The thing has been stirring ever since the nukes went off. And since that time, it has let a few people into its out-of-phase existence."

I thought about Greenland, the Polarions and those hominids in the stasis tubes. Supposedly, someone had built the complex when Greenland had been ice-free Thule. Had the white tower been hiding out here in Far Butte, Nevada since those times? Did the tower create some kind of out-of-phase field? Could our Cold Warriors testing their nuclear bombs have woken something up that should have remained asleep?

It was crazy stuff, and I was stuck in this Twilight Zone place. Was it any weirder than aliens in an orbital pirate-vessel, though? Was being out of phase any weirder than Unguls? Maybe. But that wasn't my immediate concern.

"You must realize that you've been here longer than eight years," I said. "If you came in 1951—"

"I came in 1966 when I was fifteen years old."

"Okay… That means instead of eight years you've been here more like sixty."

Debby shuddered and began to weep again.

I held her, waiting for the tears to subside.

Finally, she looked up as she dried her eyes. Our lips were very close. I kissed her because I knew I should—her lips were salty with her tears—and I held her more tightly.

Soon, she kissed me back hungrily, causing me to respond with even greater fervor.

"Martin," she whispered once.

I let that go because Debby seemed lonely. Maybe I was lonely, too, but had never let myself know it.

One thing was clear. I had to leave this place. It must have something to do with Polarions, with something inside the white tower. Maybe if I could get inside the tower, I could turn off whatever kept this place out of phase with the rest of the planet.

Debby pulled away, maybe because she sensed my drifting thoughts.

"I-I'm sorry," she whispered. "I-I shouldn't have done that."

"You needed to," I said.

Her eyes narrowed as she studied me. "You needed to," she said.

"That's true. I feel better for it, especially because now I have an ally. We're partners, Debby, you and me against that maniacal robot."

"It's no joke."

"Who's joking?"

She grabbed my fingers, gripping them tightly. "Do you mean that?"

"Yeah," I said. "I can't stay here. Aliens are threatening Earth. I have to stop them."

"How are you going to do that?"

I pulled my hands free. "Let's step outside, get some fresh air."

We slid out of the car, and I put an arm around her shoulders, maneuvering her to the biggest tree. It was colder outside than I'd realized. That was the desert for you. I leaned against the tree trunk, letting Debby rest against me.

A thought struck. I pushed off the tree and disengaged from her. I got the keys from the ignition, walked back and opened the trunk.

Behind me, Debby sucked in her breath.

We both stared at the UFO-like alien lying in the trunk. I'd killed him with my flick-knife earlier. The blade was still stuck in his forehead. I yanked it out—it made a sucking sound—and wiped the blade on his torn clothes.

"That's gross," Debby said.

"It's mine," I said, folding the blade back into the handle, sliding the knife into a pocket.

"You killed him?"

"It was self-defense. Have you ever seen someone like him before?"

She took a step closer, peering at the Ungul. Finally, she looked up at me, shaking her head.

"You're sure?" I asked.

"Positive. There are no aliens here. Who is he?"

"One of the aliens messing with Earth," I said. "I followed him to Far Butte. I wonder why he came…"

"What's wrong?" Debby asked. "Why did you stop talking?"

I closed the trunk. "The Unguls and the tower must be connected. Maybe the tower is one of the old pieces of treasure shown on the Canopus map. The Unguls definitely came searching for this place. Well, they went searching for something and found this place. Did being out of phase surprise them or surprise the Organizer? Rax didn't seem to know about this place."

"Who's Rax?" she asked.

"A friend," I said. "He can't help us now. Okay. We have the element of surprise. That means we have to keep moving in order to keep them off balance."

"How do we do that?" she asked.

I thought about it. "Can anyone else remember, even a little, what happens in the tower?"

"Parker," she said. "But I wasn't ever supposed to tell anyone."

"We have to go see Parker," I said.

"That's a bad idea. Parker doesn't like visitors. He's old, and he seems humorous, at times, but the man's a killer. You don't want to get on his bad side."

"Parker talked to you," I pointed out.

"That's because Parker likes girls."

"We're going to see Parker. We have to figure out what's going on if we're ever going to leave this place."

I headed for the driver's side, stopping when I didn't hear Debby following me. "What's wrong?" I asked.

She seemed to come out of a trance, moving suddenly, hurrying to me and looping one of her arms around one of mine.

"Maybe you're right," she said. "I've forgotten what it's like being with someone who has hope. I feel alive again, and I love it. Yes, let's go see Parker."

-31-

Parker lived a long way out of town in a rundown shack on a dusty hill. It had a two-mile driveway from the main road, three half-dead trees and a yard littered with beer cans and whiskey bottles.

We stopped in the yard. Debby pointed at several skeletons. They looked like dog or wolf skeletons and had old ropes attached to their throats. The ropes were tied to stakes hammered into the ground.

"Did those animals die here?" I asked.

"No," Debby said, looking scared as she scanned back and forth. "Parker has a weird sense of humor. He told me once he loved dogs. That's what made him think Far Butte was an antechamber of Hell. Every dog that trotted into our out-of-phase place died in a matter of days. Parker figured that must make this the other place where no one wants to go after they die."

I opened the driver's side door, and nearly jumped out of my skin as a boom sounded and a flash of flame exited a shotgun aimed at the sky.

"Hold it right there," a growling voice told me.

I froze, and then I slowly moved my head to the left.

Parker pushed off a side of his shanty, with a pump-action shotgun in his hands. He wore his black leather jacket, and his biker boots made chain-jangling sounds as he walked closer to us.

"You have three seconds to get off my—" Parker stopped walking and talking. "It's you," he said.

"It is," I said. "Can I step outside?"

"Hi, Parker," Debby said, waving at him from the passenger seat.

"You bastard," he told me. "You pulled her into this?" He raised the shotgun.

"Parker, no!" Debby shouted. "The sheriff beat him up. Walt threw him in jail. I busted him out."

"Debby," Parker said, shaking his head. "You know that will be the final straw."

"We need help," Debby said.

Parker swore, and his eyes hardened as he studied me. I saw my death in his gaze. I could feel the chill of it crawling along my spine. Finally, though, after three seconds of having a maw of a death aimed at my chest, Parker lowered the shotgun, swearing some more.

"All right, get out," the old biker told me. "Let's see if the new boy can tell us anything interesting."

***

The place reeked of alcohol with a coating of dust on just about everything except for the chopper in the living room. A dim yellow bulb gave us light as we sat at an ancient kitchen table.

Parker set the shotgun near a hand-pump faucet. I noticed there were several other weapons, too, including an old bayonet.

"Nice place," I said.

Parker's eyes might have glinted. It was hard to tell. I decided to keep the rest of my quips to myself. The old biker didn't want to hear them, and I didn't want to push him over the edge concerning me.

"The sheriff beat you up?" Parker asked, as he studied my face.

I nodded.

"You don't look beat up." He made it sound like a challenge.

I wanted to tell him I took plenty of vitamins. Instead, I said, “I heal quickly.”

His eyes narrowed, and it seemed as if he recalculated something concerning me. “You have a bit of size,” he said. “Are you strong or is it all for show?”

“He took down Walt,” Debby said. “If he hadn’t, we’d never have escaped from the sheriff’s office.”

“I’m going to have to hear about that,” Parker said.

I told the old biker what had happened.

“I don’t buy it,” he said when I’d finished. “No human could have done that to the robot.”

I glanced at Debby. She nodded. Could she already be reading my mind? She seemed to say with the glance that I could trust Parker. I decided to go with my instincts.

“Here’s my story,” I said.

I told them about Station 5 in Nevada, the Learjet, and Greenland in all its glory. I told them what Rax had done to me. I told them about the Guard-ship and the rod attack that had originated in orbit from an alien vessel. Lastly, I told them how I’d entered this out-of-phase place by trying to figure out what the aliens were up too.

As I explained these things, I watched them. The description of the stasis tubes, the Neanderthals and apelike hominids did nothing to elicit their interest or any sign that they’d heard of those things before. That eliminated one possibility for me: that the builders of the Greenland complex and the white tower belonged to the same group.

Finally, I asked Parker, “When did you come here?”

“1985,” he said, “Ronald Reagan was president.”

“You’ve been here a long time,” I said, wondering if Parker realized he’d been here a shorter amount of time than Debby had.

The biker did not respond to my comment. Could something in the tower be keeping Debby younger? Why would the thing in the tower be doing that?

“Here’s the thing,” I said, pumping energy into my voice. “It’s the reason we came to see you. Can you remember what you do in the tower?”

"Yeah," Parker muttered, as if the remembering was a chore. "I crawl into tight places. I connect couplings. Sometimes, as I do the connecting, I get shocked. That's my clearest memory. The shocking hurts like Hell every time and half my skin gets charred and hard. Others lather cream on my skin. That makes everything itch and I want to howl. I don't, though. I don't want to give whatever's watching me the pleasure."

"Who's watching you?" I asked.

Parker shook his head. "I don't know, but I can feel him. I can always feel him when I'm inside the tower."

"What does he feel like?" I asked.

Parker stared me in the eye. "Evil," he said in a breathless voice.

The way he said that reminded me of the sensation of evil I had felt inside the Greenland complex. Was there a connection between the two places?

"Have you ever heard of the Polarions?" I asked, thinking they might have something to do with the evil sensation.

"Never," Parker said.

That had been a long shot, but still, his answer left me disappointed. I was stuck in an out-of-phase place with some kind of evil inside an ancient white tower. Debby seemed to be a prize to the tower. She was one of the few, maybe the only one, to polish a giant ornament, take out cracked pieces and insert specials crystals in the empty slots. Since knowing about Rax, I had an awful feeling this ornament might be alive in some nefarious fashion.

"I have to get into the tower," I said.

"No!" Debby said. "It's over if you try that. Walt has to interview you first, assign you a number. You can't surrender, Logan."

"Who said anything about surrendering?"

"How else can Walt interview you?" Debby asked.

"I need to sneak into the tower," I said. "I have no intention of going in officially."

"Debby's right," Parker told me. "Walt guards the tower. The robot is going to be watching closer than ever. That's how it caught Martin Cruz."

“Is there another way inside?” I asked.

“None that I know about,” Parker said. “What about you, Debby?”

She shook her head.

Parker looked at me and spread his hands.

Something about that made me mad. “That’s it?” I asked. “The bad old biker wants to give up just like that?”

Parker scowled as if I’d just pissed on his boots. Maybe I should have stuck to my plan of keeping my quips to myself.

“Boy,” he told me, “you have no idea who you’re messing with.”

“Look,” I said, “you’ve been here a long time. I get that.”

“You don’t get shit,” he said.

“There’s a way to do this. But I’m going to need your help. You must have hated the Man back in the day.”

Parker watched me, the scowl sinking deeper into his seamed face.

“I have a feeling you’re still an outlaw biker in your heart. Here, something in the tower is the Man. The sheriff enforces the law. The robot tells you what to do and you ask it, ‘How high should I jump, Walt?’”

Parker’s lips hardly moved as he said, “I’m going to whip your—”

“Why get mad at me?” I asked, interrupting, running with my new approach. “I’m just saying how it is. Get mad at the hidden thing in the tower. It’s the one screwing with you for all these years. I know how to beat the robot. If I can get into the tower, I can screw with the thing that has screwed with you since 1985. Tell me a biker wouldn’t like some payback after all that time.”

“You can’t do anything to it,” Parker said.

“Not out here, I can’t. But if I can get inside the tower…”

Parker sneered.

“Hey,” I said. “I wrecked Greenland for the Unguls and the Organizer. I have a few aces up my sleeve. I’d be in a grave in the desert if I wasn’t different from the others.”

“He has a point,” Debby said.

Parker crossed his arms as he chewed that over. Finally, he asked me, "You think it's the tower that keeps us locked in this hellhole?"

"The tower does something," I said. "It's the key to all this. It has to be. We know it needs humans. Why else would the sheriff who guards the tower look like a human? Why else would people go inside the tower to do secret work? Keeping Far Butte as it is must take effort. Why do all that if the thing in the tower could dispense with humans?"

Parker rubbed his leathery face. "Not that I'm buying into your thinking, but how do you propose to get inside?"

I'd been waiting for that question. I doubted he was going to like the answer, though. I took a deep breath and told him the only way I could see of getting it done.

Parker didn't say a word afterward. Would he throw me out? Would he want to fight? Slowly, to my surprise, laugh lines appeared on his face. He shook his head.

"You have gall," Parker said in a rough voice. He walked to the sink, put his hands on the shotgun, and faced me once more. "I've been here too long, way too long." He looked at Debby. "Are you in?"

"All the way," she whispered.

"Yeah," Parker said, seeming wistful. "So am I."

-32-

I slept poorly that night even though I was dead tired. I was nervous, and I hated putting anyone else in jeopardy.

Come morning, I put on Parker's jacket. I kept his hat in a saddlebag, but I wore his old pants and boots. They were all a bit too big for me. Finally, I wheeled his chopper out of the shanty.

"Thanks," I told him.

He grinned. "You're okay, punk. Hold out your hand."

I did.

He slapped my palm with his. "This is righteous, you know."

"Yeah," I said.

"Thank you, Parker," Debby said. She stepped up to him, took his leathery face in her hands and gave him a peck on the lips.

He snaked his right arm around her waist and pulled her tight, and he gave her a real kiss. After releasing her, he said, "If I were younger—"

"I'd run screaming," Debby said with a laugh. "Good-bye," she said.

Parker gave me a solemn look. "You look after her. If she gets hurt because of you, I'm going to find you and beat you to death."

I acknowledged that with the barest of nods.

"You'll need these." Parker pulled out ancient mirrored sunglasses from his front shirt pocket. He handed them to me.

“Thanks,” I said, putting them on.

“You look good, punk,” Parker said. “Make sure you get it done.”

I didn’t have any words left, so I kicked-started the Harley. It roared into life on the first try. His place might be a junk heap, but Parker kept his hog in nearly perfect condition.

Debby climbed up behind me, putting her arms around my waist. I revved the throttle and took off, leaving Parker staring after us on his lonely dusty hill.

***

Talking on a motorcycle wasn’t impossible, just hard to do well. After leaving the two-mile driveway, getting onto the concrete, I opened up the Harley. It felt good having Debby with me. It felt good having the morning briskness blast against me. The leather jacket was excellent protection against the morning chill.

The desert terrain passed by in a blur as the sun began its journey across the sky. After ten miles, I saw the cluster of buildings and trees that made up Far Butte in the distance, with the sunlight glinting off the obscene white tower.

I slowed down and half turned my head.

“We have to do this as normally as possible,” I shouted.

“I know,” Debby shouted into my left ear.

We’d made our plans last night. I couldn’t think of any reason to change them.

There was a pickup ahead of us. I debated blowing past it just because. Then, a sense of caution held me back. The driver might be able to tell I wasn’t Parker. This wouldn’t work if someone ratted me out to the sheriff.

Nervousness hit as we neared Far Butte. I’d been able to put out of my mind what we were going to do. Now, the realization I might be dead within the hour—if we failed—made my palms sweaty and my stomach churn.

Debby must have felt the same thing. Her arms tightened around my waist. That helped me feel a little better. I’ve found that it was easier to stay cool if others around me were freaking out. Not that Debby was freaking out; she was simply scared like me.

I turned my head. “We can do this.”

She squeezed even harder.

After that, I followed the pickup to the parking lot near the tower.

“Over there,” Debby said in my right ear.

I drove to a bike rack where others were shoving front bicycle wheels into the metal rack. No one locked his or her bicycle. That was like the old days of my youth.

With my thumb, I pressed the motorcycle’s kill switch. I let Debby get off first. Then, I used my foot to push down the kickstand, leaned the Harley and swung my other leg over.

I felt exposed out here, and my face felt as if it were sunburned. This morning before leaving, Debby had applied makeup, trying to make me look older. I hunched my shoulders as I’d practiced last night, and I tried to imitate Parker’s swagger.

People milled about on the huge plastic-coated court just as I’d seen yesterday from Observation Hill. Debby walked slowly ahead of me.

The sheriff stood on the other side of the plaza. I’d seen the robot on our way in. It lacked a deputy today. I wondered how long it would take the robot to choose someone else to help it.

My stomach tightened worse than before as I saw the sheriff step onto the plaza, studying people before moving on.

Ahead of me, Debby faltered.

The tower siren blared, the shift signal. People began to part, half heading home, the others heading for the door at the base of the tower.

In a plan like this, it usually worked like a snap or it failed horribly. There were few in-between stages. If the sheriff recognized me, I’d never get into the tower. If the robot didn’t recognize me—

Debby stopped and began to turn my way.

“Hey, Debby,” I said, trotting, catching her left arm. The fear was stark in her eyes and her lips trembled. “Keep going,” I whispered.

“The sheriff’s is heading this way.”

“Keep going anyway,” I said, shoving her forward.

Debby stumbled, sucked in her breath and let her head droop. I could feel the defeat oozing from her.

I looked up. The sheriff seemed to be walking directly toward us. Was my plan a miserable failure?

At that point, tires screeched to the left of us in the parking lot. People looked up in wonder. The sheriff's car stopped, and the driver kicked open the door and jumped out. He leveled a pump-action shotgun at the sheriff. People screamed as the gunman opened fire, many of them hitting the plastic to get out of the way.

None of the shots hit the sheriff, or anyone else for that matter. Walt was standing too far away for that. The cowboy-hat-wearing robot drew its revolver and began to sprint toward the police car.

Parker, wearing my jacket with a hat pulled low over his eyes, jumped back into the prowler car. He burned rubber and created a cloud of smoke. The police car fishtailed back and forth, gaining speed.

The sheriff shoved its gun back into its holster. This time, the robot began to run with purpose, taking strides and building up speed. Soon, it was running faster than any human could have.

The biker was likely sacrificing his life for us. It had been hard to ask Parker to do it. I didn't see any other way, though. There was an off chance I could fix things before the robot caught up with Parker. But at the speed the robot was giving chase, I didn't give that high odds.

The tower siren blared a second time as if angry with the interruption.

Woodenly, people picked themselves off the plastic and began to line up slowly. Debby and I joined them. She stood in front of me. Others soon stood behind me. No one spoke, which was fine with me. I kept my head down. I wore Parker's biker hat now. I doubted it would have fooled normal people. Everyone in line seemed listless, though. Even Debby had begun to shuffle forward in a mechanical fashion.

She'd told me most of the people became zombie-like while lining up. It was different experiencing it, though.

Finally, I couldn't resist any more. I looked up. The tower door was close, seven people away from me. I squinted, trying to pierce the gloom of the entranceway. What was in there? What would happen once I stepped through?

Neither Debby nor Parker had been able to tell me anything about the immediate process. They both remembered aspects of their jobs, not the process that had brought them there. Did we cross another phase barrier at the door?

There were five more people to go, and then it would be my turn. I was finding it hard to breathe.

Four people left.

Three.

Two.

I still couldn't see anything past the dark entranceway. I couldn't detect a process or a check system before the door.

Debby stepped up, and I saw it then. A small scanner the size of a fingernail blinked blue. It blinked more, more, turned green and Debby stepped into the darkness, disappearing from sight.

It was my turn.

That's when a hand latched onto my left shoulder from behind, spinning me around.

-33-

I expected the killer robot to be smiling at me with a gun pressed against my chest. Instead, an Ungul aimed a raygun at me, with the other two flanking him as backup. Behind them, the line of remaining people waited.

"You will come with us," the raygun-pointing Ungul said.

I'd read a book once about using guns. The book had been paper-thin, more a pamphlet really. It had suggested one stay alert at all times, looking around constantly. I had failed in that today because I'd been trying to fit in and act zombie-like. One chapter in the book had always impressed me. It had been about surprise. The author suggested that surprise could help overcome terrible odds. It was a mindset thing. You had to practice it at peculiar times in order to hammer it into your brain. I had taken that chapter to heart a long time ago. That's why I'd gone on the offensive at Station 5.

I was already keyed-up standing here, waiting for my turn. The chapter had suggested that when assailants surprised you, one of the best tactics was to launch into an immediate attack. The emphasis had been on immediate. You had to jump at them and go all out. The original attacker, in most cases, would be expecting a compliant victim. The sudden assault from a position of weakness could freeze the original aggressor for a few critical moments. In that time, you had to score a telling blow.

As the Ungul swiveled me around, I'd already been thinking, *What the heck. It's over. I might as well go out swinging.*

The shock of seeing an Ungul instead of the sheriff had stung me, and a moment passed. The next moment, I recalled the dictum, "Act immediately." The third moment, I lunged at the Ungul and grabbed the end of his raygun. He pressed the firing stub, the end glowed and I shoved the weapon upward. The red ray shot up into the sky.

While continuing to keep hold of the raygun, I stepped forward and rammed a knee into the Ungul's groin. If he had been a man, I would have incapacitated him. Instead, he merely grunted, lifting up slightly.

That was enough for me to wrench the raygun out of his grip. The other two finally reacted. One reached under his suit for his weapon. The other one rushed me.

I shoved the original Ungul at him. They entangled and went down.

I could have rayed the two. Instead, I spun around and faced the dark entranceway. Before the tower scanner could scan me, I plunged toward the darkness. That darkness proved as hard as a steel door. I rebounded off it like a Three Stooges' idiot and collided with the two Unguls as they climbed to their feet. All three of us went down in a heap. They attempted to grapple me with their hot hands.

I turned into a wildcat, throwing elbows, jabbing fingers and head butting each of them. I might have won free, but there was a third member of the team still standing. He finally reacted, pressing an agonizer against the back of my neck. The shock of pain was intense, sending hot spikes of agony into my brain. I bellowed, gritted my teeth—

The agony spiked a second time. I recall arching my back, and that was the last thing I remember.

***

I woke up with a terrible sense of *déjà vu* and failure. I lay on the floor in the back of a car, with an Ungul's feet on my butt.

I hated that. I hated Unguls, but I hated worse that I'd sacrificed Parker for nothing and lost Debby. She'd gone into the tower, and I'd been unable to follow her. The Unguls had wrecked that for me. It left me bitter, with a horrible taste in my mouth.

"He is awake," the backseat Ungul announced.

I realized the taste wasn't defeat, but came from the agonizer that had zapped me into unconsciousness. Since the Unguls had caught me a second time, should I just give up? No. If Parker was still alive, he'd need help. I owed it to him to keep struggling. I also had to rescue Debby if I could. That meant I had to shift with the tide. I had to go with this. I was down. Did that mean I had to consider myself out? That wasn't my plan by a long shot.

The Unguls began a lengthy process of questioning me. It was repetitious in the Ungul manner, and it brought several touches of the agonizer against my neck. I loathed the pain and normally would have done anything to avoid it. But I figured grudging answers were believable answers. I overplayed my hand, though.

The driver and leader, Q4, said, "He is too stubborn to use, rendering him useless to the mission. Kill him."

"Wait!" I cried, switching tactics on a dime. If I couldn't win free from these bastards, I'd never save Debby from the thing in the tower. "I know about the Canopus map. Surely, you're curious about that."

The Unguls were silent for a time. By the crinkling of seat fabric, I imagined them glancing at each other, giving significant eyebrow raises, or whatever it was the Unguls did to communicate silently with each other.

"Do you refer to the Canopus Star System?" the alien in the passenger seat asked. His name was Z21.

I didn't know the name of the Ungul with his feet on my butt, although he was the one I wanted to bust up the most.

The important point was that they were curious about the ancient Canopus text. I had to play this the best I could. I took a moment to think about it, finally deciding on my strategy.

"I refer to the Linear D text found on the fourth planet of the Canopus Star System," I said. "There used to be an ancient weapon hidden there, too, but you guys lost it along with a Rigellian battlefleet."

"Could his information be true?" Q4 asked the others.

"According to my analyzer," Z21 said, "he believes he speaks the truth."

"But how can an ignorant aboriginal of this painful dirt-ball know anything about the Organizer's former events or comrades?" Q4 asked. "We do not even know those things, although the Committee heads believe this mission is related to ancient relics."

I'd been listening as hard as I could. I had a feeling I was right about privateers being like pirates. I was betting that Alien Space Pirates were similar to historical Earth sea pirates. Both sets were likely greedy. And both sets likely had leaders who kept them in the dark about the most important aspects of any deal. That was Basic Criminal Mentality 101.

"This is about more than ancient relics," I said. "This is about Polarion treasure."

That brought another bout of Ungul silence.

"Logic dictates the aboriginal has spoken to a Galactic Guard agent," Q4 said in time. "Ask the aboriginal if that is so."

"Human—"

"I heard you," I said. "This has nothing to do with Galactic whatever you said. I know because humanity has a special branch. We're not as savage as you aliens want to believe we are."

That proved to be too much for them. The Unguls began buzzing among themselves. After a time, the backseat rider rechecked my pockets.

"He has a device," the Ungul said, picking up the inert Rax.

"What is the item?" Z21 asked me.

"A cell phone," I said.

"It is inoperative," the Ungul in back said.

"Wow," I said, sarcastically. "You're kidding me? You mean you guys can call the Organizer from this place?"

They buzzed among themselves longer than before. Finally, the backseat alien pressed the agonizer against my neck. It jolted me hard, and I slumped over, unconscious for a second time.

-34-

I woke up slouched in a corner amidst other junk: jackets, what seemed to be shell cases and duffel bags. My brain throbbed, a sore neck made it hard to move my head and I was ravenously hungry. I found they'd shackled my hands and feet, with a chain linking the two.

It dawned on me that I was no longer in a car. I heard clanking outside like tank treads, and I was in a far larger compartment than before.

Right, the tanks. They must have brought me into one of the alien tanks.

I examined my surroundings. There were five Unguls at various positions. Each of them sat in a seat and manipulated controls or pressed his eyes against a periscope thingy. It wasn't like an Earth tank. There was more space and it was all one compartment, about the size of a mid-level tool shed.

I debated my options while trying to keep myself upbeat regarding my chances of ever seeing Debby again. I was still wearing my clothes. That was good. I could feel Rax in a jacket pocket. They must have believed me about the device being a cell phone.

What was my plan then? That would depend on their plan. Did they have a way of leaving this out-of-phase place?

I waited, but we kept traveling with no one paying me any attention. Finally, I cleared my throat.

Q4 regarded me. At least, I think it was Q4.

"Why didn't you kill me?" I asked.

"You have information," he said. "I do not know how you acquired this information, but the Committee will have it one way or another."

"What if the Organizer doesn't want you to have the information?" I asked.

"He will audit us at the end of the mission. That is enough."

"I guess you're saying what he doesn't know can't hurt him?"

Q4 stared at me impassively. "That is illogical. A lack of information is often debilitating. You are alive because the Committee will desire all your data concerning the Canopus dig."

I tried to shift into a more comfortable position. It proved impossible. I wondered what had happened to Debby. I wondered what the thing in the tower had thought about the Unguls dragging me away from the door. Hadn't any of the Far Butte people tried to interfere? I guess not. I was on my own, and I was sick of being in the dark. I'd have to start baiting my questions to get better responses.

"Do you realize we're out of phase here?" I asked.

Q4 didn't answer, but seemed content to stare at me as if I were some sort of museum piece. Finally, he said, "Explain the concept, 'out of phase.'"

"As far as I can tell," I said, "the thing in the tower generates a field that causes the town and surrounding area to be out of phase with the rest of Earth."

"It is a temporal or spatial shift?"

"Temporal would mean time travel, right?" I asked.

"Do not seek to equivocate. Answer the question."

"I'm guessing it's a spatial shift."

"That is our own assessment," Q4 said. "You are uncommonly scientific and observant. How do you achieve this without specialized equipment?"

"Do you mean your tanks have specialized equipment?" I asked.

"I am here to interrogate you," Q4 said. "You are not here to interrogate me."

"Sure," I said. "Don't rock the boat. I get it."

"Your statement is a non sequitur."

"Q4," Z21 said. "I have a theory as to the human's unaccountable brilliance with his accompanying ridiculousness."

"Speak," Q4 told the other.

"He may be an idiot savant," Z21 said.

"It is possible," Q4 said. "I am more inclined to believe he has gained unbelievable data from strange sources. Whatever the truth, we must assimilate the data. If the aboriginal is even partly correct, we may be able to bargain with the Organizer for a larger share of the take."

"We are all agreed with you," Z21 said.

"I did not ask for your agreement," Q4 informed him. "I am the trio leader. I decide all tertiary quandaries. Is there any in the cubicle who gainsays my authority?"

None of the other Unguls spoke up. I guess he'd just put down a semi-rebellion before it had gotten out of hand. I would have liked to know more about their social structure. As far as I could tell, the Unguls were alien cannon fodder, bottom feeders. The Min Ve and Jarnevon likely looked down on the Unguls the way that some high brass looked down on foot soldiers.

We traveled for another half hour, the ride becoming jerkier and angled more severely the longer it lasted. Finally, the treads quit churning and we came to a stop.

Q4 opened a hatch, poking his head out. He pulled his head in to buzz to the others. That was the start of a general exodus, which included me.

Instead of unshackling my ankles, two Unguls hoisted me upright and dragged me across the chamber. They thrust me through the hatch, where another Ungul dragged me over uneven rocks.

The tank was at an angle on rocks on the side of a large hill. The rest of the slope was behind us. I could see the valley floor, and I made out an area that must have been Far Butte. A glint of reflected sunlight showed me the white tower.

What would I have found inside there? Could I have defeated whatever had turned on the out-of-phase cloaking device?

Some of the Unguls set up a table on a level area. Others brought out equipment from the tank, putting it on the table.

"How come there's only one tank here?" I asked Q4.

The Ungul leader ignored me. He stood, watching the other four set up futuristic-looking equipment. Finally, one cranked an umbrella-like device overhead. He kept cranking, sending the dish much higher than seemed reasonable.

"Are you trying to contact your orbital vessel?" I asked.

Once more, Q4 ignored me.

I shifted my position, beginning to slide away.

That brought an immediate response. Q4 turned to me. "If you attempt to escape, we will cause you much pain."

"Roger that," I said. "I was just trying to scratch my back. This itch is killing me."

Q4 watched me as I slid against a boulder. It was painful work with the crick in my neck. Finally, I rubbed my back against the rock and made sighing, contented sounds.

"That feels good," I said.

Q4 turned back to the others. They continued to hook up equipment like a rock band getting ready for a show.

Fifteen minutes later, the four of them sat in chairs. A growing expectancy was building in me as they tapped screens and adjusted dials.

Q4 buzzed orders.

The tank began to hum. A section of the spherical upper canopy lifted higher on three hydraulic poles. The antennas there glowed with power. Soon, the antennas began to rotate like radar dishes.

"Are you doing something about being out of phase?" I asked.

"Yes," Q4 said.

I wondered if they were going to try to link to the energy source that would be Station 5. Was that why they had come down there at Western Sunlight?

"We are ready?" Z21 said, as he studied his screen.

"What is the status regarding points two and three?" Q4 asked.

I imagined those points were the locations for the other two tanks.

"Point three needs refinement," Z21 said.

"Tell them to hurry."

Z21 turned around to look at Q4. "Is there are a reason for concern?"

Q4 pointed in the direction of Far Butte.

Z21 turned back to his controls.

Time passed. I wondered how they could bring us back into phase. I soon realized the how didn't matter. Would coming back into phase revive Rax? If it did, would the crystal give himself away by talking before he realized the situation? What about the Min Ve's orbital vessel? Would it rain orbital rods onto the white tower?

I shook my head. Wasn't the tower the prize, or whatever was in there, the prize? If the Min Ve did attack the tower and killed Debby…

I shook my head again, refusing to go there in my thoughts. Instead, I leaned against the rock, waiting.

"Location three is ready," Z21 announced some time later.

"Synchronize your stations," Q4 said.

I watched him closely. The trio leader seemed absorbed in his task.

I began twisting my feet and testing the bonds on my wrist. Neither would give. I could possibly wear down the metal against a rock. I didn't have that kind of time, though.

I slid over rocks until I was at the farthest edge of them from the group. I suppose I could stand and hop like a fool. That might be better if something went wrong.

Our tank began to hum, and the radar dishes up there turned faster.

"Synchronize the stations," Q4 said. He didn't speak any faster or louder than earlier. Unguls always used the same tone and inflection. But there was an urgency to him just the same.

The tank's hum increased yet again.

"Synchronize the stations," Q4 said.

The four Unguls at the table worked faster.

Suddenly, the tank's hum smoothed out. The hard vibration in the air ceased. My shoulders eased, and the itchiness in my mind was gone.

Now, a new lower hum took over. It began building up, and soon, the new hum set my teeth on edge.

"Q4," Z21 said. "There is a spike on my energy chart."

I craned my head toward them so I could hear what they were saying.

"Do you detect any advanced weaponry aimed at us?" Q4 said.

I sat back against a boulder, frowning. What kind of question was that? My eyebrows rose. He must mean the tower.

I struggled up to a higher sitting position, staring intently into the valley. A wink of bright light appeared from the white tower.

I cried out, jumped up and began to hop away, with the chain between my ankles and wrists jangling madly.

"Increase the intensity," Q4 said.

"They are building up an attack—"

I didn't hear more because a terrible buzzing and burning soared overhead. I cringed but somehow forced myself to look up. A bright yellow line slashed through the air, making crunching sounds as if it burned molecules in its passage.

Abruptly, the sound and the line disappeared, although there were afterimages in the air.

I found myself panting, the air hot inside my throat. I realized the white tower must have tried to beam us but missed. Whatever lived in there had resurrected some kind of ancient weaponry.

I continued hopping, working my way up the rocky slope. The Unguls weren't paying me the slightest attention now. They were too busy working the equipment on the table.

Another searing fiery beam sliced through the air. This one was closer than before, and it was so hot I threw myself down, twisting so that I hit with my left shoulder and rolled down the rocks, landing closer to the Ungul table than before.

"The human is excitable," Z21 said.

"What do I care about that?" Q4 said. "Synchronize and give the process full power."

"The ethereal lines are strained," Z21 declared.

“I do not care,” Q4 said. “This is our only chance to communicate with the Organizer. We must use it.”

I shouted as if with terror. If the Unguls believed I was a silly, frightened human, so much the better. I rolled over and over as if frantic to get away.

“Q4,” Z21 said.

“Ignore the human,” Q4 said. “We can retrieve him once we succeed.”

I rolled down the slope, fell over a ledge and plunged. I struck rocks, banging my shins and forehead and landing on my back. I groaned, watching the white tower from an upside-down position. It was undignified, but I was out of earshot of the Unguls. That was the important point. It might be safer for Rax to revive here.

The sky shimmered strangely. Then, it seemed to shake, straining my vision. I peered at the white tower. It blurred, came into sharper focus as the fiery beam lanced out again, and blurred worse than before, leaving the rocks to my left flowing like lava.

The Unguls spoke louder at their table, working frantically. It was a race. Could the thing in the tower remember how to use its weaponry before the Unguls could break back into phase? I had a feeling the tanks were at various locations in this Twilight Zone land. The Unguls were trying to break out of here, and the ancient warden in the tower did not want that happening.

If I broke free of here, would I lose all chances of finding Debby again? I scowled. I couldn’t worry about that now. I had to worry about my planet, about my friends and family. If I didn’t do something, the Organizer might keep attacking Earth, and that could possibly include more hell-burners.

I bit my lower lip as I switched vantages.

“There,” Z21 said. “I have contacted the ship. Q4, the Jarnevon demands we come up at once for questioning.”

“Yes,” Q4 said. “Tell her we are ready for transfer.”

“Rax,” I hissed at the crystal in my inner jacket pocket. “Rax, you have to wake up.”

“Ten seconds until we transfer,” Z21 said.

“Rax!” I shouted.

“What is the human saying?”

“Something concerning Rax Prime,” Z21 said. “I do not understand—”

“A Guard Advisor Unit,” Q4 said. “That is what he is talking about. That is how he knew about the Canopus treasure site. Get him. Get him now.”

“Rax,” I said, “you have to wake up.”

“Why must I do this thing at your demand?” the crystal said in a querulous tone.

“Rax!” I shouted. “You’re awake.”

“I thought we had established that you would let me remain in meditation mode while I was in it,” the crystal said.

“Rax,” I said. “You’ve been out of phase. Unguls are coming. You have to teleport us to the Guard-ship. If you don’t, the Organizer will beam you onto the orbital vessel.”

“I am hardly awake. What did you say?”

“Cease your communication,” Z21 told me. “I forbid you to speak further.”

“Unguls,” Rax said. “This is very odd. What happened—?”

“You’ve been asleep for days,” I shouted.

Z21 leaped over a rock, crashing beside us. His knees struck my shoulder, hurling me down. An agonizer gleamed in his grip. He struggled to maintain his balance so he could touch me with it.

At that moment a wide, round red beam reached down from space, bathing us in an eerie light.

I opened my mouth, trying to shout Rax’s name. Garbled noises came out instead, and everything began to fade from sight.

-35-

It felt as if pins and needles jabbed into my flesh. Then I could almost feel my constituent atoms torn apart and turned into energy as the “I” of Logan was transported off the Earth’s surface to the orbital alien vessel.

I materialized painfully on a cold platform, my atoms seemingly shoved into an approximation of my former self. It seemed as if everything was out of order, as if my ears could smell the foul odors while I used my hands to scan the room.

The blue-skinned Jarnevon studied me. She wore a tight-fitting green garment and high-heeled black boots. She had her hands on her shapely hips, and I swear she licked her sensuous lips as our eyes met.

“Rax,” I whispered.

Unguls appeared around me in various frozen poses, no doubt teleported up from the surface along with me.

The Jarnevon smiled. It was a wicked thing and seemed to cause a spark of sensation at the back of my brain. That caused me to wonder if maybe she and I could spend some time together, preferably entwined on a big feather bed. I smiled back at her and even managed a nod.

Her smile vanished, and faster than anyone I’d ever seen, she drew a heavy-looking blaster. She aimed the pitted nozzle at me. I knew I was dead—but she hesitated pulling the trigger for some reason.

During her hesitation, the scene faded from view. It took me a second to realize why. The transportation didn't hurt this time. It was painless, seamless—

I grunted, falling several inches to land heavily on my side, my chains jangling. A second later, an Ungul landed beside me.

"Subdue him," Rax said.

I tried to leap onto the Ungul and crashed right back down onto the transporter pad inside the Guard-ship. Rax had teleported us out of the Min Ve's orbital vessel. Z21—who had apparently transported with us—opened his eyes wider than I think he'd ever done. He scrambled to his feet, and at the last minute, he remembered that he was holding a raygun. He aimed it at me.

I lunged desperately, propelled by my ankles and toes. Realizing I couldn't reach him in time that way, I spun on my side like a hip-hop artist. I whipped my legs around to strike his. My shins exploded with pain. It was like trying to chop down a tree with my legs.

The raygun glowed, and a spot drilled into the Guard-ship decking. If it went on too long, would Z21 drill a hole through the outer bulkhead and let in the seawater?

From my hips, I thrust up with my shackled feet, striking the back of his knees. That did it. He fell, stumbled down the transporter ledge, and went down hard onto his face.

I humped like a caterpillar, desperate to get to him. It was undignified, slow and maddening. I fell onto him from the transporter pad, and began a frantic struggle for control of the Guard-ship.

He had full use of his limbs, but my bulk lay on top of him. I had little reach, but his throat was right there. I dug my fingers into his flesh and refused to let go. He kneed, hit and bit me, but still I refused to release my death grip. Our eyes met from inches apart.

"Human," he gurgled. It was his last word.

Finally, he quit breathing and his alien body relaxed. Just as had happened last time, his body seemed to melt and reform into a UFO-like alien, although bulkier than most artists' conceptions.

I wanted to roll over and go to sleep. This last fight had taken it out of me.

"Hurry," Rax said. "You must get up. We are under an orbital sensor scan. The Min Ve has found the Guard-ship. He must have locked onto my transporter beam and followed us here."

"What am I supposed to do?" I shouted. "I'm shackled."

"Use the Ungul's weapon," Rax said. "Burn yourself free. Must I do all the thinking for you?"

I was tired, which meant I wasn't at my best. A person can only take so much before he snaps.

I snarled to myself, and in a black rage, I searched for the raygun. Recklessly, I beamed the shackles binding my ankles. They parted soon, leaving melted globs of metal on the floor. Then I shouted and danced with pain as the rest of the heated metal burned my ankles.

"Hurry to the control room," Rax said.

I ran, hopped at the same time, to reach the control room. As I entered, a rod slashed through the water in front of the ship. Another struck, a third, fourth and then five more in a group.

The ship shuddered.

"We're hit," Rax said.

I leaped for the controls, turning on the shield.

"Faster," Rax said. "The Min Ve is launching a hell-burner."

That doused my rage as if someone had tossed a bucket of ice water onto me. I threw myself into the piloting chair, constantly twisting up so I could use both hands—they were still chained together.

The process proved very similar to what had happened off the coast of Greenland. We had no way to stop the hell-burner. The Guard-ship was approximately one hundred miles off the Californian coast, and the alien was targeting us with another of his ultra-nuclear weapons.

I wept at my own impotence, hoping that this wouldn't kill too many people, wouldn't wreck the West Coast for years to come. Hopefully, we were far enough out—

"Logan, your mind is wandering."

I focused. I watched the screen and saw the hell-burner descending through the atmosphere for our tiny Guard-ship.

"Now," Rax said, "engage the outer transfer now."

I did. The Guard-ship transferred just like before, and just like before, I witnessed that awful hump of water that meant the detonation of a massive nuclear device. It shot radioactive water into the air. This was terrible. The wind usually blew west onto land from out here. I could hope for a freak wind, but…

From our new location, I slumped in the pilot chair, exhausted.

"Does the Min Ve still have us on his sensors?" I asked.

"I cannot detect that," Rax said. "I think we are hidden for the moment."

I nodded dully as the impact of all this struck me. The western coast of the United States was likely going to get a heavy dose of radiation, to say nothing of all the dead marine creatures.

"We must plan," Rax said.

"Not just yet," I slurred. "First, I need my beauty sleep. Afterward—" I yawned so my jaw made a popping sound. "I'm going to crash. We can talk afterward."

I stumbled to the former Guard agent's sleeping quarters. His bed was too small for me to fit in it comfortably. Before I zonked out, Rax told me about a cutting tool. I used it as my eyelids grew heavier and heavier. Just in time, I rid myself of the wrist shackles and flopped onto the bed, curling up so I could use the tiny space. I fell asleep almost immediately.

-36-

I woke up ravenous, ready to tackle the next problem—and remembered the alien hell-burner off the West Coast.

Feeling sick at heart, I showered. Afterward, I went to the galley and mechanically ate Guard concentrates. I'd have to stock up on Earth food if I was going to keep using the ship.

After burping several times—my gut ached because it was so full—I went to the piloting chamber. Rax was monitoring the sea around us.

"You have slept long and hard," Rax informed me. "Now my curiosity can take no more. Please tell me, Logan. What happened while I was in meditation mode?"

"Before we get started, I have to know what the hell-burner did to California."

"Remarkably little in overall terms," Rax said. "Your aboriginal friends have acquired luck."

"I don't know about that. Surely, the event has to be in the news."

"Explain this to me," Rax said.

I did. Shortly thereafter, we cruised near the surface as Rax picked up human-generated signals. We watched Fox News, switching to CNN later. They were covering the nuclear detonation, all right. The going consensus among the talking heads and their military experts was that the North Koreans had done it. I could understand their thinking, although I doubted the Communists over there had a nuke that big.

What surprised me was that the U.N. was having an emergency session. Normally, people didn't react this fast. Then again, normally no one was firing hell-burners into the world's oceans. The President of the United States was going to address the U.N. and list his demands regarding the North Koreans. The veiled hint was Chinese collusion with the mad Koreans.

"If I don't help to put a stop to this," I said, "the last hell-burner could be the spark that launches a world war."

"Your species does love to quarrel," Rax said, sounding superior.

"After watching the Unguls in action, I'd say that makes Earthmen about average."

"That is an interesting comment," Rax said. "You are the first person I have ever heard comparing his species to Unguls. Most Galactic races would consider that a demeaning insult."

"Why don't you shove it?"

"What causes this excessive irritation, Logan?"

"Are you kidding me? The President is ready to go to war. I wonder what the Greenland nuke has done to world opinion. The people of Earth must believe there is a vast conspiracy taking place. I have to go public with what I know."

"I have already told you that that is against Guard policy," Rax said.

"Screw Guard policy," I said. "I have to avert a nuclear war."

"The best way to do that is to stop the Min Ve. That is why the Galactic Guard is here."

I blinked at Rax. Was that the right move? How could I know? I guess I couldn't *know*. I'd have to make an educated guess.

"According to your pulse rate, you are finally calming down," Rax said. "That is wise. Hotheaded decisions are seldom the right ones."

I grunted, as that made sense.

"If you could tell me what transpired in Nevada," Rax said, "I would appreciate it. I seem to have lost time, and I certainly woke up far from where I began meditation mode."

I looked at Rax. Finally, I turned off the news. I'd heard enough. Maybe the little crystal was right. If I told the world about the Min Ve, there would be worldwide panic. I would make things worse, not better. The U.N. and the U.S. President could deal with the human crisis. I had to concentrate on the alien problem.

"I don't think you were in meditation mode," I said. "It was a lot freakier than that. Here's what happened."

I told Rax everything. I expected him to interrupt. He did not. The little crystal absorbed my words. Finally, I finished the tale, and then drained a glass of water.

"That is an astounding story," Rax said. "I am intrigued that your friend Parker Gaines felt evil in the white tower. You felt evil in the Greenland complex. It is possible the two are connected."

"I agree," I said.

"I would suggest the white structure is not a tower, however, but an ancient, grounded spaceship."

"You could be right," I said. "That makes more sense. It must have landed a long time ago, right?"

"I believe so," Rax said. "I have analyzed your tale in varying degrees. It holds logically. It is consistent with my—do you believe I was dead while out of phase at Far Butte?"

"I hadn't thought about that," I said. "But if you were dead, by what mechanism did you come back to life?"

"That is an excellent question," Rax said. "It would imply I was not dead, but in some form of suspended animation."

"Yeah," I said.

"I detect sadness in you."

"I'm sad and pissed," I said.

"You desire to find your new friend Debby?"

"Yeah," I said. "But how do I do that? Did the Min Ve blast them with orbital rods? It doesn't appear the Organizer launched a hell-burner at Nevada. We would have heard about that on the news. If the Min Ve didn't blast the tower, did the tower go back out of phase, and if it did, how can we return there?"

"We must use a spy drone's passive sensors to discover the present situation," Rax said.

I stood, walked to the hatch, turned around and walked back to the pilot's chair. I did that twenty more times.

"Does the pacing stimulate your thinking?" Rax asked.

I chewed on my lower lip. I remembered Debby's lips against mine. I remembered what she felt like pressed against my body. The other half of the time, rage tried to bubble up in a comment or have me strike a piece of delicate Guard equipment. I resisted both impulses. Yet another half of the time, I felt my impotence. The fourth half couldn't believe I was in such a crazy situation. Yes, that was far too many halves. But this was such an unbelievable problem. Could Debby really be lost, stuck out of phase in an ancient spaceship grounded at Far Butte? Had she really said her dad had died during Operation Ripper in 1951? Was the world on the verge of a nuclear exchange?

I focused on Rax, the sole representative of the Galactic Guard on Earth.

"Debby told me she polished an ornament inside the white ship. She said the ornament had cracks. She also said that sometimes, people in Far Butte found the right kind of crystal, and she inserted the crystal into a matrix, trying to repair the ornament."

"We must concentrate all our efforts against the Organizer," Rax said, "not worry about these side issues."

"I don't know if that's right," I said. "The ornament sounds important to me."

"Nonsense," Rax said. "Regarding the Organizer—"

"You wouldn't be trying to avoid talking about this ornament, would you?" I asked.

"That is preposterous. Now, if we are going to solve the problem—"

"Rax!" I said.

"There is no need to shout," the crystal said. "I am right here."

"You're trying to derail me."

"Logan, I will have you know—"

"That's not going to work, Rax. The more you try to dodge the issue, the more I want to know about the alien ornament."

"You are wasting precious time with your fixation on Debby. I realize there must be a sexual component to this. We must—"

"What is the alien crystal ornament?" I asked. "Why is it aboard an ancient spaceship hidden in Nevada for who knows how long? Why did it take nuclear weapon tests to wake it up?"

"You cannot expect me to know the secrets of lost expeditions."

"The white ship has something to do with the Polarions, doesn't it?" I asked.

"Not in a linear fashion," Rax said.

"A-ha," I said. "So you do know about the crystal ornament."

Rax did not respond.

"Is the device from Rax Prime?" I asked.

"Logan," the crystal said in a low voice. "We of Rax Prime do not like to air obscene history. It is unseemly and rather embarrassing. If you could desist from your slanderous accusations for a moment…"

I waited.

"I cannot say with one hundred percent accuracy that I know about the crystal ornament Debby described," Rax said.

"But you have an idea, don't you?"

"It is possible."

"That's good enough for me," I said. "What is it?"

"This is a painful topic. I wish you would not pursue it."

"Look, Rax, the Min Ve is dropping hell-burners on Earth, and the President is trigger-happy against the North Koreans and Chinese. Americans are the last people on the planet who will stand for others dropping nukes on them. They're going to demand retribution, which means the Earth is sitting on a powder keg. Okay. You don't like airing dirty laundry. I get that. Who does? But I have to know the scoop. I'm the military man between us."

"That is incorrect. I am the strategist and tactician."

"Wrong," I said. "I'm the man with the gun and the one who flies the Guard-ship. In the end, I have to approve all plans or they don't get done. Now, I know you have data on the white ship and its crystal ornament. I need that data if I'm going to make a righteous combat decision."

"It appears I must defer to your will," Rax said. "I find that painful, indeed. You are an aboriginal, and I am the certified Guard Unit Advisor. I advise you to forgo your unusual—"

"You're starting to piss me off," I said, interrupting.

"While I lack bodily functions, I, too, feel a surge of dislike within my matrix regarding you. If you continue this line with me—"

"Are you going to tell me or not?" I asked. "No more beating around the bush. I want you to talk or to tell me you're not talking."

"I will talk, but with extreme reluctance."

"Noted," I said.

"I will tell you but only because I have come to believe you will stubbornly refuse to continue assisting me otherwise."

I folded my arms across my chest, waiting.

"In ancient times," Rax said, "the Polarions fashioned incredible weaponry and tools. That is the myth. Certainly, no one in Galactic Civilization knows how to put a place out of phase as apparently happened to us. I suspect the Min Ve would dearly like to get his hands on such mythical technology. The Galactic Guard could use that, as well."

"Makes sense," I said. "But what does that have to do with the crystal device on the ship?"

Rax hesitated for just a second before beginning.

"Long ago, the legend goes, a Polarion wished to augment his already considerable powers. They all vied with each other in creating incredible devices. One of them came to Rax Prime. He discovered interesting properties to the crystals growing in the shallow seas of the middle continent. The Polarion experimented with the crystals…

"The Polarion became enamored with the crystals. He built a cyclopean laboratory and giant stone machines. There, he labored for many centuries, slowly bringing the crystals to a form of sentience. Some have claimed it was a blasphemous act. Yet how can that be, for I would not have been formed otherwise."

"There you go," I said.

“Others suggest that the Polarion went mad with his idea,” Rax said, as if he hadn’t heard my comment. “His crowning achievement was a vast dome of unique crystal, combining many like me into a harmonious matrix. It was a labor of love across many years, and it involved a masterful use of symmetry to augment the giant crystal’s intelligence and power.

“The dome wasn’t strictly alive yet, and it wasn’t meant to act alone. Instead, while wearing a crystal circuit, the Polarion would link himself to the dome. It would act like an exoskeleton, as it were, but instead of augmenting the Polarion’s muscles, it would augment his intelligence and power.”

“What happened?” I asked.

“The legend asserts that there was a time of brilliance. The Polarion took his crystal creation with him, doing what Polarions did in the early times of the universe. I am only privy to vague data as to what those activities entailed.

“Alas,” Rax said, “there is a record of an accident. I do not know the nature of the accident, but it weakened the Polarion. It strengthened the crystal dome, the ornament. More years passed, and the legend speaks of the crystal gaining dominance over the Polarion. In the end, the master became the slave, and the crystal dome became overbearing in its desire for power.

“Other Polarions joined against the creature that had once been the greatest of them. The creative Polarion was a puppet to what the others now referred to as the Starcore.”

Rax grew quiet.

“It’s not made from a star, though,” I said. “It’s a giant crystal dome, right?”

“Not just a crystal dome, but a special ornament with perfect symmetry and function. It grew in strength and ambition, but it also overreached.

“There was a long war between the Polarions and the Starcore. I have heard it said that the puppet died. In its creator’s place, the Starcore took other living creatures, uniting with them to give it full power. It had to have this union with a biological entity in order to function at full efficiency.”

“That’s different from you, right?” I asked.

"I, and others like me, are seared into our armored sheathing," Rax said. "One of the reasons for this is so we can never augment ourselves. We are crystals, and crystals can grow sometimes. I cannot grow. Thus, I am at the strength that I am. This limitation helps me to remain humble, which gives me proportion.

"One of your great Earth thinkers had an adage about this. 'Power corrupts, and absolute power corrupts absolutely.'"

I tapped my chin with a forefinger. "Does this Starcore have anything to do with Neanderthals and apish hominids?"

"I believe so," Rax said. "According to the ancient legend, the Starcore fashioned an empire of underlings, using them as slaves. What you call Neanderthals and hominids were merely its ship slaves, creatures to fly and fight as the Starcore expanded its realm."

"Why did we see Polarions, Neanderthals and prehistoric hominids in stasis tubes in Greenland?" I asked.

"I do not know the precise reason," Rax said. "But now realizing that you might have stumbled onto the Starcore, I would hazard a guess. The Starcore's servants built the Greenland complex. It must have put those servants into stasis for some long-lost reason. Likely, the Earth was its last outpost in an ancient empire. It may well be that those in the stasis tubes were its last servants of that distant era."

I sat down because I was starting to see implications here that I did not like.

"Are you saying the Starcore purposely hid itself in an out-of-phase location?" I asked.

"That could be a possibility," Rax said. "Or maybe the crystal's last slave killed himself while they were out of phase so the Starcore could never again run amok in the universe."

"Why would the nuclear explosions in 1951 have woken the crystal?" I asked.

"That seems simple enough to theorize," Rax said. "The nuclear explosions penetrated into the out-of-phase place. It was enough to begin something."

My eyes widened as I thought about a grim possibility. "Do you think the Starcore is using Debby as its personal slave in order to give it its unholy life?"

"The possibility exists," Rax said.

I began to pace again.

"I'm sure you've heard the old question about God," I said. "Can He make a rock heavier than He can lift?"

"I have not heard about that dilemma," Rax said. "It is an interesting query, though."

"Not really," I said. "The question comes from the belief that God can do anything. But if that's true, can He make a situation He can't handle. God is supposed to be all-powerful, right? But if He's perfectly knowledgeable, by definition He wouldn't make a situation He couldn't handle. Because if He couldn't handle a situation, He would no longer be the all-powerful God."

"Given that there is such a being," Rax said.

"Sure," I said. "That's not my point. God wouldn't be God if He could make something He couldn't handle. That shows me these Polarions were never gods."

"I simply likened them to Earth gods before to help you understand them."

"No," I said. "You told me certain Galactic races worship them."

"Yes, I suppose I did."

"Well, this Starcore shows me the Polarions were never gods, as at least one of them made a situation that burst out of his control."

"What is your point?" Rax asked.

"It's an observation," I said. "If the Polarions weren't gods, they made an imperfect weapon."

"Has my tale unhinged your thinking process?" Rax asked. "I would almost say that you are blathering about nothing at this point."

I hardly heard him. "I'm beginning to wonder if some of the Greenland personnel escaped onto the Earth before the rest entered the stasis tubes. Maybe those individuals were the first people on Earth. Wouldn't that be crazy?"

"It is a remote possibility, I suppose," Rax said. "But it is certainly not germane to our problem at hand."

"Everything in germane," I said, "as it might help us figure out how to defeat the Starcore."

"The Min Ve could defeat the crystal if he could rain orbital rods against the white ship."

"Problem solved," I said.

"But I doubt the Min Ve would willingly do such a thing," Rax said. "Likely, he will desire the Starcore above all else. The promise of great power often drives people to reckless endeavors. If the Min Ve takes the Starcore, the ancient crystal will surely be free again. The crystal entity outsmarted the greatest of the Polarions. It will have no problem outthinking the Min Ve and its crew."

I thought about that. "Maybe that's the answer. Let's help the Min Ve take the Starcore. Once the Min Ve leaves with his prize, Earth is rid of both of them."

"That is an extremely provincial outlook," Rax said in a scolding tone. "Eventually, the threat of the Starcore could come back to haunt Earth. It would likely use the Earth as a steppingstone for further conquests. Instead of being rid of the problem, it could make a bigger one the two of us could never hope to stop."

I shook my head. I couldn't believe I'd sent Debby back into the Starcore's hands. I—

"What makes the Starcore so powerful?" I asked. "I mean, if it's simply power hungry…"

"The Polarion fashioned a unique weapon. The Starcore has unique powers."

"That's what I'm getting at," I said. "What kind of powers?"

"I believe it is able to tap into the cosmic energy of the universe."

"What is that?" I asked.

"The basic form of energy binding the universe together," Rax said.

"You lost me with that one."

"I suspect the crystal's ability to use cosmic energy was severed sometime in the past. Otherwise, it would never have needed to hide from its enemies. Perhaps that is the process Debby has been engaged in all these years."

"What do you mean?"

"Some of the ornament's crystals cracked. Debby has been replacing them since 1966 would be my guess. Yet no Earth crystal could take the place of a Rax Prime crystal. Thus, the Starcore must lack its full potential. The great danger then is that its vessel regains a space drive and goes to Rax Prime to replenish itself."

I stood there stunned, staring at the little crystal.

"What is wrong?" Rax asked.

"The Min Ve thinks he came to Earth to find some legendarily powerful weapon. Instead, the Starcore must believe this is the chance of a millennium to finally start anew in the universe, to leave Earth and reenter space."

"Yes," Rax said. "That is true."

I kept staring at the metal-encased crystal. I wondered if he was in secret league with the Starcore. After a time, I realized that was the wrong fear. Maybe Debby had played me for a fool. Maybe she had stayed young since 1966 because she was the Starcore's tool. I didn't want to believe that—and I didn't know it was true. But given everything Rax had told me, it made the most sense.

I sat down at the controls. This was going to take some deep thinking. Because whatever we did next, it would be best for humanity if we made the wisest move possible.

-37-

I sat hunched over the spy-drone screen Rax used to show me what was going on at the Far Butte site. All I saw was windblown sand and yellow grasses swaying on the slopes.

"Nothing," I said. "I think the Starcore is still out of phase."

"Notice the tracks down there at the bottom of the hill."

I tapped the screen, zooming in, soon seeing tank tracks. I followed them until they abruptly disappeared.

"What's causing the tracks to appear and disappear?" I asked.

"The out-of-phase mechanism appears to be malfunctioning," Rax said. "I suspect the crippled Starcore doesn't know everything the completed crystal of the past knew. According to my calculations, its symmetry has more than a mere esthetic purpose."

"What's that mean in plain English?" I asked.

"The crystal or ornament's symmetry gives it its power and its intellect. It is a crystalline intelligence, after all. Our symmetry is critical."

"Why?"

"That is the wrong question for now," Rax said. "How that affects our strategy is more important."

"I guess so," I said. "Your point is that it's not thinking straight."

"Do you mean that as a pun?"

"What? No. It's a saying. The thing has been trying to recreate itself, hasn't it?"

"I do not follow your reasoning."

"I once saw a bronze statue in Napa, California, during a car show there in August."

"What bearing could that possibly have on our dilemma?"

"That statue reminded me of Michelangelo's David. It had that look, is what I'm saying. Anyway, the statue of a man had a mallet and chisel, and was in the process of carving himself out of stone. The statue was called, 'The Self-Made Man.'"

"Yes, I see," Rax said.

"That's what the Starcore has been trying to do. Yet, how does one make oneself? It's arrogance."

"True, as we all have a creator."

"Right," I said. "The Starcore must have blind spots it doesn't even realize anymore."

"That may not make a difference," Rax said. "The crystal was brilliant in ages past, almost as powerful as the rest of the Polarions combined. Even crippled, it will still make a formidable opponent."

"Yet, if it was using Debby," I said, "it made a mistake. If it wanted to capture me, I still managed to escape."

"Unless it wanted you to escape for reasons we cannot understand."

"We're screwed if it's that smart." I sat back and threw up my hands. "This is getting us nowhere. Why not move the spy drone and see what's happening at Station 5?"

"That will be a matter of moments," Rax said. "I have already taken the drone higher than before. I will begin a sensor sweep—Logan, do you see that?"

I bent toward the screen. It was difficult to credit my eyesight.

Five hover-pads like those I'd seen in Greenland zoomed across the desert sand, kicking up dust as they flew inches above the ground. That wasn't the incredible part. Small hominids were riding the hover-pads. The proto-humans were furry like dogs, their fur ruffling due to the speed. Each of the apelike humanoids clutched a pulse-rifle like the one I'd used in Greenland.

"It would appear I miscalculated concerning the radioactive levels at the Greenland site," Rax said. "Some of the hominids have clearly been revived and armed themselves with ancient weaponry. It appears the Starcore is attempting to storm Station 5."

"Why would it do that?" I asked.

"That is an excellent question. Possibly, the Min Ve is about to use the station against the Starcore. The crystalline intelligence must be trying to thwart that."

I could just imagine the news flash if someone from CNN saw the apish hominids in action. Could the Starcore have teleported them from Greenland to Nevada, or had there been hominids and hover-pads stashed aboard the ancient white ship and finally been taken out of storage?

As we watched, orbital rods rained down upon the hover-pads. Each rod possessed tremendous kinetic energy like a meteor. Space meteors could wreak horrible damage if they hit. Neither rods nor meteors needed any extra explosive force to destroy things. The force of the strikes was enough. The nearby rod-impacts made the crafts wobble wildly. Then a rod hit a hover-pad and obliterated it and its occupants. The shockwave upset the rest of the hovers, toppling the hominids onto the desert sand. The next few seconds ended any sign of them or their advanced weaponry, as more rods annihilated everything with repeated kinetic blasts. Finally, perhaps to hide any evidence, a new kind of rod struck the ground. A gigantic fireball devoured everything, leaving blackened soil and glassy lumps of fused sand.

"Wow," I said. "That was weird."

"The last rod was composed of dense uranium," Rax said. "That is what produced the incendiary blast. The white-hot metal vapor ignited upon the rod's impact. This strike was highly informative."

"Because you're a master strategist you understand every implication?" I asked.

"I do not rate as highly as that. In comparison to anyone on Earth, I am a *masterful* strategist. I believe that was the term I used before."

"Sure thing," I said. "What does all this tell you?"

"Station 5 must be critical to battering down the white ship's out-of-phase protection. The Starcore wishes to forestall that. Perhaps as interesting, it seems to have acquired teleportation technology."

"Why's that interesting?" I asked. "Didn't the ancient Polarions possess teleportation devices?"

"I have been taught otherwise," Rax said. "Still, if the Min Ve can force the white ship into normal phase that may give us an opening."

"To do what?" I asked.

"Perhaps we could teleport an explosive device onto the white ship, one sufficiently powerful to destroy it."

"You're that frightened of the Starcore?" I asked.

"I am petrified of the Starcore. If it can repair itself with Rax Prime crystals, it might lead to an intergalactic war of immense proportions. Better to throttle the beast in its cradle, as it were."

"More like drive a stake through its heart in its coffin," I said. "This is a resurrected evil, not a newborn thing. It might have slumbered for the rest of eternity if American scientists hadn't woken it up again with their nukes."

"Whatever metaphor we use," Rax said, "the point is to destroy it now while it is weak."

"Got you," I said. "But I can't agree to that until we rescue Debby."

"Logan, you are far too emotional. You must trust me—"

"Look, Rax, no offense. I like you. But you are a crystal. Emotions help make us human. I'm not a machine, and I can't simply murder a friend of mine and hope to live with myself. I have to rescue her."

"What if she has united with the Starcore? What if she used you earlier?"

I could see Rax's point about that. Samson had loved Delilah and it had proven his undoing. Cleopatra led Mark Anthony down the road to his destruction and Paris kidnapped Helen of Troy and brought about the obliteration of everything he loved. Sometimes the chick was a deceiver. But sometimes she brought out the best in a man. I know modern mores hated the idea of the damsel in distress. But damnit, some things were more important than fashionable or unfashionable ideas.

Sometimes the old ways were the real ways—they had gotten that way because of reality.

"What if Debby is the Starcore's slave?" I asked. "What if it has tricked her all this time?"

"You barely met her," Rax said. "You can't risk your planet for a woman."

"Debby came for me in the jail. If she hadn't taken the risk, the sheriff would have taken me for a ride and shot me in the back of the head out in the desert."

"Is that true or was that simply her story to make you trust her?" Rax asked.

The sheriff had beaten me up for no good reason at the diner. The killer robot had been coming back to the jailhouse as Debby and I had tried to escape.

"I can't give you a definitive answer," I said. "But I do know what my gut is telling me. I have to go back for her if there's a chance to rescue her. Parker took a risk on me. So did Debby. I pay my debts, Rax. That's who I am."

"This is about choosing the best strategy," Rax said.

"Jawing about this isn't going to change my mind. Can we do it? That's the question. It doesn't seem as if the white ship has a shield as our ship does. Thus, you should be able to teleport me inside the vessel."

"Your plan is too dangerous. My bomb idea—"

"I'll compromise," I said. "Give me a Guard weapon. Then teleport me into the white ship and give me thirty minutes to rescue Debby. If I fail by that time, send your bomb."

"This is all theoretical," Rax said, "as the white ship is still out of phase. If you'll notice the screen, the spy-drone's passive scan cannot penetrate Station 5's shielding. So we have no idea what the Min Ve is trying to attempt from there."

I sat stock still for a moment. I tried to think this through logically. We had a Guard-ship, an insertion vessel. We could not slug it out toe-to-toe with the orbital vessel. Our singular advantage seemed to be our advanced teleporting system. I had a plan that would use that, and would possibly help thwart the more dangerous of the two problems, the Starcore.

"I'm right," I told Rax. "My plan is a good one. Look. Maybe Debby is conspiring with the Starcore. It would make sense after a fashion. Why is she so young after more than sixty years in that strange realm? The Starcore has been keeping her young for a reason. At the same time, I believe Debby was being genuine. If she is in league with the crystal, I'm betting it's not on a completely conscious level."

"You're conceding my point," Rax said.

"I'm not," I said. "I'm saying Debby's actions toward me are a tiny foothold for us. We have to exploit our one tiny advantage to the max."

"What is this advantage?"

"She has feelings for me."

It was Rax's turn to think silently. "Perhaps you are correct," he said at last. "She is an emotional creature like you. Yet, as I said earlier, this is all moot. We don't have—"

"The Starcore sent those smaller hominids at Station 5," I said. "The logical reason was to try to stop Station 5 from doing whatever it's doing. The most rational course for Station 5 is to be doing something to batter down the Starcore's camouflage protection—the out-of-phase cloaking. We should be ready to jump whenever an opportunity presents itself. If we're wrong about Station 5's purpose, we haven't lost anything by being ready."

"Your thinking is convoluted at best," Rax said. "Yet, there is a modicum of reasoning behind it. Very well, let us attempt your plan, as there is some strategical sense to it. About that Guard weapon, though…"

-38-

Rax relented in one particular regarding the advanced weaponry. He let me take the Ungul raygun Z21 had delivered into our hands. To my delight, Rax also had a .44 Magnum in the Guard arsenal with plenty of big bullets.

Afterward, we kept watch of the Far Butte area. Finally, three hours and twenty-nine minutes later, something from the direction of Station 5 struck the Far Butte region.

"I'm detecting odd wavelengths," Rax said.

I opened my eyes and adjusted the piloting chair, bringing it back to an upright position.

"What did you say?" I asked sleepily.

"Do you notice the screen?" Rax said.

I rubbed my eyes and concentrated. I didn't see anything at first. Then I noticed the haziness.

"Can you tell me what's happening?" I asked.

"You are observing advanced physics at play," Rax said. "I doubt my scientific explanation would enlighten you to any degree, as those equations are above your head. That the Min Ve has such equipment suggests he knew about the out of phase ahead of time. The Canopus dig must have told him more than I realized."

"Is whatever the Min Ve is attempting working?" I asked.

"To a degree," Rax said.

"Do you see the white tower?"

"It is a spaceship," Rax said.

"Fine," I said. "Do you see it?"

"I detect a hazy imagine of what might be the ship. It is not yet concrete enough for me to risk your teleportation aboard it."

I licked my lips. "Maybe we should try it anyway."

"You might die if I don't do it correctly."

"I don't want to die," I said quietly.

"There!" Rax said. "The Mirror Effect is working. I see the ship. Notice, the Min Ve is attacking the ship directly. That surprises me, but I understand his greed."

Big red beams shot down from space. Armed Unguls appeared on the ground in the circular area of the beams.

"Go!" Rax said. "Go to the transporter. I will put you inside the ship if I am able. Fortunately for us, the Min Ve's transporters are much more primitive than my Guard equipment. I do not believe he can directly teleport his soldiers into the ship. That is why he must attack it from the outside."

I ran for the transporter, wondering if this was insanity. Who was I compared to Galactic privateers, ancient Starcore members, Polarions and the possible first people that had landed on Earth ages ago?

I stood on the transporter dais, panting, waiting.

"Rax," I said. "Are we going to…?" I stopped talking as everything around me began to fade.

***

I appeared on a similar dais but in a different setting. This place had gleaming metal for the floor, walls and ceiling. A squat Neanderthal in a white smock stood behind a console. He had a broad, flat nose, a low forehead and a head full of hair that would have been the envy of any Hollywood movie star.

I wondered if there was something attracting in these teleporting pads. Did such a pad draw teleporting rays the way a tall spire would attract a lightning bolt or a magnet attracted metal?

The Neanderthal looked up, and crinkle lines appeared on his low forehead.

I pointed the raygun at him. "Where's Debby?"

"This section is off-limits to you." He spoke in an Ungul-like monotone without any odd accent. In fact, he sounded like a machine. Could the Neanderthal be another robot like Walt? "Remain where you are," he told me. "I will transport you outside."

"Do you see my raygun?" I said, as I jumped off the transporter pad.

"I do," he said. "You must immediately set the weapon on the floor and step back onto the dais."

"I'm going to kill you unless you do exactly as I say."

"The Starcore would disapprove," he said. "Thus, your threat is illegal here. Step onto the dais as I have instructed you—"

I beamed him in the chest because I couldn't see his hands, and I feared others would come charging through at any second. Besides, I'd given him fair warning.

The Neanderthal glowed and turned into the appropriate pile of fumy ashes soon enough. I stopped beaming and staggered around the console where he'd been standing.

The panel had colored tabs, screens and controls. On one of the screens, I saw Unguls setting up artillery-like cannons outside the white ship. A door opened in the white tower—in the spaceship—and Far Butte people with shotguns and lever-action Winchesters charged the aliens. Parker led them as red disintegrator beams began cutting down humans.

I took a second look. Yes, it was the old biker. Parker was alive, blasting away with his pump shotgun. What had happened to Walt the Sheriff Robot? I shook my head. I didn't have any more time to ponder this. I had to find Debby before my thirty minutes expired.

I pressed an important-looking tab. The screen showing the Unguls and Far Butte humans went blank. The lights on what I took to be the teleport dais went dark, as did the majority of the console's lights.

My palms were slick with sweat as I looked around. There was a hatch behind me. I wiped sweat off my forehead, took a deep breath—and began coughing from the stink of the disintegrated Neanderthal.

I headed for the hatch, found a lever and moved it. Cautiously, I opened the hatch, peering out.

I spied a gleaming steel corridor. There were hatches everywhere along it. I stepped out with the raygun ready. Slowly, I approached the closest hatch. It had a similar lever to the first one. I turned it, pushed open the hatch and peered into a room full of humming machinery. A smell of ozone hung in the air. I kept staring, but found nothing insightful.

I closed the hatch, moved down the corridor and looked into the next chamber.

Three more Neanderthals stood at various controls. One made adjustments. The other spoke in clicks and whistles, while the third seemed to be asleep on his feet.

I must have been more nervous than I realized. With hardly a thought, I began beaming them, starting with the one making the clicks and whistles. I thought he might be summoning reinforcements.

I killed all three in short order, feeling guilty doing it. I told myself they were the Starcore's minions. I had no choice in this if I wanted to save the Earth.

An alarm sounded as I closed the hatch. My heart started beating harder than ever, and I found myself short of breath. Where was Debby?

I wanted to roar with frustration. Instead, my lips were frozen into a snarl. I ran to the next hatch, yanked it open and cut down two furry hominids. Each was in the process of slipping a harness clinking with tools or some type of weaponry over his torso.

I'd become like a blood-maddened weasel in a pigeon loft, killing because I knew no better. Something was wrong in my brain. Maybe there were alien pheromones in the air affecting my memory and my intellect so I couldn't remember anything that happened while I was in the white tower—the spaceship.

How could one fight something so strange and preposterous as the Starcore and aliens? It all seemed too huge and complex for one security officer to defeat. Instead of wilting, instead of curling into a corner and whimpering, I got furious. I shouted and swore as I yanked open one hatch after another.

At the seventh hatch, they were waiting for me. I yanked it open, saw them and fired. The red disintegrator ray stopped a centimeter short of a Neanderthal's white smock. He wore a glowing pendant from a chain around his almost nonexistent neck. I let my beam hose him, hoping I could batter down the personal shield. Instead, the shield possessed a secondary quality. A blue blot beginning at the shield traveled along the beam toward my gun. I barely recognized what was happening in time. At the last second, I pitched the raygun into the room and slammed the hatch shut.

Something exploded inside the chamber. I grabbed the handle and jerked my hand away from the intense heat.

"Consider them scratched," I muttered.

I almost continued in my frenzy. The interior explosion had helped clear my head, though. I stood there blinking.

I had to get to the main control area.

I forced myself to run down the corridor. There was a hatch at the end. I opened it and almost jumped through to my death. A small balcony like the kind Benito Mussolini used to make his speeches to Italian crowds was high above a cylindrical expanse.

I stepped out onto the balcony. This must be the top of the ship. I looked down upon many levels that abutted the central shaft. That made me dizzy, so I pulled back.

The hatch lever moved behind me. I squeezed to the side so I would be hidden behind the hatch when it opened. It did so now. A squat Neanderthal with short bowed legs and a long torso stepped onto the balcony, moving toward the rails as the hatch closed. He turned around at the last moment.

I had already begun my bum-rush. Using my right shoulder, I hit him hard, catapulting him over the rails. He was silent as he fell. There were no screams, no curses. He just plummeted down, down, down.

I pulled out the .44, yanked open the hatch and regarded three furry hominids.

Four terrific booms—four shots to the head put down two of the hominids. The last one, I forced back down the corridor.

He watched me closely. He no doubt saw the smoke curling from the barrel of my hand-cannon and realized I held his life in my hands.

"Do you understand my words?" I said.

"You are a demented creature," the hominid said in a monotone. "Surrender your weapon to me. We will apply balm to your mind so you can enjoy the remainder of your life in serenity."

"Thanks for the offer," I said. "Now, I'm going to counter. Show me how to find Debby."

"That is impossible. You must put down your weapon—"

With my thumb, I cocked the hammer, cutting off his speech. "I'm making it possible."

"You lack authority to do so," he said.

What was wrong with these hominids? Had the endless centuries in stasis made them dull-witted?

"Does it bother you that you're about to die?" I asked.

He blinked a few more times as if contemplating the idea. "There is no reason to kill me. I will give you Debby."

"You know who she is?"

"She is a worker you wish to see. More I do not know. Come, we will find Debby. You will go to her, and I will continue in my task."

"Now you're thinking. But I should warn you, if you double-cross me, you will die."

The furry hominid didn't appear to hear me as he turned around, heading along the corridor.

I followed, opening the revolver, taking out the spent cartridges and reloading with new ones from my pocket. I felt marginally better with a loaded gun.

He stopped and pointed at a hatch. "In there. You must go in there."

I remembered the room as having a hot handle. The raygun had exploded in there, or something had gone wrong.

"Open the door," I said.

"You must go in alone," the hominid said.

"Yeah, right," I said. "I don't think so. You open the door and lead the way."

"I am not authorized to enter."

"I'm giving you new authorization."

"You lack the proper certification to do so."

"Then say good-bye to life, buddy-boy," I told him.

He cocked his head as if hearing a message. “I will go in. You will wait out here.”

“What’s wrong with your thinking? Don’t you realize I can kill you at any moment?”

“I know this, yes.”

“So don’t try my patience. Do exactly as I say when I say it, and you might go home to your Starcore tonight.”

He opened the hatch, and an awful stink billowed out. He appeared unfazed by the smell. There was gore splashed against consoles. There were smoking pieces of hominid meat on the floor. Some of the consoles were plastic and had melted like candle wax.

He stopped to study the damage. “This is impressive. You have powerful weaponry. This changes the dynamics of the situation. Perhaps you would like to negotiate with the Starcore.”

“Maybe after I’m done,” I said. “We’re finding Debby, remember?”

“This is more important. The power of your weapons—the Starcore is impressed. It could use the weaponry in its struggle against the—” He made a weird sound that made absolutely no sense to me.

“Quit stalling,” I said. “Show me Debby.”

“Do you not realize the grandeur of the offer?” the hominid said. “This is a chance to change your status. Humans could become serfs instead of slaves. The Master will grant humans serf status with legally binding rights.”

“Wow,” I said, letting the sarcasm drip. “Your master really knows how to sweeten a deal. Earthmen could become your serfs. That takes my breath away.”

“It is grand indeed,” the hominid said in his monotone. “Now, describe in detail how to fashion the weapon you used in this chamber.”

“This is your last chance, Charlie. Show me Debby or you die.”

“That will halt the negotiation.”

I swore at him, unable to take any more of this. I aimed at his head and squeezed the trigger, fully intending to blast him to kingdom come.

The hominid turned around before I gave the trigger enough pressure. He went to a console and began to touch the panel. I eased pressure to see if he would do as I'd ordered.

"Come here," he said. "You must observe the females and indicate Debby to me."

I moved around the console behind him. A screen to his left, embedded in the console, showed various people. I presumed they had come from Far Butte.

"Her?" he asked.

I shook my head.

He tapped the console more, coming to a new scene.

"Her?" he asked.

"Not yet," I said.

We repeated this many times. Where was Debby?

Finally, he stepped back from the console. "Debby is not in the ship. I have shown you all the females."

"Let's try it again," I said.

"It is time to bargain for your weapon."

"One more time," I said.

"You are uncommonly stubborn."

"It's been said," I told him.

He went through the same procedure. I watched him closely this time, seeing what he did with the controls. I'd seen Debby some time ago, but had been trying to figure out the control panel. I distrusted the mind-controlled hominid. He meant to screw me, to help the Starcore screw humanity. The human race wasn't going to be anyone's serf if I could help it.

Finally, as the creature continued to show me images, I shot him in the back of the head. Yeah, it wasn't knightly. But this was for the soul of humanity.

I ran from the chamber back to the one I'd originally entered. The controls here were similar to the ones I'd been watching.

I pressed the tab that had turned everything off before. Lights came on the panels and power hummed all around me.

I wiped the back of my right wrist across my lips. Then, I did what the hominid had done when he'd shown me Debby. The dais glowed as it had earlier.

"Here goes nothing," I whispered.

I ran for the dais, standing on it as the chamber began to fade. I hoped I was about to appear where Debby worked.

-39-

I appeared in a room with gleaming metal. I panned the .44, looking for somebody to shoot, but the place was empty. It was the size of a regular high school classroom but had no furniture, no nothing expect for three closed hatches.

I ran to the left hatch, planning to open it and jump through. Instead, I used the back of my left wrist, feeling the opening lever for residual body heat. I went to the others and did the same. I couldn't feel anything.

Which hatch should I use? I could waste precious time if I went through the wrong one. Would Rax insert his bomb onto the spaceship? It seemed he was wrong about the ancient Polarions lacking teleporting ability.

Stepping back, I regarded the hatches. I decided to do what I'd done all my life during multiple-choice tests. The rule of thumb was to follow your first instinct unless you had a good reason to switch answers.

I went to the leftward hatch, clutched the lever and almost yanked it open. At the last moment, I eased the lever and did the same with the hatch as I opened it.

A round egg clanked at my feet, rolling—

I bent, picked up the egg-shaped thing before it could roll too far and pitched it back. I slammed the hatch shut, almost getting it closed. Then, I heard a crump sound and the hatch blew backward, knocking me onto the metal floor.

I lay there and might have blinked a thousand times in confusion if I'd let myself. Instead, I climbed to my feet before I realized someone had tossed a grenade at me.

I laughed in an unhinged manner, reopening the hatch. I stepped through smoke and spied blasted-apart hominids. Gore dripped down the corridor walls. That had been some grenade.

The smoke stung my eyes, causing them to tear up. I inhaled too much and coughed explosively, finally vomiting and spitting onto the deck. I wanted to get the taste out of my mouth.

In a stagger, I passed the dead hominids—three of them with blackened harnesses on their charred and now hairless bodies. The corridor curved around as I staggered faster.

A side hatch opened. I fired at the hominid poking his head through. He dropped with a big hole in his forehead.

I stepped over the dying creature and entered what looked like a surveillance room. Screens showed various chambers—horror chambers. Unguls were strapped to different types of restraints. Needles jabbed some of them. Electrodes were attached to others. Some writhed in agony. Some screamed with their faces turning stark colors. A few of the screens showed Neanderthals in white lab coats regarding the tortured aliens. Each of the men held slates, jotting down notes.

I finally saw Debby. She stood behind a lab-coated Neanderthal. The scientist hunched over a prone man, delicately slicing open a portion of the man's chest. The scientist must have spoken, because Debby mechanically picked a small round item off a tray, handing it to him.

I tried to study her face. It seemed wooden, hypnotized perhaps.

I felt soiled witnessing this. I hated the Starcore. This was monstrous. It was evil.

I noticed a symbol under the screen showing Debby.

While heading for the hatch… I halted, turned to the main security console and began tapping. I had no idea what these controls did, but what the heck, I was a monkey throwing my own kind of wrench into the system.

A klaxon blared.

Feeling righteously murderous, I dashed out of the room and sprinted down the corridor. I noticed symbols by the hatches. It was some kind of numbering system.

I sprinted until the klaxon's blare lessened, until I panted from the exertion. Finally, I quit running and walked as fast as I could. Sweat dripped from my face and my side hurt.

Eventually, I saw the symbol I'd been looking for. I tried the opening lever. It wouldn't move.

I put my mouth by the hatch where it touched the wall and shouted as loudly as I could, "Debby! Do you hear me? Open the hatch, Debby! Open the hatch!"

It was a long shot. I hammered on the hatch with the butt of the .44. I bellowed some more. I hammered—

I heard a click. The lever moved.

Jumping back, I raised the .44, holding it with two hands. The hatch swung open. I licked my upper teeth, readying to blast—

Debby stared at me with blood smeared across her face. She blinked with incomprehension, tried to form words and collapsed across the bottom of the portal opening.

-40-

I would have stopped and inspected her, but the stakes were too high for me to indulge my more tender emotions just yet.

I leaped across her, landing in an antechamber. Motion caught my eye. A man with hairy forearms and blood oozing from his chest advanced in a staggering lurch. I recognized him from the diner. When he saw me, he did a one-eighty, staggering away.

I shot him, and he toppled through an entrance into another area. The dying man tried to drag himself across the floor. I ran up, expecting others.

A Neanderthal in a white lab coat rushed me from around the entrance. He held a spark-emitting rod, silently thrusting it. The end of the rod connected with my chest. A terrific shock jolted, knocking me off my feet, sending the .44 skittering across the floor.

I groaned, managed to open my eyes enough to see the Neanderthal coming at me, and tried to slide away.

"You are dangerous," the Neanderthal said in a monotone. "You are an amok man sentenced to immediate death. I therefore adjust the setting so."

He twisted the bottom of the rod so it sparked more fiercely.

I scrambled to my feet, pulling out my flick-knife. I trembled with exhaustion as the spring-assisted blade snapped into position.

"Surrender," the Neanderthal said.

“You surrender,” I said in a slur. The shock had affected me more than I realized.

He advanced on me with the shock rod held out like a sword. I circled around him as I dragged my left foot. He stopped, looked at the .44 on the floor—

I charged as fast as I could, hoping to stab him. He turned and lashed at me with the rod. I desperately twisted and barely avoided what I imagined was the killing stroke.

He jabbed. I scrambled back, tripping over my bad foot and sprawling onto the floor. I hit my left elbow hard, jarring it, making pain flare up the forearm. Even so, I crawled backward on my back to get out of range of the probing rod.

He stopped. I began getting up—he lunged faster than he had before. I threw myself back as the rod reached for me. It touched my jacket and emitted a spark that hit me in the face. I yelled, and he might have had me there.

Debby screamed as she leaped onto his back, trying to bear him onto the floor. He twisted around and began bringing up the rod to touch her with it.

I threw myself at him, stabbing him in the chest. My momentum threw him back against a wall, and Debby grunted in pain, caught between him and the wall. His rod hit the wall, and it exploded with a sizzle of raw power.

That knocked all three of us onto the floor. Debby went rolling. The Neanderthal landed flat on his chest, and I hit my side.

I was groggy and a raw burnt odor filled the room. The Neanderthal regarded me, his half-charred face oozing blood. He no longer held the rod. It lay on the floor, looking as if it had short-circuited.

“You are destructive,” he said in the same monotone as before.

I hurt. I was scared of losing, and I still feared that bastard of a shock rod. This Neanderthal had proven more deadly than the rest. I came at him on my hands and knees. He watched me. Maybe he couldn’t move. Maye he was playacting. I had no idea. Probably at this point, I didn’t care. I retrieved my knife and stabbed him in his good eye, killing him.

Afterward, I crawled on my hands and knees to Debby. She was breathing, but she looked dead-beat. I checked her for cuts. I couldn't find away.

"Are you okay?" I asked.

She frowned severely at me.

"Logan," I said. "It's me, Logan. You know me from Far Butte."

The frown deepened, which hadn't seemed possible.

"You work in the white tower, remember?" I said.

She opened her mouth, trying to speak.

"Did you hear me calling you from the other side of the hatch?" I asked.

She began blinking, finally nodding.

I went for my gun then, climbing to my feet. With the .44 ready, I checked the larger chamber.

It had a high ceiling, with big lights that were turned off, and was crammed with medical equipment along the walls and what looked like old-style computer banks. In the center of the room was a table with a naked man strapped to it. An overturned cart with various scattered surgical tools lay nearby.

With my .44 ready, I approached the torture table. What looked like an electrical wire had been partly inserted up the man's left forearm. The wire was attached to an electrical box on a stand. He wore a half-mask that covered his mouth and nose. Anatomically, he looked human with good musculature and white hair. If he was the same man that I had seen on the screen earlier, the cut on his chest was no longer there.

His eyes were closed at first. Maybe he heard me, as he opened his eyes. They were starkly blue. He stared at me for a long moment before closing them again.

I removed the mask. Something hissed from it. I followed the tube line attached to the mask to a tank. I turned the tank's valve, stopping whatever gas they'd been feeding him.

I looked at the wire in his forearm and hated it. I put one hand on his wrist, grabbed the wire and yanked it out.

He moaned and opened his eyes again.

"You okay?" I asked.

He stared at me with incomprehension.

"Yeah, you're beat," I said.

I studied the table, soon unlatching him from it. I wondered how much time we had before Rax sent his bomb, the Starcore sent reinforcements or the Organizer's Unguls won through onto the ship. Seeing that he was alive, I went back to Debby.

She sat up against a wall, hugging herself.

"Get up," I said in as close to a monotone as I could, trying to sound like the Neanderthal.

She stood up obediently. I wasn't sure I liked that. What did it mean concerning her free will?

"Stand here and wait," I said.

She stood stiffly.

I opened the hatch and glanced down the corridor both ways. I couldn't see anyone. I shut the hatch and locked the lever.

"Stay with me," I told Debby.

She moved behind me as I reentered the scientific torture chamber.

The naked man stood behind the torture table with blood running down his forearm. He had an alien gun, and he fired at me as I entered.

-41-

The shot scored the wall to my left, leaving a big smoking hole.

"Stop!" I shouted. "We're friends. I'm the one who let you off the table."

I don't know why I thought he was free from the Starcore's control. It must have been his face. It was twisted with agony. The others—the Neanderthals, apish hominids and Far Butte people—had all had wooden faces. I must have instinctively believed the Starcore controlled them.

The naked man aimed the gun at me. He reached out with his other hand, steadying it. He looked dazed and confused but seemed determined.

"Can't you recognize me?" I said. "I just released you from the table."

He kept aiming, blinking, aiming— "Friend?" he asked.

"Yeah," I said, slapping my chest.

He flinched at that, and I figured he would fire by instinct.

"Take it easy," I said. "I'm Logan from Earth. I was trapped in Far Butte earlier. I think we're still on the Starcore's spaceship."

Some of the confusion left his eyes. He lowered the gun, setting it on the torture table. Then, he looked around, saw something and headed for it.

I almost lunged for the alien gun or raised my .44 at him. Instead, I watched. He went to a crumpled uniform in a corner.

He grabbed it, shoved his feet inside and soon closed his metallic looking one-piece. It had several stars as adornment.

Could he be one of the Polarions I'd seen several days ago in a Greenland stasis tube? It seemed likely. If the Starcore had been reviving the Neanderthals and hominids, why not the Polarions—who I'd taken to be Polarions, in any case.

The man looked at me. He had clear blue, intelligent-seeming eyes, and there was something else as well. It wasn't quite arrogance. Maybe it was majesty. He seemed higher than I was, regal, perhaps. It was obvious that he figured he was the highest-ranking person in the room.

He moved back to the gun, picked it up and walked past me to the hatch. He didn't look back to see if I was following him. He opened the hatch, poked his head through, looking both ways, and hurried into the corridor.

"Stay with me," I told Debby.

She did just that, trying to give me a flat tire several times by stepping on the back of my boot heels. We hurried after the Polarion.

He moved briskly, which was pretty good for a man waking up from hideous interrogation.

"Grab my hand," I told Debby.

She did, and we ran after the Polarion.

I suppose I could you give a detailed rundown of the next half-hour. It was a blur of activity. We climbed up access tubes, raced along corridors and snuck through hatches.

By that time, I figured Rax had tried and failed to teleport a bomb onto the ancient spaceship. We were still here, so he must have failed.

For ten minutes, the three of us hid in an access tube as others hurried past. Their footsteps dwindled, and it was silent again. Soon, a pair of people walked past. The Polarion burst out of hiding without warning. I don't know what calculus he used to figure it would be safe doing so with these two.

The Polarion moved like a cat, coming up behind the two men. He fired without hesitation, his weapon spewing an electrical-type discharge.

The two staggered as their pseudo-flesh melted, revealing gleaming metal underneath. They were robots. Had the Polarion known that, and if so, how had he known?

The two dead machines clanked onto the deck, sparking and sizzling as they did.

The Polarion moved swiftly. He scooped a tablet off the deck. One of the robots had dropped it. First pressing his weapon against his one-piece—it stuck there—he began to access the tablet.

The Polarion read the tiny screen, tapped faster, and made a hissing sound.

I'd been listening and watching the corridor for more adversaries. As the hiss, I glanced at him.

He stared at me before abruptly hurrying to the right. He broke into a run. Debby and I ran after him, finding it difficult to keep up.

Finally, he stopped before a red color-coded hatch. It seemed like an important area. He put his weapon on the floor, cracked his knuckles like an old-time safecracker and began to manipulate a keypad beside the hatch. He stopped for a time, staring at the keypad as if he could figure it out through sheer brainpower.

A klaxon began to wail. That had taken long enough to occur. The blaring sound made me nervous. I turned around, looking down the corridor, expecting to see a horde of security people attacking us.

One thing seemed sure. The spaceship was a whole heck of a lot larger inside than it had looked outside.

The red hatch clicked. The Polarion picked up his gun, opened the hatch and jumped through.

As I entered with Debby, the Polarion made clicks and whistles in an obvious imitation of the Neanderthals earlier. Lights snapped on and machines hummed into life. This was a huge chamber with a high oval ceiling. The floor shone with a metallic sheen and proved slippery to walk on.

The Polarion moved carefully to a bank of machines on a wall. He manipulated panels, pulled levers and tapped his fingers on screens.

On the far wall, an archway glowed with light. I heard machines roar into life from somewhere nearby. They were loud and powerful-seeming. The mechanical sounds increased. A sense of foreboding grew.

The Polarion ran to another set of controls. He worked feverishly, glancing at the glowing archway from time to time.

The archway started pulsating with many colors. Instinctively, I stepped away from it, drawing Debby with me.

The Polarion barked a savage laugh. I glanced at him sharply. His eyes seemed to shine as he studied the archway. Then he went back to madly tapping controls.

The nearby machines thrummed with even more power. It sounded as if they might be going into overdrive. Was the Polarion destroying the spaceship? I wished I knew the man's game plan.

Debby squeezed my hand before pointing at the archway. It showed a frozen hell with snow and hard-blowing wind. It made me cold just looking at it.

The Polarion moved across the floor. He gripped his gun, grabbed me by my right bicep and pulled me with him toward the bitter archway.

I'd already guessed it was a portal of some kind. Maybe this was how the Starcore had been collecting his Neanderthals and hominids.

The machine noises had become thunderous. The room began to shake. An explosion from a panel caused smoke to billow.

The Polarion looked at me. I had no idea what he was trying to impart with his look. Then he moved the final distance to the portal and dragged me with him. I was still holding Debby's hand.

The three of us moved through the portal together. I felt a momentary stretching. It felt as if my lungs were on fire. Then, I staggered into a snow bank as frigid wind blew against me.

The Polarion still gripped my bicep, dragging me. I looked back and could see into the gleaming room we'd left. Everything still seemed to be vibrating in there.

The Polarion dragged us to the side, away from the portal opening. A distant, muted explosion sounded. A gout of flame burst past me from the portal, warming my skin. Then, both the flame and portal disappeared. Fortunately, the Polarion had dragged us far enough to the side that we'd been out of the blast's line-of-fire.

That told me he'd done this deliberately. Had he killed the rest of the people aboard the spaceship?

I began shivering from the intense cold. It felt as if he'd transported us to the North Pole. The wind howled in this place, and the sky was darkly menacing. That didn't seem right for Greenland. It was summer, meaning it should be light almost all the time in Greenland. Maybe this was the mother of all storms.

My teeth started chattering. Debby's face had already turned bright red.

The Polarion dragged us through the wind and snow. He seemed indomitable. How could he even tell our position? He hurried as if he had a destination in mind. The snow blew harder, and icy particles struck my face. I wasn't going to last much longer.

Soon, I couldn't feel my hands, and it was nearly impossible to think. He brought us to a cliff or a wall of stone. That cut down on some of the windy blast, but it wasn't going to save us from the freezing weather.

He released me, bent low, scraped away snow as if looking for something and seemed to touch an area in a certain sequence. I could hardly think at this point. But it looked like the upper portion of an entrance slid open near the ground. It was like an elevator that had only reached a floor with the upper quarter of its door. He lowered himself to his stomach, shoved his feet through the tiny opening and squeezed out of sight like a gopher.

I barely had enough sense left to shout at Debby to do likewise. I had to push her into the hidden place. Finally, I followed their example, sliding into a cold, bleak chamber the size of a principal's office.

"W-What is this place?" I asked, shivering.

The Polarion motioned to us. He led us through a door into a small hall, entered another room and manipulated yet another hatch that soon opened.

The next cold room had a central machine with controls along two walls. Heaters glowed on the ceiling. They smelled of ancient dust, as if this place had remained empty for centuries. Could that be true? It gave me the willies just thinking about it.

The heat was a blessed relief just the same. Debby and I stood under one heater, shivering uncontrollably.

As we tried to soak up a modicum of the heat, the Polarion went to the machine and pressed a switch. A panel slid out of it. He manipulated the panel fast, his fingers blurring over controls.

Finally, he pointed at me, and then pointed to an area with a painted outline. He seemed to want me to stand over there.

I didn't want to move, as the heat had increased. Reluctantly, I left Debby and stood inside the painted outline on the floor.

He put a headset over his ears with a small microphone before his mouth. Then he tapped the panel, waited and tapped more.

Intense red lights snapped on over my head. That bothered me, and I started to move away.

"No," he said.

I saw him move his lips, but the words came from a speaker to my left.

I pointed up at the red lights. "Does this translate my words?"

"In a manner of speaking," he said. He tapped the controls again.

Abruptly, the red overhead lights snapped off. He removed the headphones and microphone.

That didn't make sense. Didn't he need the machine to translate? Maybe the machine had already absorbed my speech patterns, though. If he was a Polarion, surely he had incredibly advanced technology.

"Who are you exactly?" I asked.

He shook his head. "We both know who I am. The question is: who are you and how did you get aboard the Starcore's spaceship?"

The words came directly from his mouth now. He no longer needed the translation speaker. Could the machine have "read" English speech patterns from my mind and transferred the knowledge to his mind?

"I'm Logan," I said, "but I have no idea who you are."

He stared at me and laughed, louder this time, shaking his head. "It would appear you are a natural."

I was tired of innuendoes and hints. With a scowl, I said, "How about clueing me in as to what you're freaking talking about, huh?"

He pressed another control—

I head a sharp, overhead sound. I clamped my hands over my ears, and tried to stagger away. That's the last thing I remember.

-42-

When I awoke, I found myself in a small capsule, strapped into a bucket seat. A tiny screen was level with my eyes. I saw no way out of the capsule, no one in here with me and no means of changing my fate.

Why had the Polarion done this to me, especially after I'd helped him escape from the Starcore? Just what—

The screen made a slight hum, coming on. I saw the Polarion in his one-piece. He stood in a room surrounded by machinery. There was no sign of Debby.

"It is unfortunate I had to take such abrupt action with you," the Polarion told me.

He had a rich voice and an even more regal bearing than before. I wondered how much time had passed since he'd rendered me unconscious.

"I could no longer afford the contamination of your presence," he added.

"What contamination?"

"It is self-evident," he said.

"Well, not to me, it isn't."

"That is because you haven't allowed yourself time to think," he said. "You react too quickly at times. Yes, you are a natural, and that is what the Ancient Book says naturals do. But taking time to think could dramatically change your life."

"Who are you?" I asked.

"You already know."

"You're a Polarion?"

"I do not answer rhetorical questions," he said with a frown.

"Look. I saved your hide—"

"I am aware of that," he said sharply, "and I am…grateful," he added in a softer tone. "That is why I am lowering myself to speak with you."

"What? Lowering yourself? Just who do you think you are?"

His eyes seemed to swirl with power. I imagined that was how Zeus might have looked when Hera had angered him.

Maybe I was taking the wrong approach with him. After all, I was the one trapped in a capsule. I couldn't believe he'd done this to me.

"You have a sharp tongue," he said, "a reckless tongue. To forestall any misunderstanding on your part, I will inform you that your companion has told me about Far Butte and the atomic testing that woke the Starcore."

"What have you done to Debby?" I demanded.

"We have similar features, you and I," he said. "Maybe your mistake lies there. Know that I am not human the way you are human. I can die, but I am also ancient. You might even think of me as an immortal. Perhaps, then, you can understand my…*dislike* at having a puppy like you question me. I am making allowances for your brutishness because you have done me a service. It is possible you saved my life. For that, I give thanks."

I told myself to relax. He was a Polarion. He obviously thought highly of himself. Now, he claimed to be an immortal. He knew stuff. It was clear he was dangerous. Maybe it would be best to keep thinking of him as Zeus. I might be able to talk my way out of the capsule that way.

I cleared my throat. "You're welcome for the help…sir," I said. The *sir* was the right touch. I was sure of it.

"Ah," he said. "You have a modicum of wit after all. It is clear you desire me to do you a favor in return for your service."

"That would be nice…sir."

He nodded. "Your companion says your Earth has alien intruders."

“It does,” I said.

“I am unsure how to explain this to you in a manner you will understand.”

“Maybe it will help if you know that I’ve been to Greenland,” I said.

He stared at me.

“I’ve been to Thule,” I said. “It’s covered in ice these days. When you first came to our planet, I imagine Thule was like everyplace else on Earth. I’m also guessing that you’ve been asleep or in suspended animation for a really long time. Were you one of the Starcore’s prisoners, or one of its slaves?”

Color appeared on his cheeks. “I am no one’s slave.”

“So you must have been its captive,” I said. “Look. You’ve woken up in the middle of a crisis. I’m trying to save my planet from destruction, and I don’t know if you’re a help or a hindrance.”

His eyes narrowed. I had the feeling few people had ever spoken to him like that. Finally, he took a breath. “Explain your meaning,” he said.

I told him about Earth being a banned planet. I told him about Station 5, the Min Ve privateer, the Galactic Guard, Greenland, the stasis tubes, and finally, about the hell-burner.

“A moment,” he said. With a few manipulations, he brought a floating screen before him, studying it for a time. Growing decidedly more thoughtful, he made the screen disappear. Finally, he eyed me anew.

“You are a natural,” he declared.

“You said that before. What is that even supposed to mean?”

It looked as if he might tell me to mind my manners while speaking to him. In the end, he simply said:

“Some people are exceptionally athletic. Some are computational wizards. Others have an affinity for games, for any particular activity under the sun. There are a rare few who have exceptional…” He drummed his fingers on the console. “Some say naturals are unnaturally lucky. I do not believe it is luck, but it is a thing akin to luck. A natural makes an exceptional soldier or spy, the activities you have been engaging in the past few days.

"I am tempted to have you assist me," he said. "But..." He shook his head. "I have an ancient score to settle with the Starcore. I cannot worry about your planet. It is possible you would try to thwart me if I was forced to take extreme measures."

"I saved your life," I said. "You can't destroy my planet in return."

"You lack the proper respect while addressing me," he said. "I find my desire to chastise you growing by the moment. Thus, I am correct in my assessment regarding your nearness." He pondered his next words. "It is difficult to know the best procedure for dealing with the situation. The orbital privateer hesitates because lust for gain causes the commanding Min Ve to believe he can acquire the Starcore for his own use. My own era as well as the last several thousand years shows me the folly of that kind of thinking. The Starcore is incredibly dangerous. I cannot allow it to survive, not under any circumstances."

"What are you going to do to me?" I asked.

"You have the Guard-ship. I'm granting you your life. Use the ship and flee this planet while you can."

"What about Debby?" I asked. "Why are you keeping her?"

"Your impertinence at questioning me brings you dangerously near to destruction. This once, I will answer you. Debby is linked to the Starcore, but she still possesses some free will. Both the crystal and the girl find you interesting. It is why you still breathe. Because I can use this linkage, she will assist me in destroying the crystal."

"I want to destroy it, too."

"That is no doubt true. But you lack my resolve and sense of purpose, to say nothing of my power. I will bring down the entire solar system if I must to kill the perverted crystal creature."

"May I ask, sir, if Parker is linked to the crystal?" That would explain how the biker had managed to survive Walt.

"Parker and Debby are the Starcore's prime creatures," he said.

"The crystal toyed with me, then?"

"Of course," he said. "It has always been curious and always too arrogant. This time, I will use those qualities against it. I will not fail. I dare not."

I started to ask him another question.

He waved his hand and my screen went blank. At the same time, my capsule began to buzz with power.

I struggled against the restraints. If he thought I would leave Debby behind, he was crazy.

"Hey!" I shouted. "I'm not done talking to you."

Instead of receiving any answers, the capsule hummed louder than ever, shaking until I could no longer see straight.

***

I'd never been angrier in my life. I'd saved the Polarion, and he'd taken Debby from me. To add insult to injury, the capsule whined down as a hatch lifted in front of me. My straps burst off and the chair catapulted me from the capsule. I flew through the air and landed with a jolt, sprawling across sand. I looked back and saw my transportation shimmer and disappear.

I couldn't believe it. It felt as if the Polarion had picked me up and pitched me out of his saloon. I climbed to my feet shaking with indignation. I'd saved his butt and this was his thanks?

I didn't know who to hate more, the Starcore or the Polarion.

Finally, I took a communicator out of my pocket and clicked it on. "Rax?" I asked. "Can you hear me?"

"I hear you, Logan. Where have you been? I need your help. The Organizer—"

"Rax," I said, interrupting him. "Get me out of here. Bring me back to the ship."

"Yes," the crystal said. "That is an excellent suggestion. I will begin the procedure."

-43-

"I feared you were dead," Rax told me as I entered the piloting chamber. "I would have been stranded in here until the Guard-ship lost power and sank to the bottom of the ocean. I might have spent the rest of my life down there. You have no idea how frightful a fate that would be."

I was still nursing my grudge against the Polarion. Of all the black-handed—

"You seem upset," Rax said. "What happened to you? How did you come to be in the middle of the desert?"

I told him about my adventure in the ancient ship, the escape and my subsequent conversation with the arrogant Polarion.

"That is fascinating," Rax said. "You spoke with a living, breathing Polarion. Do you know how many beings have desired to do that? Millions, I'm sure. It is possible the number runs into the billions or even trillions. They are real, then."

"What do you mean, they're real? They were in the stasis tubes in Greenland."

"It appeared that was true. Finding out for certain is a different matter altogether. This will change many planetary histories. It might well change Earth's history and the original causations to many—"

"Rax," I said, "forget about Galactic history. The Polarion changes the dynamics of the present situation. He's royally angry and wants to get even with the Starcore. He's talking about destroying the solar system if he has to in order to take down the crystal."

"That makes sense," Rax said.

"No, it doesn't," I said. "That's like using a hammer to crush the fly on your face. The cure is worse than the problem."

"For you, that is true," Rax said. "The same does not hold for the Polarion. Likely, his home is a wasteland, obliterated by the Starcore during the prehistoric Galactic conflict."

"Well, it's true for me," I said. "We have to stop the Polarion."

"Better to try to stop the tide."

"That could be done, too," I said. "All you'd have to do is blow up the moon."

"Granted," Rax said. "But the magnitude of the task would be daunting in the extreme."

"Which is why we have to get started immediately," I said. "Thus, this fancy theorizing is finished as of now. We have to take action."

"What kind of action do you have in mind?" Rax asked.

That stopped me. I didn't know. Maybe a little theorizing wouldn't hurt, after all. The least I could do was to find out what had happened while I'd been unconscious. I was still so angry at losing Debby that I could hardly think straight.

"Did the Unguls successfully storm the white ship?" I asked.

"I lost visual of the fight," Rax said, "but what I saw leads me to believe the Unguls failed. The Far Butte humans stormed the enemy position, slaughtering the Unguls as they set up their heavy weapons. I could replay what I recorded so you could see for yourself."

"Not just yet," I said. "Did the humans kill all the Unguls then?"

"Eighty percent of the Unguls died, while roughly twenty percent of the humans perished. At that point, a second team of hover-assisted hominids struck Station 5. I focused my concentration on the new battle. The hover-riding hominids must have taken a long detour and seemed to have avoided the orbital vessel's scanners. Perhaps they used a cloaking device to do so."

"The hominids overran Station 5?" I asked.

"That is correct," Rax said.

"So, the Starcore's hominids control the Western Sunlight Station?"

"Negative," Rax said. "Once the hominids slaughtered the last Station 5 Unguls, the Organizer destroyed the installation with a hail of orbital rods."

"Those things are proving to be pretty handy for the Min Ve," I said.

"They are the perfect weapons to use against the aboriginals of primitive planets, as they leave no sign of alien interference. At best, the aboriginals put it down to the 'gods' sending an unusual number of meteors. In fact, I suspect certain ancient folklore—"

"Are you telling me Station 5 is in ruins?" I asked, interrupting him.

"Affirmative," Rax said.

"And the Starcore's white ship is out of phase again?"

"That is my suspicion," Rax said.

"You don't know?"

"I have been unable to scan the region to confirm my suspicions."

I blinked at Rax. "So, we're right back where we started."

"That is false," Rax said. "I have been analyzing your tale and have come to several interesting conclusions. The Starcore is possibly baffled at this point in the affair."

I ran a hand across my face, turned around and started telling myself to calm down. Getting enraged at Rax wasn't going to help me. I had to think carefully…just as the Polarion had suggested I do.

"All right," I said. "Lay it on me. What do you have?"

"I have begun to suspect that Debby was the Starcore's biological linkage," Rax said. "The crystal must have united with her—"

"That's totally wrong," I said, heatedly. "She broke me out of jail, remember. She went to Parker—"

"Please, Logan, bear with me. You must stop interrupting me as I speak. It is very annoying and time-consuming."

I grunted a monosyllabic answer.

"Debby has remained young," Rax said. "That is one point. At his place outside town, the biker Parker lived like a hog in a pigsty."

"Why does that matter?" I asked.

"Recall what you told me about Far Butte. It was pristine. That makes perfect sense. We crystals abhor a mess. We yearn for symmetry. According to you, Parker has beer and whiskey bottles strewn about his property. He has dog skeletons lying around. His home is a mess. That would indicate Parker isn't completely controlled by the Starcore."

"Well, that destroys your point right there," I said. "The others of Far Butte were under deeper control, proving—"

"They were mindless slaves," Rax said. "The Starcore acted in union with its chief biological units. It united with them, allowing them more of their former personality."

"Is this mere logical deduction, or are you accessing ancient memories concerning the Starcore?" I asked.

"The latter, of course," Rax said. "I have come to suspect that the Starcore humored its two chief biological units. It is also possible it was running a deception campaign against you for reasons of its own."

"I hate that idea," I said, sitting down. "But that doesn't mean you're wrong."

"I would also like to point out that while trapped at Far Butte you had a flimsy plan for storming onto the white ship. The fact that Parker so readily agreed to the plan also leads me to my conclusions. Moreover, there is the fact that Parker survived the robot sheriff. That is a damning piece of evidence."

"Why did Debby let me into the torture chamber then where I freed the Polarion?"

"Yes," Rax said. "That is an oddity. It causes me to question a few of my assumptions. Perhaps Parker was the Starcore's focus all along. Maybe Debby was the focus until Parker arrived. Parker or the Starcore decided to keep Debby afterward."

"Why would either of them do that?"

"I could think of any number of reasons," Rax said. "Perhaps the chief one is the obvious one. Parker liked the curve of Debby's legs. Did she not say that Parker likes the girls?"

I glowered at Rax for a moment and then looked at the sea outside the Guard-ship's window. The crystal's thinking seemed so convoluted, so twisted.

"The Polarion took Debby," I said.

"Precisely," Rax said. "That is the telling point to my belief concerning her. I believe he did so in order to bait the Starcore. I believe the Polarion knows more about the ancient crystal than anyone alive."

"So what do we do next?" I asked.

"I imagine you are against leaving Earth as the Polarion suggested," Rax said.

"That doesn't even deserve an answer."

"I thought you might feel that way, even though the critical element is to destroy the Starcore. Everything else is secondary to the main goal."

"That's where you're dead wrong," I said. "Saving Planet Earth is first. Rescuing Debby is second. A distant third is destroying the Starcore and lastly, stopping the Organizer."

"You are I are at cross purposes then," Rax said.

"Wrong again," I said. "You're the advisor unit. I am the decider. Your job is to advise me, not to try to set the agenda."

"Logan, I am a Galactic Guard Unit Adviser. Surely, you see that my first allegiance—"

"Why are we arguing?" I asked. "We can't get at the Starcore because it's likely out of phase again. We can't do anything to the Min Ve if he stays in orbit. The only one we can affect right now is the Polarion, provided he's somewhere in Greenland."

"That is logical, as far as it goes. But why would we try to stop the Polarion, as his goal is the same as mine?"

"Maybe it's not a matter of stopping him, exactly," I said. "Maybe he'll need help, and he's too proud to know it. The Starcore captured him once. Maybe it will do so again."

"That is an interesting point."

"You're darn right it is," I said. "So, our next step should be to go back to Greenland, preferably to the underground site."

Rax was silent for a time. Finally, he said, "I strongly advise against having me teleport you there."

"Yeah," I said. "We need to scout the place first. Why not send your spy drone over there?"

"I suggest we refrain from that. The Organizer spotted my previous drone and beamed it out of the sky."

"Do you have a spare drone?" I asked.

"I have one backup unit. I am loath to simply toss it into the furnace."

"Do you have another way of spying?"

Rax was silent again, although not for as long. "I do," the crystal said. "Before we do anything else, though, we need to refuel the ship."

"Roger," I said. "Let's get started. You can tell me the rest along the way."

"Logan, I must warn you. I will not work directly against the Polarion if he is actively attempting to destroy the Starcore."

I let that sink into my brain and nodded.

-44-

I sat at the Guard-ship's controls, cruising through the depths back toward the Hawaiian Islands. It was much like last time as I avoided any underwater sensor devices—mostly American—and submarines. I did notice more U.S. naval activity. The vessels headed east toward China and North Korea. Were they headed for a military showdown?

I had to put that out of my mind for now. I already had too much on my plate.

After we reached a location that put the Earth between the Min Ve orbital vessel and us, I took us nearer the surface.

"This is good," Rax said.

I tapped a control, launching a buoy with a line to the Guard-ship.

"I will begin monitoring," Rax said.

The crystal hacked into sophisticated spy satellites. It took Rax ten minutes before he was fully integrated with the NSA, Chinese and Russian systems.

I waited. He had explained this method during the cruise. It had its own dangers, the biggest was that one of Earth's tech people would discover Rax's piggybacking. According to the crystal, it was a way that "primitive" people could infer alien interference.

"This is evidence that you are correct concerning the Polarion's location," Rax said. "There is greater activity at the Greenland site than I'd imagined there would be. Look to your left and you will see what I mean."

A screen maneuvered into place beside me, switching on so I saw four different camera angles. Each angle was from a different spy satellite. I saw snow and ice—

I leaned closer, spying the former Greenland ice canyon. There were fresh machine-made tracks on camera two and several armed hominids picking through the destroyed Ungul warehouse on camera four.

"What spy satellites are observing this?" I asked.

"The Chinese and American," Rax said. "I have already begun to cause different signals to reach the Earth receivers. They will no longer see what is really happening in Greenland. In fact, I will cause malfunctions in all line-of-sight satellites. It is better this way."

I wondered what the Chinese and Americans made of the hominids for the few moments they had seen them. Maybe they would believe the hominids were small men in furry parkas. What would they think about the destroyed warehouse in the middle of nowhere and the radioactive levels from an exploded hell-burner off the Greenland coast? What if instead of believing that each other had exploded a nuclear weapon, some Chinese and American intelligence agents had already concluded there was *alien* activity in Greenland? Wouldn't a superpower want to get hold of extraterrestrial technology for their side alone? What would each side do if that were the case?

"Are there any Chinese or American troops heading toward Greenland?" I asked.

"That is an interesting query," Rax said. "Give me a few moments for study."

As Rax did his thing, I kept watching the four camera angles. As I did, I spied a small hover zipping across the snow. I would have liked it to zoom in so I could see who was driving it. Before I could get to that, something small and fast from above zeroed-in on the hover.

"Another orbital rod," I whispered.

The rod headed straight for the hover. The driver appeared to look up and raise his left hand. It glowed, creating a buffer between him and the space-launched missile.

The rod slid along the curvature of the buffer, slamming into the snow and exploding with released kinetic energy.

The hover lifted as if riding an out of control energy wave. The driver clung to the hover's controls. I was surprised the machine hadn't already burst apart. Then, I noticed the same glowing buffer but now at the bottom of the hover. Finally, the driver brought the hover level with the ground again. He sped toward a dark opening.

Two more times, an orbital rod should have annihilated him. Each time, he did the glowing-hand trick, deflecting the rod. Finally, the hover zipped into the underground opening, disappearing from sight.

"Did you see that?" I whispered.

"Indeed," Rax said. "Before we delve into the meaning of the activity, I should inform you that I have discovered an American naval task force heading to Greenland. It contains two aircraft carriers—"

"Forget about that," I said. "If the Starcore is out of phase, I'm guessing it isn't sending or receiving any more personnel to or from Greenland. That would mean the little hominids checking out the destroyed warehouse are on the Polarion's side. Maybe the Polarion was driving the hover. The driver's actions just now sure seemed godlike."

"I am playing back the hover image just before the first orbital-rod strike," Rax said.

On camera two, the hover image expanded. A white-haired man was driving the vehicle. He was wearing the star patterned one-piece. Was that the Polarion I'd rescued from the torture table, or was that *another* Polarion freed from his Greenland stasis tube?

"Focus on the hand," I said.

"This is the best I can do," Rax said.

The image had become grainy, so it was difficult to tell. The raised hand began to glow. After that, the image blurred considerably.

"What did he activate that caused his hand to glow like that?" I asked.

"Unknown," Rax said.

I drummed my fingers on the top of the screen.

"Maybe we should use your nuclear device on the orbital vessel," I said. "I'd rather help the Polarion than the Min Ve."

"I agree," Rax said. "Unfortunately, a shield blocks a teleportation beam. This is well known."

"Does that work both ways?" I asked. "I mean, does the Min Ve have to lower the privateer's shield in order to teleport Unguls onto the surface?"

"Yes. Do you suspect the Min Ve will do this?"

"Don't you?" I asked.

"That is a logical possibility given the new evidence. But we do not know *when* the Min Ve will lower his shield. There is also a time-lag element involved in the equation. I would have a better chance of placing the nuclear device if the Guard-ship were nearer to the privateer. The odds of success would climb even higher if the Guard-ship was in orbital space when we made the attempt."

I studied the screen showing the four satellite images. The alien privateer was in orbital space and would stay there for who knew how long. The Min Ve would continue to do what he'd been doing. I had to stop him from dropping more hell-burners or from using orbital rods against the American carriers. I couldn't just stand by while that happened.

"Right," I said. "It's time for us to make our play."

I strapped myself into the piloting chair and began pressing tabs at Rax's instructions. Soon, acceleration struck as the Guard-ship blew out of the water. We roared for space. It was a heady feeling to realize I was now entering an elite group of Earthmen who had piloted a space vehicle.

We lofted for orbit while the alien privateer was on the other side of the planet from us. In that way, we shielded ourselves from the Min Ve.

"This is not good," Rax said.

My teeth rattled as we continued to climb. "What's the problem?" I shouted.

"The Min Ve has begun destroying all satellites," Rax said. "If he does, we will no longer be able to watch the Greenland site to time our nuclear-device attack against the privateer. That means I will have to risk using Guard scopes."

I might have said something regarding our bad luck, but the shaking had become too violent for me to speak. Therefore, I endured.

-45-

Weightlessness made my stomach churn. The Galactic Guard-ship had reached orbital status as we moved around the blue-glowing curvature of the most beautiful sight in the galaxy. The oceans and continents spread out below us as we headed away from Australia toward Asia at an angle. Cloud drifted in places. We were much higher than the Learjets had flown. This was true space. I wondered what was going on in Greenland. What would happen if the white ship came back into phase and the Starcore sent robots and humanoids to the ancient Thule facility?

I couldn't worry about that just yet. I had to adjust to this new environment as fast as I could.

"What happened to our ship's gravity control?" I asked.

"We are attempting to act like space debris," Rax said. "That mandates weightlessness. The privateer's sensors would instantly pick up any gravity-control emanations if we used them. That is why we are drifting now, no longer under acceleration."

"That makes sense. Are you scanning the privateer?"

"Not yet," Rax said. "The orbital vessel is not yet in sight. When I do scan the ship, it can only be with passive sensors. Otherwise, I will give away our position."

"Can't they see us anyway?"

"Space is huge, Logan. We are tiny. As long as we keep our power usage to a minimum, it is unlikely they will spot us while they are concentrating on the surface."

I nodded, rubbing my stomach, trying to get it to settle down.

The minutes ticked away as our ship drifted through space. Ten minutes passed, fifteen, twenty, twenty-five—

"I have extreme visual contact," Rax said finally.

I looked out our window first. All I saw was the curvature of the Earth and the vastness of the star field. The Sun was presently behind our planet. I studied my screen next. It showed an outline of a cloaked orbital vessel.

"Is the privateer's shield up?" I asked.

"Yes," Rax said.

"So what do we do now?" I asked.

"We wait for our opportunity," Rax said.

That was always the hardest part, the waiting. But I was beginning to learn that waiting was one of the components of space combat. The greatest similarity on Earth would have been WWII carrier-aircraft combat. Back in the old days, the Japanese and Americans had had long, drawn out carrier battles. Each side had sent out squadrons of planes, searching for the enemy. The carrier commanders had had to do a lot of waiting, even in the middle of a battle. The key to that had been judging distances and remaining hidden in the vastness of the ocean.

Space was even bigger than the oceans. It took time for a spaceship to maneuver into position. It would take time for missiles to reach their target.

"Greenland will soon be visible," Rax said.

The privateer outlined on my screen wavered for a second.

"Did you see that?" I shouted.

"Indeed," Rax said. "The Min Ve has released bundles of orbital rods."

"Are the bundles inside or outside its shield?" I asked.

"Why, they are outside, of course," Rax said. "That was why the shield shimmered for a moment. So the bundles could pass without harm."

"We should have launched our nuclear device then."

"I cannot teleport the device in a second of time," Rax said. "The Min Ve is playing a cagey strategy. It is placing its weapons outside the ship's shield so it can activate the rods through comm signals."

"What if we destroyed the orbital bundles?" I asked.

"First," Rax said, "we would have to close with the bundles and the privateer. The Guard-ship's laser cannons are relatively short-ranged weapons. Second, we would necessarily give away our position by firing. Our usefulness would be at an end, as the privateer could easily destroy our small craft."

"But Debby is down there in Greenland," I said. "What if the Min Ve launches hordes of rods at the ancient site?"

Rax did not reply to that. A few seconds later, he said, "Look."

"Look at what?" I shouted

Rax zoomed in on the screen. Three bright dots climbed up from the ocean near Greenland. Those dots must indicate missiles. Had the Polarion launched the missiles, or were those American submarine-launched missiles? Whatever the case, a red line slashed down from the orbital vessel. The line was a bigger version of the disintegrator ray. The ray touched each bright dot in turn, creating a bloom of light, indicating a destroyed missile.

Soon, no more missiles climbed into space.

"From this demonstration," Rax said, "it is clear that the side with the high orbital position has the advantage."

"Why's that?" I asked.

"Because of gravity," Rax said. "It is easier to beam disintegrator rays or drop rods down than to send rockets up."

I could see his point. The Earth was at the bottom of a gravity well, as it were. As anyone who has had the opportunity could tell you, it was easier dropping rocks into the well than heaving rocks up to the top from the bottom.

The rockets surprised me. Who had launched them? Occam's razor suggested the Polarion had done so. The U.S. probably lacked anything sophisticated enough to see the cloaked privateer. Therefore, the Americans had likely not used submarine-launched missiles. Yet, if the Polarion had launched the missiles, I would like to know where he'd gotten them, why he targeted the alien privateer and why he had failed.

The Polarion was supposed to be godlike. Shouldn't his weapons be able to defeat a mere privateer?

"Can the Min Ve fire his disintegrator beam through his shield?" I asked.

"Not precisely," Rax said. "There is a special mechanism. It turns the shield off for the split-second the ray beams outward. The instant the ray quits, the shield is back online. Naturally, teleportation beams require the shield to lower for a longer amount of time."

"Rax, I want to go down to Greenland."

"That is not logical."

"Sure it is," I said. "I have to coordinate with the Polarion. It will also give me an opportunity to see what's happened to Debby."

"The Polarion dismissed you," Rax said. "Legend holds that they are notoriously vain. He might eliminate you in a fit of royal anger if he sees you again."

"The rockets changed the equation," I said. "If the Polarion launched them…"

"Your meaning escapes me," Rax said.

"I'm going down to Greenland."

"The Min Ve might detect that," Rax said.

"It's a risk, sure, but I think it's worth it."

"Very well," Rax said. "I agree that there are variables in play that I do not understand. I will remain here while you go."

I studied the little crystal in his metal case. Then, I unbuckled, floating for the hatch.

-46-

I had my .44 Magnum, wearing it outside the metallic one-piece I'd taken from the Greenland site during my previous visit. On the other side of the belt was the communicator linking me with Rax.

The Polarion had called me a natural before. Maybe he was right. I had an instinct about this. I was doing the right thing. Yet, if that were true, why was my gut churning the way it did?

"I'm ready," I told Rax.

"I suggest you reconsider this," the little crystal said. "I am detecting heightened energy readings from the privateer. According to my calculations—"

"Enough, Rax," I said. "Just do it."

"You do realize this is a highly emotional decision?"

I did not respond. Several seconds later, the Guard-ship's transfer chamber began to fade…

***

I appeared inside a huge chamber and realized that two efficient-looking Neanderthals flanked me. That seemed to indicate that they, or the Polarion, had known I was teleporting down. Before I could react, one of the Neanderthals drew my .44 from its holster. The other put a huge hand on my left elbow, propelling me toward a vast screen in the center of the chamber.

On the screen was the outline of the alien privateer. Even fainter than the outline were the girders and modules making up the orbital vessel. I'd forgotten about the true shape and manner of the privateer. Clearly, it was a deep space vessel, never meant to enter an atmosphere.

As the Neanderthal propelled me, I had a chance to look around. I noticed various personnel occupying stations with screens and controls. This place reminded me of NORAD, but instead of Air Force officers in white shirts and ties, I saw Neanderthals and apelike hominids. None of them spoke, although they all worked fast at whatever they were doing.

Most of the chamber was dark. The small station-screens created some illumination. The greater amount of light came from the giant screen. It should have been in a football stadium, it was so big. The lowest part of the giant screen was fifteen feet off the floor. That should give you some idea of the size of the place.

The Polarion stood alone before the giant screen. The white-haired humanoid had folded his arms across his chest as he gazed at the Min Ve privateer.

The two Neanderthals brought me toward him. The Polarion turned and raised a bushy white eyebrow.

"The natural," the Polarion said in his rich voice. "I gave you explicit instructions to stay away."

I remained silent.

The Polarion nodded ever so slightly. One Neanderthal released his hold on my arm.

"I saw you earlier," I blurted.

The Polarion waited.

"Earth satellites were watching you," I said. "Rax had broken into the satellite systems. We saw the Min Ve try to assassinate you with an orbital rod."

The Polarion simply continued to watch me.

"You destroyed the rod with a flick of your hand," I said.

The Polarion held out his left hand. I had no idea what that meant. One of the Neanderthals must have, though. He approached the Polarion and gave the man my revolver.

The ancient white-haired superman turned the weapon over several times, studying it. Finally, he opened the cylinder, dumping the bullets into his other hand. He squeezed the bullets while his hand glowed with power. I noticed he wore a strange ring. Did the glow originate from it?

In any case, inadvertently, I took a step back from him.

The Polarion looked up at me. I held my ground after that. He fixated on his hand, squeezed harder as the glow brightened, and suddenly opened his hand. His shoulders seemed to sag the slightest bit. The glow left his hand, although a nimbus surrounded the bullets. Soon, that glow faded as well.

He handed the bullets to me.

I accepted, not sure what I should do with them.

He nodded at my belt. I thought I understood and slid each bullet into an individual slot on the belt. Once I'd finished doing that, he handed me the .44. For a millisecond, I thought about reloading. Instead, I holstered the empty gun.

He gave another of his minimalist nods. The Neanderthals departed, leaving the two of us alone before the giant screen.

"You may call me Argon," the Polarion said.

It was my turn to nod. He didn't seem as arrogant as the last time we'd spoken. He did have that majesty, though. It radiated more powerfully than ever.

"Can I ask you a question?" I said.

"Ask," he said.

"Where's Debby?"

His nostrils flared. Then, he turned to his left, walking swiftly. I had to jog to catch up, following as he passed under an archway.

I halted in shock as an electrical noise focused my attention. I saw a huge ball of blue lightning hovering twenty feet off the floor. Inside the ball of blue lightning, Debby floated with her hair radiating in all directions. She wore her bra and panties, but nothing else. Her eyes were a silver color, and she tried to mouth words.

My heart went out to her as my right hand dropped onto the butt of the .44. Then, I realized the revolver was empty. With a conscious effort, I lifted my hand off the gun.

"She is unharmed," Argon said.

"What are you doing to her?" I asked in a voice I hardly recognized.

"Using her as a communication device," he said.

"What's that mean?"

"I have instructed you to think, Natural. This is one of those instances where you must do so. I will not answer the obvious."

I admired the Polarion and yet I hated his guts. The former emotion won out this time.

"She can talk to the Starcore?" I asked.

"The Starcore and I have bargained," Argon said with a touch of dry humor. "To date, the Starcore has refused my offers."

"May I ask what you're offering?"

"Rest for the weary," Argon said. "I have offered the ancient device its destruction for the good of the universe. The construct stubbornly resists me. In fact, the Starcore demands I return Debby. I have thus far declined to do so."

Argon turned to go.

"Wait," I said.

A touch of annoyance crossed the Polarion's noble features. "We lack time for debate, and I have a few items to relay to you. It may well prove critical. Come."

I wanted to grab an arm and shake him. I figured that would put me flat on my back at best. The Polarion was inhuman in ways I could sense but didn't understand. I felt as if he could swat me out of existence like a proverbial fly. Thus, I followed him.

I did glance back at Debby, though. She tracked me with her silver eyes. I shivered because I could feel the Starcore's hatred.

I hurried after Argon. Soon, we stood before the giant screen again. The rest of the people in the chamber worked silently at their stations.

"I have begun to regain my former abilities," Argon said. "We Polarions have aspects. You might call them powers. I can control various electromagnetic situations."

"You do this mentally?" I asked.

"It is unimportant how I do it," Argon said. "I have revived ancient weapons systems in record time. I doubt the Starcore believed me capable of doing so this quickly. I have already stymied several of the construct's plans."

I waited, realizing the Polarion had a reason for telling me all this.

He sighed.

"I have slept for an age," Argon said. "I find it difficult at times to maintain my equilibrium. My ego is strong. The emotions needed to battle against the Starcore—that comes and goes. It is almost as if life wearies me. Do you not think that is strange?"

"I am not a Polarion," I said.

"No," he said after a time. "You are not."

Argon resumed his study of the orbital vessel. He compressed his lips as if debating an idea. Finally, he spoke again. He did not turn to me, but kept his focus on the Min Ve privateer.

"The Starcore is like me, ancient beyond reckoning. Yet, it is a construct. It has not lost its zest because it never had it. The white ship is old and brittle. According to what I've gleaned from Debby, the Starcore doesn't trust the white ship sufficiently to engage in star travel with it. Perhaps as important, the Starcore's creatures are busy repairing the damage you and I inflicted on the white ship."

I took that in.

"I suppose I should tell you that I assisted you in your initial rampage through the white ship's control areas," Argon said.

"How could you do that?" I asked. "The Starcore's scientists were torturing you."

"True," Argon said. "That made the effort more difficult. Still, I hindered the Starcore's responses. That left its slaves incapacitated, giving you the needed margin to kill them and damage important equipment."

"Why did the Starcore revive you if you're that dangerous?"

Argon shook his head sharply, as if the subject angered him too much to speak about it.

"Did the Starcore revive other Polarions?" I asked.

"I am alone," Argon said quietly. "I am all alone in this distant era. It is a strange sensation." He shook his head again as if ridding himself of something useless.

"I am hindering the Starcore," Argon said. "The construct yearns to leave Far Butte. It seeks to return to normal phase. Soon, the Starcore will succeed. I must destroy the privateer before that happens."

"Can I ask why?" I said.

"The privateer is a modern starship. Thus, the Starcore wishes to possess it as its own. If the construct can do that, it will race to Rax Prime. There, it will finally repair itself, regaining full use of its deadly ability to wield the cosmic force."

"That's greater than electromagnetic control?" I asked.

A look of pained majesty crossed Argon's face. The look frightened me in a way that was hard to describe. It made me want to go down on one knee and bow my head before him.

He chopped his left hand through the air, as if cutting the feeling from my heart.

I staggered, blinking in surprise.

"The Starcore has *strengthened* the privateer," the Polarion said, ignoring my stumble. "I may not be able to destroy the orbital vessel in time. We shall see. The Starcore wants me dead. That is certain. The construct is willing to risk its ticket out of the solar system because it knows I will revive to even greater strength in the next few hours."

"How did the Starcore strengthen the privateer if the construct is out of phase?" I asked.

Argon held both hands before him. Electricity played between his fingers and the ring glowed brightly. At the same time, his features hardened.

"It has begun," he said.

"The privateer is going to attack this place?"

"Of course," Argon said.

"Maybe I can help," I said. "Rax and I plan to teleport a nuclear device—"

"Cease your prattle," the Polarion said in a commanding voice. "The Min Ve has unleashed a sub-atomic blast against your Rax Prime crystal. I do not believe the Min Ve has detected your Guard-ship, but he must have reasoned its presence. You will be unable to teleport up or teleport your nuclear device for the next ten minutes at least. The battle will be over one way or another before that."

"What battle?" I asked.

"Yes," Argon said. He raised his hands. The electrical power emanating from them grew. And a most amazing sight greeted me.

-47-

On the giant screen before me, I saw something rising out of the ground from the ice canyon in Greenland. Snow and big white chunks fell from it. Several seconds later, I knew exactly what I saw.

A great barrel—like one of the giant WWI artillery barrels—moved out from an even bigger turret. The turret spun. The barrel climbed until its orifice aimed into the heavens.

I laughed in astonishment. Perhaps this was the reason why few alien vessels had ever returned from scouting the banned Earth.

Tension seemed to mount inside the command center. That's what I was standing in, I realized. I had been correct about the NORAD feel to this place. Vast machinery roared with power from somewhere nearby. I could feel the floor shake. Ancient sources must be attempting to energize the equally ancient cannon.

Energy flowed from Argon. It was a staggering sight. I backed away from him. His fingers writhed as if he were a master pianist playing his greatest piece.

On the giant screen, an orange ray bolted from the orifice and pierced the sky as it climbed into orbital space.

At that point, the giant screen split in half, at least in what it showed. I saw the giant Greenland cannon, and I saw the privateer.

The orange ray struck the privateer's shield. That caused the cloaking invisibility to shimmer and then vanish. The orbital vessel was visible as individual girders and modules. Before the mass, the shield glowed with power.

Inch by inch, the Greenland beam pushed the shield closer to the orbital vessel. I wondered why the privateer didn't fire back. What was it waiting for? Would Argon solve the privateer problem for Earth?

Finally, I realized the Min Ve's plan. Clearly, he did not want to time the shield shutting down for even a millisecond in order to fire back with the ship's beams. He would let his shield absorb the horrendous punishment while he struck back another way.

Orbital rods now rained at us like meteors as the Min Ve used his prepositioned bundles.

My gut clenched as I realized that I was as much a target now as Argon.

"The Starcore still hopes to capture this site," Argon shouted in a strange voice. "I will not give him that option."

I wasn't sure what that meant exactly, but it sounded ominous.

One thing it meant was that the great barrel was no longer aimed at the privateer. The turret spun, and the huge cannon swept from side to side. The orange ray moved around the sky. Each time the beam touched an orbital rod, the missile burned up at the intensity.

The Min Ve had rained many rods, however. Maybe he'd realized the power of the surface-to-space cannon. Instead of a handful, *hundreds* of orbital rods shrieked down from the heavens. Each one left a luminous trail in the sky as it plummeted toward its target.

What would any watching Chinese or American soldier make of those trails?

The surface-to-space cannon obliterated more rods than I would have believed possible. In the end, though, several rods made it down all the way.

The first struck the turret, leaving a harmless, baseball-sized chunk missing. The second did that to a lower portion of the barrel. More rods hit, gouging out more little holes. Despite the terrific meteor-like velocity, the individual rods did negligible damage to the great gun. More kept raining down. More kept hitting. The Min Ve's targeting was something else.

Now, uranium rods struck, creating fireballs. And an enemy orbital beam finally struck at Greenland. The ground-to-space cannon no longer fired at the privateer, but smoked still more rods. Maybe because of that, the Min Ve was finally willing to lower his shield each needed microsecond in order to beam a disintegrator ray.

With the suddenness of a falling tree, the great barrel splintered. The cannon fell onto the ground, breaking into several large pieces. At that point, a giant fireball ignited, blowing those pieces into hundreds of smaller ones.

"What just happened?" I asked.

Argon didn't answer. Instead, he staggered, clutching his gut. I didn't understand. It seemed as if the giant barrel's destruction had physically hurt him.

Several seconds later, Argon twisted his head to look back at me. Pain was etched across his features. Slowly, he removed his hands from his gut, straightened and sighed.

"I kept some of the larger explosions at bay for a time," he whispered.

"You can do that?"

"When I released my hold, all the contained explosions united at once. That is what you just witnessed."

I blinked several times as I tried to figure out what he was saying. Could he dampen a blast? I guessed so. But he could only do so for a time, it would seem. That was one crazy aspect. That was what he'd been talking about before. He could control—

"Launch the missiles," Argon said in a harsh voice.

It took several seconds. Then, the floor, the giant screen and the Neanderthals and hominids at their stations began to tremble and finally shake. I stumbled to the right and to the left as I tried to compensate.

On the screen, gigantic missiles lofted from hidden silos. They were bigger than any ballistic missiles I'd seen on TV. The roar of their passage was amazing. The big things seemed armored and frankly indestructible. They climbed slowly at first, but soon gained velocity. More silo caps blew into the air. More giant missiles left their ancient lairs.

"The missiles have been waiting since the dawn of time to fly?" I shouted.

Argon focused on the screen. I was certain he heard me, but I guess he was busy.

A red disintegrator beam struck down from the heavens. It hit a giant missile's hardened nosecone. The armor took the hit for a long moment before finally beginning to smoke.

"Are you doing that?" I asked.

Argon shook his head.

The entire missile exploded at once, reminding me of the Challenger shuttle explosion I'd seen in a documentary.

The disintegrator ray focused on a new missile. At the same time, orbital rods attempted to strike the rising missiles. One hit, smashing the missile off course but not annihilating it. Those armored nosecones were tough sons of bitches. The rest of the orbital rods streaked earthward.

Giant red beams now reached down like the ones I'd seen that night in Nevada. One part of the giant screen showed the result. Inside the circle of a red beam, the Ungul's boxlike tanks and Ungul soldiers appeared. In other red-beamed circles, I saw small one-man flyers with Unguls lying prone on them. Those flew toward the underground openings.

I glanced at Argon.

"Form combat teams," the Polarion said in a loud voice.

The Neanderthals and hominids rose from their stations. They picked up rifles and grenades, racing for the exits.

I studied the giant screen. It seemed as if the Min Ve were emptying his privateer. He'd sent down a small army of Unguls. Argon's pitiful few wouldn't stand a chance against them.

"Can you destroy the Ungul army with your aspect?" I asked.

Argon glanced at me, his features unreadable. Afterward, he focused on the giant screen, on the part showing the climbing missiles.

The privateer's disintegrator beams knocked out more missiles. The Min Ve's people no longer targeted the armored nosecones, but the less armored rocket areas.

Argon made a grinding noise in the back of his throat. I heard an agonized, "No," torn from him. He raised his hands, and power sizzled from them. He stepped closer to the giant screen, staring at the privateer. It seemed as if the Polarion concentrated with awful intensity. He staggered, and air whooshed from his lungs.

On the screen, I witnessed a new sight. Something dark appeared near the privateer. Then, what looked like an EMP blast started as a tiny light from the darkness. The light expanded rapidly, one portion of it striking the privateer's shield. In that moment, the glow of the shield disappeared. The Min Ve's disintegrator beams no longer poured from the various cannons.

The remaining Greenland missiles lofted unharmed toward their orbital target.

I shouted with glee, pumping a fist into the air.

Argon glanced at me. He did not appear elated.

Frowning, I watched the privateer. I saw point defense cannons beginning to fire solid shot. By the magic of the Greenland sensors, I could see the solid shots heading at various missiles.

I winced every time I saw a PD shell hit an armored nosecone. The armored missiles were tough, but one by one, they shredded apart under the merciless PD assault.

"Use another EMP blast," I said.

Argon shook his head sadly. The Polarion looked haggard and old. It seemed like a chore for him now just to remain standing.

"So the Starcore has won?" I asked.

That seemed to revive Argon a little. He spun around, racing to an abandoned station.

Two of our missiles yet remained. The second-to-last missile exploded under a PD hail. That left the last one.

Argon stood at the station, tapping controls. Finally, he looked up at the giant screen.

PD shells hammered the last missile.

I stepped closer to the giant screen. Tiny rods sprouted from the armored nosecone. At that moment, the great missile ignited its nuclear warhead. The nuclear blast unleashed terrible forces, but too far away from the privateer to do it much harm. Then, through the Greenland sensor "eyes," I saw the gamma and X-rays reach the sprouting rods a millisecond before the nuclear blast destroyed them. The rods focused the gamma and X-rays at the privateer in a coherent beam.

Those gamma and X-rays raked the alien privateer. The rays shredded and twisted girders and destroyed a few modules outright. In others, I had no doubt any alien beings would die of radiation poisoning.

An entire fourth of the privateer went dark.

"You did it," I said. "You hurt the Min Ve's ship."

"What is your saying?" Argon asked. "It is too little, too late."

I cocked my head. I could hear fighting in the corridors. There were Unguls in the ancient site. How long would the handful of Neanderthals and hominids resist them?

Argon inhaled deeply, shoved off the station and walked solemnly toward me. He still looked old and worn, having lost much of his majesty in the process.

"What's the next move?" I asked.

"Remember," he said in a tired voice, "the Starcore has the terrible power of mental domination. You have one hope against the construct, in case you ever come into its presence. Your own Rax Prime crystal can act as a hindrance to the mental domination for a time. That will render your crystal mute during the process."

"Ah…okay," I said, wondering what that was about.

"I have one play left," Argon said quietly. "I can harden the Min Ve's mind against the Starcore's domination. I doubt—"

The Polarion looked up at the giant screen.

I turned around as my stomach tightened. The privateer launched a missile of its own. I'd seen the type before. The Min Ve was playing hardball. He had launched another hell-burner. It drifted from the girder-module spaceship, forced away through cold propulsion.

"You must leave," Argon told me abruptly.

"I'm taking Debby with me," I said.

Argon cocked his head as if seeing something. He sighed a moment later, shaking his head.

"You gave it your all," I said. "Now—"

The Polarion moved toward me as his hands glowed. Something must have radiated from him to me. I was frozen. He reached me, took hold and did something I couldn't perceive. Then, faster than it had ever happened before, the underground Greenland chamber began to fade from my sight.

-48-

I reappeared on the Guard-ship's transfer pad. I couldn't believe it. The Polarion had forced me to teleport by the touch of his hands.

I had a feeling it hadn't been that easy. Did Argon truly possess godlike powers?

I staggered off the pad and hurried to the piloting chamber.

"Logan," Rax said in surprise. "How did you get aboard?"

I told him in as few as words as I could. Afterward, I asked, "What's happening with the hell-burner?"

"A moment, please," Rax said. "I have been out. A form of EMP—"

"Bring up the scope," I shouted.

Rax did. Hot exhaust powered the deadly missile. The hell-burner plunged toward the atmosphere and toward Greenland far below.

I struck the screen with my fist, but not enough to shatter anything. Why had Argon refused to give me Debby? I could have saved her. Now, it was too late.

A small part of me wondered if the Polarion had a last trick up his sleeve.

"The Min Ve appears to be teleporting Unguls up from the surface," Rax said.

"Can you get a fix on them? Maybe we can teleport Debby out of their grasp."

"What makes you think the Unguls had time to capture her?"

I didn't have an answer, but I did have a gut feeling.

The hell-burner couldn't reach the surface all at once. It took time to leave the orbital vessel, race through space and the atmosphere, and reach Greenland. At last, though, the hell-burner screamed for the surface. It plunged down, down, and right before reaching snow, the warhead blew. I saw everything on the Guard-ship's scope.

The warhead burst apart, but there was no thermonuclear explosion. The missile smashed against the surface. The velocity caused the rest of the missile to shred into nothing. But there was still no explosion.

"I do not understand this," Rax said.

"Argon is holding the blast at bay," I whispered in awe.

"What does that mean?" Rax asked.

Before I could explain, a titanic explosion caused a mighty mushroom cloud to bloom in Greenland. Argon had lost the battle. Did that mean the Polarion, Debby and any prehistoric people still stuck in the stasis tubes were dead? Had the Min Ve beamed up all his people in time, or had a number of Unguls perished in the devastating nuclear blast?

My chest hurt. I couldn't believe a being as powerful as Argon could have lost.

"It's over," I said.

"I do not agree," Rax said. "I am preparing our own nuclear weapon. I am..."

I heard the hesitation in his speech. I hardly cared now. Would the latest hell-burner start a nuclear war between Earth's superpowers? Maybe the first hell-burner had ignited without any Earth people other than me noticing. It was certain the second had focused the world's attention. The world's premier soldiers must have seen this one, too. I felt a bitter taste of defeat in my mouth.

"Logan, I am going against my better judgment in telling you this," Rax said. "I can guess with a high degree of probability what your reaction will be. Yet, I need your command to do this, given that we are working under the Antares Clause."

"What?" I asked.

"I have located Debby."

I looked up. "She's alive?"

"Indeed," Rax said. "She is on the privateer. Do I have your permission to teleport our nuclear device onto the Min Ve vessel? We must do so immediately if we wish to achieve success."

"The device would kill Debby, right?"

"Affirmative," Rax said.

"No, you don't have my permission. I want to save Debby."

"Yes, I realize that. But, Logan—"

"Can it," I said. I could feel the energy flowing back into my body. It told me what I needed to know concerning Debby. Sure, I'd seen the silver eyes, and I know what Argon had said about her. But if I could save her, I could use her to help me destroy the Starcore. Then she would be free to be Debby again. I liked her—a lot. Ever since my divorce, I'd been searching for a good woman. That night in Far Butte with Debby had solidified something in me. I couldn't just toss that away.

"We only have a few minutes to do this," Rax said. "I detect rapid repairs over there. If we wait to thrash this out—"

"I said no," I told him. "I'm going to rescue her. Did the Min Ve beam up Argon, too?"

"Who?" Rax asked.

"The Polarion," I said.

"Unknown," Rax said.

"Do you know Debby's location on the privateer?"

"Yes."

"Then beam her here. What are you waiting for?"

"The privateer could detect such a teleportation—"

"Now, Rax," I said, "teleport her here now."

"I am initiating—no, it is too late. A shield has energized."

I studied my screen. I could see the shield as a dull glow around the orbital vessel. I made a few manipulations on the screen. I was starting to get the hang of this.

"According to this," I said, "the shield is at seven percent of its former strength."

"That is true," Rax said.

"Seven percent is enough to stop teleportation rays?"

"Yes."

"Then let's knock down the shield," I said.

Rax did not respond.

"I've had enough of this," I said. "If you don't want to help me, fine. I'm going to—"

"Logan," Rax said. "Desist at once."

I had brought up the fighter controls. I hesitated for just a second, though.

"There is a better process," Rax told me.

"Better start talking while you can," I said, "because I'm about to go postal on you."

"I do not understand your reference."

"What's your better process?" I asked.

"The privateer's shield is at eight percent of its former strength and climbing. We will have to attempt this at once. If the shield reaches fourteen percent of its former strength, our odds for success will be so low that I would mandate a cancelation of the effort."

"Rax!" I said.

"You must head for the teleportation chamber. There is a stealth-suit in the number three locker. I also suggest you take weapons two, three and nine. They will be in the number four locker."

I jumped up, heading for the hatch, taking Rax with me.

"What's the plan?" I asked.

"I will attack a small portion of the shield with a sonic drill. It is a Galactic Guard commando technique. At the precise instant I do this, I shall make a tight-wave transfer onto the enemy vessel. At the present shield strength, that gives us a fifty-eight percent probability of success."

"That low?" I asked.

"It is a highly dangerous technique. But I am assuming you are willing to try nearly anything to rescue the Earth woman."

"I'll try a fifty-eight percent commando attack," I said, "especially since I don't have anything else I can try."

"That had been my internal prediction concerning your answer," Rax said.

"Unless…" I said. "I can capture the Starcore and make a trade for Debby."

"I cannot believe you are serious. That must be yet another attempt at crude Earth humor on your part."

"That last hell-burner means we're almost out of options. What good is it if I win and the Earth is a radioactive mess? I want to have a home to come back to."

I'd entered the transfer chamber. I now opened the number three locker, finding a strange sort of suit and bubble helmet.

"This is the stealth suit?" I asked.

"Affirmative," Rax said. "You must put it on while I instruct you in its functions."

I would have a three-hour supply of air, and could run the camouflage unit for a combined length of sixty-seven minutes. It also had a bulky hydrogen pack, allowing me short spurts of spaceflight. The boots had a switch that magnetized the soles.

The combination suit was heavy, and it wasn't a perfect fit, binding me because it was too small for my stature. Still, it would work.

"We are moving too slowly," Rax said. "The privateer's shield is at eleven percent and climbing."

"What's next?" I shouted, the words reverberating inside the bubble helmet. I would mourn Argon later. I was sure the Polarion had died. I did remember Argon saying something about helping the Min Ve break the Starcore's hold over him. That kept itching in the back of my mind as my subconscious worked out a plan. Before I let myself think about that plan, I wanted Debby safely aboard the Guard-ship.

I also had time to worry about this spacewalking attack. I had a bad feeling that this wasn't the best way to learn how to use a space-slash-stealth-suit. But I didn't have a choice if I was going to rescue Debby. That was one of the reasons I was going to take Rax with me. He could keep an eye on the suit and tell me before I attempted something that would kill me.

I grabbed grenades, a dual-purpose rifle and several magnetic mines. It seemed like far too little against the Min Ve and his remaining crew.

"I still don't see why you can't teleport-grab Debby after making the sonic penetration of the shield," I said.

"With the shield hindering me, I no longer have a fix on her location," Rax said. "It is easier to deposit you inside than to grab her, as you say."

"Sure," I said, as I climbed onto the transporter dais. "Are you ready?"

"Give me a moment," Rax said. "I must adjust for our continued velocity. Analyzing…analyzing… Logan, prepare for teleportation."

I stood on the dais, clutching the rifle harder than ever.

"Three…two…one…" Rax said.

Nothing happened. The room did not begin to fade.

"What's the problem?" I asked.

"I have enough time for a secondary try. There was an unforeseen surge of power to the enemy's shield. Logan, I suggest we abort—"

"Make the transfer!" I shouted, wincing at the echo in the helmet.

"I would like to lodge my protest—"

"Now, you bastard," I shouted. "Transfer now."

"Two…one…zero…" Rax said.

I thought the crystal's second attempt had failed, too. Just as I began to speak again, the chamber began to fade.

-49-

This was the strangest teleportation of all. Everything faded from view, I could feel myself stretching and the world around me seemed faint. It solidified, grew fainter again, staying that way far too long, and finally solidified once more.

I found myself floating several feet away from a large moving girder.

"Warning," Rax said.

The girder struck me, knocking the wind from my lungs as a loud *crack* sounded from the helmet. An immediate hiss made the helmet foggy up and down along the length of a hairline crack. The crack zigzagged across the helmet, making it difficult to see perfectly, like wearing a pair of fogged sunglasses.

I clutched onto the girder, trying to get my bearings.

"Given the rate of oxygen loss," Rax said, "our timeframe has changed from three hours to one hour."

"Doesn't this thing have a patch kit?" I asked.

"It does," Rax said. "But a helmet patch would negate the suit's stealth function. We will likely need the invisibility more than the excess time. However, our margin for error is rapidly dwindling."

"Are you saying I have to listen to this constant hiss the entire time I'm out here?"

"Affirmative," Rax said.

"What about the fogged faceplate?"

"Do you have any visibility at all?"

"That's not the point," I said. "This is my first time spacewalking. Not being able to see—"

"Logan, we have no more margins for error. Thus, we must change our tactics. We do not have time to exchange opinions with each other."

"Right," I said. As I clung to the giant girder, I looked around.

We were in the upper part of the Min Ve privateer. As I'd said earlier, the spaceship was really a maze of girders with modules and engines seemingly placed at random.

Thrust presently glowed blue from two rearward engine modules. A third module had terrible rents along the sides. The gamma and X-rays from the last missile must have done that. There were other damaged modules, as well.

The two good engines presently propelled the privateer around the Earth in an orbital pattern.

I counted nine good modules, what Rax referred to as living quarters. There were four engine modules and seven huge cargo modules.

"Where's Debby?" I asked.

"Pull up the display pad if you would," Rax said. "It is on your left pectoral."

I found it, detached the pad and watched as Rax activated it. He put up a schematic of the privateer.

"The red-colored module is the transporting area," he said.

I studied the display pad and then looked around at the privateer. I soon found the targeted module.

"She's in there?" I asked, tapping the pad.

"Logan, you are drifting."

I grabbed the girder again.

"Use your boots," Rax said. "Magnetize yourself to the metal."

I shifted position while turning on the magnets of my boots. The first time, I found that I couldn't yank my boots off the girder.

"You have the boots at the highest setting," Rax said. "Do half that rate."

It took a minute before I got the hang of it.

“This is an inauspicious beginning to the commando mission,” Rax said.

“You said we don’t have time for negative comments, remember?”

“You are correct. Let us proceed.”

“Let me ask again,” I said. “Is Debby there?”

“I am unwilling to use the suit’s sensors just yet,” Rax said. “That would undoubtedly give away our position.”

“The only other way is to go and look inside the module.”

“Therefore, we must go there now,” Rax said.

I judged the distance. “Right,” I said. “How do I use the thrusters?”

“The thrusters use cold propulsion,” Rax said. “But using them will likely also give away our position. I suggest you walk there.”

I studied the maze of girders. I’d have to walk across a module or make a detour to get to my location. I asked Rax about that.

“Walking across the modules could create telltale sounds. I suggest you make the detour.”

I laughed sourly. “Do you hear the helmet hiss? That means we don’t have any excess time. We’re going to have to make an educated gamble. I can’t run along the girders because I don’t have the knack down yet. I don’t dare waste time, either. So I have to use the sensors to pinpoint her or use the thrusters to fly to the targeted module. Which choice presents the least risk?”

“Give me a moment please,” Rax said. “I have many considerations to calculate.”

The seconds ticked away as my nervousness increased.

“The thrusters seem like the best choice,” Rax said. “However, they take delicate precision to use correctly. Clearly, you lack any skill in the art. This will be clumsy flying at the best. At the worst—”

“I know,” I said. “All our options are lousy. But beggars can’t be choosers. Let’s get started. Any pointers?”

“Be gentle with the trigger throttles. Remember, the faster you go, the harder you will have to brake at the end of the flight. There is negligible friction in space. It will be easy to injure yourself if you fly too fast."

"That makes sense," I said. "Here goes."

"Wait," Rax said. "You must demagnetize your boots before you begin."

"Roger that," I said.

I shut off the magnets on my soles, shoved off with my legs, and let myself drift to get the hang of it. I took a deep breath.

"I forgot to mention," Rax said, "you must turn on your internal gyro-stabilizer first."

I decided to view this like a military jet. With Rax's help, I made a preflight inspection. There was more to this than I'd realized. Finally, I was ready.

I gently squeezed the throttle trigger. A slight push shoved against my back. I twisted around and saw a trail of white hydrogen exhaust. That was the propellant. It was like having a can of Raid on your back, pressing the nozzle to give yourself motive power.

Fortunately, the white trail rapidly disappeared.

I focused on the selected module. Then, I forced myself to look around. I remembered reading about WWI dogfights. Most of the shot-down pilots never saw the enemy because they didn't look all around all the time. I started looking around now. It was strange flying past the girders and various modules. The aliens were in there. Maybe one of them already had me on his screen.

I exhaled, shook my head and wondered if I should have turned on the stealth equipment. When I asked Rax about that, he explained that that would be a waste of suit energy as long as I was using the thrusters.

Finally, the selected module neared.

"You must twist around," Rax said, "so your thruster is aimed at the module."

I tried twisting around, and had to ask Rax the trick to doing it. His explanation failed to make sense right away. By the time it did make sense, the module was rushing toward me at what seemed like ramming speed.

I twisted, grunted and finally viewed my backward flight on the display pad. I used the thruster, but squeezed too much hydrogen spray.

"Stop, stop," Rax said, "or you will send us back to where we first appeared."

Twisting and grunting, I faced forward again. I felt as if I was moving in slow motion. It seemed to take forever for us to close the final few feet to the module. I did not feel like a ninja commando. I felt like a lead-footed beginner.

"You have the element of surprise," I whispered to myself.

Finally, the bulkhead was almost within reach.

"Get ready," Rax said.

I did, but it still felt as if three linemen slammed me at once. I crashed against the module, the wind knocked out of me again. Fortunately, I kept the helmet from crashing against the module, preventing the crack from lengthening.

"You must ease your boots onto the bulkhead," Rax said.

He had to tell me three times before I got my bearings.

I put the boots at one-quarter magnet strength. As gently as I could, I put my sole down. Despite my best effort, at the last moment the magnet pulled my boot down by surprise. It must have caused a clang inside the module. Outside, I could not hear a thing, as sound did not travel in a vacuum. I did manage to put the second boot down more lightly.

"Where's the hatch?" I asked.

Rax told me.

I walked across the module as quietly as possible. It was hard to know if I was making noise inside or not. Since I couldn't hear anything, I had to trust that I was doing it correctly. The module walking should have been easy. My thighs soon burned at the effort of pulling my boot free and making sure the soles didn't land too hard on the bulkhead.

At last, I reached the hatch, out of breath and sweating as the suit's air-conditioning system blasted me with cooling drafts. During the walk, I'd been doing some hard thinking.

"Rax," I said. "This isn't going to work. I don't know how to use your suit efficiently. I'm already out of breath."

"I have been analyzing our chances," the crystal admitted. "Watching you in action has led me to the obvious conclusion that they are rapidly dwindling to nothing. You are green in space and need extended practice. Normally, a Guard commando—"

"Let's skip the history lesson," I said. "I need to think." I was going to follow Argon's advice.

"You are wasting precious time."

"Shut up, Rax. Let. Me. Think."

"As you wish," the crystal said, almost sounding sullen.

I stood outside the hatch to the privateer's transfer module. I'd already been in it once when the Jarnevon had teleported me up to their ship from Far Butte.

I studied the girders, the modules—the good ones first and then the damaged ones. I thought about the Greenland-privateer battle. We still had to stop the greatest menace of all—the alien Starcore. Could I race through these modules invisible with the too-tight stealth-suit?

No. I didn't have the energy or the training to do that. The ninja idea had looked good in theory. In practice—

"Scratch that," I whispered to myself.

The answer came to me in a flash from my subconscious. Maybe Argon had buried the idea there. I don't know. Like most great ideas, though, it erupted full-blown like Athena from Zeus's forehead.

I had to keep using my greatest asset—the Galactic Guard teleporting tech. In order to give it full scope, the privateer's shield had to go. I did not have the firepower to batter down the privateer's shield. But maybe I could surprise and rush one module, hopefully an empty one.

"Rax," I said. "Which module would I have to knock out in order to short-circuit the ship's shield?"

"Working…" Rax said. "Working… I have it. You would not need to enter a module at all. Do you see the central node to your right?"

"Just a second," I said. I tore the display pad from its pectoral location, switched it on and had Rax pinpoint the node on the ship schematic. Yes. I could see it now.

"That is one of the shield generators," Rax said. "If you rendered it inoperative, it would take several minutes at least for the Min Ve or his crew to reroute the other nodes. In essence, the privateer would lack a shield during that time."

"All right," I said, snapping off magnetic power to my boots. "I have a change of plans…"

-50-

I used my spacesuit's thrusters to maneuver toward the central node. I was finally getting the hang of thruster flying.

"Don't get cocky," I warned myself.

I could space-maneuver better than I had at first. That didn't make me an expert. Whenever I thought that I was the cock of the walk, I usually made my worst mistakes. But when I took pains in what I was doing, I usually did a good job.

Today was the time to take great pains.

"Warning," Rax said. "Enemy combatants are exiting a hatch. They are suited and armed. We must assume they have spotted us and are taking action."

My heart hammered. This was just what I needed. I'd been getting ready to twist around in order to put myself in a braking position.

"Where are they?" I shouted.

"You must remain calm."

"Just tell me where they are?" I shouted.

"To your lower left," Rax said. "I spy five suited adversaries. They are unlimbering weapons."

I activated my suit's stealth function.

"That will not work," Rax said. "They will see us as soon as you begin to brake."

"I'm not braking just yet," I shouted.

"In that case you will either crash into or miss the central node altogether."

"Exactly," I said. "Now shut up for a moment so I can think." I grunted and twisted, turning so I faced the enemy. Then I squinted, scanning the strange spaceship, looking for my foes. "I can't see anyone," I said.

"Precisely," Rax said. "They are wearing dark suits. I doubt you will spot them visually. You will need the display pad for me to point them out to you."

"My helmet's visor should have a heads up display," I said. "Even I know that much."

"Criticizing Guard apparel—"

"I'm freaking out, Rax. Let me bleed off my nervousness without turning everything into an encyclopedic explanation."

I used the display pad, having Rax pinpoint the enemy flyers. I finally saw them, and I saw streaks of dark hydrogen spray now. The enemy flyers squirted the spray in tiny bursts. That was clever, showing their better vacuum-combat training.

If my rifle had a more sophisticated targeting scope, I might have tried taking them out. Yet doing so would likely render me visible to them. Their survivors could target me in turn.

I slapped the display pad onto my pectoral and put the rifle in its shoulder harness. I wouldn't need either of those for this. I twisted around so I faced the direction I was traveling again. I wasn't going to worry about the five enemies just now. Instead, I detached a magnetic mine from the suit. I set it, watched the central node coming up…coming up—

I threw the mine at the node. I ripped a second mine off the suit and did the same thing.

"Are you ready?" I shouted.

"Explain your tactic," Rax said.

"I'm going to use the thruster. I have to move or I'm going to hit the central node."

"The others will use your hydrogen-spray trail to target you."

"I know," I said. "So we have to time this just right. The mines are nearing the node. You're going to have to ignite them at the right moment. I'm hoping the shrapnel doesn't kill me."

"I am beginning to perceive your idea."

"Good," I said. "Once the privateer's shield goes down, you have to find Debby pronto. Once you do, you're going to teleport me to her. I'll kill anyone around her. Afterward, you teleport us back to the Guard-ship."

"It is a simple plan," Rax said.

"Yeah," I said with a dry tongue. "Well, here goes. It's been good knowing you, Rax."

I pressed the trigger throttle. Spray thrust from the pack. I jetted upward in relation to the rushing-near node. A second later, I detached the straps of the thruster pack. I shoved it away.

"That was foolish," Rax said. "How will you slow down?"

Three red rays beamed at the thruster pack. One enemy ray barely missed me—my position had shifted slightly from my hurling the ballast that was the thruster pack away from me.

For every action, there was a reaction. That was Newton's Third Law of Motion.

I flew past the node. "Blow the mines, Rax," I shouted. "Do it now!"

I twisted back to look. Two bright explosions showed me the igniting mines. Some of the blasts and shrapnel struck the central node, taking it out.

Red rays beamed once more. Some of the rays struck space junk. The others missed me, which was all that really mattered.

"Is the ship's shield down?" I shouted.

"Yes," Rax said. "You were successful."

"Have you pinpointed Debby?"

"I am scanning....scanning... I have found her, but there is a problem. It appears the Jarnevon is in the same chamber with her."

"That doesn't matter," I said. "You're going to teleport me into that chamber. First, I have to know this, though. Can you bleed off my velocity during the teleportation?"

"Indeed I can, Logan. I had already foreseen the need and calculated the process. It will be a tricky—"

"Great!" I shouted. "Are you ready then, or are you going to jaw about it all day?"

I finally began to fade.

***

I managed to grab my Galactic Guard rifle before I completely faded from my present position. Thus, I had it level when I appeared inside a large chamber. The problem was that I was facing the wrong way.

Each module must have possessed gravity control, because I stood normally in the chamber. I could feel the gravity keeping my feet in place.

I turned around as a beam lashed me. Instinctively, I threw up my rifle in front of me. It took the brunt of the Jarnevon's beam, melting in places.

Several things flashed through my mind. The Jarnevon's weapon must have been locked onto a weaker setting because she was inside a spaceship and wanted to make sure she didn't breach a bulkhead. I also saw that she was stunningly beautiful in her tight leathers, but she was diabolically evil for what she was doing to Debby.

Debby was stark naked with electrodes attached to her skin. She wore a vicious-looking helmet with electricity zapping through it. Debby arched and writhed on the torture table. Her eyes bulged as she silently screamed.

Something snapped in me seeing that.

I pitched the rifle at the Jarnevon. She dodged, but she also lowered her gun and quit beaming me.

I charged in what seemed like slow motion in the bulky suit. That gave the Jarnevon time to slip to the side, aim and fire. I took the beam on my suit, which must have possessed beam-retardant skin. Thus, I closed the distance and almost managed to grab the lithe Jarnevon. She slipped to the side again, keeping the beam on me.

An alarm rang in my helmet. She was about to breach the suit.

"Surrender," she said.

I hurled a grenade underhanded at her. In my haste, I hadn't armed it. That was just as well, though, as I didn't want to kill Debby or myself. The grenade struck the Jarnevon in the stomach, making her grunt and taking her beam off me as she lashed the ray against the deck.

I charged again, ripping a second grenade off my suit.

The Jarnevon retargeted but at a different spot on my suit. I hurled the second grenade. It struck her right shoulder, upset her balance. She tried to duck but I latched my space-suited gloves onto her gun-firing wrist.

I pulled down while ramming a knee against her hand. Her gun went skittering across the floor.

The Jarnevon hissed like a cat, and I could feel the strength in her arm. Maybe she originated from a heavier gravity planet. Allowing her no time to slither away or to attack me, I bashed her against a console. She grunted. I used a wrestling move from high school and took her down hard, landing on top of her.

"Others are coming," Rax said.

I hardly heard. I'd seen what this witch had done to Debby. Before I thought it through, I grabbed the force blade from my outer suit, switched on the energy and killed the Jarnevon.

That brought me back to sanity with full force. I climbed to my feet and staggered to the torture frame. Any remorseful feelings I had for killing the Jarnevon fled as I saw poor Debby again.

I shut down the power, tore the leads off her sweaty skin and gently removed the sinister helmet. I had to use the force blade to cut off her restraints. Finally, I picked her up, holding her against my chest.

I'm not sure I was thinking straight just then. I'd seen Debby earlier in Greenland. She'd had silver eyes and Argon had told me he was using her to communicate with the Starcore. Maybe Debby was a Trojan horse.

I actually hesitated. Then, I remembered that the Jarnevon had been torturing Debby. That implied that Argon had succeeded in turning the Min Ve from the Starcore's mental-dominance control. And that meant…

It was too complicated. I was going to try to save my girl, or the woman I hoped to make my good friend, at least. Debby wouldn't hurt me. I was sure of that.

"Can you teleport us out of here?" I asked Rax.

I fully expected to hear the crystal tell me there was a problem. The next thing I knew, the chamber began to fade from view.

-51-

I carried a sobbing Debby into the Guard-ship's sleeping chamber. Her eyes were normal-looking except for all the tears pouring out of them. I laid her down, pulled the covers over her and stepped back.

"She is seemingly distraught," Rax said.

"What do you mean seemingly?" I asked quietly.

"I have been running tests using advanced Guard equipment. I was unable to do so while we were on the privateer—or behind its shield, at least. The point is this, Logan. I have detected strange emanations in her mind. I believe that she is linked to the Starcore. Your Debby may be playacting."

I'd been refusing to believe that, but…

It felt as if a fog lifted from my mind. I don't know what caused that. I realized that I had to consider the brutal facts, if for no other reason than to save the Earth. I felt soiled for killing the Jarnevon. I shoved that into a deep part of my mind, sealing the area. I didn't want to think about that right now. I had other things to consider.

With a start, I realized I was wearing a ring on one of my fingers. Why hadn't I noticed it before? Could Argon have done something to my mind? Yes! And that something had just revealed itself. I remembered what the Polarion had done to me at the end in Greenland. Argon had put his ring on one of my fingers. Then he had "touched" my mind, likely so I wouldn't notice the ring or his actions until now.

Debby stirred on the bed. I focused on her.

"Who are you?" Debby whispered.

That seemed like a strange question until I remembered that I still wore the cracked bubble-helmet. I removed it.

"Logan?" she asked.

I nodded.

"I didn't know you were a spaceman."

"I wasn't until a few days ago," I said. "Debby…" I let my question hang. I hated the idea that she was linked to the Starcore.

She wiped her nose and dried her eyes. They were bloodshot and red-rimmed.

"Do you know what the Starcore is thinking?" I asked.

The question changed her demeanor, making her seem more calculating.

"What do you know about that?" she finally asked.

I wasn't sure, but it seemed as if a different intelligence shined through Debby's eyes then. It was as if I had a greater clarity of thinking and could see things I wouldn't have been able to before. The realization made me sick at heart.

I tried to speak, but couldn't.

"Cat got your tongue?" Debby, or the thing in her mind, asked archly.

The Starcore might have meant that in a playful manner, as if to use Debby's femininity against me. It hadn't come out that way, though. Maybe she or the Starcore recognized the mistake by the horror on my face.

"Logan," Debby said. "It's still me. You like me, don't you?"

"I do," I whispered.

"We're friends, and you kissed me. I liked it when you kissed me."

"You killed Martin Cruz," I said.

Debby blinked rapidly as if trying to work that out. The alien presence in her eyes diminished a little. I don't know why I'd thought that would be a good thing to say, but it had. Maybe Debby's love for Martin Cruz was one of the things the Starcore hadn't been able to change in her. Could it be a lever to wrest her from the construct's mental domination?

"What are you talking about?" Debby asked softly.

"Martin Cruz was murdered," I said. "You once told me that Sheriff Walt killed him. Why did Walt do that? It must have been at the Starcore's orders."

Debby shook her head, although tears began to ooze anew.

"Do you want the Starcore inside your mind?" I asked.

That changed her on the instant. She seemed crafty again, not anything like the Debby I knew.

"You are meddling in affairs beyond your understanding," Debby said in a strange voice. "If you attempt to thwart me, you will die. Help me now, and I will reward you in ways that you cannot conceive."

"What are you really?" I asked. "A demon?"

"I am the greatest thing in the universe," the Starcore said in Debby's voice. "I was wronged long ago. But this is a new age. Help me, Logan. Gain my good graces. Do you want Debby? If so, I can give her to you, body and soul."

I couldn't disguise my disgust. I wasn't going to bargain for a woman as if she were a slave to buy and sell. I would win a woman's love the old-fashioned way or not at all.

"Do not play coy with me, Logan. I know you want the girl. You went to extreme lengths to save her. You did me a favor in that. You—"

"Warning," Rax said. "The white ship has come into phase and it is launching. I believe the vessel will attempt to reach orbital space."

"Who said that?" Debby asked. "I detect a Rax Prime crystal in your close proximity. I could use the crystal. Perhaps you and I could make a trade."

"Logan, you must go to the piloting chamber at once," Rax said.

"What do I do about her?" I shouted.

"Lock the door behind you," Rax said.

I began backing up.

"No," Debby said, as she whipped aside her covers, revealing her nakedness "Don't you want me, Logan?"

I hated the Starcore for using Debby like this. I couldn't believe it was her asking this. I didn't believe she had voluntarily let the Starcore into her mind, either. In some unholy fashion, this alien construct was using Debby. I was sure I had talked to and kissed the real Debby before. I didn't know how the Starcore could control her from afar, but I was certain it was.

"I won't let this stand," I said, hoping I could speak to the Debby inside her own mind.

"Logan, let us make love," she said, climbing out of bed.

I turned and stumbled for the door. I felt like an old-fashioned prude afraid of seeing a woman naked. Another part of me was ashamed for Debby. The thing used her body as a bargaining chip. I hated that. The hatred beat in me even more strongly than when I'd slain the Jarnevon.

I was going to destroy the Starcore. I would do it to free Debby, if for no other reason.

I slammed the hatch behind me and locked it.

"Can she escape?" I asked.

"Not quickly," Rax said. "Please, Logan, hurry to the piloting chamber. I think the final showdown is about to take place."

I sprinted down the short corridor, burst into the piloting chamber and literally threw myself at the chair. I strapped in, pressed controls as if I knew what I was doing, and activated the Guard-ship's shield and laser cannons.

-52-

The white ship shimmered as it lifted off from Nevada.

I saw it on the Guard-ship's screen. We raced to intercept the vessel, increasing velocity as we tore over Middle America while high in orbital space. The privateer was ahead of us and had greater acceleration.

It wouldn't be long before the white ship had sufficient velocity to escape the planet's gravitational pull. I thought about that. Argon had said the Starcore wanted the privateer for its own. The construct did not trust its ancient vessel as a starship.

How many centuries had it been since the white ship had flown? Likely, Greenland had been Thule back then, a regular land instead of the ice-encased wasteland it was now. Had the Starcore brought captive Polarions in its cargo holds, or had the Starcore's soldiers slipped into the Thule compound and conquered it? Did it matter today?

I supposed not. Still, I would have liked to know. Would I ever know? Heck, would I be alive an hour from now, twenty-four hours from now?

"There is an incoming message," Rax said.

"Put it on the screen," I said.

The screen shimmered before Parker Gaines stared at me from it. He seemed different than I remembered. He seemed much wiser although more evil than last time. I had no doubt the Starcore was in full control of his mind. The belief solidified into certainty as I noticed a crystal bracelet around

Parker's right wrist. It was actually fused to his flesh, which couldn't be a good sign.

"I should have killed you that night outside my house," Parker said.

"What happened to you, Parker? When did you become the alien thing's slave?"

Something seemed to flicker in his eyes. It passed almost right away. Parker shook his head.

"That won't work," he said. "This one is not Debby. He has no feelings for you."

"You don't like me, Parker?"

"You are playing for time," the Starcore in Parker said. "I have offered you the girl. You refused my gracious gift. Now, you will die along with the pup of an alien in his damaged starship."

"I thought you were trying to capture the privateer," I said. "You need it in order to travel to Rax Prime."

"You have no idea of my plans," the Starcore in Parker said. "But I will tell you this. Help me, and I will spare your planet. I will also give you the woman. Resist me, and I will drop all the hell-burners on Earth once I control the privateer. I will wash your backward planet in nuclear fire. It will be as if the human race never existed."

"Nice," I said. "But all you're saying is that you fear me. Thanks. I wasn't about to quit. Now, though, I know I can win. I just have to figure out what you're afraid of."

"You think I fear you?" the Starcore in Parker asked. "You are little better than an ape, a capering fool with delusions of grandeur. You have spurned my last offer. Now, I shall surely destroy you and your pathetic race."

The white ship roared into the edge of orbital space. At this pace, it would reach our height before we were close enough to use the Guard-ship's laser cannons. If the white ship continued to accelerate at this rate, we'd never catch up with it.

"Warning," Rax said.

The connection between us and the white ship snapped off. At the same time, a heavy disintegrator beam slashed from the privateer. It focused on the white ship's back area where the exhaust left the ancient alien vessel. The Min Ve's goal seemed clear. He wanted to cripple the white ship so it couldn't leave Earth or the solar system.

Somehow, Argon had freed the Min Ve's mind from the Starcore. Maybe it had been the Polarion's dying gift. The Min Ve appeared to be up to his original goal: he wanted the Starcore for his own. That meant the Min Ve wanted to cripple the white ship so he could take the Starcore at his leisure.

At that point, the white ship changed or deployed an odd sort of field. It appeared as if a giant fireball encircled the ship. Like a roaring ship-sized comet, the ship hurtled upward into space.

On our screen, I watched the disintegrator beam strike the fireball shield. According to Rax's sensors, the beam sizzled against that area but was seemingly unable to penetrate through to the ship underneath.

"Is the fire-shield impervious to the disintegrator beam?" I asked.

"I am analyzing…analyzing…" Rax said. "It is a complex shield of a fiery nature. I detect elements of cosmic energy in the fireball defense. You are correct in doubting that the disintegrator beam will be able to breach the shield any time soon."

"The Min Ve should use a hell-burner against it," I said.

"Clearly, that would be against a privateer's basic nature," Rax said. "The Min Ve surely came to Earth to acquire the Starcore. Destroying it would mean his mission was a failure."

A searing beam slashed from the white ship. It reached across space to the outline of the privateer. The orbital vessel's shield blocked the beam, blocked, blocked—

"The Starcore is targeting the command module," Rax said. "I suspect the Starcore is personally attempting to assassinate the Min Ve. First, it must batter down the privateer's shield."

That made perfect sense to me. Likely, only the Min Ve wanted to fight the Starcore. If the Starcore could kill the Min Ve, the crystal construct could mentally dominate the rest of the crew and still gain a workable starship.

"Rax," I said. "I know what to do."

"We can do little," Rax said. "We have one effective weapon, our nuclear device. Even if we could enter the fight in time, our laser cannons would be ineffective against either vessel."

"Listen," I said, as the Polarion's ring glowed faintly from my finger. "We only have minutes at most to do this right. Are you listening?"

"Yes," Rax said. "Tell me your plan."

-53-

The white ship behind its cosmic-fireball shield rose into orbital space. At the same time, its searing beam battered at the privateer's shield. Every iota of the Min Ve orbital vessel's power went into keeping the shield intact.

I reentered the piloting chamber with sweat on my face. I was short of breath from having maneuvered an excessively heavy object onto the transfer pad.

"Well?" I asked.

"The privateer's shield has weakened considerably," Rax said. "That is the good news. The bad is that it is still much too powerful for us to implement your plan."

I sat down, increasing the Guard-ship's velocity. "I'll have to add our laser cannons to the attack then."

"That is a joke," Rax said. "The Guard-ship's lasers are short-range weapons. We are too far away and will not reach there in time."

"Then we have to try the sonic drill this instant."

"Logan—"

"No more arguments, Rax. This is our only hope."

Rax was silent for several seconds. "Yes. I have calculated several scenarios. This is the only one with even a few percentages of possible success. I am amazed you derived that before I did."

"I'm a natural," I said.

"It would appear the deceased Polarion knew what he was talking about."

The white ship's incandescent ray continued to strike the privateer's shield. The shield withstood the beam, but it lost power as it did so.

"Now," I said, as I watched a shipboard meter. "Do it now."

The Guard-ship's engines whined with power. Everything went into the sonic drill. Nothing now powered the drive that had built up our velocity. The sonic drill struck the weakened privateer's shield. It attempted to bore through at one precise location.

"I have almost made the breach," Rax said.

"Transfer the device now!" I shouted.

The ship's engines suddenly whined to a lesser level. Our craft shuddered, and the engine noises changed dramatically once more.

"No," Rax said. "The teleportation attack will not succeed. The sonic-drill apparatus has sustained heavy damage because I strained it beyond its normal capacity. I cannot now place our nuclear device behind the privateer's shield. Perhaps as important, the Min Ve has begun to strengthen the shield. This is amazing. I wonder what tech he is using. Your idea was a gamble, and that gamble has already failed."

Frustration that had been growing in me finally erupted. "Place the nuclear device outside the shield."

"That will not help us."

"Rax, I'm ordering you to do as I say."

A second passed. Then another.

"Very well," Rax said. "I will do as you say, since you are a natural and may possibly have stumbled onto the answer."

The truth was that I was desperate. I meant to do something, because something was always better than doing nothing.

Several seconds later, our thermonuclear device appeared outside the privateer's shield. The device ignited, hitting the shield with blast and heavy radiation. The privateer's shield buckled—and went down! I had no idea how much radiation struck the various modules then. I had no idea—

The white ship's ray struck the privateer at that moment. The incandescent beam targeted the Min Ve's module—the command center of the vast starship. I think the thermonuclear device had caught the Starcore by surprise. The construct might be beaming the privateer with more power than it would have wanted to if simply trying to incapacitate the interstellar voyager until it could take it over.

According to my readings, the Min Ve's main module was more heavily armored than the others were. The terrible ray chewed through the armor plating in a matter of seconds, digging into the hardened ablative foam underneath. The furious ray burst into the module. Air exploded out of the breach, even as the ray continued to smash inside the module.

The white ship's ray finally stopped beaming. The Starcore must understand the danger to its plan.

I held my breath. Would my idea work? I had helped weaken the shield in a surprise move, hoping the ray would do more damage than the Starcore wanted.

Struggling beings burst through the breached module. A red glow—

The command module burst apart like a grenade. That hurled broken pieces of armor plating in every direction. The command module was near the very center of the starship. Heavy shrapnel shredded another module even as they cut girders in half. The second module erupted with a furious explosion. Maybe it had been a weapons locker. The intense blast sent even more shrapnel spinning against girders and others modules. A chain-reaction event was occurring—my fondest hope for my gamble.

The great Min Ve privateer began to come apart at that point. An exploding engine compartment added to the destruction.

While some of the enemy personnel might still be alive, the privateer as a singular vessel was dying before our eyes. In time, perhaps, one could collect the largest intact sections and try to remake an interstellar voyager. I didn't plan to give the Starcore that luxury.

"This is amazing," Rax told me. "It appears as if the first part of your plan has succeeded. That was well thought out, Logan. Now, the Starcore lacks a useable starship in the near future."

"It's always good to get lucky," I said, unbuckling myself from the piloting seat.

"I would not call this luck," Rax said. "You suggested the Polarion called you—what are you doing, Logan?"

I'd grabbed Rax, stuffing him into the front pocket of my combat vest. I sprinted out of the piloting chamber, racing down the short hall into the transporter room.

I already wore a weapons belt, but lacked a spacesuit. I didn't need one, though, for what I planned. Jumping onto the dais, I said, "Do it, Rax. Teleport us to the white ship to these coordinates." I spoke them fast.

"This is madness," Rax said. "It is a suicide pact, as we cannot teleport past a shield. I am not suicidal, Logan. Let the white ship attempt to leave the solar system. Its vessel is ancient and has little chance of surviving an interstellar voyage. We should wait for a Guard fathership to appear. I can give a full report—"

"Rax, we're running out of time. The white ship will be out of teleportation range soon. It has built up too great a velocity for us to match. This is our last hope to stop a terrible menace."

"Did you not listen to me, Logan? We cannot teleport past the shield."

"What if the white ship reaches wherever it plans to go and then returns to Earth before your fathership does?" I shouted. "The Starcore will destroy the Earth to kill every human. In that way, no one will ever tell your Galactic Guard anything. Besides, I have a way past the shield."

"That is impossible," Rax said.

I made a fist, showing the glowing Polarion ring to better effect. "This once," I said, "I can add energy to the transfer that will help us pass the shield."

"What is that on your finger?" Rax asked. "It is giving off incredible readings."

"It will give us a power boost," I said, not sure how I knew this. "I think Argon might have foreseen this moment. I don't know how he did, but it's our last hope."

"Very well," Rax said in a resigned voice. "Let us make this final attempt."

-54-

Technically, the white ship didn't have to flee anywhere. The Greenland site was history. Argon was dead. The Min Ve was either dead or defanged. We had spent our single nuclear device. The Starcore could exit the solar system at its leisure. Probably, its wisest course would be to decelerate so it could come and kill us. Of course, that was given that the Polarion ring could even help us teleport onto the white ship.

Rax began the transfer between our two vessels.

This was a huge, crazy gamble. But what else could give us even the slightest chance of victory now? I had no idea, so I rolled the dice one final time. I think it would have been impossible to teleport the nuclear device onto the white ship, as the ring actually had to make the journey to the teleported target to add its power.

Argon had told me something before he died. The Starcore was curious and arrogant. Those were the crystal entity's twin failings. There was another thing. The Starcore had shown a great interest in gaining Rax. The Starcore also believed it could mentally dominate any human. Rax could act as a shield for a time against the Starcore's dominating ability.

All those thoughts roared through my skull as the Guard-ship's transporter chamber faded from view. Would I know I was dead if we couldn't pass through the fiery shield? Would I live long enough to know—?

A chamber appeared around me. The walls scintillated with terrible brilliance. The first part of my gamble seemed as if it was going to pay off.

I'd given Rax precise coordinates I had no way of knowing. He transferred us into the hardest to reach area of the white ship. It seemed reasonable that that area would hold the fabled Starcore.

As I appeared in the new place, I noticed the ring on my finger. The gem had burst open, showing tiny electrical discharges. The ring sizzled and fused as a tendril of smoke rose. With a furious shake and a pull, I tore the hot ring from my finger, dashing it onto the floor. Whatever powers the Polarion ring had possessed, they were gone, destroyed by this attempt.

I had appeared in the brilliant chamber and found the brightness too much. I tried to look around, but it was like the time in Spokane during winter when I'd been a kid. The sun had shone too brightly off the snow, giving me snow-blindness. It had been brighter than the brightest day on Turlock Lake in Central California.

It seemed wrong that we wouldn't even have a chance because it was too bright in here. Had I wasted the priceless ring for nothing?

I laughed, drawing Parker's sunglasses out of a front area of my combat vest. I'd transferred them from my former clothes to the Polarion garment and then to this vest.

I slid the sunglasses onto my face, no doubt making me look like an old-time 70's cop. I tried to look around again, and found that by squinting I could actually see.

There was a giant crystal dome in the exact center of the chamber. It took up half the space and glittered with greater wealth and power than any diamond. I realized that mirrors set at cunning angles reflected the crystal dome's brilliance back at itself.

Every place I looked, I saw mirrored rows upon rows of the beautiful crystal. I craned forward, realizing that the brightness hid cracks in various crystals that made up the dome.

"Well, well, well," I said. My voice sounded strange in this room. It sounded small and weak. Still, it was my voice.

A pressure struck my mind, and I stumbled. I took Rax out of hiding, attaching him to the front of my vest. The terrible pressure receded enough for me to think again. It was like a balancing act. If I tilted the wrong way, the awful pressure would crush my free will and make me the Starcore's slave.

Despite the remaining pressure, I grinned at the great dome.

"You must leave this instant." The voice sounded mechanical, lacking the crystal's bright beauty. "This is holy ground, reserved only for my choicest servants. If you will not leave willingly, I will—"

I staggered to the side, and my free will almost succumbed to a heavy surprise assault.

"Parker," the Starcore said in a loud, robot voice. "Hurry to the holy place. A two-legged species of vermin stands before me, profaning the air with its tainted breath."

I concentrated with everything in me. I let my hatred of the Starcore fill my being. At the same time, I drew the .44 Magnum. I flipped open the cylinder and put the bullets Argon had held into the separate slots.

I don't know how, but I knew energy weapons would have proven useless against the Starcore. Argon must have planned this event.

"You must stop at once," the Starcore said. "I can offer you great power, if you do."

I flipped the cylinder into place and thumbed back the hammer.

"This is a perverted monstrosity," the Starcore said. "You cannot hurt a divine being like me."

I held the Magnum with both hands.

BOOM!

The heavy Polarion-enriched bullet smashed against crystals, blowing some of them away and plowing deeper into the massed substance.

"No!" the Starcore said. "What are you doing? This is gross sacrilege. You must stop this instant or I will—"

BOOM! BOOM!

I sent two bullets at two different points of the great crystal dome. I shattered more of the Rax Prime crystals that made up the Starcore. I also caused cracks to appear in other parts of the dome.

"Please, Logan, you do not know what you are doing."

"Wrong," I said. "Remember Debby, you devil."

BOOM! BOOM! BOOM!

I felt each shot. I watched my hand-cannon rise. I listened to shattering crystals with great delight. I might have been grinning like a maniac at this point. It felt good to destroy the demon that took over people's minds. I was sick of aliens by this point. I could conceive of no better way to end the Starcore's menace to my planet.

I opened the cylinder and let the spent cartridges tinkle onto the smooth floor. I reloaded as fast as I could. My fingers were steady. With a snap, I clicked the cylinder back into place. I think the Starcore had weakened enough so regular bullets could damage it.

"Logan...I beg you. Ask me...anything. Logan...this is...wrong."

BOOM! BOOM! BOOM! BOOM!

I kept firing, reloading, firing and... Everything began to fade from view as a panel slid open. Parker rushed inside with his pump shotgun. He leveled it at me, and he began to fire. Walt the Robot was hot on Parker's heels. The ex-sheriff of Far Butte had drawn its pistol and fired with Parker.

Those two were the last things I saw on the white ship as Rax teleported me out of there.

***

I reappeared on the Guard-ship, stumbling as I did so.

"That was great timing, Rax," I said.

"That was pure luck," the little crystal said. "I realized we were almost out of teleportation range. Fortunately, as the Starcore died, the cosmic energy-strengthened shield went down. Even so, it is amazing we made it back onto the Guard-ship at all."

I stumbled off the dais, dropped my .44 and walked around the chamber in a daze. I began laughing. I tried to stop, but I couldn't. I laughed, began coughing, laughed louder and finally put my hands on my knees as I wheezed from coughing too much.

"Are you well, Logan?" Rax asked.

"I don't know. I feel spent, Rax. But I don't think it's over yet."

"We must return to the piloting chamber."

"Yeah," I said.

I wanted to sprint there, but I simply lacked the energy. Soon enough, though, I sat down with a grunt. I used the long-range scope. The white ship was moving fast, still gaining velocity. It would reach the Moon in a short time. It would—

"Warning," Rax said.

I didn't need the little crystal to tell me anymore. This time, I didn't even need the Guard-ship's scope. A white explosion caused the window before me to glare with brilliance. Fortunately, I was still wearing Parker's old sunglasses.

In a moment, the glare vanished.

"What happened?" I asked.

"I believe the badly damaged Starcore lost its ability to control its remaining cosmic energy. The energy must have ignited the ancient engines. The white ship is gone. We have truly won, Logan. We have completed our mission."

I sat at the controls, letting that sink in. A grin spread across my face. There was no Starcore now to screw with Debby's mind.

A second later, the grin vanished. Argon was dead. All the Neanderthals and apish hominids had surely died. Was there anything at all to salvage from the ancient Thule station? Before I dwelled on that too long, I realized that all the Far Butte people had died as well.

"Logan, I am detecting life-readings on the privateer."

"Right," I said.

I headed for the wreckage of the privateer. There was no mercy in me for them. They had nuked the Earth too many times. Because of those detonations, the world leaders were outraged at each other. If I could, later I would try to help defuse that situation.

First, I was going to use the laser cannons to finish the pirates and force the various ship pieces into the atmosphere.

There, they would burn up, eliminating the starship and alien corpses from curious eyes.

It was part of my bargain with Rax to do this. I'd made the crystal promises that I intended to keep.

-55-

After completing that grim chore, I went into stealth mode. The privateer had already taken out all regular satellites. Still, a few agencies attempted to make contact with me as I destroyed what was left of the privateer. By their questions, they didn't know exactly what had happened, although a few seemed to have a good idea. If it was possible, I wanted this to be another UFO mystery.

I also wanted to cruise underwater with Debby for several weeks, getting to know her better. I was in a unique situation, possibly the weirdest in all human history. I had a Guard-ship, a Rax Prime crystal, perfect health, increased vitality and strength, and…I had more knowledge about what was going on than anyone else on the planet. Hmmm….I wondered if that was completely true. Debby must have extensive knowledge, too. She'd also been young for possibly longer than anyone else in human history.

The first thing I did after inserting deep into the Pacific Ocean was talk to her, asking her how she felt.

Debby was in the sleeping compartment, wearing some of my clothes. She wouldn't look at me and mumbled something about being horribly embarrassed by all the things she'd said and done.

I tried to tell her those things weren't her fault.

"No," she whispered. "That's not how it worked. I…I…could have resisted more."

"After sixty years in the Starcore's control?" I asked.

"Give me some time, Logan," she pleaded. "Let me go somewhere so I can think things through. I need that."

There was no way I wanted to do that. I'd gone to the ends of the Earth to rescue her. Didn't she understand that? Wasn't she grateful?

"Sure," I said, keeping the hurt out of my voice. "I think that's a good idea. Where would you like to go?"

She looked up at me for a moment before looking down. "Where do you suggest?" she asked in a small voice.

I thought about that and decided I should drop her off in Kauai, the Garden Island of the Hawaiian Chain.

Suiting thought to action, we used the transfer chamber three hours later, appearing near the car rental agencies close to the Kauai airport. There was only one on the island.

I'd had Rax manufacture a Kansas driver's license and a Visa card for her. I helped her rent a jeep from Avis and drove her around for a while. An hour later, I got her set up in the Koa Kea Hotel. It was right on the beach and had fantastic service.

"The ocean is beautiful," Debby said that evening.

We stood together on the sand, the hotel behind us. I had so many things I wanted to tell her. The way she had come for me while I'd been in the Far Butte jail…

"Everything you need is within walking distance," I said. "I suggest you rent some snorkeling equipment later and swim in the ocean. Talk to one of the hotel desk women about setting you up for a helicopter ride, horseback riding and inner tubing…anything you want to try. Relax and enjoy yourself for a time. Walk on the beach and think. Relax in the hotel Jacuzzi. But you should know that some men are going to try to pick up on you."

Debby smiled at me. "Don't worry, Logan. I've been around awhile."

Her smile made my heart thud. I wanted to hold her, but I held myself back by sheer force of will.

She stared at the waves washing onto shore. "This is wonderful. I think your suggestions are exactly what I'm going to do." She frowned, becoming serious then. "I don't think you understand. You're trying to, and I appreciate that. I've had the

Starcore meddling in my mind for a long, long time. I have to get used to being myself again."

I nodded.

"But Logan…"

I looked at her.

"I want you come back for me," she said.

"I will."

"Promise?" she asked.

"Cross my heart," I said, grinning.

She touched my forearm before turning around and heading back for the hotel.

I watched her go. She looked great. I wanted to be with her, and I wondered about the guys who would be hitting on her soon.

Finally, I took out my communicator. "Rax," I said.

"Here," the crystal replied.

"Bring me aboard," I said. "We have work to do."

-56-

The Chinese publically backed the North Koreans. They said the Koreans hadn't ignited any nukes. The Chinese spokeswoman on TV said the only people on the planet who had ever fired a nuclear bomb in anger were the Americans. The spokeswoman also accused the Americans of going mad, launching several terrible tests in Greenland.

Publically, none of that sat well with the President of the United States or with the American people. They were angry, and there were growing demands to teach the North Koreans a lesson. If the Chinese stood in the way, they could learn those lessons, too.

The Chinese publically made veiled threats regarding American carrier groups stationed several hundred miles off China's coast. The Chinese said they had ways of dealing with any American submarines as well.

That wasn't all. There were news reports of people having seen UFOs. Some of the more scandalous newspapers actually had headlines about alien space battles having taken place around the Earth.

I always used to think those outlandish stories were as fake as could be. Now, I wondered if those rags were the only papers left that told the unvarnished truth.

It was crazy.

I was on the Guard-ship after having been to Vegas. I'd watched TV and Internet reports. I'd listened to people talk as I'd wandered around some of the casinos.

"Rax," I said. "I don't know what to do. The standoff between the superpowers is getting worse. The idea of real live aliens out there has gotten stronger. Should we show them the Guard-ship and tell everyone what really happened? I think some people already know."

"Under no circumstances shall *we* do that," the little crystal said. "That is against all Guard regulations. You have acted like a provisional Guard agent throughout the emergency. Until the fathership returns, you have a duty to the Galactic Council to help keep the peace on this backward, banned planet."

"How do I do that? Earth is about to start a nuclear war."

"You must defuse the situation," Rax said.

"Yeah, I know that. What I don't know is the right method of getting it done."

"Analyzing…analyzing…I have a possible solution."

"Let's hear it," I said.

"We must destroy all the Earth's nuclear weapons."

I laughed, shaking my head. "First, I don't think we can do that easily. The various militaries would soon start setting traps for us. Second, I don't want to make Earth weaker. What if more aliens show up?"

"You and I will take care of that problem," Rax said.

"Maybe and maybe not," I said.

"If you will not disarm the aboriginals then you must help them see sense."

"That," I said, "is easier said than done. Too bad I couldn't…" I snapped my fingers.

"What is wrong?" Rax asked.

"I have an answer," I said.

"Tell me."

"You're not going to like it. In fact, you'll say it's against Guard policy. But it's the only thing I can think of."

"Please, Logan, tell me your plan."

I did, and I was right, Rax hated it and refused to play any part. I kept at the crystal, though, and two days later, he finally relented and said I might as well try.

By that time, it seemed the Chinese and Americans would launch at each other any hour.

***

I'd been studying the situation for several days already. I had made my pick. Well, Rax had made the analysis and told me the right choice given my parameters.

First, I donned a special piece of Guard equipment. It fit around my neck, giving me a holoimage disguise over my features. I figured it was best to keep my true identity a secret as long as possible.

Afterward, I transferred into the U.S. Secretary of State's bedroom. The man was asleep in his bed and alone, as his wife was visiting their daughter in Cleveland. It was dark in here, although the drapes were open, admitting starlight and some nearby porch lights.

As quietly as possible, I grabbed some of his clothes, socks and shoes. Then I went to his bed and gently shook his shoulder.

The older man smacked his lips, clearly not ready to wake up.

"Sir," I whispered. "I have something to show you."

"Go away," he said in a groggy voice.

"I can't do that, sir. World peace depends on you."

He opened his eyes and looked up at me. He had messy white hair and craggy features.

"Who are you?" he asked in an even voice.

I smiled, saying, "We're ready."

"Roger," Rax said from my communicator.

The Secretary of State bolted upright in bed. He began to shout. As he did, the bedroom faded from view.

We reappeared on a lonely hill in Virginia, with Washington D.C.'s lights visible from here, although I don't think he knew that yet.

The Secretary of State fell back to his prone position. I staggered, each of us having fallen an inch from the air.

The older man jumped to his feet, staring at me in shock. He was a bigger man, an inch taller than I was. He wore tighty-whiteys and seemed to be in relatively good shape given his age.

"Here," I said, shoving his clothes at him. "I don't want you to get cold."

He accepted the items meekly, which surprised me. The Secretary of State was known as a bulldog. His shoulders squared once he tied his shoes. He ran thick fingers through his snowy-colored hair.

"Who are you?" he asked.

"That doesn't matter."

"It certainly does," he said.

I sighed. "Look, sir, I'm trying to avert the end of civilization. I've been studying the U.S. leaders. You strike me as the only one among them with enough of a logical mind to hear me out."

He blinked several times, scowled finally and nodded. "Are you a Chinese agent?"

I laughed. "Right. I teleported you out of your bedroom in order to assassinate you. First, though, I gave you all your clothes."

His scowl deepened. Clearly, the man did not like anyone laughing at him. Soon, he turned away. His head swayed. I think he noticed the D.C. lights in the distance.

"Is that Washington?" he asked, pointing.

I said it was.

"I don't believe I'm hallucinating," he said to himself.

I told him he wasn't.

He looked at me. "You're going to have to tell me who you are and how I got here."

"I'll tell you this," I said. "But I doubt you're going to believe me right away. I stumbled on an alien invasion about a week ago."

He stared at me.

"I know," I said. "It sounds crazy. But I'm sure you've seen some strange reports about happenings in orbital space."

"Go on," he said slowly.

"The aliens abducted me, but I got away. That happened in Greenland."

"The nuclear detonations," he said. "They're your fault?"

"Not a chance," I said. "But I know who dropped them on Greenland and off the West Coast. That's not as important between you and me. Long story short, I stumbled onto an alien vessel with fantastic technology. It also had an entity onboard."

"A what?" he said.

"The alien ship I found had a creature that's been helping me. Again, long story short, we destroyed the other alien menace, but not before it launched several hell-burners. You know about those."

"I know there have been several massive nuclear detonations. The whole world knows that by now. I also know there have been far too many missiles launched into space, and all the satellites are gone."

"Right," I said. "The point I'm making is that the North Koreans and Chinese had nothing to do with any of it. The aliens did all those things."

He stared at me harder than before. "Why would these aliens do this?"

I smiled without any humor. "You'll love this, sir. The aliens wanted an ancient extraterrestrial treasure buried somewhere on Earth. The aliens found the extraterrestrial treasure but also woke up an ancient menace. The aliens got themselves killed in the process. I slew the ancient menace."

"You expect me to believe such nonsense?" he asked.

"Soon," I said. I took out my communicator. "Rax," I said. "Transfer us…" I looked up at the Secretary of State. "Where would you like to go, sir? You choose our destination."

He stared at me as if he thought I was a lunatic. "There's a castle in Germany. It should be empty right now, as it will be dawn there."

"What castle?" I asked. "You have to be specific."

He was.

"Did you hear all that?" I asked Rax.

For an answer, the little crystal transferred us to the castle in Germany.

***

The U.S. Secretary of State put his hands on the castle's stone battlements. Below us, several early-morning joggers moved past. In the distance, the Sun barely peeked over the horizon.

The older man turned to me. He seemed perplexed. "I can't deny my senses," he said. "You clearly possess this teleporting technology. That doesn't necessarily make the rest of what you say true."

"It sure helps, though."

He rubbed his chin as he studied me. I was gladder than ever that I'd worn a holoimage disguise. I imagine he would to go to the best police sketch-artist later to help make a wanted poster of me.

"Do you have a raygun, perhaps?" he asked.

I detached a Guard weapon from my belt, aimed it at a small tree below and beamed it out of existence.

The older man stared wide-eyed at the burning tree before looking at me with fear in his eyes.

"Rax," I said. "Transfer us down."

***

The Secretary of State and I were in the Guard-ship's piloting chamber. We cruised through the depths. I sat in the piloting chair until I dogged an American submarine several hundred miles off the Chinese coast.

"Amazing," the older man said. His knees seemed to weaken. He leaned against a piece of equipment for support.

I waited.

After a time, he straightened, studying me carefully. "What do you plan to do with this all this incredible technology?"

"Not much," I said. "Wait for the Galactic Guard fathership to show up."

"What does that mean?"

"This is a Galactic Guard insertion ship," I said. "You could think of it as an advanced form of shuttlecraft. A fathership will show up in time to reclaim it. They're a peacekeeping force as far as I can tell. They don't want low-technology aboriginal beings like us to know about them or the greater Galactic Civilization."

"That means…?"

"That I'm playing by their rules. If any more bad aliens show up, I'll try to stop them. Once the fathership shows up and reclaims this vessel, I'm back to being a regular person."

The secretary shook his head. "You must realize that the Galactic Guard will not allow you to stay on Earth."

I shrugged.

"You're taking a lot on yourself, young man," he said.

"Maybe."

He pursed his lips. I don't think he liked me saying that. "Why show me all this? What are you expecting me to do?"

"You know the truth now, sir. But here's a very important point. Only *you* can know the truth. I believe you're the kind of man who can keep a terrible secret. You also have the power to help put an end to this stupid showdown with the Chinese."

"I see," he said. "Is that all?"

"I don't know what the future holds. But I'd like one person in authority to know the score. I picked you because you seemed the most level-headed and honest."

"I might blow your cover and that of this Galactic Guard."

"Do you want worldwide panic, sir? Things are already getting out of hand. I'm sure others out there have guessed the truth, but that's different than knowing for certain."

He studied me.

"Maybe you can help get the ball rolling for the right kinds of technological advancements," I said. "Humanity needs to get out there, but I guess it has to do so under its own steam."

"You seem to think I should trust you," he said.

"Yes."

"Why should I do that? You have too much power without any oversight."

"I did the right thing this time," I said. "Besides, how much power can I really wield? I could threaten Earth, I suppose. But when the fathership returns, I'll be in deep, deep water with the Galactic Guard. I don't think I want that."

He thought about that, finally nodding. Then he studied the depths for a solid ten minutes. At last, he turned to me.

"Thank you, son," he said in a softer voice. "I appreciate your vote of confidence in me. It's time to send me home. I have a lot of work to do if I'm going to help defuse this madness between the Chinese and us. I also give you my word of honor to keep your secret. I may be a politician, but I have always kept my word."

"That's one of the main reasons I came to you, sir." I stood and we shook hands. Then, I had Rax send him home.

-57-

Three days later, the worst standoff since the Cuban Missile Crisis began to wind down.

The Secretary of State had kept his word so far. I wondered if he could keep it in the long term. I decided that wasn't my worry today.

Instead, I went to Kauai. I rented a car, bought some new clothes and swim trunks, and went to the Koa Kea Hotel.

For the next few hours, I lay in the sun, soaking up rays. I had a few beers, ate a beef sandwich and watched people.

Finally, I had the awesome reward of seeing Debby in a bikini. She carried fins, mask and snorkel, returning from the beach. She went to the outdoor shower, rinsing the saltwater from her.

She was tanned, seemed content and looked better than the last time I'd seen her. Debby returned the equipment to the sports shed on the side. Then, she crossed the big lawn to her apartment.

"Hey," I said.

She ignored me.

"Debby," I said, louder than before.

She turned her head, saw me, stopped and smiled so beautifully that I allowed myself the faintest of grins.

I got up, walking to her. Without thinking about it, I took both her hands in mine.

"You did it," she said. "The standoff with China—"

She wasn't able to say any more because I kissed her then. As I kissed her, I held her tightly. Finally, I let go.

"Hello," I said.

"*Hello*," she said with a smile.

"Would you like to go out to eat?" I asked.

"I'd love to."

"Great," I said, taking one of her hands.

I didn't know what the future held for us. I didn't know if any more aliens would show up or not. I didn't know if the Secretary of State would try to form a secret cabal to try to hunt me down. What I did know was that today the human race had averted a terrible disaster. I also knew that I was going have dinner with a beautiful woman.

I was looking forward to it, and to whatever would happen after that.

The End

SF Books by Vaughn Heppner

DOOM STAR SERIES:
Star Soldier
Bio Weapon
Battle Pod
Cyborg Assault
Planet Wrecker
Star Fortress
Task Force 7 (Novella)

EXTINCTION WARS SERIES:
Assault Troopers
Planet Strike
Star Viking
Fortress Earth

LOST STARSHIP SERIES:
The Lost Starship
The Lost Command
The Lost Destroyer
The Lost Colony
The Lost Patrol

Visit VaughnHeppner.com for more information

Printed in Poland
by Amazon Fulfillment
Poland Sp. z o.o., Wrocław